Kiakora

A Flame of Sorrow

Allyson Martinez

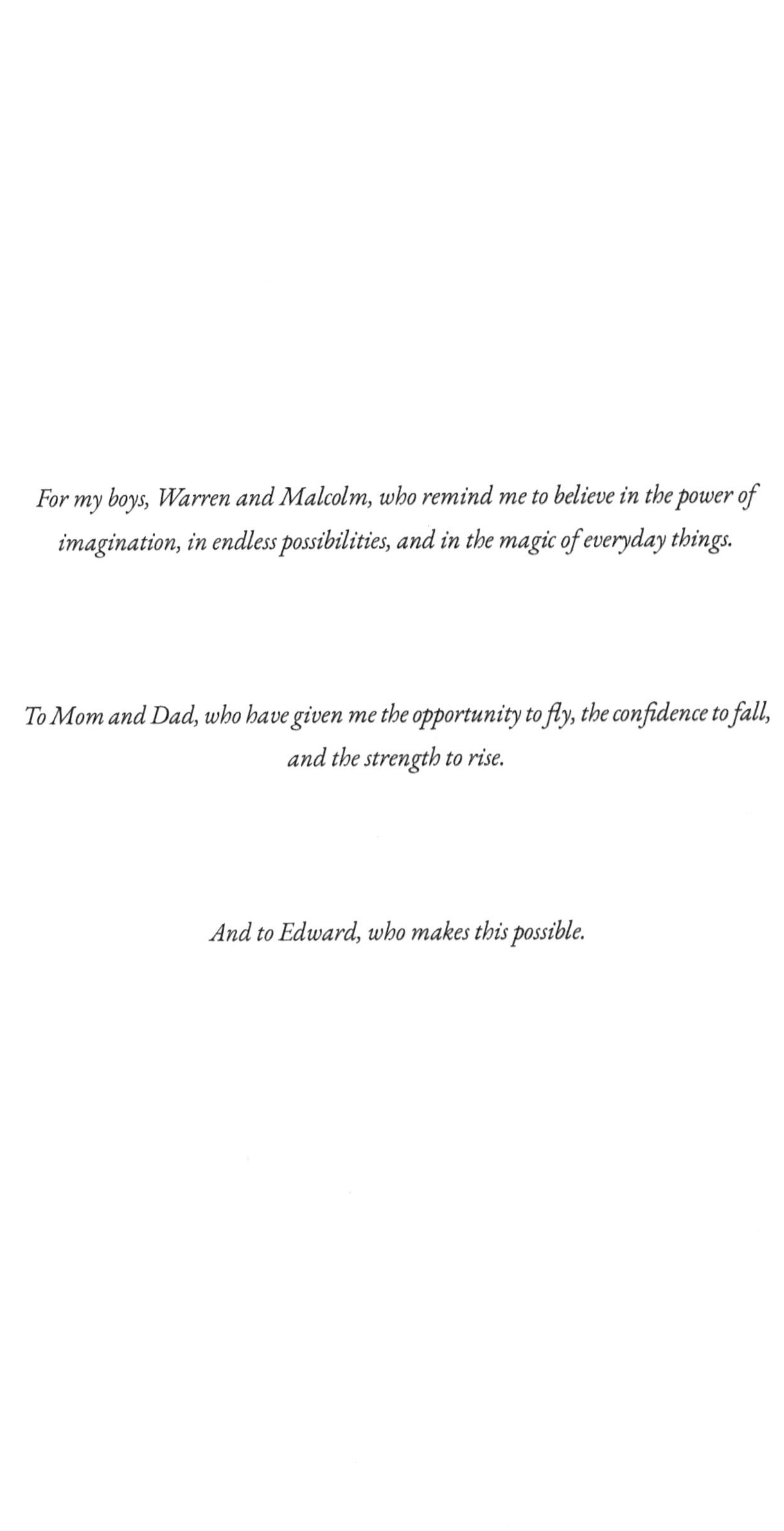

For my boys, Warren and Malcolm, who remind me to believe in the power of imagination, in endless possibilities, and in the magic of everyday things.

To Mom and Dad, who have given me the opportunity to fly, the confidence to fall, and the strength to rise.

And to Edward, who makes this possible.

KIAKORA
THE RANGI MOUNTAINS
KIROMAR
NAGRIMAR
RIMEAN
EASTERN MOUNTAINS
THOL WOODS
HAFRA FOREST
Orchard Clearing
Mound Ruin
MISANDREE
THE ANCIENT FOREST
AODHEN
FIRA
Lake Luun
Marshlands
HAWA
Hawa Sandsea

1

*R*un!

The scream came from somewhere behind me. The village. Mother. Dried leaves crinkled under my bare feet as I padded back through the forest. I smelled the fire before I saw the blaze. Burning. Burning our homes. My mother. More screams joined the crackling of burning wood, creating an unusual cacophony of sounds that shattered the once-peaceful night. Mother. I had to get to her.

Bright green eyes pierced the darkness.

I bolted upright. Breathing heavily, I took in my surroundings. The cot. The wooden walls and floors. The small window with drawn, pale-yellow curtains. I let out a long breath. I was in bed, in my home.

My forehead and hair were both soaked with sweat. I pulled the thin sheets off, glancing at the cot across the room. Naleiri slept serenely, unaware of whatever noise I might have just been making. My shorts scrunched up my thighs as I swung my feet to the chilled floor and walked to the small washroom tucked in the corner. It jutted out from the living space, which doubled as our bedroom.

We had done little in terms of decorating, leaving the cottage pretty much the way we'd found it. Nestled in the forest, the exposed beams lining the ceiling matched the wooden exterior, making it feel like we lived inside of a hollowed-out tree. A thin blue rug lay on the oak floor in the middle of the room. We purchased it from the market a couple of weeks ago to bring some warmth to the space now that winter was almost upon us.

The cool water was refreshing as I bent over the small white basin and doused my face. Grasping either side, I leaned into the mirror. Small purple bags bulged under my eyes. This was the third night in a row I had awoken with the same dream. Sometimes I saw figures attacking the village. Sometimes I felt a wave of power surge into my chest, knocking me from my feet. Always, I saw those piercing green eyes.

I knew it was from my past. It was how I ended up alone with no memory of my family, or my home. I wished I could remember enough to piece together what had happened. What was real? What were creative additions from my subconscious mind? Whose eyes were those? Who was I?

The soft light pierced the tree branches. I loved the way the forest looked in the morning. Peaceful, almost gentle. Tall oaks and maples towered over giant ferns. Bright green grass, the evidence of all the rain we'd had lately, covered the ground of the clearing. The cottage was old and small, hidden in the Hafra Forest outside the city of Aodhen. It was the only real city in Fira and also home to the House of Fira, rulers of the west.

Running was my only release. I wore tight leggings, a loose-fitting tunic, and my well-worn, soft leather boots, a gift from Naleiri that she had bartered for at the market. They were old, creased in all the wrong places, but were finally molding to my feet.

I turned right out of the cottage onto the path that would lead into Aodhen. I wouldn't be going that far. My brisk walk quickened as I felt the leaden weight of my nightmares melt from my legs. Naleiri didn't understand my desire to expend energy needlessly, but my mind was never clearer than when I was running.

The muscles in my legs loosened, jumping to life to keep up with the pace I was setting. I reveled in the slight increase of my heartbeat and the controlled air I released from my mouth in steady breaths.

In my periphery, the forest animals greeted the day. A rabbit left its burrow, nose twitching, timidly assessing whether it should venture farther from safety. Chattering squirrels darted up a tall oak in a frantic game of tag.

Fall was my favorite time of year. The leaves were just starting to change color, and the musty smell of the forest clung to the crisp, clear air. Soon the forest floor would be a marbled swirl of brown and green as the fallen leaves mixed with the never-changing Snowgreens. I loved the seasons, witnessing the slow shift through the natural cycle of life. Sweat dotted the bridge of my nose and hairline as I pivoted back toward the cottage.

My thoughts roamed to my arrival in Aodhen three years ago. I'd awoken on a small cot, in a single room shared with a bunch of travelers and nomads. Across from my cot, a beautiful girl was sleeping peacefully. That was the day I had met Naleiri. I had no idea how I got there or what had happened. I couldn't recall my memories though I felt them there, just out of reach, shrouded in shadow. I knew my mother, from snapshots in dreams, but also from a warmth that burned in my chest whenever I smelled cinnamon and lemon. I couldn't remember her voice, but somehow, I knew she'd told me to stay hidden. That I would be hunted. Maybe just as she had been that night that revisited me so frequently. Were the green eyes the ones that took her from me?

Trying to grasp at my memories was like holding water in my hand, watching it seep out of every crack and opening left for it. Only flashes from that night permeated the fog in my mind.

The cottage clearing appeared in the distance. Naleiri was the one who really felt at home in the forest. I could take it or leave it. Naleiri and I had become fast friends after we'd met that day three years ago. We'd tried to stay in Aodhen.

At first, we'd thought city life would be more conducive for two young Eleiyon trying to scrounge for food and doing the odd job here and there to earn some pyra. But Aodhen was always crawling with Archai taking advantage of the residents for more than they owed. The Archai enforced the strict rules of the House of Fira. No one dared stand up to them. They were known to be the top soldiers in Kiakora, and even if someone did stand up to them, they'd have to answer to the Lord of Flame, who was even more feared than they were. I slowed to a walk as I entered the clearing. That was what had driven us into the forest.

There had been a riot. It was Market Day, same as today, and all the Eleiyon of Aodhen hauled their goods to Center Square. Some had wagons, some had stalls set up, others were selling out of their wheelbarrows, bags or blankets arrayed with trinkets or crops.

It happened right in front of me. A soldier snatched an apple from the wheelbarrow of a little boy, typical behavior for an Archai.

The boy didn't stand down, though. He shouted after the soldier, "Hey, that'll be three pyra."

The Archai stopped and turned on his heel, staring incredulously at the boy. The boy mumbled something. I caught "mother," "tax," "hungry" over the noise of the market. Whatever the story was, the soldier didn't care. He grabbed the bottom of the wheelbarrow and flipped it. Apples rolled everywhere. Some Eleiyon ran to fill their aprons with free apples and others gathered to help the boy. They raised their voices, shouting, jabbing, and then, the Archai attacked. They conjured flames and spewed a hose of fire at the crowd. Screams rose above the shouts as some dropped to the ground to stamp out their burning clothes. Stalls went up in flames, and the crowd started running, scrambling to get out of the square as quickly as possible.

I had sat there watching with Naleiri. We looked at each other and wordlessly gathered our basket of fruit and left the square. It was that day we'd decided to leave the city and ended up here.

We found the cottage and decided we could make it our home. It looked to have been abandoned years before. The cottage wasn't so far from Aodhen, and Naleiri felt more comfortable in the wild than in the city. So we stayed. The first time we entered, cobwebs draped the ceilings, and a thick layer of dust covered every surface. The sweet smell of mildew greeted our nostrils as Naleiri declared, "It's perfect." Raising an eyebrow, I thought, *a perfect place to hide.* Perfect for two friends who had found each other when they needed to, the orphan and the girl who was no one from nowhere.

I made my way up the two dilapidated cottage steps. We hadn't gotten to those yet.

Naleiri was downing her last bit of Fizzed Horcha. Taking in my sweaty face and matted hair with a quick glance, she said, "We'll need to buy more in the city today as well. Don't let me forget." She dropped the tin cup into the basin.

She was already dressed in a green tunic and leggings, complimenting her fair, freckled skin and brilliant blue eyes. Her red hair, dulled by the winter, fell to her waist. In the summer, it would have streaks of blond as it gathered the sun's rays. She often braided vines into her locks or tucked flowers behind her ears. She was naturally beautiful, like a wildflower. Dirt smudges blushed her cheeks, and grime gathered beneath her nail beds.

"You better wash up and change. Otherwise no one will want to buy goods from us at the market," Naleiri said, eyeing my tattered gray shirt and sweaty hair.

I pulled on a pair of tight black bottoms and an oversized brown shirt that hugged my shoulders and chest but dropped loosely to mid-thigh. Naleiri was outside when I emerged from the washroom, arguing with a couple of squirrels who'd found their way into the bags of goods she'd already packed.

"We need those. It's Market Day," she explained to the pair.

Another round of squeaky chatter.

"I told you already, the jam was made from blackberries we collected months ago. You know they're seasonal." She pointed to the dehydrated mushrooms. "You can find more of those down by the stream."

The squirrels seemed satisfied with that and scurried away. I remembered collecting those berries. Naleiri's bag had been laden with the plumpest, juiciest berries I'd ever seen, and I suspected she'd aided a bit in their development. I somehow never managed to be as successful a forager as her.

"Are they looking for an easy meal?" I nodded after the squirrels.

"You know……It's that time of year." She shrugged.

I was always amazed by her gift. Naleiri was Eleyi. A sect of Eleiyon that broke off millennia ago to live in the forests rather than the developing societies the Eleiyon were building. This sect mixed with the native Forest Nymphs, and later generations developed a unique gift because of their bloodline. The Eleyi could hear Kiakora. Naleiri learned to listen to the trees, communicate with animals, even bring small flower buds into bloom. The Eleyi could connect in intimate ways with the natural world, and often they were able to do it instinctually, with little training.

Naleiri had grown up with her grandmother in a small community of Eleyi. She observed how they used their gift and learned traditions that were older than even the stories themselves. When she'd lost her family, she was on her own, just like me. But her tug back to the natural world was much stronger than mine.

It was one of the reasons she'd fallen in love with the cottage when we found it. It reminded her of living with her family in the forest. She'd told me they lived for a time in the gigantic, hollowed-out trees of the southernmost part of Fira. I'd never traveled that far south, that I could remember, but I'd heard tell of trees so tall, they scraped the sky, and wide enough for ten Eleiyon to walk through side-by-side.

No, it wasn't my connection to the natural world that drew me to the forest after leaving Aodhen; it was restlessness. Aodhen had grown small around me, and the community room where we stayed, even smaller. The Archai were a constant nuisance and a ready-made excuse to leave. Naleiri could have convinced me to move anywhere. A slightly dilapidated and isolated, but otherwise charming cottage in a seemingly never-ending forest sounded like a wonderful change of scenery.

The walk into Aodhen was pleasant. Naleiri enjoyed hearing the chatter of the forest from the trees that lined the path and the animals that scurried about. It gave me time to think, try to collect the broken pieces of my memory to form some coherent story of myself.

"No matter how many times we do this, going into the city still makes me uneasy." Nalieri's clear voice rang over the other sounds.

"I know. I'm not jumping with joy either," I said. But I couldn't help the flutter of excitement in my chest as the trees parted to reveal a small meadow with a winding dirt trail that headed into the city. As eager as I had been to leave Aodhen behind for the forest, I now looked forward to the energy and excitement it offered.

The last line of trees swayed as we passed, sending a rippling farewell to Naleiri through their leaves. She returned a smile.

2

"It's unusually busy today, Aila," Naleiri noted, looking at me over her shoulder.

It was indeed. The hustle and bustle of a typical Market Day infused the streets with energy. Vendors were traveling in from surrounding areas, the same as us, lugging everything from fresh vegetables to crystals and amulets. As we entered the city limits, the dirt road became worn concrete. It was cracked and pitted from too much traffic and not enough care. The aroma of fires and caramelized treats wafted toward us. To my left, I saw a group of kids huddled together, kneeling. They were entranced by something happening in the middle of their circle. As we passed, a young boy turned to look at us, revealing two, foot-long lizards. One of the boys was holding a small cloth bag full of silver pyra as he took final bets on the upcoming death match. To my right, a man and woman struggled to pull their heavy wagon of pickled vegetables through their front door and into the street.

City dress was about the only thing Naleiri and I had taken with us to the cottage. The women all wore leggings or tight pants with tunics of bright colors that didn't hinder their movement. Some older women still opted for long dresses with shawls drawn over their shoulders to shield from the strong gusts that wound through the city at any moment, particularly this time of year.

City noises filled the air as we made our way toward Center Square, along with most other residents. The sizzling of street meat marked the food vendors' early preparation for the coming onslaught of customers. Children ran wildly through the maze of people, playing their imaginary games of Search and Find or Catch the Fairy.

The entrances to Center Square could be found at each of the four corners of the plaza, manned by two Archai. The square was a large open space in the heart of the city, bordered by buildings on three of the four sides. The buildings were all different colors, most in need of refinishing. They were made of wood, but if you peered closely enough, some still exhibited evidence of hawastone foundations from another time. On the fourth side, where we entered now, there was a trellis-covered path. The green vines that bloomed with beautiful flowers of every color and tangled themselves around the top of the trellis in the spring and summer had already turned brown and dry.

As we were about to enter the square, a tattered poster zoomed into my hand. Surprised, I looked in the direction it had come from. An older Eleiyon sat at a table, lazily enchanting a stack of posters to find their way into the hands of market-goers. I looked down. A brown design looked back at me. The same one I saw every day in the mirror: the brown ink curved into the crest of an ocean's wave, morphing into the swirl of wind and the peak of a mountain, before ending in the point of a single flame. My heart fluttered to a stop and then plummeted. Naleiri's face was the picture of terror. I hadn't seen one of these signs in over a year, when they'd adorned every single doorway. *Why were they passing them out again now?*

Naleiri knew what I was, of course. She had seen the mark that branded my collarbone. She never asked about it, about my family or my powers. I honestly doubted I had either. As far as I knew, I was a Nulk. I felt a hum of energy, sometimes beneath my skin, nestled between my heart and my mark, but I never saw it. The only thing I knew about my past, besides the small glimpses I got through my nightmares, was to never, ever, show my mark. If I didn't have power, good riddance. It would only cause trouble for me anyway.

"Don't worry about it. Let's just sell our stuff and get out of here," I said calmly to Naleiri who, I was certain, was preparing to turn around and head back to the cottage. Sure enough, her tense jaw softened, but her gathered brows told me she was ready to argue. I squeezed her hand reassuringly and turned to enter the square. I felt her follow reluctantly.

3

Most vendors were setting up having already claimed their spots for the day.

"How about over here?" I asked Naleiri, motioning to the small space available between a storyteller and a food vendor. Candied apples wouldn't be competition, and the storyteller might draw in potential customers.

Naleiri nodded her approval. As we laid out our own blanket and started to display jams, pelts, and dried herbs, a group of children ran up to the storyteller.

Flicking him two pyra, the oldest child cried, "Tell us the one about Liro, the great sea-dragon of the west!" The storyteller snatched the two silver pieces greedily. They all plopped down cross-legged in front of the storyteller, pushing each other for the best view. A hush fell over the children as they eagerly waited for the tale to begin.

The teller turned the two pieces over in his leathery hand before launching into his story. "A great choice. It is one of the best stories of Kiakora."

Liro is a terrible and wonderful creature, and for most, the mere thought of him sent Eleiyon running for shelter in their homes. It is said he could drown an Eleiyon with only a look into his swirling eyes. But it is also said that he favored us in the west, even before the creation of territories. Long ago, millennia before you were born, before even your parents were born, there were no territories. There wasn't Hawa in the south, or Rimean in the east. The north wasn't Kiromar and we were not known as Fira. There were no gifts. There weren't even Eleiyon. There was just one Kiakora. The lakes were lonely; the forests longed to be explored; the mountains yearned to be seen; and so, the great dragon Liro rose from the darkest depths of his underwater home to hear their pleas. He too agreed that Kiakora was lonely indeed.

Liro was so immense that if he left the water, he could wrap himself around Kiakora twice. He was strong enough to strangle all Kiakora with his powerful serpentine body. His mouth was so gigantic, he could have eaten the moon that now dangles in the sky. Each of his teeth was the size of a full-grown Eleiyon. Liro wanted to help Kiakora. He didn't want nature to suffer in solitude anymore, and so, he decided to create a species that would enjoy its wonder and beauty.

"I love this part!" squealed a mousy-haired boy in the back.

"Shh," said a serious-looking girl, turning emphatically back to the storyteller as if to let him know that it was now okay to continue.

He breathed fire from his mouth, scorching what is now Fira. The city of Aodhen was built on the exact spot where Liro burned the land all those eons ago, and thus it has become the heart of the west. It's where you and I sit now and why the gift of flame flows through our veins. Anyhow, he waited for a species like no other to rise from the ashes, but only more trees grew out of the scorched land. They created the beautiful Hafra forest, but they too were alone.

"My father says the stories about Liro are nonsense. He says that we came from somewhere else. Another world... or something," a chubby boy interrupted from his place next to the bossy girl. He looked at his feet after receiving her imperious glare.

"Your father is not the only one to believe that. Let me ask you, young sir... what do you believe?" the storyteller asked.

"I..." the boy started.

"I think," declared the bossy girl, "that whether we come from Kiakora or not, and whether Liro is real or not, doesn't matter. This is a story...and I'd like to get his two pyra worth," she finished firmly, cocking her head toward the boy who'd shelled out the pyra. The other kids who'd considered entering the debate promptly closed their mouths.

"Shall we then?" said the storyteller, raising his eyebrows slightly at the young girl's demeanor.

The trees pleaded; the animals begged. Liro once again felt their cries. He wept for their loneliness. His tears fell, splattering the surface. And where they fell, deep trenches carved the land, becoming the rivers that stretch across Kiakora. He waited for a new species to emerge, but only the animals that already called Kiakora home crept out of the forests to drink from the fresh, running water.

Finally, seeing that nothing else would work, Liro plucked four golden scales from his own body, one for each of the elements in Kiakora. He scattered them about, and these became the four elemental gifts of the Eleiyon. Liro placed the gift of Land in the south. Fire was planted in the scorched land here in the west. He dropped Water in the flowing rivers, which carried the power across Kiakora and with his dragon's breath, he blew the gift of Air into the wind. The root of all our gifts comes from his four scales.

Today, Eleiyon possess a single elemental gift. Sure, there are those who don't have any power at all, which sparked the Nulk War, a story for another time and another two pyra, but most of us have a gift from Liro. And as--

"What about Elementals?" interrupted a small girl with two long braids.

The old man's eyes widened in mock shock. With the emphasis he'd placed on "single elemental gift," something told me he'd anticipated the question, even prompted it. "Most Eleiyon only have one gift, but there are those amongst us, a small few, who can wield multiple gifts. We call them Elementals. Elementals are an anomaly, some mutation from Kiakora's influence. No one knows for sure how they were created, or why."

"What happened to them all?"

His eyes saddened now. "For their difference and for their power, they were feared. They were hunted almost as soon as they were discovered, and for millennia ever since. After the Nulk War and the creation of the territories, there was a renewed search for them, but only a few were found. They were driven from the cities. If there are any left, I'd imagine they keep themselves hidden for fear of persecution."

"But the posters around the city? Why are the Archai looking for them again?" another child shouted.

"That, my child…is a question for the Lord of Flame." He took a breath, ready to continue his story, but another kid piped up from the back of the circle.

"What about Liro? Where is he? If he is so powerful, what happened to him?"

The storyteller's eyes twinkled. "Now that is something only the Ancient One might know."

"We should go on a quest to the Ancient Forest and ask!" said a boy firmly.

"Yeah!" another agreed. "We could find out what happened to Liro." His excitement rose. "Maybe even bring him back!" he exclaimed.

A dark look passed over the storyteller's face. "Traveling that far from Aodhen is no longer safe," he cautioned. He added mysteriously, "Even the Ancient Forest yields to the darkness to protect itself."

The kids continued coming up with theories on what happened to Liro and why he'd disappeared from Kiakora, each one wilder and more farfetched than the last. The storyteller entertained them all, adding a few of his own theories. His crinkled skin smiled beneath his white-and-black peppered beard.

I had heard this legend a thousand and one times. It was impossible to live in Fira and not hear it. Everyone knew Liro. The legend of how the great dragon, protector of the west, created the Eleiyon; about the Elementals who were hunted and feared for their difference. I had no idea why that single slice of knowledge penetrated my otherwise murky past. I know it was more than difference though. They were hunted for the threat they posed to those in power, or those who would seek it. It was the reason I was hunted. The reason only Naleiri knew what I was, and why even now, I felt an uncomfortable tingle on the mark that grazed my collarbone. It was why I had no family to speak of, why I was never trained in magic, if I had any to begin with. I was an Elemental.

"Aila," Naleiri called as if from a distance. "Aila," more sharply this time. I started and turned to Naleiri, breaking away from my thoughts.

There were a few customers gathered around our blanket, pointing at the jams and dehydrated mushrooms. One woman was inspecting the rabbit pelt I had finished last week.

Leaving my thoughts behind, I said to the woman, "Six pyra for that pelt."

By midday I was hungry. Grabbing four of the pieces we made selling our goods, I turned to Naleiri. "I'm gonna get us something to eat."

"Grab a Fizzed Horcha for me too, please."

The wooden stalls that lined this part of the market were adorned with woven fabrics of every color and style. There were thin, bright scarves for summer and dark wool cloaks to shield from the harsh winter that was coming. The woven fabrics changed to leather satchels, belts, and bags as I walked farther along. The vendors stood by their stalls, beckoning anyone who locked eyes with them to admire their merchandise. It was just as crowded now as it had been this morning.

Where there were no stalls, vendors with small tables and wheelbarrows lined the street, like Naleiri and I. These were the less wealthy vendors, selling what they could to make a pyra or two. I passed a large group of Eleiyon gathered to watch an entertainer juggling balls of fire. Next, a hunched woman, cloaked in black, stood behind a small table of large crystals and amulets. No one was approaching her table. I knew I wouldn't buy anything, but maybe my interest would help the old lady attract other customers.

I walked over, eyeing the pieces she had carefully displayed. There was a dark emerald amulet encased in silver snakes that slithered into a chain. The row across the back of the table were large amethyst crystals, the smallest the size of my fist. There were amulets of every stone imaginable: citrine, topaz, onyx, scattered at the front of the table, ready to be strung onto a cord. My eyes were drawn to a dark green, oval-shaped orb with crimson specks and swirls, no more than an inch long. I picked it up, admiring the way the bright red melted into the dark green.

"Ahh, the bloodstone. Interesting choice," the old woman said, looking not at the amulet in my hands but into my eyes. "A choice for courage and for destiny. What secrets, I wonder, does your blood tell, child?"

My eyes flicked to hers, assessing her angle. She was old. The soft lines betrayed her years, but her eyes held only kindness.

I turned my attention back to the polished stone. I could just make out my reflection in its smooth surface. The tawny color of my skin was lost in the deep green of the stone. The red specks in the rock competed for space with the few dark brown freckles on my cheeks. *If only I knew.* I pushed the thought aside.

"Thanks." I placed the amulet back on her table and hurried away.

I felt her eyes bore into my back as I continued down the crowded path. *Yes! Mushroom turnovers.* I made my way toward the stall in the far corner of the square. My feet crunched on the small gravel covering the dusty ground, the only thing that prevented the path from turning into a mud pit on Market Days. I didn't see who bumped my shoulder, spinning me almost completely around. My arm reached out instinctively to catch my balance and I unintentionally grabbed the arm of an Archai.

This wasn't just any Archai. His muscled arm tensed as I clutched it. He turned to look down at who had grabbed his arm just as I gazed up at him. His hazel eyes locked onto my brown ones. He was handsome. His sun-kissed skin matched his shoulder-length, wind-blown hair. His maroon-and-brown leather uniform fit perfectly across his broad chest, ending in capped sleeves that revealed strong shoulders. The Archai symbol, a black triangle, was fire-branded over his heart. Brown leather guards covered his wrists and forearms, up to his elbow, accentuating his bulging triceps.

"You okay?" he asked, grabbing me under my other shoulder to set me upright.

"Yeah. Sorry. Thank you," I muttered, instantly dropping my eyes to the ground and trying to maneuver around him.

"You seem scared." He side-stepped swiftly in front of me, cutting off my path to my mushroom stall salvation. The guards behind him snickered as if watching a predator play with its catch.

"I...no. I'm just getting food for my sister. She's waiting on me." I hoped the lame excuse would be enough for him to lose interest. I dared another peek at his face. His angular jaw was clean-shaven, and his skin, tanned golden from the sun rather than his natural coloring. His hazel eyes creased as he smiled.

"My apologies for holding you up." And he stepped aside to let me pass as he turned back to his slightly disappointed friends.

4

The mushroom turnovers were getting cold as I hurried back to Naleiri. I juggled the food and the Fizzed Horcha which sloshed about if I moved too quickly. I silently cursed her sweet tooth. Naleiri came into view as I passed the last fabric stall. She looked angry. A raised voice cut through the space between us.

"You can't sell here without buying a permit. You pay me now and I don't report you. Simple." Two Archai towered over Naleiri. The kind crinkle in the eyes of the Archai I'd just met was missing from their faces. The bigger one sneered at Naleiri, holding out an expectant hand.

The altercation was already starting to draw attention from the other market-goers. I gathered my courage and marched over to them. "Excuse me, sirs... Is there a problem?"

"I was just telling your friend here that you are selling illegally. To be a vendor in this market, on Market Day, you need a permit." The soldier's eyes looked me up and down, taking in my worn shoes and dusty black pants. He lingered on the curve of my hips before his smug eyes settled back on my face. We had no bargaining power here.

I tried anyway. "Our apologies, sir. We thought the larger vendors with the stalls needed the permits. We know of many Eleiyon who come here on Market Day to sell their goods without purchasing permits."

"But we're talking to you two." He extended his hand to me this time. "Ten pyra should do it." I couldn't help the quick mental tally of what we actually sold. Four jars of jam at three pyra each. The rabbit pelt for six, two bags of dried mushrooms and five bags of dried herbs for one pyra each. That was twenty-five pyra. But I had spent four on the mushroom turnovers and Fizzed Horcha. Half. They wanted half of what we made today.

"Unless you'd like to pay us in some other way," the soldier snickered, passing another lustful gaze over my hips.

I looked at Naleiri trying to send a mental message to her. Understanding flashed across her face as she grabbed the bag to pack the remaining items. Thankfully, there wasn't much left.

I raised my voice a bit. "Surely that's a little unreasonable. That's half of what we made." I ignored their last comment. The two men turned their attention to me completely. *That's it.* I went on, "We pay our taxes. I don't see why we should pay an additional cost when no other vendor here without a stall is doing so." I chanced a quick look at Naleiri out of the corner of my eyes. She held our coin satchel and the bag. I gave a slight nod.

In a split second, we were in motion. Naleiri slung the bag over her shoulder and took off at full speed, using the gathering crowd to shield her direction. I threw the Fizzed Horcha and turnovers, splattering the Archai, turned on my heel, and ducked simultaneously as the big soldier made a wild grab.

I ran in the opposite direction of Naleiri, chancing a look behind me. The two soldiers were chasing me. I was the easier prey, since I hadn't had the head start and crowd cover. I was always the bait, but I was faster than Naleiri and if I were honest with myself, I knew I would never let her put herself in danger for me. She was what I wanted to be: carefree, innocent, and happy. But no matter how much I wanted to, I couldn't shake the shadows that haunted me.

"Stop her!" The soldiers yelled above the noise of the market. I bumped into the jostling crowd as I made my way once again past the fabric stalls. I tried to weave in and out of the leather stalls to lose my pursuers. The fire juggler was still at it. I ran straight into the crowd gathered around him, folding into the onlookers as I slowed my pace.

My pursuers slowed as well. The larger Archai's fat face peered over the shoulders of the crowd, red and splotchy from exertion. *Him, I could definitely outrun.* The other one looked in better shape but less committed to the chase. I backed farther and farther away, retreating from their bobbing heads. The little one caught my eye and pointed. Not waiting another moment, I shifted to top speed and ran... right into the strong grasp of another Archai.

I turned to look at my captor, even as I struggled against his grip.

"We have to stop meeting like this," the same smooth voice from earlier hummed in my ear. My breath caught, and for some reason, my heart skipped at seeing his face again. His hazel eyes, noting the fear in my expression, flicked to the two Archai quickly making their way to us. His hands were soft but firm against my arms as he held me in his grip.

"General Kyran. I...I didn't realize you were here today. I..." The plump solider stammered.

I looked in shock at the man holding me. *This was General Kyran? General of the Archai, son of the Lord of Flame, heir to the House of Fira. Liro's balls.*

"What has she done?" General Kyran nodded toward me as he spoke.

"She didn't pay for a vendor permit. We were in the process of collecting her dues when she and her friend ran."

"I see. Thank you, gentlemen. I'll take it from here." His grip slid to my elbow as he spun me around and started a determined march away from the soldiers and the crowd who had gathered to watch my public humiliation. Behind me, the four remaining soldiers were laughing, no doubt at whatever consequence I was about to receive at the hands of the general.

He grasped my elbow tightly until we were out of Center Square. I quickly assessed our location. We were on the south side of the market, the farthest point from the forest. With a tug on my arm, General Kyran had me facing him again.

"What's your name?" I looked up. There was no malice in his eyes. He seemed genuinely curious.

"Aila."

"Nice to meet you, Aila."

"No one but the stall vendors pay for the permit on Market Day, you know. It wouldn't be worth it for us small sellers," I said smoothly, deciding to plead my case.

"I know. Those guys were taking advantage of you. I will deal with them later." Something like utter shock must have passed over my face, because General Kyran let out a laugh. "What? You thought I'd be awful? Make you turn over the twenty pyra you made and throw you in a cell?"

Shame burned my cheeks. The way he casually said twenty pyra as if it were nothing. Of course, it was nothing to him. He grew up a prince, living in a palace of servants, having his every need attended to, not to mention having everyone terrified to disobey any of his commands because of who his father is.

"Am I free to go then?" I asked defiantly.

"Of course. I can escort you home if you'd like, just to make sure our two friends don't catch up with you again." He tilted his head toward Center Square.

"Thanks. I don't live in the city though." A look of slight disappointment crossed his face. I wasn't stupid enough to not take him up on his offer. So, I added, "You can walk me to the other side of Center Square. I'll be fine from there."

His smile reached his eyes, seemingly pleased that he would accompany me for a few more minutes. "You know. It's only proper since I saved you for you to offer me something in return."

Something in his tone was playful, not cruel, despite him being the leader of the Archai. I smiled. "I have nothing you would want." Thinking of the old cottage in the woods, the makeshift wash basin and the twin cots that were shoved in the corner. What could I possibly offer that he did not already have?

"How about your time? You agree to meet me here again in… three days."

"For what?" My voice faltered.

He must have noticed because he stopped walking and grabbed both my hands by the fingertips. His smooth fingers clasped my rough ones, and once again, my heart betrayed my calm face with a flutter.

"I'm not going to hurt you. I just want to get to know the beautiful Eleiyon who fell into my arms today. Twice." He winked. Actually winked.

I couldn't help the blush that was surely evident on my cheeks and the slight tug on the corners of my mouth as my lips involuntarily curved into a smile. "Deal," I finally acquiesced. I hadn't noticed that we'd reached the other side of Center Square, and the curved path out of the city toward the forest was just ahead. "Nice talking to you, General Kyran," I said lamely.

"Please, call me Kyran. And the pleasure was mine, Aila."

5

I kicked myself for my giddiness as I walked home. I was not a fan of Archai; in fact, I harbored a healthy fear of them. And for good reason. Today was not Naleiri's and my first negative encounter with them, nor, I'm sure, would it be our last. But for some reason, General Kyran...Kyran seemed different. My face tingled again as I recalled the feeling of his hands grasping my fingertips.

He had called me beautiful. My honey-brown hair was streaked with strands of blond and auburn. It was shoulder-length, curling into tight ringlets when wet and frizzing up into a mane of wild wisps, escaping the neatly bound curls as it dried. I often wore it tied back, like today, or in two tight braids. Freckles dotted my face, and my dark brown eyes stood out, even against the ochre of my skin. Beautiful, he had said.

I reached the cottage. Naleiri's bag was out front on the porch, a sure sign she had made it home safely as well. I cleared the two steps in a single leap and entered the cottage.

"I don't think you should go." Naleiri's brow furrowed with concern. It was the second time she had said as much since I'd told her about the deal I'd struck with the general. "He's an Archai. He's the leader of the Archai. It's not a good idea."

"And it's a better idea to ignore the deal I made and have him come looking for me?" I countered. "He knows I don't live in Aodhen and he walked me right to the path that leads here. What if he comes?" Part of me believed the concern I now presented to Naleiri, but the other part of me was simply excited to travel back into the city for something other than Market Day. To meet him. To join the rest of the world, even if it was just this once, and just for a short time.

"You know what they're capable of, what they did to my family, my forest." Her voice shook slightly. "They have no respect for life, for the world around us. Mark my words, they'll consume everything around them in their quest for expansion or power, or whatever it is they're after...just like the fire in their blood," she finished, a coldness in her voice so markedly different from her usual demeanor. I couldn't blame her. She'd told me how the Archai had burned through her forest, sending her family fleeing for their lives in the middle of the night. "My grandmother is dead because of them." The Archai hadn't killed her grandmother intentionally. They'd burned the forest to create more farmland to supply Aodhen, but they hadn't known about the clan of Eleyi living there. Nevertheless, Nalieri's grandmother had stayed behind trying to rescue as many animals as she could. She'd died, and Naleiri, alone, ended up in Aodhen.

"I know," I said quietly. "But this is different. I won't be in any danger. And I won't share anything personal," I guessed at Naleiri's real worry. "He won't know what I am," I said after a few moments of silence, trying to assuage her fear of losing another loved one to the Archai.

"I'm just saying, it seems like an unnecessary risk is all. I'm worried about it." She let out a breath, signifying defeat, and turned back to a pot of simmering vegetable broth she had been preparing when I arrived. "What do you think he wants anyway?" She stirred the soup intently, revealing the chopped carrots, onions, and potatoes cooking in the hot liquid. She added the small bag of dried thyme and parsley mixture that didn't sell today at the market.

"I don't know. He seems...nice," I finished cautiously. And he did seem nice. But I would be foolish to trust an Archai, and Naleiri would be the first to let me know it. "He's probably just bored with his quaint palace life. Having all those servants wait on him must be exhausting." I raised my voice a notch to imitate an imaginary servant. "Yes, General Kyran. No, General Kyran. Whatever you wish, General Kyran. Please let me wash your feet, General Kyran." I gave an exaggerated bow to emphasize my point, the ends of my hair grazing the floor. Naleiri laughed.

"Maybe. Or maybe His Highness has a thing for the mysterious Eleiyon from the woods," Naleiri offered, raising her eyebrows and inflection slightly. It was a statement laced with a question, ascertaining my own intentions.

"Doubtful."

And yet, he had insisted on walking me to the edge of town. He had saved me, or at least saved our money, from the other Archai. His face had seemed genuine when he asked my name. And the deal he made—why? He knew I had nothing to offer him. To ask for time with me? To what end? My cheeks flushed again. Silly. The Prince of Flame was not interested in me.

"Just do something for me, please. Remember who he is. He could be dangerous if he ever discovered what you really are," Naleiri finished as she ladled soup into a bowl and slid it across the table.

6

I spent the next two days doing chores around the cottage. Neither Naleiri nor I knew how to perform even simple enchantments like warming our house, so Naleiri wanted to prepare for winter early. I chopped log after log of wood for our small fireplace. The cottage was not well insulated, which was fine in the spring and fall, but in the summer and winter, it could be deadly.

"How much do you think is enough?" I called over my shoulder as I leaned my weight on the axe, exhausted.

Naleiri eyed my pile as she hoisted a sack of walnuts up the stairs. "That looks good for now. Let's stack it up. I saw another fallen tree near the stream we can use when we run out."

We never cut down the trees. Naleiri reminded me of the old ways in Kiakora, the way the Eleiyon used to live and the way the Eleyi still do, as a part of nature, not instead of it.

It was good foresight to prepare now. The harsh, toe-numbing cold of winter made chores even more difficult. Not to mention that snow would soon cover the ground, hiding the resources we needed. So, like squirrels, we gathered and prepared in advance.

I piled the logs on the tarp we used to keep the wood dry and lugged them to the side of the cottage. Evidence of my previous work was already stacked against the wall. I added the logs, one by one on top, and stepped back. The pile was up to my shoulders and wider still.

"Good," I uttered under my breath. I flung the tarp over the logs. My hands were swollen. As I balled my fists, a sting radiated off my palms, telling me that I would have callouses forming over the next couple days.

———

Butterflies fluttered in my stomach as I made the trek into Aodhen the following day. The air was crisp. The leaves had already started changing colors, bringing a golden glow to the forest that had nothing to do with the sun. Soon they would be falling, covering the path, and blanketing the ground with their crunchy, dried bodies. I loved fall and always thought of the transitioning leaves as beautiful. I'd never thought of them as dying until, inevitably, winter came and the shriveled, brittle remnants crumbled to dust in my hands or disintegrated beneath my footsteps.

I wore a snug pearl-colored tunic that clung to my body. My dark blue leggings were tucked into my favorite brown boots that laced up to my calves. They had molded to my feet over the years and were the most comfortable footwear I had. I was devastated when the stitching finally started to come apart last spring and my pinky toe wore a hole through the thinning leather. By luck, I'd found a vendor at the market who offered a cheap enchantment to restore the shoes. Normally frugal, in this case, I had been overjoyed to pay the price: five pyra. The moon had gone through five phases since then, and the boots still looked brand new.

The canopy of trees thinned, a sign I was near the forest opening where the path that led to the city connected to the forest. My chest pounded. I took another step and willed my heart to calm like the complete stillness of winter in a snow-covered forest. My hands unclenched, my heartbeat slowed, and my face cooled as I held the image of a white winter and silent snowfall in my mind. I took the final step into the meadow clearing.

"Hello, Aila." General Kyran's voice rang through the quiet, empty meadow where he stood waiting for me.

"General Kyran," I answered, proud at the steadiness in my voice. I surveyed his loose hair and his tightly fitted black shirt with maroon panels stretching from hem to armpit. The maroon Archai insignia was stitched over his chest, just as it had been on his uniform the other day. He had on black pants that were tight enough to show his muscled form, but not too tight to hinder movement. I assumed all the Archai's clothes were designed for combat.

Reading my mind, he said, "Flame resistant." He plucked the fabric at his shoulder. "It's training gear. It can get pretty... heated... in the ring." His eyes flicked up to meet mine as his lips twitched at his own pun.

"Very funny." I only allowed a small smile to crack my lips. "Are you accustomed to having people fall over themselves at your jokes?"

"Only the clever ones—which that one certainly was, by the way." He gestured toward the path, motioning for me to continue walking.

I felt his eyes on my back as we walked the path into Aodhen. Something about an Archai walking behind me made me uneasy. I turned, catching his eyes snap up quickly to meet mine from wherever he had been looking. Pretending not to notice, I dropped back to walk at his side and ventured, "So what do you have planned for me today, General Kyran?"

"Can you please call me Kyran?" The insistence in his tone made me wonder if he was in fact interested in getting to know me. Most Eleiyon in his palace and protected by his walls would probably never consider calling him something other than General.

"Okay, Kyran. What are the plans for today?" I asked again, placing unnecessary emphasis on his name.

He turned his gaze on me, light dancing in his hazel eyes. "I thought we'd take a walk in Aodhen. I know you've seen Center Square and the market, but have you had a chance to explore the rest of the city?"

———

The usual activity of Aodhen's Market Day was gone. Pedestrians walked the streets with more purpose, and I hardly saw any vendors preparing their carts or wheelbarrows. It had been over a year since I had been here on any other day, and in the short time I had lived here, Naleiri and I had stayed close to the inn. Inn life hadn't exactly motivated me to explore other parts of the city. I recalled the pickpockets returning at the end of Market Day to count their loot. We had toyed with the idea of learning from them but couldn't bring ourselves to do it. Most of the Eleiyon who attended Market Day were only slightly better off than we were.

"No, I haven't," I said, deciding that was enough to share for the moment.

"Right this way, Aila." He gestured again with a sweeping arm, allowing me to take the lead down a hidden side alley just before Center Square.

The alley was narrow and lined with the same wooden structures with sandstone foundations I saw near Center Square. The foundation stood out more here though, because of how narrow the street was. I could have reached out and touched the rough wall. The smooth paved surface we had been walking on turned to an uneven cobblestone, giving an old look to the street.

Kyran narrated what we saw. "This is the Old Quarter. At one point in our history, this was all there was to Aodhen. The streets down here are all like this: cobblestone, and some buildings, like that one, are still entirely made of sandstone." I followed his outstretched arm pointing at a small building down the street to the left. It was ancient. The brown stone was smudged with green and black, probably splatters of the dirt and grime that caked the streets, mixed with water damage from rain.

"Did your family help build this city?" I had never considered how Aodhen got here. Our history, Eleiyon history, was so long. I'd picked up most of what was common knowledge in the three years I'd lived with Naleiri. But maybe Kyran had additional information. I eagerly listened to the Prince of Flame to see if I could glean anything new.

"Yes. My family are some of the oldest residents of Aodhen. This city has been here for millennia. My ancestors founded it. We were not a ruling family back then. In fact, there were no ruling families at first. Of course, you know the story: the four territories were established after the Nulk War. Before the war though, Aodhen was known for metal-working and weaponry. Young blacksmiths from all over Kiakora came here to apprentice. My ancestors were the finest blacksmiths the world had ever seen. Because of our gift of fire, it came naturally. More and more Eleiyon with fire came to Aodhen because of that reputation. The Hawa were here too. They used their gifts to build the city entirely from sandstone." Kyran shrugged, adding, "After the war, it seemed natural for Aodhen to become the capital of Fira."

"When did the architecture change to wooden buildings?"

"Not long after that. The war drove a wedge between us. The Hawa moved South and we separated more and more based on our gifts. Without them, we needed a way to expand and rebuild. The Hafra Forest provided the easiest resource, so..."

"You cut it down," I finished. Naleiri was right.

We paused our walk next to an arch carved into the sandstone wall. It had dried vines growing up the side until they curved over the top of the arch. The inside of the building was visible. Its floor was made from uneven tile. A waist-high counter, covered in every tool imaginable, lined three walls of the room. In the center was a table, and on the floor, a metal bucket filled with different-sized hammers. It smelled like burning wood and melting iron. Heat radiated from the entryway as I stepped closer to peek around the archway. A huge forge took up almost the entirety of the hidden wall. The fire inside burned calmly and slowly.

"This forge has been here since the beginning of Aodhen. It is the one my family used to run. Nobody is working today, but the House of Fira still gets weaponry from here," Kyran explained, avoiding my comment about the trees.

Swords and axes adorned the walls. I reached up and cautiously stroked the wooden handle of one. "The same forge used to create the weapons used in the Nulk War." It wasn't a question. "What side was your family on?" I asked, though I suspected the answer.

Kyran let out a sigh. "My family has always been on the side of Fira, even before we were a territory."

"That's not really an answer," I said.

He took a moment before responding. "There was a growing riff, back then, within our species, about the Nulk's status as Eleiyon. And while I'm sure that was the catalyst, there were also a lot of other issues. City expansion, growing borders, neighboring factions with different powers encroaching on Aodhen..."

Naleiri and I had debated these points endlessly in the sanctuary of our cottage forest. "Yes... on one side." I added, "The destruction of forests and pollution of rivers on the other..."

"Perhaps. It's impossible to truly know all the factors that were at play, I suppose. But I'd imagine that could have been part of it. Even today, you see Eleiyon who have abandoned the great cities to reconnect with nature. I, for one, think that building cities is an evolution of our relationship with Kiakora. The land provides for us; it makes all of this possible." He spread his arms wide as if to encompass the city streets around him.

"But at what cost?" I asked, completely disagreeing with his interpretation of a positive relationship with Kiakora.

He turned to me, appearing to contemplate my question as we continued our walk. Apparently, he would stop at contemplation, because he didn't respond.

The road started winding up again. We strolled deeper into the old city. These were topics most shied away from; it was nice to discuss them with someone besides Naleiri.

After another moment, I asked, "What about you? If the Nulk War were fought today, which side would you be on? Do you think the Nulks are still Eleiyon?"

Kyran blushed. He took a moment before responding. "Well, I think what makes Eleiyon Eleiyon is our gifts, and since the Nulk don't have gifts, that makes us fundamentally different, doesn't it? Even if we are all descendants of the same species."

"Well, I'm a Nulk. So how do you feel spending the day with me? Am I so much different than other Eleiyon?" I asked, perhaps more defensively than I intended.

His face shone bright red now, and he squirmed at my directness. "Ahem…" He cleared his throat uncomfortably. "Well…I…I just assumed that… I mean, at the core of it, our differences prompted the war," he said, launching into a history lesson and ignoring my comment. "Eleiyon with different gifts distrusted each other. They started to create towns and cities only welcoming their own kind, even before we had any defined territory borders. Ultimately our beliefs in how we should run Kiakora and govern ourselves drove us against each other. Then there were…ahem…the Nulks. I think they envied the Eleiyon with gifts. They saw society fracturing, the gifted Eleiyon taking the leadership roles, and got fed up. I don't have anything against Nulks, I just don't know that they can be called true Eleiyon."

"I could see that happening, I suppose. Though there must have been enough gifted Eleiyon who recognized the unfair treatment and sided with the Nulks for there to have been a war." I knew there were still many Eleiyon, like Kyran, who continued to separate themselves from the Nulk on the sole basis of their being gifted. "Or maybe there weren't that many. Maybe the Nulks were just supported by the most powerful of all of us." I smirked, thinking that he would brush off the comment for the instigating jest it was.

Instead, he turned grave. "The Elementals were very rare, even then. And now...all but disappeared. Though, I'd say they are the only reason the Nulk even had bargaining power in the Treaty of Gifts."

The mark on my collarbone tingled as our eyes locked, his face serious. There was no hint of the playful general from earlier. I broke the stare first to look down at my feet, hugging my tunic tighter around me. The mark burned my skin like a brand reminding me of the extraordinary legacy of that mark and the embarrassing reality that I had no gifts.

"Yeah," I said lamely. "So how did your ancestors become the ruling family of Fira then?" I asked, trying to lighten the mood and shift the conversation to anything but Elementals.

"The Treaty ended the war. It outlined the four territories we have today, Fira, Hawa, Kiromar and Rimean, as I'm sure you remember from your schooling. Couldn't have been that long ago, could it?" He was right. Even though I couldn't remember the details, I couldn't have gone through First Mark that long ago. "Well, when they drew the official territory lines, each territory determined how they wanted to govern themselves. Fira decided on a ruling House, and since my family was the most powerful, they were naturally selected as the ruling family. It was my grandfather who was the first ruler of the House of Fira. The north, Kiromar, also selected a single ruler, though they lack commitment and give in to the whims of their people. Hawa is a free-for-all; they govern as a committee, and Rimean, well, they just scattered into a bunch of isolated towns. No wonder they're so backward over there." He shook his head in disgust. "With the territories established, they became the solidified homes of each gift. It wasn't necessarily spoken, but Fira became the home of Eleiyon with the gift of fire. Back then, they were much stricter on letting any...any Nulks inside our borders, but we've since become much more tolerant, as you can see." He said it proudly, like the words he spoke were true. Did he not know how his beloved Archai treated the Eleiyon in Aodhen, particularly the ones who couldn't defend themselves? "Now we are not so divided based on being Nulk or Eleiyon, but by our gifts," he continued. "My father has made a lot of changes during his rule to better Fira and one day, it will pass to me," he finished heavily, as if the weight of those millennia already rested on his shoulders.

"Are you excited to rule?" I was genuinely curious. I, for one, didn't envy his position.

"My father is still young. He was born right after the war." *Young*? I did the calculations. *That must mean the Lord of Flame was thousands of years old.* I tried to hide my surprise, but I couldn't help the next question.

"And you?" I blurted.

"I only have sixty years or so under my belt." He gestured to a belt he was not wearing, his playful tone returning. "I mean, who's counting. Hardly any Eleiyon I know keep track once they reach First Mark. Seems pointless when you live for so long. I don't expect to rule any time soon. But when it is my time, I will uphold the reputation of the House of Fira—our strength, and our traditions. My father has me training the army just as he did for his father before." He was proud of his family and his traditions, perhaps even of his future role.

We talked like that for the rest of the morning, wandering around the city. He would stop now and then to point out an old structure or a building that held stories from the beginning of Aodhen. He told me about the Water Weavers who used to live by the Mill, helping the town to grind grain for all the local bakeries. I'd all but given up on figuring out what had happened to me three years ago, but something about hearing these stories made me think I could rediscover my past. The truth might be here somewhere, just hidden from view, like the sandstone foundations of the oldest buildings, reminding anyone who looked closely of another time.

We stopped for lunch at a small domed building that stood slightly apart from the rest. It was also made of sandstone, with only wooden additions here and there, mostly in the door frames. The same tiled floor from the forge was just barely visible under a cloud coating. But instead of the putrid smell of melting metals, the aroma here was heaven. The sweet smell of baking dough wafted through the open doors of the building, beckoning customers to come in. Flour covered the floor and filled the air. The counters were lined with waxed parchment pieces and dough in varying stages of preparation. I saw stencils for cookies and pastries. Rolling pins danced solo carrying out their enchanted instructions to roll the dough to the perfect thickness.

A squat, rosy-cheeked woman bustled into view, wearing a light blue dress covered by a white apron that did nothing to shield her clothing from the mess of the bakery. She greeted Kyran with a wide smile. "Kyran!" Pure delight sounded in her voice as she hurried over to stretch her too-short arms to Kyran's face.

"Tansy is the best baker in all of Aodhen. She bakes for the palace, but I admit, I sneak down here sometimes just like I did when I was young to grab freshly baked pastries." He winked at Tansy, who turned red at his compliment and busied herself putting together a massive plate of sweet and savory pastries.

"Now, I have some rolls in the oven, Kyran, but why don't you get started on these? Freshly baked this morning. I have ham and cheese turnovers, mushroom tarts, and your favorite, chocolate scones." She placed the pile of pastries on the small table in the middle of the bakery and folded some linen cloths next to each of us. And then, as if forgetting an important ingredient, she popped over to the corner and pulled out a chilled bottle of milk and a pair of glasses. "Kyran always knows what to say to get a girl all flustered," she finished as she placed the glasses next to each of us. I noticed her second use of his name, Kyran. She was the only one, besides myself, not using his title. "And you, my dear, what's your name and how did you come to be spending time with this troublemaker?"

I smiled. Her welcoming nature put me at ease enough to say, "My name is Aila, and Kyran over here is calling in a bet to spend the day with him, which I was forced to make in a moment of sheer desperation."

"HA!" She burst out laughing. She looked from Kyran to me. "I like you. He needs someone to ruffle his feathers once in a while. It's good for him." She reached up and tousled his hair before returning to her rolls, which had turned a beautiful golden brown over the fire.

The pastries were exquisite. I wrapped a couple up for Naleiri who would go crazy over the mushroom tarts.

———

"So, we spent the whole day together talking about me, my family, the history of Aodhen, and I don't know anything about you, other than your name and, apparently, that I'll have to fight you over any future chocolate scones," he said as he gently bumped into my shoulder. It was the end of the afternoon, and we started back toward Center Square.

"Well, you should have asked more questions instead of talking about yourself the whole time," I teased. I was actually terrified of what he might ask and had purposely peppered him with questions about the city in any moments of silence.

Surveying our distance to the edge of the city, he said, "We have just enough time for me to learn at least one thing about you... You look about my age, but it's always difficult to tell once the aging slows down after First Mark."

Liro's balls. I have no idea. "Twenty-five." I threw the number out without thinking. "Just under half the time you've been around, old man."

"Very true." He stopped and grabbed my fingertips so swiftly I wouldn't have been able to pull them away, even if I had wanted to. "But that means I have a lot of experience. I can teach you things." He scanned my face, taking in my freckles and dark eyes, lingering on my lips.

"Hmm, like what?" I pulled my hands from his and turned to keep walking past Center Square toward the path that would bring me home and away from whatever this was.

"What would you like to learn?"

"How about how to kick the butts of jerk Archai who don't mind their own business so that I don't need you to step in and help me?"

"Done," he said quickly.

I turned to face him.

He had stopped walking, prolonging my departure. In response to the disbelief that surely crossed my face he added, "Really. If you want to learn combat, there's actually no one better to train you than me. It's part of my job, after all." He smiled that easy smile again.

I had said it as a complete joke. But now that the offer was out there, I contemplated it. How many times had Naleiri and I had to create distractions to escape Archai? I was lucky to have accidentally run into Kyran the last time; otherwise, where would I be? In the best-case scenario, twenty pieces poorer, in the worst, in a cell somewhere under the city. I looked down at my hands; I was weak. A Nulk. No gift to speak of. What else could I do to defend myself? This was my best option. Part of me also longed for this, some kind of action, something outside of my routine, just like today had been. And now, even better, this was an activity with a purpose. I supposed I didn't hate the idea of spending more time with Kyran either.

"Okay. I'd like that. When shall we start?" I looked back up at him to find him grinning widely. He tucked his long hair behind his ear to prevent it from blowing in the breeze that had just whipped up.

"Tomorrow—same time."

Perhaps it was his smile that urged me to walk toward him then. His face turned serious as I approached, entering his space. I grabbed his fingertips, just as he had done to me twice today. He looked so intently at me that I had to ask, "Why? Why make this deal with me? To spend the day with me?"

He smiled. "Because when you bumped into me the first time, I thought you were the most beautiful Eleiyon I had ever seen, and I just let you walk away. The second time, I knew Liro had given me another chance." My cheeks warmed as he reached up to my face, letting his finger gently caress my cheek as he tucked a strand of loose hair behind my ear. His hand lingered for a moment. I grabbed it, lowering it to where our hands met.

"Thank you, Kyran. I enjoyed our walk through Aodhen today. And I will likely enjoy kicking your ass tomorrow during training even more." I gave him a smirk and walked away before he had the chance to reply. One thing was for sure, though; Naleiri would absolutely hate the idea of me training with an Archai, if she ever found out about it.

Smoke filled my nostrils.

It was so dark. Too dark to see anything. And then the fire rose above the tops of the trees.

I hurtled toward my house. It was the last one on the street, closest to the forest. Panic gripped my heart, but if I could just...

Something cold grabbed my arms and yanked me off my feet. I flew into the thorny bushes and opened my eyes. Thick smoke and...

Piercing green eyes loomed above me.

I gasped. The heavy smoke that filled my nostrils just a moment before was gone. Blinking, I cleared the sleep from my vision. I was home. Naleiri slept soundly across the room. I rubbed my temples with my fingers and closed my eyes, massaging little circles until my heartbeat calmed.

"It's not real," I whispered to myself.

I lay back down, resting my head on the soft pillow, and stared into the darkness of the cottage. I knew these were flashes of a memory. My memory. Why couldn't I remember? What happened that night? Questions floated across my mind. Like a shepherd with her flock, I counted them one by one as I drifted back to sleep.

7

It could have been the restless night or the excitement for my first day of training, but I woke, bathed, and dressed before the sun was anything more than a pinprick on the horizon. I grabbed one of Tansy's blueberry muffins from the stash I had brought home and stepped out the door before Naleiri could wake and ask me any questions.

It was another brisk fall day. I pulled my layers of clothing closer around me. As I set out to Aodhen, I tried to piece together the shards from my dreams.

I always woke when I saw those green eyes. It was like they pierced through the veil that separated sleep from consciousness. The dream was never exactly the same, but I knew each was a different piece of the same memory. If only I could somehow piece them together, I could get the whole story.

I wasn't from Aodhen. That much was clear. The smoke. The fire. My town had been attacked. For some reason, from what I could gather, I had not been at home but off somewhere in the woods when the attack started. Why hadn't I been able to get back? What happened to my mother? The questions tumbled, one over the other, until a gripping pain crushed my chest, as if buried beneath the weight of it all. Tears welled in my eyes. Why had no one come looking for me? And it was the unspoken answers, not the questions, that forced the tears out of my eyes and down my face in silent streaks.

I arrived at the meadow clearing well before our agreed-upon meeting time and found a flat boulder on which to perch as I waited.

Right on time, Kyran marched into the meadow. I caught his eye, and he slowed, gesturing for me to come the rest of the way. Hopping off the boulder, I strutted to him in what I hoped was a walk that exuded confidence in my ability to participate in whatever he had in store for me.

"Good morning, Aila." His eyes caught on the swerve of my hips as they did a quick assessment. "Shall we?" He started walking before I responded. "We are going to train for a bit just you and I before joining the rest of the Archai. I want to get you warmed up," he continued.

I swallowed audibly. I should have assumed, but I hadn't thought of training in front of anyone else.

He either heard my unattractive swallow or he guessed at my thought, because he said, "Don't worry. You're with me and training as my guest. No one will bother you." Adding his playful touch, he said, "If I didn't know better, I'd say you were scared, Aila." He nudged my shoulder gently.

"Not a chance." I said with as much of a steady, calm voice as I could muster, knowing that public humiliation was in my very near future.

I was delusional in thinking that the kindness Kyran had shown me yesterday would extend to the training field. It did not. His demeanor turned serious as soon as we entered a small training ring connected to the palace grounds. I couldn't see the House of Fira from here, and only then did it dawn on me how big the estate must be. Surrounding the ring were manicured green lawns lined with bushes and red maples whose leaves were beginning to fall. Low stone walls jutted out in different directions to create a maze of pathways and tranquil gardens. The ring was connected to one of these walls, made from the same stone but much higher, several feet above Kyran's head. I was grateful for the walls. At least I would have some privacy.

That feeling quickly dissipated as we began training with what Kyran called *warm-ups*.

"I want you to start with lunges from here to the opposite wall. Touch it and sprint back. Do that ten times." His commands were short and serious. The playful general was gone, replaced by the leader of the Archai.

He watched me intently as I performed the task. I finished, breathing hard in front of him. I was proud of myself for having completed this first task relatively quickly.

"Good. Your legs are strong. Looks like you've worked up some muscular endurance there. And it seems you have a certain cardio stamina built up as well." How he gleaned that from this single task I had no idea but assumed it could only come from someone who spent a lot of their time evaluating soldiers' physical performance. "Let's see where we are starting in terms of upper-body strength."

My stomach sank. I had never done an upper-body exercise in my life.

"Twenty push-ups," he ordered.

I did five before collapsing on the ground at his feet.

I thought I caught a smirk slide across his lips before it was quickly masked by his impassive general's face. "And this is where we'll start," he stated.

There was no actual combat that entire morning with Kyran. Despite my protests at wanting, and having agreed, to real combat training, Kyran insisted this was the foundation.

"You won't last a minute in hand-to-hand combat with someone who is trained to fight if you don't have the strength to keep your shoulders up to protect your face. Now, arms back out... straight Aila, don't get lazy." I felt the burn in my shoulders as I locked my elbows. "Give me five more, sidestep to the wall and back, and DO NOT LOWER THOSE ARMS. Go!"

My body sank to the ground when Kyran finally called the end of the practice. It was only midday, but my core and my shoulders were the soupy, sludgy mess snow turns into after falling on a heavily trafficked road.

"Good job today, Aila. You pushed yourself. I think another couple sessions like this, and you'll be ready to add some basic techniques." I looked incredulously at him. *Another couple sessions — what had I signed up for?* He must have misinterpreted my silence for agreement, because he said, "Great. Now let's head up to the main field to get a feel for some weapons training with the soldiers. Don't worry." He stopped my protest before it started. "You're not going to be wielding any weapons today. This is more to observe what we're working toward down here."

I got wearily to my feet and followed Kyran out of the training ring. The grounds were not only big, but they were also beautiful. The red maples I'd caught a glimpse of earlier lined each gravel pathway, creating a maroon canopy. The small stone walls were covered in mossy patches here and there, giving the entire space an ancient feel. The winding barriers created landscaped gardens with short green grass and what I was sure would be flowering rose bushes in the spring.

"It's right up there," Kyran called from a few feet ahead of me, pulling my attention away from the beauty of the grounds. The gravel crunched under our feet as we walked deeper into the garden.

I followed where he was pointing but paused on an immense stone building with a maroon roof. Up ahead, the ground sloped downward so the palace was half hidden, but it was still bigger than any building I'd ever seen. It had three different sections: a massive, rectangular building at the center, and on either side, two tall stone pillars topped with pointed maroon roofs and a House of Fira banner. In front of the building was a spacious courtyard built three feet up from the ground. The raised court-yard bled into a grand stone staircase that led up to large oak doors, each sporting the Archai insignia.

"Is that your...?" I started. My voice caught on the question. I knew the answer by the building's sheer immensity.

"That's the palace. The House of Fira. Residential quarters are in the back. You can't really see them from here, but yes, that's my home."

Shame crept up my neck as I thought about the small cottage tucked in the forest. A man's deep voice pulled me from my thoughts. "General. I have the soldiers working on sword techniques right now. We went through archery drills this morning. I thought we'd break into one-on-ones for the rest of the afternoon." It was posed as a statement, but he still waited for Kyran's confirmation.

Before giving it, though, Kyran turned toward me. "Aila, this is my second-in-command. He is my right hand in combat, and in pretty much everything, come to think of it." He smiled cheerily, a distinct contrast to the man who now stood before us. "Cyrus. Cyrus, this is Aila. She'll be observing us today."

A questioning look flit across Cyrus' sallow face before he slid back into the impassive look of a solider ready to follow orders. "Sure, General."

"I'll spar with the soldiers today." That seemed to be the confirmation Cyrus needed, because he dismissed himself with a nod and started corralling the soldiers and separating them into sparring partners. Kyran motioned to a long wooden bench off to the side.

The main training field was a big rectangle. Large sheds lined either side, full of weapons, I assumed. Grass covered the ground in some spots, but just as much of the area was bare, packed dirt. Black patches dotted the field here and there, curling the grass or surrounding divots in the dirt. *Scorch marks.*

Kyran waved his arm, and white circles appeared on the training field, each five feet in diameter. There were at least twenty of them spanning across every inch of the field. Seemingly without a command, the soldiers broke into pairs, each marching onto the field armed with swords. They were sparring circles. Kyran stood inside the one in front of me, across from another soldier. As he turned, I saw that it was Cyrus.

Another unspoken command, and the dueling began. Kyran and Cyrus were impressive. Their swords clanged as they met each other's blows time and again. They twisted and turned, somehow always able to block the other's strike just in time. *They must train together regularly to know each other's movements so well.*

Just then, Cyrus side-stepped Kyran's strike. The maneuver threw Kyran off balance, leaving an opening for Cyrus to deal a blow with the butt of his sword to Kyran's exposed cheek. Instead of balking, Kyran leaned into the momentum of the blow, spinning with it while extending his sword, coming full-circle. His blade met Cyrus' stomach. Kyran held it there, to prove his strike would have been lethal. Cyrus dropped his sword, grinning. "Ahh, I thought I had you that time," Cyrus said, clapping Kyran on the shoulder.

"Well, you got my face for sure, Liro's balls." Kyran put his hand to his jaw, wiggling it a bit. A red mark was already sprouting up. It would undoubtedly become a bruise if it weren't for the Eleiyon's fast healing abilities.

The pairs kept rotating. The winner remained in their circle while the loser of the match moved to the right. Kyran's next match was a massive soldier who towered over him and was twice his girth. He proved to be too slow for Kyran's swift footwork. Kyran had him pinned in half the time he took with Cyrus.

After a couple matches, Kyran removed his shirt, revealing a chiseled, sweaty body. Muscles rippled under his skin with each movement. His forearms and triceps bulged with each extension; his abdominals curled with each downward blow. Kyran was lethal, in every way.

The final match finished, and the soldiers walked off the training field, some of them throwing curious glances my way. Kyran plopped down on the bench next to me with his own jug of water, sweat dripping down his forehead and beading on his bare chest.

Trying to look only at his face, I said, "Pretty impressive. I take it from the scorch marks that you sometimes train with your gift?"

"Of course. Magic and hand-to-hand are equally important in battle. We can be drained of energy when we use too much magic. That's why we can never rely solely on it. Many Eleiyon neglect their physical strength because of their magic, but eventually, they will find themselves in trouble. It's important to train with weapons, and to train our bodies, so that we are always ready to fight." He looked out at the rings that still sprinkled the field. "We'll work up to this, Aila. But when I'm done with you, you'll be kicking butt in these circles." He offered me that playful smile that had been missed all day.

I grinned, genuinely happy at the idea of kicking some Archai ass. I reached up to give him a playful shove, but my muscles had already started to stiffen, and an immediate burning across my shoulder halted my movement. "Oww!" I said, grasping my shoulder with my other hand, which caused an equally painful burn in that shoulder. "Yeah, that won't be happening any time soon."

He let out a true belly-laugh.

8

I was the last bit of honey stuck to the bottom of the jar as I inched out of bed. A full six days of training had caught up with me. Every muscle protested movement as I stood to search heaps of clothes for leggings. Pulling them out from under the cot, I made a mental note to wash clothes after breakfast. I finished getting ready, tying my hair in two tight braids down the side of my head. I had been skirting chores the past week and had a lot to catch up on. I wanted to get an early start to prevent Naleiri from noticing exactly how many of my chores I had not done. I slipped into the kitchen and bumped into Naleiri who was standing with her arms crossed, blocking the door.

"I'm not stupid, Aila. You've been disappearing every day for the past week. You never come home with any nuts or herbs. You've rushed to bed before I can ask you anything. It's clear that you're avoiding me. I know you're going into the city, and I'm sure it's to see that general. What's going on?" Her tone was accusatory.

I didn't know why I was the slightest bit surprised. I hadn't exactly developed an elaborate scheme to trick her. I hadn't even thought to collect a basket of mushrooms on the walk home from the city to possibly lead her into thinking I was out gathering each day.

"I'm going to catch up on all of my chores today, Naleiri, I promise."

"I don't care about your chores, Aila. I care about you. You're messing around with the General of the Archai, the Prince of Flames. How do you think that's going to turn out when he discovers what you are? What are you doing all this time with him anyway?" Her anger turned to concern, and mine melted away at once.

"He's not going to find out. There's no reason why he would." I paused, quickly calculating whether to tell her about training or not. I hated keeping things from her. Deciding to lay it all on the table, I said, "He's been training me." I realized I was staring at the floor to avoid her eyes and lifted them to meet her gaze.

It was incredulous. "WHAT? He's training you? In what, Aila? You need to end it. What has been the entire point of living out here if you are just going to bring yourself right into the hands of the people that would see you captured or killed?"

"It's just hand-to-hand combat training. Not magic. He doesn't think I have…I don't even know if I have magic. He trains me by myself in the mornings, and then I watch the rest of the Archai training in the afternoon. That's it." I was defensive. Now that my days with Kyran were in jeopardy, I realized how much I wanted to continue training.

I felt Naleiri's anger radiate off her in pulsing waves. I just stood there, waiting to see what else she would say. I wasn't going to let myself get mad at her. I knew this was coming from a place of concern for me.

"And what if he finds out, Aila?" She repeated her question softly. I knew this was what it was all about— not the chores, not hiding it from her, not the training—it was about my safety.

"He won't," I repeated firmly. I couldn't imagine a scenario in which he would find out. We weren't using magic. Even if I tried to train in magic, I might not have a gift. And for all he knew, I was a Nulk. I told him so. There would be no reason for him to suspect otherwise. "The only way he could find out would be if I revealed my mark, which you know I would never do," I explained.

I'd missed spending time with her this week. My stance softened, and I added, "After I do some chores this morning, want to head up to Orchard's Clearing? Maybe there's still some apples, even though it's late in the season."

She gave a weak smile. A sign she wasn't over it, but she wasn't going to punch me if I approached her. I walked the couple steps to her and gave her a tight hug, rocking her to the right and then to the left. "Come on, Naleiri, smile. You can't stay mad at me forever. I know you want to spend the day with me."

She laughed and hugged me back. "Okay, fine. But we need to finish chopping that wood. I won't be surprised if we get snow by the next moon phase."

———

Orchard's Clearing was our name for the place. It was a hike up the rolling foothills northwest of the cottage. They were the beginning of the Rangi Mountains that rose to the north, in Kiromar. We found it accidentally one day while tracking a deer and named the place Orchard's Clearing for the apple trees that grew there.

The clearing was just as it always was, untouched by Eleiyon. A circular grove of apple trees waited for us; their leaves had already turned yellow, so I doubted any apples would be left on the branches. The sickly-sweet aroma of rotten fruit hung in the air, confirming my suspicions.

The midday sun shined through the yellow-tinged leaves, warming my cheeks and fingers as we left the shade of the forest and entered the clearing. Scattered throughout the grove were the wrinkled remains of the apples deemed unworthy by birds or other animals. Despite the chilled air and lack of edible apples, the clearing was still beautiful and worth the hike.

The apple trees swayed in greeting to Naleiri. A couple of squirrels ran over to her, circling wildly around her feet and then bracing their front paws on her legs. She knelt to greet them, handing them an acorn she had collected on our march up. They chattered gratefully and scurried off into the forest. I admired her gift. Untrained as it was, she was a natural. She could have so easily bent the world to her will, all of nature on her side, but she was content to live amongst the wildlife rather than rule it.

"I never get sick of this view," I called to Naleiri over my shoulder.

The clearing stood on the side of the foothill overlooking the western-most part of Fira below. Although I couldn't see it, I knew Aodhen was behind us. Sprawling out to the west and north was seemingly endless forest. Naleiri and I never ventured further. The city was full of newcomers lately with whisperings of change in that part of the forest; stories of destructive raids and dangerous, wicked creatures crawling down from wherever they'd been hiding for millennia. It could have been a trick of the light, but it looked like the woods to the north were darker somehow, cast in shadow.

My eyes scanned the treetops, looking for the telltale sign of the small town that I knew stood at the southern edge. Sure enough, I spotted the break in the trees that was a narrow river and traced its path to the small clearing, revealing the town's location. Farther to the south was Lake Luan, glistening in the sun against the darkness of the forest, like a full moon in the night sky. The lake was believed to be patrolled by a gigantic sea dragon that could breathe fire the likes of which no Archai could match.

Naleiri and I plopped down on the soft grass, looking out over the beauty below us. By the time Naleiri spoke, the sun had moved from its spot directly above us to where it would become part of the view over the western expanse. "We should have built a cottage right here, so we could look out over this every evening." She followed my gaze.

"True. We still could...build our own place here." They were empty words, because I knew the last thing either of us would want would be to destroy the serenity of this place by building something here.

A lone yellow flower still stood in the clearing, braving the coming cold. It swayed in the light breeze in front of my feet. Its glorious, colorful days behind it.

"What does that remind you of, Naleiri?" I nodded toward the flower. She turned in the direction I pointed. A smile played on her lips as her eyes landed on it.

"The day we met," she said simply. "I woke up and you were sitting across from me, staring. You just followed me around Aodhen that day, completely silent, like you were in some kind of trance or something."

"I was lost," I agreed, remembering that day waking up on the cot, trying to piece together what had happened.

"All of us were lost in that place. Misfits from somewhere else. I'd only just arrived a few phases earlier, after... after my grandmother was killed."

"Those first few days were hard for me." The emptiness I'd tried to fill over the last three years still hung in my chest, reminding me of how I'd felt that morning. "I remember we sat on your cot and just talked into the night. And you took out that dried flower you had in your satchel." Her smile widened as she too recalled the memory. "When you pulled it out, I remember being surprised it hadn't crumbled to pieces considering how brittle it looked. And just as I reached for it, it transformed. The stem became green and plump. You breathed life into the petals. They became the happiest of yellows."

"I remember," Naleiri said softly.

"It was my first time seeing your gift," I remembered fondly.

We sat together quietly for a moment, lost in our shared memory. Then she asked, "Why is the training so important to you?"

Why was it so important to me? The truth was I hadn't felt this alive since I awoke on that cot in Aodhen. And not knowing how I'd ended up there, or why, still haunted me. I thought back to the countless times she and I had been chased by the Archai. "I don't want to have to rely on anyone, Naleiri. I want to be able to protect the ones I love. To be able to do something if I ever have to," I finally answered.

She nodded silently. "That's why I like the forest. If you respect it, it respects you. Everything is living off the same land, just trying to survive. And survival is easier when you help each other. It's much harder with the Eleiyon: the hidden motives, the selfishness, ambition, destruction. The forest is simpler," she ended with a shrug.

I didn't disagree with her. "Do you think you could be happy here forever? In the cottage, I mean?"

The words came out light, but they voiced an unspoken something in my heart that had begun to stir over the past week. Training in the city with Kyran had awakened a feeling that I hadn't known was there. A restlessness.

"I could," she answered softly after a moment. "I think it's the Forest Nymph in me. The Eleyi were only nomadic out of necessity. They were constantly chased from one village to the next, or out of one forest and into another. When my grandmother found a place in the forest that could support us for a time, we set down roots, just like the trees. Stayed as long as we could. That's when I was happiest." She paused her recollection. "I know you can't, though. I've known it since we moved out here, that it is too quiet, too small a place to hold you." She looked at me sadly. "I'm just not sure where I fit in." She blinked a tear away and turned her head to look back at the forest stretching out beneath us.

I hated this. Letting someone stick me repeatedly with Dendro Needles felt preferable to putting voice to the thoughts running inside my head. Part of me wanted to tell her that I didn't know either. That staying in the cottage, even if it was with her, would lead to a slow wilting of everything I was, like a flower left in the blazing sun, with no water to nourish it. *Who was I kidding? A flower?* More like one of these rotting apples, left to be picked at by scavengers and slowly disintegrate into the ground around it, until it was nothing.

The other part of me loved Naleiri so much that I wanted to protect her, even from myself. I had too many feelings. Feelings that were unfocused and undirected, not meant to hurt her, but if I ever let them loose, they would. So, I swallowed them.

"You fit with me. We're in this together." And I wanted so badly for it to be true. "I'm not leaving, Naleiri." And even though a chain tightened its grip around my heart as I said it, I meant it. I had no one else in the world but my best friend sitting next to me. No memories. No past. No family. Why would I leave the only person in the world who looked at me, knew what I was, and loved me?

"Enough of this blubbering talk," she said, casting me a sideways smile. "Tell me about training."

I held her eyes for a moment to see if she really wanted to know. "Exhausting," I said, finally deciding on the perfect word. "I've been learning a lot. Honestly, Kyran has been great. He's taught me so much in such a short time..." I paused for a moment, letting thoughts come together. "I wonder about him. He doesn't seem bad. Sure, he has his biases. I don't agree with his position on Nulks for example, but... I wonder how much of his beliefs are his own. You know?"

"What do you mean?" Naleiri asked.

"I mean...how much choice do you think he has as the Prince of Flame? Born into a way of life. No one there to challenge him to see things differently."

"Ahh. I see." Naleiri nodded, exaggerating her understanding. "You think you can change him."

"No. I'm just saying maybe he'd be open to change is all."

She looked at me for another moment. "Maybe," she said quietly. Her lips curved into a soft smile that didn't reach her eyes. Then she stood, brushing away the dried grass pieces that clung to her bottom. "We should start heading back now, so that we make it home before dark," she advised.

"Right," I agreed, following her to my feet.

The way down was always faster than the way up. The western side of the mountain was an easier descent. The heavily wooded slope created a canopy overhead, shielding the sinking sun and leaving us in relative shade despite the clear blue skies peeking through the branches. Two bluebirds flitted this way and that, high above us, jabbering away. They took a dive toward us, seemed to think better of it, and landed on the branch of an elm tree. Naleiri stopped to watch them.

"What is it?" To me, their squeaking chatter sounded exactly as it always did, but Naleiri's brows furrowed.

"They're not from around here. They want to talk to us. Well... to me. Surprisingly, they're scared of you," she said sarcastically, raising her eyebrows in mock astonishment.

"Me?" I mouthed dramatically, feigning insult. I felt the warmth of her magic emanate from her body as she called the birds over. They considered it for a moment before flying down to perch on either of Naleiri's shoulders.

The conversation was a series of chirps and tweets, but Naleiri nodded in understanding before the birds flew off.

"They are from the woods on the northern border, but they had to leave. It's sinking into darkness...they said creatures long believed to have vanished from Kiakora, have returned to the forest, prowling at night, killing everything they see. And there's...something. They said it's a decay, growing on the trees and over the ferns. Like a poisonous mold... but... unnatural. Choking the life out of the forest. They escaped. I guess many birds were able to, but everything else has been... consumed." She stared off in the direction of the northern woods as if she could see all the way to the borders where the darkness was smothering the forest. I knew she was listening for the secrets carried on the leaves.

She added quietly, "They said it's spreading. They warned us to leave the forest. It will not be safe here for long." Her eyes shimmered in the soft light. Naleiri could not bear to see nature harmed. The roots that sprawled beneath the forest ran through her veins as well. She loved it more than anything. Well, perhaps second to me.

"Let's get home. We can talk about what to do there." I reached for her hand, still warm from the magic. "Maybe we can save it." I meant the words as encouragement but felt the hopelessness that weighed on them. *What could we do?*

9

The bluebirds' story preoccupied my entire walk to the city the next morning. I couldn't help but look for signs of the darkness they warned about, but the serenity of the forest seemed unbroken. Kyran was waiting for me in the clearing as usual.

Should I tell him? Did the Lord of Flame know what was happening within his borders? Would he try to stop it?

I turned the questions over and over, trying to find all the angles they could be viewed from. I knew anything I shared with Kyran would bring attention back to Naleiri and me. His first question would surely be, *how do you know?*

So what? Naleiri was Eleyi. She could commune with nature. It was a rare gift, but everyone knew about the Eleyi and their shared bloodline to the Forest Nymphs. It was not unheard of to find one in the city. The real worry was if the story would lead to questions about me.

"Lost in thought?" Kyran's deep voice pulled me out of my internal banter. I flashed a smile.

"Just admiring the view."

"Why, thank you. I did spend some extra time picking out my outfit today." He stretched his arms, checking himself out.

"I meant..." I placed heavy emphasis on the words, "the view of the meadow." The dew that normally danced on the tips of the long grass had frosted over, making them look like long eyelashes that had caught falling snowflakes. I clutched at the collar of my white turtleneck, pulling it higher to my jaw to prevent the cold from seeping into my skin.

Kyran feigned insult before pivoting toward the city.

———

The ring was set up differently today. Kyran had stretched two ropes from one wall to the other. Off to the right were three posts with thick pads tied around them. They poked out of the ground like big sticks skewering marshmallows.

"We're going to start working on technique. Don't worry, we'll still do plenty of endurance and cardio as well," he said, giving me a reassuring look, as if I had somehow expressed concern over not spending all day lunging across the field.

I picked up the ropes quickly, bobbing and weaving up and under, across the field, moving forward and backward. This was the first step to avoiding and blocking oncoming attacks, Kyran explained.

"Subtle movements! You don't need to exaggerate so much," he critiqued after I squatted particularly low to dodge the rope. "Remember, eventually these are going to be punches and kicks. I need swift, concise movements so that you are always ready for what's next," he warned.

The posts were a bit harder. I got the concept of sticking a punch fine enough, but Kyran insisted on perfecting my stance.

"Don't square up. You leave your entire body open to attack when you do that." He took a short wooden stick, lightly prodding my side, my gut, and my ankle to demonstrate his point. I couldn't dodge any of the strikes. "Turn your body to the side, like this." I felt his warmth as he came up behind me. His hand lightly pushed the back of my hip forward, rotating my body. I couldn't help my breath catch as he grabbed the back of my left thigh, positioning it farther forward. He backed away, barking a few more orders. "Turn your head to face forward. Arms up. Always protect your face." He tapped the outside of both of my hands, demonstrating how they created a barrier for my head. "Now, stay on the balls of your feet, and no matter where you move, keep your feet this distance apart so that you always maintain your balance." He indicated the shoulder-length space I'd created. "On the balls of your feet!" he repeated, rapping my boots with the stick.

"I might rip that thing out of your hands and hit you with it if you keep poking me."

"Oh, right. Sorry. Just a habit, I guess." He set it down on the ground sheepishly.

It took well over an excruciating hour for him to be satisfied with my stance. My shoulders burned, and all I'd accomplished was standing correctly. Once he approved, he finally taught me the basics of throwing punches and kicks at inanimate targets.

"Am I training with the Archai today?" I asked as we trekked up to the main training field.

"Not yet." He looked me up and down, assessing my form. Although the look appeared calculating, his hazel eyes lingered too long to be purely objective. He added, "You need a little more time practicing the basics before getting in a ring with a trained soldier."

———

The Archai trudged off the field, grumbling. Training had gone overtime for the third day in a row. Cyrus and Kyran were still engaged in a brutal battle. I took the opportunity to run to the washroom situated just behind the bench. The clanging of the swords stopped, replaced by angry voices that floated off the field. My hand paused on the doorknob.

"You've missed morning training for a full moon phase now. You know I had to report it to your father. And for what, some low-class Nulk?"

"She is training hard," Kyran responded after a moment of silence. "She could be useful."

"She can't be. She doesn't wield fire. She doesn't have any gifts at all, does she? Your father would never allow it, and neither would half the Archai on this field."

Kyran didn't respond.

"Listen," continued Cyrus in a softer tone. "I get it. You have some kind of crush on this Nulk, for whatever reason. That's fine. Get it out of your system and don't do it during training. That's all I'm saying."

"Cyrus, you're my best friend. But you don't give me orders." His voice was harsher than I'd ever heard it. "Aila will train with the Archai until I see fit to let her go." Another beat of silence. "And if my father has a problem with it, tell him to bring it up to me." His last words lost the bite of the first. *He wouldn't stand up for me against his father, regardless of what he might tell Cyrus.*

Silence.

Then, "Yes, sir." I heard the rustle of clothes as Cyrus must have bowed. I waited another minute, hand still on the doorknob, before stepping back onto the field.

"Sword training is always fun." Kyran's easy smile greeted me as I walked over to the bench. His face was clear of emotion. "Let's get you back home."

We walked in silence, each of us lost in our thoughts. The sun had warmed the air considerably since this morning. *Why was he spending all this time with me? Would I even want to be an Archai, if that were a possibility?* I couldn't shake Cyrus' words: "get it out of your system," "low class Nulk." As painful as it was to hear aloud, it was true. I knew what the Archai thought of me. And compared to Kyran—I almost let out an audible chuckle—I was nothing.

As if hearing my thoughts, Kyran spoke, "You know..." He reached for my hand, lightly tugging my pinky to spin me toward him. His touch sent a tingle up my arm, warming my face. I allowed it. "I've enjoyed the time we've spent together."

Alright, here it is. The goodbye. I guessed he had considered what Cyrus had said and decided he agreed after all. I waited for my dismissal.

After sensing that I wasn't going to reciprocate, even though I too had enjoyed myself, more than he needed know, he added, "We could meet more often... outside of training, I mean." Even though it was phrased as a statement, the question dangled in his eyes.

I could have just said yes. I hadn't known it, but now that he said it, I realized I wanted that too. Without the pretense of training and the distraction of the Archai, or the serious persona Kyran couldn't seem to help but adopt on the field. Spending time with just him would be perfect. Maybe it was my pride, or out of hurt, but instead of yes, I heard myself saying, "Why? Why, Kyran?" My lips framed his name. It was intimate, the way I said it, like he and I had some kind of relationship that justified it. *We didn't.* "What do you want from me? Why are you hanging around a *low-class Nulk*?" I spit Cyrus' words back at him.

Hurt and understanding crossed his face. He looked down, dropping my hand. "I'm sorry you heard that." He looked back at me, his eyes earnest. "I don't agree with him. I don't think that. It's just..."

My tone softened slightly. "It's just what? He's not wrong. I can never be an Archai. But that doesn't answer why, Kyran. Why are you investing so much time in me?"

His eyes searched my face as if he could find the words he was looking for hidden there. He warred with the same question, his expression passing from curiosity, to desire, to anger, to shame. He understood just as little as I did about why he was going to such great lengths to be in my company.

After what seemed like ages, he finally said in a husky voice, "We're spending so much time together because I want to. We are training because you want to. The rest of it is a problem for another day. Now..." He reached for my hands again, his smooth palms clasping my own in a strong grip. "Would you meet me, the day after tomorrow?"

"That's the Festival of Flame."

"I know. There's nothing quite like the Festival of Flame in Aodhen." He smiled, and then, not quite pleading but close to it, "Will you come?"

Despite my screaming instincts telling me this could not, would not, end well, and despite my acknowledgment that the growing feelings blossoming in my heart could only ever serve to break it, I said, "Yes. I'll be there."

He flashed his easy smile. His smooth hand reached up to tuck another strand of loose hair behind my ear. Goosebumps tickled the back of my neck as his fingers grazed my cheek.

"Get home safely, Aila." And with that, he turned and walked back into the city. I was left standing in the meadow, completely unbothered by the sting of the chilled air on my palms as the warmth of his touch left.

10

The morning of the festival arrived, and I hadn't picked an outfit. After bathing, I sifted through my limited clothing options for the third time, searching for something halfway decent. I finally settled on one of my two high-neck knitted tops to shield myself from the early winter air. This one was black, faded from overuse, but it fit nicely. I pulled it on over the tight, dark green pants I had already chosen.

"So, is this like a date or something?" Naleiri appeared at the doorway to the bathroom as I fussed with my wet hair. I finally decided on pulling it back into the same tight tail that I wore almost every day in training, not having the time to wait until it dried or the patience to figure out another style.

"No," I said too quickly. "It's just us meeting up outside of training is all."

"Yeah, for the Festival of Flame. I'd imagine that's a pretty big deal to the General of the Archai, Heir to the House of Fira, His Gloryship, and all," she mocked.

"I doubt it. It's probably old news for him. Growing up in the middle of it every year? It just seems like a big deal because we've never seen it." We'd always purposely stayed far away from the activity of the city during the festival. The number of Archai that wandered the streets would surely double.

"There will be light shows and fire dances. It's supposed to be quite beautiful, so I've heard." Her tone changed to genuine curiosity about the festival.

"You want to come? I'm sure Kyran wouldn't mind." A sudden twinge of guilt at leaving her alone tonight mixed with my excitement.

"I'm sure he would, actually." She grinned mischievously. "I have a lot to do around here, anyway. The squirrels say it's going to snow soon. Besides, I'm not interested in being the third wheel on your not-date... And stop messing around with it." She grabbed my hands from attempting to retie my hair for the umpteenth time. "You look beautiful."

Aodhen transformed for the Festival of Flame. It was only midday, but it looked as if the entire city was out preparing for that evening's celebration. Black, maroon, and orange banners, the colors of the House of Fira, lined the sidewalks. Streamers of the same colors draped across the city streets like clothes hanging out to dry, blowing in the light breeze that swept through the city.

It was more crowded than a typical Market Day. Vendors prepared their stalls, some boycotting their traditional merchandise for festival-themed goods. One stall had already managed to gather a crowd of children. The peddler was demonstrating to his wide-eyed audience an enchanted stick. He waved it rapidly through the air, slashing up and down. As soon as the stick stopped moving, the word "LIRO" burst into flame, suspended in the air where he had been tracing moments before. The words transformed into a long-tailed dragon and chased the children. The kids clapped, some running off to beg their parents for the four pyra that the enchanted stick would cost them.

As I made my way closer to Center Square, our agreed meeting place, a delicious aroma drifted from the side street stocked with vendors. The sweet smell of candied plums and pecans floated over the sea of smoke coming from an alley. Before my cravings could draw me off track, Kyran's muscular form caught my eye. He was talking to two other Archai. He motioned to each of the four corners of Center Square in turn, probably ordering sentries to be stationed there.

Not sure whether to approach him while he was clearly "on duty," I settled for fiddling with one of the festival flags displayed in the stall next to me. The flag came in each of the House of Fira colors with a gold triangle stitched in the center. I jumped as a small bead of flame blazed to life in the bottom left corner of the triangle and traveled to each of the remaining points before returning to where it had started. The flags were piled into a large barrel next to a long rectangular table laid out with other House of Fira merchandise. I watched the fire bead make another round on the triangle. Naleiri might get a kick out of one of these.

"Excuse me," I called to the vendor's back. He was probably selling them for a killing. "Excuse me, how much are these flags?"

"Six pyra each," the vendor answered cheerfully as he spun around.

I jumped back, almost knocking over the barrel of flags. The vendor's bright green eyes latched onto my own, so similar, yet so different from the haunting eyes of my dreams.

"Is something wrong?" he asked, his cheerful expression slipping into concern.

"No...I...Never mind. I have to go. Thank you," I sputtered, excusing myself as quickly as I could.

I wandered through the gathering crowd. I was still on edge after seeing those eyes when a firm tug on my shoulder sent another wave of adrenaline through my system.

Kyran wore a maroon silk shirt, unbuttoned at the top, revealing a peek at his marble chest. The collar sported the typical black triangle, which matched his black pants.

"You look..." he started. I glanced down at my own outfit. A different shade of what I wore every time I saw him.

"Exactly the same as always," I stated, finishing his sentence. My heart returned to its normal rhythm.

"I was going to say stunning, actually." He smiled. "May I?" he asked, holding out his hand for my own. The playful smile that I remembered from the day I'd met him was back. There was no sign of the drill sergeant who I had come to expect in the training ring. I accepted his outstretched hand and felt a slight thrill as his warmth enveloped my own.

"So, when did the Festival of Fire become a propaganda party for the House of Fira?" I said jokingly, nodding at the various tables of merchandise.

He grinned. "Since my father saw an opportunity to make money without increasing taxes and unify our people around the House of Fira at the same time. A win-win, I'd say." He said it proudly. *Taxes.* The Archai protected Aodhen and the rest of Fira, but I wondered how much of the tax money went to that, and how much lined the lord's pockets. I didn't bother asking.

The afternoon went by in a blur of street food and craft stalls. It seemed like every hour Kyran was buying me a different must-have festival treat. Vendors demonstrating their own fire gifts charbroiled steaks on skewers with spouts of flame and heated tubs of sugar to be whipped into bags of sweet pull-apart candy. Kyran insisted on blackened corn: a chili-seasoned corn on the cob literally seared in the hands of the vendor. It was delicious. We paused to admire the craftsmanship of a glassblower who shaped giant globes of molten glass with steady streams of his own flame, adjusting the heat and intensity to form striations of different colors.

As evening descended, we made our way to just outside of Center Square where the fire dance performance was set up. I cradled the warm hot chocolate Kyran had just bought. I'd never tasted something so rich. I'd watched as the vendor spewed an endless stream of fire to melt the chocolate down from solid chunks for each cup. She added milk and cinnamon to the thick concoction. I didn't even protest when Kyran suggested we try it.

I tried to ignore the questioning looks and behind-the-hand gossip as I followed Kyran to the first row of reserved seating for the dance.

"You are the talk of the town tonight," Kyran whispered as we took our seats.

"I think they're probably more concerned with you than me." I couldn't help glancing around as I said it, catching the eyes of a couple who quickly looked away.

Kyran leaned over so that his lips brushed my ear and his warm breath, still sweet from the hot chocolate, filled my nose. "Let's give them something to talk about." His whisper was sensual, sending my heart into overdrive and shivers down my spine.

"I don't think they need any additional motivation." I pressed my hand against his chest, gently pushing him back in his seat. But my face warmed, and my heart thudded against my chest.

He leaned back into his chair with a casual wink. I rolled my eyes. He snickered and turned to look at the stage. Something told me Kyran was very used to getting everything he wanted. And more.

The performance started with cascading jets of fire and then a flood of performers swirled on stage. The females wore cropped tops and long black skirts slit open on the sides. Beads of fire ran continuously along the seams of their flowing skirts, creating endless streams of light as they twisted and twirled. The men wore maroon pants, cut short to show off their chiseled calves. Flaming rings of fire decorated their wrists when they stood still and morphed into streaks of orange as they performed acrobatic feats across the stage. The music flared with intensity, the beating drums dictating the speed of the performers' flips and spins. A male performer would occasionally launch a female one into the air, where she would shoot streaks of flames in wide arcs before falling harmlessly into the awaiting arms of another performer.

As the dancers somersaulted, becoming balls of fire moving across the stage, a warm weight slid over my thigh. Kyran's heavy hand gripped my leg tightly before beginning to rub small soft circles with his thumb. My body tensed. I wasn't ready to give him the satisfaction of knowing I enjoyed his touch. I ignored it, keeping my eyes trained on the stage, even as my mind wandered.

The performance ended with the dancers forming a pyramid of bodies. In the final moments, they blasted fire from their palms, creating a wall of flame in the shape of the Archai triangle. It stood for a moment before the dancers tumbled through the wall of fire, unharmed, holding each other's hands for a final bow.

Kyran's hand slid from my leg as we stood, applauding the performers.

———

"That was the first time I've seen the Fire Dance. It was spectacular," I added, still impressed by the flying acrobats of the dancers. We'd begun our walk back to the edge of the city.

"Really? I'm surprised. It's one of the oldest aspects of the Festival of Flame...the merchandise came much later," he said with a smirk, plucking a House of Fira banner from a vendor's bucket as we strolled by.

"Naleiri and I always just celebrate together," I explained.

"What about before that? Your family?" he asked, his face genuinely interested in hearing my story.

"I don't remember much about my family."

"I see," he said softly, thankfully deciding not to press me for more details. "Well, the Fire Dance actually dates back to before the official founding of Aodhen. Fire has always been the element most naturally controlled by the Eleiyon. It is the only original element that doesn't come directly from the land. Fire exists outside of the natural world, born from it, living in it, but still separate." He kindled a small flame on his open palm as he spoke, demonstrating his point. "It needs to be molded, manipulated, and fed to exist." He spoke of the fire lovingly, as if it were his loyal companion. "That's what the fire dance represents, and what is at the heart of the entire Festival really, our connection to our gift. A reminder that we have the ability to control fire, but if we don't respect its power, it can consume us." He clenched his palm, extinguishing the dancing flame.

I'd gotten so lost in Kyran's explanation that I didn't realize how quickly we'd arrived at the edge of the forest. It was already time to leave.

A small object appeared in Kyran's hands. He fiddled with it, opened his mouth, changed his mind, and closed it again.

"Is there something you want to say, Kyran?" I couldn't handle the suspense any longer.

We stopped. He continued to toy with the object in his hand, looking past me into the forest. "I was waiting for the right time to give this to you, but the evening went by so fast."

"You didn't have to... I mean, tonight was more than enough..."

"I know. I wanted to. Here," he said, pressing a brown leather holder with a matching strap into my hand. The strap was braided. It connected to a sheath where a bone-white handle poked out. I slowly withdrew the small dagger to reveal a blade the size of my palm. Along one side, the blade was etched with swirls that looked like flames.

"It's beautiful," I whispered quietly. The moon caught Kyran's reflection in the shiny silver. His flaming eyes were on me, no attempt at hiding the desire he felt. I brought my eyes to meet his. The smoldering look was gone, replaced by something more unsure.

"Do you like it?" he asked tentatively.

"Yes. Yes, I do." I sheathed the blade again, sliding it nicely into its leather pocket.

"May I?"

I offered him the knife. He stretched the braided strap between his arms, straightening it. Kneeling at my feet, he fitted the strap around my mid-thigh.

His fingers grazed the same spot where he had placed his hand during the performance. His touch sent more sparks flying up my spine, and my heart launched into palpitations. He tightened the strap until it fit securely but comfortably on my leg.

"Perfect," he said, getting to his feet. "It's a small blade," he added, his tone suddenly reverting to the trainer I had grown accustomed to, "so use it as an extension of your jabs. No need to change your form to fight with it. It is part of your fist." He cast an apprehensive glance at the forest. "Why don't you live in the city anyway? Marching into the forest every day has to be exhausting."

I'd told him this on more than one occasion but repeated the answer just the same. "My best friend is like a sister to me, and she likes the forest. Besides, the family that runs Aodhen charges too much in taxes." I grinned a half smile, tempting him into a debate.

He didn't fall for it. Instead, he said, "Well, are you sure you don't want me to walk you home? It's dark."

"Thanks for pointing out the obvious," I joked. "I've walked this path a million times. It's fine. It's not that late anyhow, and now I have this." I motioned to the dagger strapped to my thigh. The thought of the bluebirds' warning fluttered into my mind, but I brushed it off. Naleiri and I hadn't noticed anything out of the ordinary since that afternoon.

He considered my argument for a moment before glancing uneasily at the dark woods. His eyes surveyed the tree line, performing a soldier's calculation of the risks. His expression cleared, and he stepped closer so that his face was just inches from mine. "I had a great time with you tonight," he said softly.

"Me too. Thank you...for the gift and for all the food. Hopefully it doesn't slow me down in training tomorrow," I said, unconsciously placing a hand on my overstuffed stomach.

"Hopefully not. You're going to start training with weapons tomorrow...and sparring with the Archai." The flutter in my stomach had nothing to do with the shrinking proximity between us, or the food in my belly.

"Good night, Aila." He bent down, placing his warm lips on my cheek. My nostrils filled with his warm vanilla and sandalwood scent. The intense desire reflected in the blade earlier lurked for a moment behind his carefree smile, and then it was gone. Straightening, he added, "Get home safe."

I felt his eyes boring into my back as I disappeared into the forest.

11

The brush of Kyran's lips lingered on my cheek as I walked home. I savored the secret glances he shot me throughout the night when he thought I wasn't looking. While thoughts of Kyran flitted through my mind, I couldn't help the creep of doubt that tried to ensnare them. *How much could I trust him? What if I was just a momentary distraction?* I tried to shake the feelings already planting roots in my heart. *This could not be good.*

I was nearing a familiar bend in the path that would lead me slightly southwest of Aodhen when I felt it. The delight from just moments before disappeared in a sudden burst of adrenaline. Something was watching me. My ears strained to pick up the sound of a snapping twig or the unavoidable crunch of dried leaves.

Nothing.

I peered into the darkness behind my right shoulder. It was the unmistakable chill of something stalking me. I searched for the glowing eyes that would give away an animal.

Nothing.

Fingering the short blade strapped to my thigh, I pulled it out and held it ready. I felt, more than saw, the sudden agitation of the still darkness in front of me. Without a second thought, I raised my dagger, deciding not to run until I knew exactly what I faced. And another dreadful thought: how many of it I faced.

Red eyes emerged from the bushes, towering over my head. They loomed in front of me, as if suspended from the branches, before the rest of the massive creature crawled into the open. It was a gigantic insect, half the size of the tallest trees. Its curved body had a permanent arch, supporting two thick legs that ended in sharp talons. They were poised to stab its prey at any moment. The thorax was covered in short, swaying hairs, making its exoskeleton look alive. The rest of its centipede-like body was carried on dozens of squirming legs. Just below its glowing red eyes, stretching almost entirely across its triangular head, was a large, salivating mouth filled with rows of razor-sharp teeth.

It clicked and snapped as it crawled forward, moving its head jerkily from side to side. It gnashed its jaws, producing more saliva, which started to pool and drip to the forest floor, where it dissolved into the dirt with a smoking hiss.

I backed away slowly. *Liro's balls. What had Kyran said? The dagger is an extension of your fist.* All the hours of training came to me as I slid my left foot forward and turned my body sideways. The creature immediately responded by trying to circle toward my front. *It wants a large target.* I moved on the balls of my feet to prevent that. I circled opposite the creature, keeping my eyes locked on its deadly claws.

A short, quick step forward tested the creature's reaction. It skittered quickly to my right before continuing its circular dance. Tossing the dagger to my other hand and holding it ready, I made the same quick step forward with my left foot, slightly bigger this time. Anticipating the creature's move to the right, I spun and ducked, swinging my blade-wielding arm with all my strength, jamming the creature's soft underbelly with the dagger.

It let out an ear-splitting squeal and slammed its claws down where I had been moments before. I was already back on the balls of my feet, poised for the counterattack I knew would come. Black blood oozed from its wound. It was deep. *Good.*

No more circling. The creature attacked straight on with a swift slash of its left claw. The point just grazed my arm before I dive-rolled out of the way. It left a superficial scratch across my bicep, ripping the sleeve of my tunic. Not giving me a chance to gather my bearings, it launched itself again, this time with its right claw. I slashed out with my dagger, severing the claw at its first curved joint. Another shriek as more black blood poured from the new wound. It was lopsided now.

Kyran would tell me it was time. *Don't wait for it to regain its composure, go for the kill.* I heard his voice in my head. *Now!*

I threw myself forward. I barely noticed the gust of air that propelled me higher. I held the dagger over my head and rammed it into the creature's forehead. The creature fell, its red eyes dulled with death. My dagger protruded from its head.

The pounding of my heart in my ears drowned out the silence of the night forest. I took a step back, dislodging myself from the lifeless body. I bent to collect my dagger, pulling it from the creature's head with a sickening squelch.

As I turned, two more clicking creatures appeared from the depths of the forest.

Having assessed my fighting style with their comrade, they wasted no time in attacking straight on. I dodged the first one with a dive to my left, but not in time. An excruciating pain pierced my calf and radiated up my leg. The shriek I heard now was my own. I looked back; bright red blood poured from a gaping hole in my calf. My vision blurred, and ringing started in my ears. Both creatures reared up for their final death blow.

And then the night was on fire.

The insects let out their otherworldly squeals as flames consumed their writhing bodies. The intensity of the heat burned my face. I turned away, dragging myself farther from whatever new terror I was going to have to face.

The creatures fell to the ground in charred masses, and Kyran stepped through the remaining flames. His face was pure fury. Then his eyes caught mine.

Relief. His features relaxed slightly as he made his way over to me. His eyes tightened at the site of my wound. He scooped me up in a single, fluid motion.

"I'm sorry, Aila. I shouldn't have let you walk home alone. Are you okay?" His voice was worried as he tried to both inspect my wound and carry me back toward the city.

I was slowly drifting out of consciousness. The blood continued to gush from my calf. "Naleiri," I muttered weakly.

"What?"

"Naleiri. My sister. You have to get her. She's there alone. In the cottage off the trail... you'll see it...not safe...please." And then a darkness more absolute than the night itself enveloped me.

12

*F*ire crackled loudly.

"She's not here."

The voice was strong and clear, rising above the noise of the raging fire as it consumed the house.

My village. My life.

The suffocating smoke choked my lungs, but I ran, feeling my legs lock into the familiar movement.

My mother. I knew that voice anywhere. It could be stripped from me a thousand times and I would still recognize it. The melodic notes that sang away my cuts and bruises or carried me off to a soundless sleep, hidden now beneath fear.

"She's not here." Stronger this time.

CRACK!

My eyes snapped open.

———

"What were you thinking?" Naleiri did nothing to hide the accusation and worry in her voice.

"I know... I wasn't, I guess." Kyran was sitting in a small chair in the corner of the room, hunched, his head in his hands.

"How long have you known?" Another accusation.

"We didn't. I swear on the Ancient One."

"That's sugsack and you know it! You and the rest of the Archai do nothing but patrols. How long have you known the creatures moved this far south? How long have you known and continued to let Aila walk home alone after your training sessions?" She didn't give him a chance to respond. "You just don't care. The forest isn't important enough for you to bother. Let the darkness have it." Her voice dripped with anger and pain.

"That's not true! We didn't know about the northern border until it was too late."

"Who is talking right now? You, or the carefully crafted lies of your father and his court?"

"Careful now, Naleiri." Kyran's tone changed. He stood, anger burning in his eyes as well.

"Hey, can you both stop arguing please? Can't a girl recover in peace over here?" I added weakly, trying to lighten the mood.

They both spun to the bed as I spoke. Naleiri, seething a moment before, smiled wider than I had seen since we had splurged on Fizzed Horcha and chocolate pastries a couple Market Days ago.

She bounced the few steps to my bed and hugged me tightly. "How are you feeling?"

"Fine," I squeezed out through her tight hug. "Good as new," I said, raising my leg and seeing that it was completely healed thanks to my fast-acting blood. Healing quickly was part of the Eleiyon package, gifted or not.

"You're lucky Kyran found you. That creature's claw is venomous. Your blood wasn't enough to heal the wound on its own," Naleiri explained. I shuddered against the thought of what would have happened if Kyran hadn't followed me into the forest.

Kyran paced awkwardly behind Naleiri. I was in a small room with dark wooden floors that matched the bookcase directly opposite me. A small circular table was placed next to the chair Kyran had been sitting on. It was topped with a red-based lantern that glowed tangerine from the flickering flame. A bay window cast dimmed midday light into the room despite the thin, white curtain draped across it. To my right, a small metal cart with various medical instruments, gauges, and ointments stood ready for the next patient.

"Where are we?" I asked, looking at Kyran.

"This is the infirmary... in my house."

I gulped. We were inside the House of Fira. "Thank you...you know, for saving me," I said awkwardly.

Kyran flashed a proud smile. "You did great by yourself. I can't believe you took out a Myriapod on your own, and with no powers. Incredible."

"Yeah; too bad there were two more of those things." I shivered at the memory of their clicking gait. The conversation I had woken up to drifted back to me. "Why were they here? Will the Archai do something about it?"

"No." "Yes." Naleiri and Kyran answered at the same time, glaring at each other.

"Yes. I am organizing a search party. We'll be out in the forest a couple of days, traveling north to see if we can figure out where the creatures are coming from," Kyran answered, casting an annoyed glance at Naleiri. "Though I'm sure they are gifts from the Shades." He sneered the last part.

"I'll get my things." I made to slide off the bed.

"You're not coming with us, Aila," Kyran said firmly.

Naleiri looked at me incredulously. "Are you crazy?" Her voice rose a decibel. "I told him about the bluebirds, he *claims* to have had no idea." She glared daggers at Kyran. "It's clear the forest isn't safe anymore. You almost got mauled to death and you want to go back out there? To do what?"

"To do something, Naleiri." My anger flared. The flood of restlessness I'd felt over the last three years surfaced. "I can't just sit here and hope everything is going to be okay while others are out there doing something about it. That's not me." She cringed at the veiled insult and the unsaid words. *That's you.*

"I get it," Kyran interrupted. "But you're just healing. It's a small, trained patrol. We need to move quickly. It's more of a scouting mission really, and if we do encounter trouble, I can't be worried about keeping you safe." His tone was final. It was his drill sergeant persona and there would be no swaying him.

I slouched back into the bed. "So, what now?" I said, more to Naleiri than Kyran, thinking about our home in the woods, which now might be too dangerous to enter.

But it was Kyran who answered. "Now... you go check out your new home." His expression became light and happy at the confused look on our faces.

The home was luxurious. I shouldn't have expected anything less from the Prince of Flame, but I was still overwhelmed as I stood in the open atrium. Despite its location in the city's center, the noise of the busy streets and Center Square, visible from the front window, didn't penetrate the house. An enchantment of some kind, I assumed, after watching a large group of Eleiyon talking animatedly but seemingly silently right outside the window.

It was pristine, nothing like the old buildings Kyran had shown me on that first day we spent walking through the city, or like the dilapidated tavern where I'd first met Naleiri three years ago. This was bright and open. The furniture elegant but tasteful. The atrium opened into a large living space with two heather-gray sofas, each draped with a maroon throw. They sat facing each other with a low, glass table between them on which sat an arrangement of dried wildflowers. As was typical of any house in Fira, a large fireplace took up most of the far wall. The mantel was lined with shining obsidian rocks of all sizes.

It was too perfect, far from lived-in, which was confirmed by the hint of staleness that hung in the air.

"The kitchen is straight back," Kyran said, indicating a hallway directly across from the ornate door. "And a washroom and two bedrooms are on the second floor," he added, pointing at the narrow staircase along the right wall. "The house is stocked with everything you need, but should there be something, just call for Gillie and she'll be sure to get it for you."

I jumped, having only just noticed the slight girl with pale skin and short blond hair hovering timidly at the end of the hallway.

"Gillie takes care of the house and any occupants," Kyran explained. "She doesn't stay here, but if you call her name while you're in the house, she can hear you and she'll pop over. Right, Gillie?" Kyran smiled, looking at the girl for the first time who still hadn't moved. She nodded fervently in agreement and disappeared into the kitchen.

Turning to Naleiri, Kyran continued, "The library is just down the street to the left, at the end of the block. You can't miss it. Caeru is expecting you." Naleiri nodded and even offered a half-smile to Kyran.

When Naleiri had found out about this place, she insisted on doing something to earn her keep. Kyran attempted to protest but quickly gave up when he realized she was not going to budge. He suggested the library, I suspected because of its proximity to the house. He had made a strong case for it, though, claiming the librarian was complaining about the amount of work it would be to reorganize all of Aodhen's most ancient texts with the new addition of the patron reading room on the lower level. Naleiri was happy with the task, and I was grateful for the distraction.

As Naleiri made her way up the stairs, no doubt to claim the bigger of the two bedrooms, Kyran turned to me. He cradled my hands in his own, as had become our customary departing gesture. "I'll be back in a couple of days. Stay safe."

"Are you absolutely sure I can't come then?" I said beseechingly, trying to muster every ounce of persuasion I could without dropping to my knees and begging.

"I'm sure…" He tucked that disobedient strand of hair behind my ear. "Besides, you need to keep up your training. Don't forget, you *will* be joining our sparring sessions when I get back." His emphasis on "will" had me gulping.

I pulled myself into his arms. Perhaps it was my recent near-death experience that made me do it. Standing on the tips of my toes, I hugged him tightly, breathing in warm vanilla and letting my lips brush against his ear. "Be safe," I whispered.

His body stiffened in my embrace, and he wrapped his arms around me, resting his hands on my lower back. Unless I was mistaking it for my own, his heart beat faster beneath my chest as he held my body against his.

"I will." He relented, pulling away just enough to look at me as he said it. He bent down to place a soft kiss on my cheek. His lips were warm and smooth on my skin. He looked at me, his face inches from my own. Desire for something more shone in his eyes behind the question that he didn't voice but which I knew—whether I too wanted more. Not finding the answer his eyes craved, he flashed his easy smile.

"Goodbye, Aila." He walked out the front door, leaving me standing breathless in the empty atrium.

13

The library was a stone building that took up the entire corner of the block at the end of our shared street. The Hawastone dated it as one of the oldest in Aodhen, though the interior looked anything but.

It was massive. The front doors opened into a huge space with high ceilings from which hung an iron chandelier the size of a horse. At least fifty white candles adorned the chandelier whose flames' stillness made me think they were enchanted to burn endlessly. The front desk was directly opposite the entrance, stretching the length of the open space. Its light cherry finish shone in the candlelight. Behind the desk were shelves and shelves of books: endless rows of bound knowledge collected over eons. My breath caught in my throat. I hadn't expected the welling of emotion, but I'd never seen so many books in one place. I could spend hours here, days even, and not scrape the surface of what it offered.

Off to the left of the main entrance was a room in complete disarray. Cushions and writing desks were strewn about. *The patron reading room,* I registered. Swirling up to the right was a grand wooden staircase that wound up the side of the wall where more bookshelves were built into the cavities of the building itself. The stairs led to a second floor that was filled with even more shelves.

I took a step forward and only then noticed movement behind the front desk. An ancient woman with wrinkled skin looked up. I was immediately struck by her glasses. I had never seen an Eleiyon with glasses, assuming our vision would always be perfect, but she wore large, thick ones with beaded straps framing her angled face.

"Hello? Caeru?" I said, my voice faint, lost to the vast openness of the room. I moved closer to where she stood behind the desk expectantly. Her skin had a faded blue hue, and the strands of hair she had left were stark white. She was old, and apparently, nearly blind, but even so, she looked fierce.

"Ahh, you must be Aila." Her facade crumpled into a wrinkled smile. *So much for fierce.* But something told me that my initial instincts were right. "General Kyran told me you would join your friend a little later. She's in there." She pointed a long, thin finger to the mess of a room off to the left, where Naleiri, her hair tied in a loose knot, was picking through a pile of boxes.

"Thanks for joining me... finally," Naleiri said as I entered the room. The space was deceptive; it appeared small from the entrance, but sank back into the canals of the library, initially hidden from view. Despite the feigned annoyance in her tone, I knew she was in her element. She loved to organize stuff like this, and it looked like she had full rein to turn this reading room into something spectacular.

"Hey, did you notice Caeru's glasses? I didn't think we would ever need them." The question had been tugging on my mind since meeting Caeru.

"Eventually we might, if we get old enough. Our senses can fade just like those of other species, Aila. Besides, Caeru is not Eleiyon. Didn't you notice her pointed ears and blue skin? Granted, that too has probably faded over the millennia. If you met a younger one, I don't think you would mistake her for Eleiyon." Exasperated by my bewildered look, she added, "She's a Mangi, Aila."

A Mangi. The mountain sorcerers from Rimean? They were reclusive, rare...and extremely powerful. What was she doing as a librarian in Fira?

"And to answer your question, I doubt she needs those glasses," Naleiri said, contemplating a moment before adding, "They probably complete the friendly librarian look she's clearly going for."

I turned around, gazing through the open doorway at Caeru, and could have sworn I saw her smirk, as if she'd heard Naleiri's comment.

When Kyran didn't come home for a third day, I couldn't hide my disappointment. When had our relationship turned into this...whatever this was? It felt like more than friendship: the way my heart fluttered when I saw him; the shivers his touch sent through my body; the excitement for each day that I would get to spend with him.

I lounged at one of the writing desks in the reading room waiting for Naleiri to give me my next order. Instead, she said, "I'm sure he's fine. Kyran is powerful and the Archai are exceptionally trained."

"I know. I am a little worried, but more than anything, I want to know what's going on. If they found anything...Don't you?"

"Sure, I do. I've been so busy here, though, that I haven't had much time to think about it." She paused, assessing my reaction. "Here...why don't you help me with these boxes. We need to bring them upstairs to be sorted." She motioned with her foot at two large boxes that had been pushed to the door.

We marched up the spiraling staircase laden with our boxes. The upstairs smelled like mothballs and dust. Naleiri set her box on a wooden table on the landing. "So Caeru wants to convert these two aisles to the ancient texts and scrolls from downstairs." She pointed to the two rows of shelves at the far left. Some of them were already bare. "Obviously for the scrolls, we'll have to get creative. These bookshelves just won't do," she said, holding up a musty yellowed scroll that would probably just roll off the shelf and unravel onto the floor.

"What is all of this stuff?" I asked, peeking into the box I had just unloaded. It was full to the brim with leather-bound volumes. I didn't see many titles written in a language I recognized. It was mostly runes and symbols printed across the covers.

"Caeru said these are all part of the Lord of Flame's personal collection. I guess they're some of the oldest texts in the library. They come from all over Kiakora. Some of them might date back to before there even were territories." She started emptying the contents of the box and carefully spread them out on the table.

"I don't recognize all of the languages." I flipped through the pages of yet another book. This one was filled with black dots printed in varying combinations and configurations.

"Yeah. That isn't Eleiyon—there could be books about the Mangi here." A glint of mischievous curiosity glowed in her eyes at the thought. I knew nothing beyond general knowledge about the Mangi. I had to admit, I was curious, and Naleiri seemed just as willing to shirk work to see what we could find. An opportunity I had to capitalize on. I was suddenly full of questions. *Did something happen that led Caeru to Fira? Would we find something in these books about the reclusive Mangi civilization in the Eastern Mountains?*

We spent little of the next two hours shelving anything. Instead, we poured over the tattered scrolls, manuscripts, and old, thick volumes of Kiakoran history. Naleiri found a species book that documented all of the known creatures in Kiakora: what they looked like, habitats, food, even their mating behaviors.

"Look!" I called after rifling through the book.

There was a crude sketch of the creature that had attacked me in the forest. The text read:

The Myriapod is a giant insect in the Myriapodomorph family. It has a hard exoskeleton along its thorax and abdomen with a soft, vulnerable underbelly. They live deep in the caves of the northern Rangi Mountains and rarely venture out, feeding mostly on bats and other nocturnal animals who seek shelter in their rocky lairs. Their red eyes have evolved in the darkness of the caves to see in pitch-black night, making them superior nocturnal hunters. Their movement is typical of other smaller insects, a tripod gait, and may be accompanied by clicking and hissing noises, which are used to alert their pod of prey in the area. They kill with massive, sharp, venomous front claws or with acidic saliva, which can eat through even the toughest animal hides. They prefer to corner their prey using coordinated attacks.

I suppressed a shudder at the memory of the creature's clicking movements, now realizing that it had been calling out to the others to join it in a hearty meal. *Why had they ventured so far from the Rangi Mountains?* I pushed the thought aside. "Okay, that's enough of creatures wild and wonderful for me," I said, slamming the book shut.

"Here, look at this, Aila," Naleiri whispered. She held a large volume open to the middle of the book. Curling letters topped the page: Mangi. There were no images to accompany the text here, but I hungrily read the next few lines:

A fierce and feared species that dwells in the Eastern Mountains. The Mangi draw much of their power from nature. They ultimately retreated from the mainland of Kiakora to separate themselves from the Eleiyon, preferring to live in isolation rather than participate in the systematic destruction of the natural world. There was a time when the Mangi lived amongst the Eleiyon, sharing their secrets. However, there are no records from the last six millennia of any interaction, suggesting any cohabitation between the two species is ancient history.

Mangi are intensely magical and masterful spellweavers. They harness the power of the natural world to strengthen their own enchantments. The secrets of how they do so have been lost to the ages and are known only to the Mangi themselves.

Several attempts have been made to enter the Eastern Mountains and reopen dialogue with the Mangi, none of which have been successful. Those who have returned alive remember nothing of their journey nor of having met any Mangi.

Their accounts should be met with skepticism as we do know the Mangi are just as capable of creating powerful curses and binds as they are of casting spells.

Naleiri and I finished reading at the same time, my own curiosity reflected in her eyes as we looked at each other across the open book.

"So, if Mangi communing with Eleiyon is so unheard of, why is she here?" I asked.

"I don't know... but whatever drove her out of the Eastern Mountains had to be pretty serious," Naleiri answered quietly.

"Exiled?" I mouthed the question.

Naleiri opened her mouth to respond—

"Kyran told me you two wanted to work, not jabber like a bunch of school-age Eleiyon." The shrill voice cut through our silent conversation. Caeru appeared at the side of the table effortlessly carrying another two huge boxes. She dropped them with a bang.

"Of course. Just a quick break." I smiled while I casually flipped to another page, hoping she hadn't noticed what we were reading.

Not returning my smile, she walked toward the stairs mumbling something that sounded like, "In my day..."

I arrived home from the library later than I'd planned. I said a silent thank-you to Gillie as I searched the packed cupboards for something to snack on. Naleiri wanted to stay later to perfect the shelf organization.

"I have a note from His Highness," a meek voice called from behind where I was rummaging through another cabinet stuffed with sweet treats. I jumped, colliding with the cabinet door I'd left ajar.

"Ouch! For Liro's sake, Gillie. You shouldn't sneak up on someone like that." I closed both cabinets with a snap, rubbing the emerging lump on my head.

"You have a message from Kyran?" I hated the giddiness I felt at hearing his name.

"Yes. A note." She extended a skinny arm with a folded piece of paper.

"Thank you," I said, taking the note from her. She turned and vanished before even reaching the kitchen exit. The note was brisk and business-like:

We will continue our training tomorrow. Come to the ring at dawn.

Disappointment settled in the pit of my stomach. As if I, too, were another of his servants, obligated to appear if a service was requested by His Majesty. I cursed myself then, because of course, I was no better than a servant, and certainly not entitled to special treatment. *Why would I expect Kyran to treat me any other way? Did he give intimate farewells and spend entire afternoons with his other subjects?* A little voice piped up from my heart. Certainly not based on the sliver of conversation I had overheard between him and Cyrus. That didn't mean there weren't others, though. The thought slowly occurred to me now as my cheeks burned. *Why hadn't I considered that sooner?* Of course, he would be entertaining others, much more suitable others.

Deciding I wasn't so hungry after all, I made my way upstairs and climbed into bed. I wasn't entirely sure if it was Kyran I missed, or the training sessions. The feeling of purpose over the last couple of weeks had erased the looming cloud of restlessness that had hovered over my cottage existence. How much of what I felt was because of this note, and how was resentment for being left behind while he ventured out into the forest?

"Ughh," I growled to the dark room, frustrated by the never-ending spiral of questions. "You'll never fall asleep like this, Aila." I tried to silence my mind and shelve the questions for later. I finally managed to drift into a fitful sleep of green eyes and smoke.

14

"Find any more creatures lurking in the forest?" I broke the silence with all the lightheartedness I could muster. Kyran stood in the training ring, adjusting a display of deadly weapons laid out on the ground.

"Straight to business, huh? *How are you, Kyran? I'm happy you returned unharmed,*" he mocked. "Didn't you miss me while I was gone, Aila?" His tone was suddenly intense and serious as he closed the gap between us in two fluid steps.

"I..." I wanted to yell, *Of course I did!* And slip into his strong embrace, wrapping myself in his warm vanilla scent. But pride got the better of me and I settled for, "I kept myself busy. Not enough time to really dwell on it." I hoped he wouldn't notice the heightened pitch in my voice. Perhaps I made up the shadow of disappointment that crossed his features as he turned to point out the array of weaponry on the ground.

"As promised." He waved an arm over the options as if showing off a prized stallion. "Where would you like to start?"

My eyes raked over the double-edged axe the size of my leg; the quiver of arrows set against a massive wooden bow; a gleaming sword with a brass hilt; but my attention caught on a matching pair of weapons the length of one of those ancient volumes I'd been lugging around the library. Each had three prongs, and the middle one reached straight out, far beyond the other two. The two side prongs curved up from the meeting point of all three at the base, just above the handle.

"How about these?" I indicated the curious weapon with my index finger.

"Ahh...twin sai. Interesting choice." He swooped down to pick them up. "Not a personal favorite, but I admit, when wielded well, they are both lethal and versatile. Generally used for an up close and personal kill." He held one in each hand and performed a quick one-two combination with swift, powerful jabs. "But, with practice..." He turned suddenly and chucked one of the weapons. It somersaulted through the air and sank into the target across the ring, its three prongs halfway buried. "It can be used from a distance."

I clearly did a poor job of hiding my enthusiasm after Kyran's demonstration, because he chuckled at my expression. "Okay, killer, let's start with how you grip them."

We spent the rest of the morning perfecting a secure grip and practicing feints and combinations using the twin sai. He showed me how the two side prongs were used for blocking and parrying attacks from an armed opponent. Kyran countered my strikes with strong blocks to my forearms, trying to loosen my grip on the two weapons. He only succeeded the first time. I was so enamored with the sai training that I completely forgot to dread the afternoon's sparring session with the Archai. That is, until Kyran interrupted my fourth time through a one-two combo with a sidestep and a left-hook finish to remind me.

"We have to get up to the main field. Don't want to be late to your first match!"

My insides lurched at the excitement in his voice.

The march up to the field felt like a forced, humiliating walk toward an agonizing death. I was perfectly fine just training with Kyran. *Why did I need to spar with the other soldiers?* Maybe I could convince Kyran that Caeru needed me at the library with Naleiri and that the commitment had completely slipped my mind. I calculated the odds of not coming off as an absolute coward as slim to none before abandoning the idea.

Kyran wouldn't let me go in there if I were hopeless, right? I mean, what would the point of that be? Then my annoying internal voice: *maybe to make sure you don't get too carried away by your successful encounter with the Myriapod?* I shoved the voice aside as we entered the field.

I was met with a mixture of curious and annoyed glares. Cyrus stood at the edge of one of the circles and muttered something to two muscular Archai. Kyran must have warned them that I would be joining today.

I had overheard Cyrus' thoughts on Kyran's and my relationship but was still surprised at the anger that flashed across his face as he looked me up and down, no doubt assessing how long it would take one of his Archai to chew me up and spit me out. I followed closely behind Kyran, trying to settle my pounding heart. We stopped at the center, in front of one of the sparring rings. Kyran spun to face me.

"You ready?" Excitement gleamed in his hazel eyes.

"Hardly," I muttered, trying not to reveal the absolute chaos that was ravishing my insides.

He ignored the judgmental glances of the passing Archai as he placed his sturdy hands on my shoulders. "You can do this, Aila. I wouldn't put you in here if you weren't ready to be competitive. You killed a Myriapod on your own, remember."

For just a moment, my heart sailed. The milling Archai disappeared around me, and I stood alone on the field with Kyran. Relief swept over me; he thought I was ready. That was what I needed to hear. My confidence surged. *Why else had I been training this hard if not to test my skills against an opponent?* I was ready.

I gave Kyran a reassuring smile and turned to the ring.

Waiting inside the circle was one of the massive Archai I had seen talking to Cyrus. He was just as tall as Kyran but much larger. The sun shone off the dark skin of his bald head; his eyes, darker still, were cold as they trailed my advance. There was no kindness in his face. I looked back at Kyran. Cyrus stood behind him. *He was here to teach me a lesson.*

I searched Kyran's face for some kind of clue about what I was facing, some hint of hesitancy to call this whole thing off. But his face was smooth. Impassive. Observant.

Thankfully this session was going to be hand-to-hand combat. I was even less ready to wield a weapon against a seasoned soldier. I slid naturally into my fighting stance, my opponent mirroring the movement. I heard a whistle, but from the corner of my eye, I saw that neither Cyrus nor Kyran had moved an inch. Magic. The match had begun.

My opponent started to circle the ring, like a wolf trapping a scared, motherless fawn. *But I was no fawn.* I echoed his footsteps, staying light on my feet as I circled across from him. I felt the eyes of the other Archai on us, even as they were supposedly engaged in their own matches. Taking a deep, steady breath, I released, freeing myself from the Archai's stares and the debilitating nerves. It was just me and him, my prey. *This time, I was the hunter.*

I took a quick step forward with a single left jab, ensuring that I kept out of his range. He didn't falter his circling like the Myriapod had. He knew I wasn't close enough to land anything. What had I expected? He was an experienced fighter. *Okay. Keep testing him. Look for an opening.* Kyran's lessons flooded back to me.

We circled for another minute. His eyes assessed my movements, evaluating the space between my feet, the position of my fists and shoulders. One chink in my stance and he would capitalize on it.

Then I saw it. His back foot pivoted ever so slightly, preparing to launch himself forward. I anticipated his attack and slipped under the slicing jab, spinning and kicking my left leg out in a wide sweep, knocking his front leg forward and throwing him off balance. He caught himself before he fell and spun around quickly to face me. I was already on my feet, fists up protecting my head. I was quicker than he was. That would be my only advantage, I realized. He was more experienced and clearly more powerful. One blow and he would knock me out cold.

Our deadly dance continued. I concentrated on the subtle changes in his footsteps, knowing that would signal an attack. It would be my only chance to block, dodge, or counter. We seemed evenly matched. I anticipated his movements and slipped beyond his reach again and again. I sensed his mounting frustration. I was waiting for this: *a frustrated opponent is a sloppy opponent.* Kyran's warning rang in my mind. *Just a little bit longer and I'll have my chance.*

There.

Rage and impatience consumed his features as my opponent gave in to his brute strength. It was his only shot at a quick victory. He charged, completely abandoning his defensive stance, squaring his body. *The bigger the opponent, the bigger the target.*

He extended his arms to grab me, leaving his face unprotected. I threw a sharp jab to his nose, intended to stun, not stop. He faltered; his right hand instinctively went to the blood pouring from his nose. I twisted my hips, bending my knees to gather all the power I could, and landed a strong right uppercut to his stomach. He doubled over with a gasp, the blow emptying his air completely. This was it—the close shot. A knee to his face would do it. I positioned my right leg, extending my left to add more momentum to the blow and—

An excruciating pain seared across my left arm.

A wave of flames lapped at my neck and collarbone as I stumbled back, away from the spray of fire. And then voices. Loud voices were shouting, pulling me out of my daze. My opponent stopped his fire hose, smirking at my scalded arm and stunned expression. He advanced one step forward to finish the job.

Before he could act, a lasso of fire looped around his body, shackling his arms to his sides. The rope tightened, eliciting a yelp of pain. Kyran entered the circle, his eyes blazing with fury. The other end of the fiery rope was in his hand. He tugged, bringing the sweating and now terrified Archai to his knees. Flames erupted in a ring around the three of us, preventing the other soldiers from stepping in.

"This was a hand-to-hand sparring session. No powers." Kyran's anger palpated in the small circle.

"She doesn't deserve to be here, General. She's not one of us," the kneeling soldier barked gruffly.

Another wave of pain that had nothing to do with the blisters already dotting my arm washed over me.

"Maybe she should be. She would have beaten you if you had kept the fight fair." The anger lacing his words silenced the man on the ground, who looked up at Kyran, defeated.

"You're right, of course, General. No honor in an unfair fight," he said through clenched teeth. He hung his head in shame. His voice, however, was robotic, and his words were far from sincere. This man would stab me in the back if he ever got me alone. Literally.

The flames around us died, and the blazing lasso disappeared. Kyran turned to me, his eyes tightening at the shining, red skin and singed remains of my sleeve. Some of the fabric, I now realized, had melted into my skin leaving behind the charcoal smell of charred flesh. Without removing his gaze from my arm, he ordered, "Get them out of here...now."

"Dismissed." Cyrus' voice rang in my head, but he hadn't opened his mouth.

The rest of the soldiers responded to the command by filing off the field toward the bathhouses, some glaring in my direction. Cyrus was the last to leave, waiting for my opponent to get to his feet and follow his fellow Archai. He glowered at me over Kyran's shoulder, his eyes filled with a hatred I didn't understand.

We stood silently in the circle, my arm throbbing. "I'm sorry, Aila," Kyran said weakly, not lifting his eyes from my arm to meet my gaze.

"It's not your fault." I stepped toward him, touching the bottom of his chin with my good hand, turning his face to me. "I'm okay. This will heal in no time." I nodded at my arm.

He clutched my hand and led me to the bench. Kneeling in front of me, he looked into my eyes. The emotion on his face surprised me. The anger was still there but subdued now. Behind it, was guilt and something else I couldn't quite place.

He gently kissed my blistered hand. I flinched slightly as his warm breath irritated the burn. He looked up, evaluating my reaction before continuing cautiously, ever so softly kissing the angry blisters up my forearm. I let him, surrendering to the lovely blend of pain and relief that twisted together as he planted each kiss.

"You have no idea, Aila," he whispered into the crook of my neck, "how furious it made me to see him hurt you." His lips trailed down my neck to my chest. I cradled his head as he nestled himself between my legs. "You have no idea," he said again between tender kisses, "how much I want...certain things." His throaty voice dripped with desire.

Feathery kisses sent shivers up my arm, raising the little hairs on the back of my neck. His closeness intensified my own yearning. My body longed to know the way his lips would feel. But the searing accusations I'd just heard from the man in the ring stung more than the burn I nursed.

"Not quite as much as you want other things." I know he heard the unspoken words—*to be respected; to live up to your father's expectations; to lead.*

"Let's go up to the infirmary. Achillea Ointment quickens the healing of burns," he said abruptly, getting to his feet and pushing aside the tension that moments ago had been thick enough to pierce with my twin sai. "Trust me, I would know," he added with a wink.

In my periphery, Cyrus lurked in the shadows. I wondered briefly if Kyran had sensed him there as well, and whether that was the reason for our sudden departure.

15

Kyran was right. The Achillea Ointment did speed up the healing process considerably. I escaped to the library, mumbling some excuse about scrolls, shelves, and Naleiri.

Slumping into one of the chairs in the reading room, I succumbed to the weight of my thoughts and admired Naleiri's progress. Almost all the boxes were out of the downstairs room. She'd arranged large black-and-maroon body cushions throughout the reading room for lounging patrons who'd found a good read. I somehow doubted these would be used very often. Along the back and side walls were individual desks set up for independent study. Spread across the room in the center were three long, rectangular tables, each ending with bookshelves filled with small volumes that did not look as intimidating as the ones we had been sorting through yesterday.

"It looks like Liro's got you snared," Naleiri observed.

I snapped my head up, only just realizing how completely I'd been lost in my thoughts.

"What are you thinking about?" Naleiri asked, concerned, sliding into the seat next to me.

"It's nothing..." Naleiri wouldn't want to hear my warring feelings about Kyran and the rest of the Archai. She hadn't thought training with them was a good idea in the first place.

"You can tell me," she insisted. And I knew I could. Naleiri would never judge me. She would sit and listen and try to understand.

I thought for a moment. "I like Kyran," I admitted. "I do," I repeated. "But he's part of a world that I don't belong in."

"You belong, Aila. The Eleiyon are great at drawing lines, telling us who belongs where, but those lines only exist if we believe in them."

"Hmm...when did you become so wise?" I said slyly, smiling. She was right, of course. "I'm not sure I even want to belong..."

"I think..." she said after a moment, "you need to decide what it is you like about the time you're spending with Kyran, and what has you so bothered about not *belonging* with the Archai. You've never cared about that before, why now?"

She picked up the stack of books she'd been carrying and stood. "This caught my eye, thought you might find it interesting," she offered, sliding a thin book across the table.

She left me with a new pile of feelings to sift through. She was right. Why did it bother me that the Archai didn't accept me? Why was I surprised?

I opened the book. It was on weaponry. About halfway through, the corner of one of the pages had been folded in, marking it. It was a chapter on the twin sai. I smiled. I had only mentioned the type of weapon I'd been training with once to Naleiri, but she'd remembered.

The chapter outlined different fighting techniques using the sai, accompanied by images of the technique in action. I was just getting to the section on parrying an attack using the side prongs—

"Ahh. The twin sai," came a sharp voice from behind me.

Startled, I jumped up and closed the book with a thud.

"Don't let me stop you," Caeru crooned. I still struggled to get used to her thin, silky voice.

"No. Sorry, I'm just a little on edge today is all," I stammered.

"Is it whatever caused the burns that has you wound up tighter than a spool of yarn?" she asked knowingly.

"What...?" I glanced down at my arm. Fully healed. No trace of the burns. "How did you know?"

She pointed a bony, blue finger to her nose. "Achillea Ointment has a distinct smell. It's made from the Astera Bush, you know. Very rare in the Eastern Mountains, much more plentiful here," she added.

I turned over the information thoughtfully. I hadn't noticed a strong smell coming from the ointment, but then again, I hadn't been thinking about it. "You know the twin sai?" I decided to change the subject. I didn't feel like hashing out the events of this morning with her.

"I know it well. It's one of the preferred weapons of the Mangi, you know." Her cadence was slow, deliberate. She pondered for a moment, seemingly lost in a memory before adding, "The twin sai, yes. Of course, we Mangi rely more on our magic, but there are many who grow their own sai. Powerful weapons...more powerful when linked to nature, as are most things." She looked at me gravely.

"What do you mean, 'grow their own sai'?" Had I heard her wrong?

"Yes, grow," she confirmed. "From Kiakora of course," as if it were the most obvious fact in the world.

Noting my blank look, she continued, "The Mangi... we,"—including herself as an afterthought—"we are connected to the natural world in a way that you Eleiyon have forgotten. It's from where we draw our power. We have... secrets of how to harness the power of nature and give it form, shape it to our will, or guide it for a specific purpose. Growing sai is a tradition as old as our kind, Aila." She paused, perhaps to gauge my interest. I greedily listened for more. "Crystals form naturally from hardened minerals, under millennia of immense pressure.

Even though we are eternal, we are the mountains compared to the babble and turmoil of a mortal existence; or perhaps more like the rivers that carve into the land, appearing and disappearing across millennia... anyhow, even we are not that patient. We know how to..." She searched for the right word. "...expedite the process and can cultivate crystals. We can form them, imbibe them with additional powers besides that which the crystals naturally draw from the land. Our sai almost always have powers beyond the typical ones. And, of course, are much more beautiful than a hunk of cooled metal...But to each her own, I suppose." She shrugged.

Fascinated, I looked at her, surprised by her sudden openness. It was the perfect opportunity to push my luck. Maybe, just maybe.

"Why did you leave?" I whispered. I didn't know why I whispered. Her steely eyes glazed and went distant suddenly, haunted by a faraway place of snow-capped peaks, the gusting winds swirling behind her gray eyes.

It seemed like she wouldn't respond, but then, "Sometimes there are no easy answers to even the simplest of questions," she finally responded. "Maybe one day, there will be a reason, a precious enough reason, to drive you from your home...from the ones you love." Her eyes flicked upstairs to where Naleiri was unloading more boxes.

Her wall shuddered back into place almost as soon as the last words left her thin lips. I wouldn't get more out of her today. Her expression was wistful, catching my eyes. Then she left.

Naleiri popped up behind me, ripping me away from my thoughts for the second time. "Hey Aila, I didn't think you'd be here today." And then, in typical Naleiri fashion, "Since you are though, come up here and give me a hand, would you?"

I smiled a greeting. "Sure."

"I saw you talking to Caeru. What did she want?"

"Hmm? Oh, nothing. She said I could take this home if I wanted," I answered, holding up the book Naleiri had given me. "Thanks, by the way, it's great." I followed her silently up the stairs, still lost in thought, deciding to keep my discussion with Caeru to myself.

16

I woke up hours before I was supposed to meet Kyran. For the first time, I wasn't sure I wanted to go. Yesterday had created a whirlwind of emotions that hadn't completely settled. *A quick run before training. That's what I need.*

Winter had finally descended on Aodhen. Cold air whistled through my ears as I ran through the city streets. It wasn't as convenient as running through the forest trails, but it was early enough that not many pedestrians were out. Yesterday's events tumbled over each other in rapid succession as I veered right to run the perimeter of Center Square. I'd been humiliated in the ring, both by the burn and the insults, which I knew the other Archai had overheard. Kyran had to come to my defense, which only proved their point further. And then there were Kyran's tender kisses on my wound, and our sudden, unexplained departure to the infirmary. I made it back to the apartment just in time to get dressed for training and still hadn't worked out how I felt.

Who would be waiting for me in the ring today? The drill sergeant who I'd come to expect? The playful friend who had shared his city with me? The torn general ripped apart by competing desires?

It was none of those Kyrans who greeted me. He was more serious than I had ever seen him outside of training, but more open and somehow more vulnerable than he ever allowed himself to be on the field.

"I thought we'd do something else today. The Archai are off in the forest for tracking practice..." He tilted his head toward the expanse I'd just come from. "And it's been too long since you and I have spent time together, outside of training, I mean."

I momentarily lamented losing time with the twin sai, having memorized some techniques from the book. I was planning on trying them out today. But Kyran's expectant, hopeful expression made me say, "Okay. I, uhh...yeah, that'd be nice," I finally managed to get out. "Where are we going?" I asked, genuinely curious as we left the ring and turned away from Aodhen.

"To my house," he said nonchalantly. As if he had no idea that his "house" was the House of Fira.

———

It was even more beautiful than I could have imagined. If the house in the city center was luxurious, then this was majestic, making the former look like servant's quarters. *Which is precisely what it is, Aila, as you, Naleiri and Gillie are the only ones who ever actually stay there.*

A grandiose, white marble staircase with black and gold railings greeted us in the foyer. A crystal chandelier hung from the vaulted ceiling, casting sparkling light as the winter sun dazzled through a large circular window above us. The walls were a deep maroon that gave warmth to the otherwise cold and open space. Hallways and gaping rooms jutted out from the foyer in every direction. Kyran led me to the staircase.

"We're going upstairs," he said quietly, as if his movement toward the staircase didn't tip me off. I wondered if his father would approve of his son's house guest.

Kyran brought me to the second door off the landing. It was simple, polished oak with a gold doorknob that creaked slightly as Kyran opened it. Inside was a spacious room with the same maroon walls. The floor tile in this room was black. In combination with the maroon walls, it felt like we were walking into a velvet box, a coffin.

Adorning the walls all around us were massive paintings set in ornate golden frames that stretched from floor to ceiling. All the faces looking down at us, and there were at least ten of them, had the same hazel eyes as Kyran. In some of the paintings, the subject was seated on a jeweled throne or locked in an epic battle; in still others, he was surrounded by collections of books.

One portrait caught my eye. It was the last one, all the way to the right, in the back of the room.

The background of the portrait was black, and emerging from it, like a candle in the darkness, was a middle-aged-looking man with cold eyes set in a stern, angular face. His mouth turned into a grimace, like someone had placed rotten cheese beneath his nose. He cast an imperious gaze down at his viewers, confirming their position beneath him.

Besides his pale face, the only other colors emanating from the image were the golden broaches and medals decorating his uniform and a blazing orange triangle, symbolizing the House of Fira, glowing on his chest. I knew who it was before Kyran said it.

"My father."

I'd never met the Lord of Flame but I knew his reputation. I had heard stories at the Market about his inflexibility when it came to taxes, even in poor harvests or difficult winters. I knew from the Archai's behavior I'd observed countless times in Aodhen that their intolerance for the Nulk echoed their leader's sentiment. This picture somehow made those stories more real. He terrified me.

I felt an ounce of pity for Kyran who, despite living a privileged life, had to try to earn the approval of this man. I wondered if he even attempted to win his affection.

"Have they all been Lords of Fira?" I asked, turning to Kyran. He stared up at his father's image. Something between reverence and loathing gleamed in his eyes.

Without turning to me, he answered, "Not all. There have been only three lords since the territories were established. That's my great uncle over there." He pointed to one of the portraits, its subject surrounded by books. "He never ruled, but he created the library where Naleiri and you are working. He traveled all over Kiakora, requesting volumes from different territories to grow the collection." The tinge of sadness that coated his words stopped me from asking what happened to him. "Besides those three and my uncle, the others date back to before Fira officially existed. My family have always been...leaders. Nobles, I guess you could say. Aodhen has followed us, looked to us for protection, stability, even before the formal title. I mean, my family helped build Aodhen, like I told you. We're the ones who fought back the forest and claimed the space for Eleiyon. It helped us earn respect and eventually the right to lead."

The passage about Mangi floated back to me: *the destruction of our natural world*. "Were there Mangi in Fira back then?" Curiosity was getting the better of me.

"Mangi? They left millennia ago. Jealous of the power and progress of the Eleiyon. They exiled themselves in the Eastern Mountains, disappeared like many of the species. I, of course, was not around. But I've heard stories from my father, who heard from his and so on. The Mangi never wanted Eleiyon to succeed. Even now, they are biding their time in the mountains, waiting for any sign of weakness to come down and take the territories for themselves."

Such a different version of events than Caeru had shared. Another thought tumbled out. "What about Caeru?" I asked.

Kyran was quiet a moment before responding. "She came to Aodhen years ago looking for a safe place to live and work. The Mangi believe that the Eleiyon are an abomination, and they refuse to have any contact with us. Caeru was trying to persuade her people otherwise, and she was exiled for it. She had to leave the Eastern Mountains, and when she came here, ancient as she is, my father thought she'd do well with the library, caring for the ancient texts collected by my uncle. Caeru has more than you or I could fathom. You never know when having access to information like that could come in handy. If we ever need her, or what she knows, she owes us." He shifted his weight uneasily from one foot to the other, as if he'd revealed too much. "Not sure if that's what you're asking," he added.

Interesting. It was all a game. Nothing was done for free. A good deed done by the Lord of Flame in exchange for an old Mangi indebted to him. "I see... Your father must have a deep interest in the history of Kiakora." Kyran's brow creased in confusion. "His personal collection is massive, and mostly made up of the oldest volumes," I explained. The entire second floor of the library was closed to the public.

Kyran's face smoothed in understanding. "Yes. He's become quite...obsessed. Even more so lately." He turned to look at the portrait, not caring to elaborate on his father's recent obsession.

I followed his gaze, trying to find an inkling of compassion in the Lord of Flame's likeness. There was none. So much history hung on these walls, and yet, what had really changed? "It's been centuries since the war; will Fira ever view the Nulk as equals?" The question tumbled from my mouth before I could consider whether I should really voice it.

I could tell by his expression that he heard my real question. *Will you ever see me as your equal?*

"I don't have the power to change centuries of prejudice or the thoughts of others, Aila." His voice was soft as he stepped toward me. "I don't believe those things...what Cyrus said about you..." Anger flashed behind his eyes as he said his second-in-command's name. "You are special." He stepped closer to me. "I've never met anyone like you. You make me feel...like me. Like I can be me. Everyone else wants something from me. Expects me to be...to be a certain way." He looked up at the faces of his ancestors gazing down at him. "I hoped seeing this, you'd understand what it's like for me. Everyone judging, waiting, expecting me to be the next leader. I guess it's nice to just be. That's what it's like when I'm with you."

I waited, my heart pounding.

"I guess what I'm trying to say, Aila, is that it's complicated." He was close enough now that he reached up and gently stroked my cheek with the back of his knuckles. "There's me and what I want, and then there's this"—he gestured to the wide room—"who I am and everything that comes with it." There was pain in his eyes as he searched my face. For what? For acceptance?

Tears welled in my eyes, not out of sadness, but out of anger. "I know who you could be, Kyran, if you could get out from under all of this." It was my turn to wave a wild arm at the looming portraits and their eternal, condescending sneers. "I've seen glimpses of the real you, the one you're afraid to be. It's you who doesn't know who you are, Kyran. Or maybe you do, but you're just a coward."

I checked my voice, sensing that it had risen a few decibels since I'd started speaking. I said softly, feeling a rogue tear streak down my cheek, "You don't have to rule the way he has." I nodded toward his father's likeness. "You can be different. You can change everything—bring us all together, make us stronger, help us to remember the connection we have to each other and to Kiakora." I stepped toward him, closing the gap between us and cradling his large hands in my small ones. "I understand the pressure you're under. But I will never understand the way the Archai prey on us, or the things your soldiers have said about me. I refuse to believe that the Eleiyon can't repair the damage we've inflicted on nature, or that we can't remember that we, too, are a part of Kiakora.

I won't accept things the way they are just because they have always been that way" I finished , breathless.

"You know..." His voice was husky. "I didn't keep you in that apartment when I went to the forest because you weren't my equal; I kept you there because I like you, Aila. And the thought of something happening to you...if I can't protect you. I wouldn't be able to take it." I knew he was thinking about the Myriapod and the botched sparring session.

"I don't want to be protected, Kyran. Not by you. And not from you," I added softly, thinking of Naleiri. "Why did you bring me here?" My voice turned to a whisper. "So that I could be deemed unworthy by the entire House of Fira's royal line?" My sarcasm was biting, even in a whisper.

"To show you that, despite millennia of pressure and tradition, of knowing that this will never be accepted by the others, and certainly not by my father... I can't stay away from you." He reached a strong arm behind me, grabbing my waist forcefully, and pulled me to him. His eyes never left mine as he searched, waiting for any sign of protest from me. I gave him none. Lowering his head, he kissed me. His warm vanilla scent flooded my senses as his soft lips parted my own. He slipped his other hand to the back of my neck, pressing me against him. His kisses became more urgent, as he slid his tongue into my mouth with a sweetness I hadn't expected. I gave into his hunger, winding my own hands around his neck and into his loose hair, pulling him to me. Had what we'd discussed moments ago been that important? I was lost. Lost in his touch as he slid his hand down to my bottom, gripping it in tight fistfuls. I reveled in the tingling sensation traveling up my spine, coaxing goosebumps from my scalp as I parted my lips from his to catch my breath. He didn't stop, moving his kisses to my neck.

"Aila," he grumbled into my skin.

We both stiffened as we heard it. The quiet click of a turning doorknob. We bounced apart, Kyran running a hand through his hair to smooth it while I adjusted my top.

I feigned interest in the portrait on the opposite wall as the door creaked open. We both turned to see Cyrus standing in the doorway, his face impassive. "Your father needs to see you...now," he said, looking only at Kyran. "We just finished a briefing, so if you're...done here"—his cold eyes flicked to mine with his typical disapproving look—"then we need to make plans about how we're going to proceed with...the situation." He clearly did not feel comfortable sharing any further details on the "situation" while I was standing there.

Cyrus didn't wait for a dismissal. The door clicked closed behind him. "Don't worry about him. He's just...he's loyal to my father, and to me. And right now, when it comes to you, he's stuck between two competing sentiments. Give him time," Kyran explained.

"Would your father disapprove so greatly if he saw me with you?" I asked softly, not sure I wanted to hear the answer.

Kyran sighed. "I want to be honest with you, Aila. The reality is, my father is consumed by his own endeavors; he barely notices what I do or who I am with," he admitted, hurt in his voice. "His strength as a leader comes from his adherence to tradition as much as it does from his gifts," he explained. "There are differences too ingrained in his mind to overcome. You being a Nulk is one of them. And because of that, if he cared enough to notice, he would not approve," he said heavily, as if facing this hard truth for the first time himself.

This didn't surprise me. And even though I didn't like what I heard; I knew I'd finally gotten the truth from him. "Will you ever stand against your father for what you know is right?"

"You give me too much credit, Aila. Even if I dared object to some of my father's beliefs, you are wrong in believing he would listen," he said quietly.

He waited for me to argue. When he saw I wouldn't, he added, "I really should be going." He looked at me for a moment, deciding something, and then said abruptly, "I want you to come to the Solnas Ball with me. As my guest."

The Solnas Ball was for the Archai and the elite, most of whom lived in the city of Aodhen, although there were a few estates scattered across the rest of

Fira. The average Eleiyon were not invited to the palace to celebrate the Solnas Ball for Solnascor. My head was still spinning, trying to remember exactly how I felt. *Was I still angry? Had anything been resolved? Where did this leave us?*

"Are you sure?" I managed.

"Absolutely," he said, resolve on his face now. He gave my hands a small squeeze, perhaps trying to convince himself that was true.

"I have nothing...appropriate to wear to something like that." I felt the tingle on my cheeks that meant they had turned a damning shade of red.

"The Ball is not until the next full moon. You'll be able to find something at the stores in Aodhen by then. I'll let them know to expect you," he added, noting my expression at the mention of a city store, which would surely be out of my price range.

Before I considered it further, I blurted, "Can Naleiri come as well? To the Ball?" If he wanted me, he needed to take all of me, and that included Naleiri.

He considered momentarily and then said, a little tightly, "Of course. You're sort of a package deal, I guess." He slid so easily into his playful tone that I was sure I imagined anything else.

I gave him a joyful hug, happy that he understood how important Naleiri was to me. Laughing, he peeled my arms off saying, "Alright. I better hurry to meet my father, or I won't be around to take you to the Ball."

As I left, curiosity tugged at my thoughts, but my heart sent them in a different direction. I imagined Naleiri and me attending the Solnas Ball in our fancy dresses.

I envisioned Kyran escorting me to the dance floor, Naleiri on the arm of some equally handsome Eleiyon. We were both twirled gracefully to an unknown composition while the other guests watched.

I sat at the rectangular table on the second floor of the library, fiddling with the corner of one of the giant tomes with one hand, supporting my head with the other. Kyran had sent another message through Gillie to cancel training. It would just be a few days, but I was finally getting used to the twin sai. I recognized my spiral of doom for what it was and forced myself to recall the exact wording of Kyran's message.

Planning for a situation affecting Fira with Cyrus and the Archai. My father is counting on me. I have to cancel training for the next few days. I'll miss you.

Just a few days. A few days, I repeated to myself.

I still had gotten up hours before dawn, deciding that I would continue to train whether Kyran was there or not. I practiced with the twin sai, using the strikes and parries described in the book I now read nightly. Tomorrow I would try chucking them at a target and see if I could achieve the desired aerial somersaulting that Kyran had done rather effortlessly.

My thoughts carried me down the last two aisles. Naleiri had added a few shallow baskets on some of the shelves to display scrolls. Each one had an orange string tied to a small label tag, indicating the scroll's topic or author. For the scrolls in better condition, there was a contraption designed to display the scroll and allow the potential reader to browse the contents. I examined it more closely. It was a small wooden spindle that protruded from the side of the shelf with a thin slit running the length of it. The scroll slid in, catching on the slit to hold the end of the parchment in place. As the reader tugged, the scroll unraveled, making it easy to read and neat to store.

I marveled at Naleiri's ingenuity. Caeru, I was sure, loved the invention. Between the two middle panels, Naleiri had created at least twelve of these spindles, all holding a scroll. One caught my attention as I looked at the display. It was second from the top and was slightly unfurled to reveal a sketched foot behind which the pen etchings and hashmarks created the impression of swirling darkness.

I fingered the label tag. It just read, "Beginning."

Placing my fingers gingerly on the bottom corner of the scroll, I pulled. I could feel the document's age. It was made of thick, cloth-like parchment. Humidity and temperature had affected it over the years, making it crinkle with the slightest movement. As I pulled, the delicate scroll revealed a beautiful Eleiyon woman. She was breathtaking, despite being a simple black-and-white rendering. Her long hair flowed in some ancient breeze. Her left leg was raised, bent at the knee, and her right foot flexed, angling down, as if she were floating in midair. Both of her arms were lifted slightly away from her sides, contributing to the feeling that she was suspended in an eternal jump. In one hand, she carried a dagger with an ornate handle, decorated with a single circular stone. I couldn't tell what kind of stone it was from the colorless sketch. Her clothes fit tight to her body, perhaps made of leather, based on the texture of the drawing. Each long sleeve ended in a triangular point that matched the triangular neckline dipping at her chest and secured with a laced string.

To say she was otherworldly was an understatement. Her fierce expression contradicted her soft, feminine features. Though there was no indication, I knew she was powerful. It emanated from the scroll, across whatever time and space separated us.

The scroll was completely open now. I examined it. No other markings, No date. No name. Who was she? Where and when was she from? What did she do to be immortalized in a sketch that had been saved for millennia?

"Briggid," an all-too familiar voice whispered behind me.

I whirled around. Caeru peered over my shoulder at the stunning figure.

"You know her?"

"I know of her. She was before even my time." *Ancient.* Not wanting to offend my only source of information, I decided not to risk asking exactly when that might be.

"Who was she?" I asked curiously.

"The first Eleiyon in Kiakora," Caeru answered. Amazed, I turned back to the dazzling woman as Caeru continued. "You Eleiyon have your creation stories, the great Liro, but the truth is, your species arrived here from somewhere else. Another world. Some Eleiyon know this, even though they still give credence to the Liro legends. It is said that Briggid entered Kiakora through a tear in the fabric between worlds, in the very veils that separate us all. She brought with her a small band of Eleiyon who colonized Kiakora. Your ancestors." Her voice was solemn, hushed as if speaking a forbidden topic in a sacred temple.

"What happened to her?" I whispered back, mimicking her tone. I was not as surprised as I thought, hearing for certain that the legends of Liro were just that.

Something hardened behind her eyes. Assessing. Sifting through millennia of information and deciding what she should share. "Kiakora is full of secrets. The ancient stories are like puzzles; pieces are scattered across time. You can only know the truth by connecting them all," she finished cryptically.

"And what piece of the truth do you have?" I abandoned any attempt at pretense.

She eyed me thoughtfully. "Truth cannot come from ignorance. The Eleiyon do not know their own history. The Mangi...we have lost our way, huddling in the Eastern Mountains for too long..." Her eyes took on that faraway gaze, transporting her out of the library. She opened her mouth after a time to continue, but it was Naleiri's voice that broke the heavy silence.

"What do you think?" Naleiri asked brightly, admiring her handiwork with the shelves.

"Fabulous," Caeru exclaimed as if that was what she was going to say all along. "Well, I won't keep you then." And she glided off as I stared daggers into her back.

"Ever wonder why she doesn't just use magic to reorganize this place? Why all the heavy lifting?" I asked. With a final look, I carefully wound up the Briggid scroll.

"She told me that some of the most sacred texts are magical themselves; wards and such woven by their authors to prevent theft. To protect their secrets. That's why the House of Fira went through all the trouble of traveling across the world, petitioning for some of these texts. I doubt they can be magicked at all. Or, knowing Caeru, it could just be that she is lonely and wants company in this place. It must get boring. Not exactly full of patrons, is it?" Naleiri joked.

Both sounded like plausible explanations to me. "I have something to tell you," I said, deciding to get through this as quickly as possible. Just like ripping off a bandage. I took a deep breath and let the rest of the words spill out. "We've been invited to attend the Solnas Ball as Kyran's guests. I told him we would go." I rushed the last part before I lost my courage. Bandage off.

Naleiri's eyes widened with rage. "You WHAT?"

"Absolutely not. No. Aila, no. It's a bad idea." She slammed her ivory fist against the table to emphasize her point. We had moved our conversation to the library's upstairs landing where we could sit at the table.

"Why are you so adamant that we not do anything different?" I lifted my hands in frustration. "You're stuck in your ways. You're just as bad as him!"

"Not true. Not even close to true, Aila, and you know it," she said angrily, clearly trying not to raise her voice and alert Caeru downstairs.

"Fine. Maybe not quite, but Naleiri, you're not even open to giving him a chance." I looked up at her from where I was sitting as she slid into the seat across from me.

"Why would I be? He doesn't deserve it. He doesn't deserve you. He gets you all excited about this training, and then abandons it when more important things come along. He has you train with the Archai, where his soldier tried to maim you, Aila. And I don't care what you say, he took their side. You're not training with them anymore are you? Not that I disagree with that part, honestly."

I twiddled my thumbs aimlessly, staring unseeingly at the table in front of me as she listed the reasons we should hate Kyran, all of which were true and all that I'd considered before myself. "He knows you won't be accepted as part of his *real* life. And I'm not saying that he doesn't like you or whatever, I'm saying that he's clearly not trying to complicate things for himself by including you. How long will this be enough for you, Aila?"

"You're not wrong. Everything you said is true. And I said as much to him the other day." I raised my eyes to hers. Maybe she saw my hope there, because she clasped my hands on the table. "Maybe this is his attempt to change. Inviting us to the ball. His father will be there. And Cyrus," I added. *Was I trying to convince myself?* Even as I said it, I questioned whether I believed it.

She sighed heavily. "Aila, you know I support you. But just because I support you doesn't mean I need to agree with you. I'd be behind you whole-heartedly if I thought he was good for you. I know that's none of my business, and if I thought you truly wanted him, that would also be different. But I know you, Aila. I know what's drawing you to him. I know the sense of purpose training has given you. It has somehow reminded you of who you are, of who you were before you lost it all. You don't say it, but I know you feel trapped here."

"No... Naleiri. I..." I interrupted as the crack in her voice was like a chisel to my heart.

"Let me finish, Aila. I just don't want you to trade one cage for another. I want you to be happy. Don't be afraid to follow your heart, even if it leads you away from here." A tear rolled down her cheek as she finished quietly. My throat burned as my own eyes blurred.

"I will. I promise," was all I could say.

She huffed, expelling the swell of emotion and offered me a teary smile. "And you know I'll go to the stupid dance. I'm not going to have you there alone in a room full of Archai." She got up from her seat and hugged me tightly. Her voice muffled by my neck, she asked, "What are we going to wear?"

17

Gillie found us in the kitchen one evening. She stood timidly, half hidden by the door frame.

"Hi, Gillie," said Naleiri, noticing our silent observer.

"Hi," she peeped, sliding a little farther into the open and raising her hand in greeting. "Umm...His Highness...um, General Kyran. He asked me to make sure you got this." She had a squeaky voice that matched her petite frame. She extended a small hand that held a faded piece of paper.

I walked across the kitchen and took it from her. "We were just about to eat. Would you like to stay?" I offered, thinking that she looked entirely too skinny.

Her eyes darted to the kitchen table like a frightened deer eyeing an escape route. "Oh...thank you. That's very kind," she blushed, dropping her head to gaze at the floor. "I really can't though. I should be going. Thanks again." She ventured a look at us before stepping quickly back behind the doorframe and into the hallway where the invisible portal Kyran had set up took her to wherever she called home.

I turned back to Naleiri shrugging. Three names of city shops were scrawled across the paper in what was presumably Kyran's handwriting. "Well, I guess we know where we're going tomorrow." I raised my eyebrows and gave a cheeky grin to Naleiri, who simply rolled her eyes back at me.

———

"For someone who was so against this, you sure are being particular." I said to Naleiri as I slumped on the gray leather cushion in the dressing room of the last shop.

We'd gone to all three that afternoon. I found my dress in the first store, but Naleiri wasn't happy with anything she found there, or in the next one. We were three dresses into this store, and it didn't look promising.

The shop assistant pulled back the heavy black curtain to the changing stall, revealing Naleiri wearing a beautiful royal-blue gown. It strapped around her neck, accentuating her bustiness, and then billowed out at her hips. The bottom was streaked with crystals that sparkled with her movement, like shooting stars across a midday sky.

I could tell she hated it.

"This is awful. Too...poofy." She pulled the sides of the billowing skirts out for effect. "I hate the bulkiness of the bottom, and the halter is going to drive me crazy. Uh, maybe I'll just find something from home that will work."

"Nothing we have at home will work. We'll find something," I said, trying to remain positive and hide my mounting frustration at the same time. "How many do you have left?"

She stuck her head behind the curtain. "Two more. The black one and the yellow one."

"Let's see the yellow next." I'd picked that one out for her. She disappeared behind the curtain followed by the assistant, who I could have sworn let out a heavy sigh. I couldn't blame her, getting people in and out of these big ballgowns was not a job I envied.

The assistant reemerged, nearly hidden behind the folds and billows of the unwanted blue dress. She carefully hung it up before returning to Naleiri. After a couple more minutes, she came out, slowly opening the curtain behind her.

It was perfect. The fabric was the color of sunflowers, bringing out the cool undertone of her fair skin. The dress clasped at the base of the neck with a thin collar that followed the collarbone to capped sleeves ending just beyond the shoulder. The solid fabric parted in the center of her chest, creating a diamond of bare skin that tastefully revealed the tops of her breasts. The dress was corseted around the waist. It was the only part of the entire gown where the solid fabric was decorated with textured swirls of stitching that led to the hip where the dress flowed out loosely. Thigh-high slits created tendrils of fabric that looked like flickering flames as she swayed, turning to look at herself. The back mirrored the front except for a nearly invisible zipper up the middle.

"You look stunning," I said simply. Her face glowed with agreement.

Casting one more glance over her shoulder at the mirror, she said, "Alright, let's get out of here."

18

I woke to the first snowfall of the season. It wasn't like the dense quiet blanket that coated the forest. In the city, the whiteness of snow only lasted so long before the trudging of residents turned it into a mushy brown mess. Surprisingly, the snow generated even more activity. It covered the roofs and sidewalks. Neighbors were out earlier than ever, removing it with enchanted shovels. Kids ran about excitedly, building snow forts, and those that could, were enchanting snowballs to fly over the barriers to strike their unsuspecting opponents.

I missed the stillness of a forest winter. "Naleiri. Do you want to check out the cottage? We could finally grab that purple tunic you've been missing," I tempted as I wandered back to the kitchen, leaving the winter city scene at the window.

I knew she'd also want to get out of the city, but we hadn't been in the forest since the attack. I wasn't sure how permanent our relocation was, but I wasn't in a rush to return, and surprisingly neither was Naleiri. Kyran had made sure all of our belongings ended up here. Although now I was almost certain that we really had Gillie to thank.

Naleiri looked out the small kitchen window to the side alley that ran between this and the neighboring building. The only proof of snowfall was the bright white flurries that stood out against the red siding of the other building before they passed our tiny window and fell to the ground. I knew she missed it too.

"Okay. Let's go," she said, smiling widely.

———

"Do you think they might have some winter boots in here?" I called up to Naleiri as I rifled through the downstairs closet that was situated under the staircase. I tossed aside brooms and a duster, snatching up two matching, black winter coats with a strip of what looked like fox fur running around the hood. Well, Naleiri wouldn't care for that, but she'd have to deal with it. Closing the closet door, I turned back to the kitchen when Gillie appeared out of the hallway portal with a faint pop.

"Ah!" I jumped, clutching a hand to my chest. "Gillie, for Liro's sake, what did I tell you about that? You scared me."

"I'm sorry, madam," she said, bowing her head.

"Oh. No, please...don't bow. And don't call me madam. It's okay. It's not your fault. Just...wasn't expecting you is all."

"You didn't ask for boots?" she asked, holding up two pairs of heavy-duty, brown winter boots.

"Yes! In fact, I did," I said, recalling the request I'd shouted up the stairs. I forgot that Kyran had mentioned that all we had to do was ask for what we needed, and Gillie would get it. "Thank you." I reached out to take the boots from her. She only bowed in response.

Loud thuds signaled Naleiri's excited descent. Holding up the boots, I announced, "Look what Gillie brought us."

"Great!" She took a pair from my outstretched hands.

"Thanks again, Gil—" But Gillie had already disappeared.

The snow had petered out to a light flurry by the time we reached the forest. The coat and boots were perfect to combat the knee-deep snow and occasional harsh gust of winter wind. Naleiri and I knew the path so well, it didn't matter that it was currently hidden.

Snow dusted the branches of the evergreen firs, making their dark green needles stand out even more. Beneath the largest trees, there were small circular stretches of bare ground where the snow hadn't quite been able to reach. We stood in awe, taking in the absolute hush of the forest. What a contrast to city life. I'd forgotten. It had always been one of my favorite observations, to watch flurry after flurry fall quickly and soundlessly to the ground, adding its tiny form to the fluffy veneer coating.

Not wanting to disturb the coveted quiet, we walked wordlessly down the path. The last time I had been on this trail, I'd almost died. That was two moons ago now, before winter had gripped Fira. And it had been at night. I didn't feel even a twinge of fear now; whether that was bravery or stupidity I wasn't sure. A part of me knew Kyran would not approve of our winter stroll, but what Kyran didn't know wouldn't hurt him. Besides, he was off gallivanting around, doing only the Ancient One knows what. I looked at Naleiri to see if she sensed anything out of the ordinary from the surrounding trees. She smiled pleasantly, content to be back in the wild. All must be good.

The cottage looked just as it had the last time I'd seen it, which seemed ages ago now. A thick layer of untouched snow frosted the roof and completely hid the two front steps. I was walking toward them when I lurched, pulled back suddenly by Naleiri's hand at my elbow.

"Someone was here," she whispered.

The light breeze drew my gaze to Naleiri who was looking up at the leafless branches rustling above us. The sudden warmth indicated she was using her

magic to interrogate the oaks. The branches bent and clacked together in response. "It was dark, but... definitely a female Eleiyon. And creatures of some
kind. Creatures the trees fear to mention, even now. They went into the house.
They were searching for something. Or for us. I don't know," she finished.

"How long ago?" My hand instinctively reached for the dagger strapped to
my thigh. My eyes strained to discern the slightest movement in the clearing.
There were no traces in the snow, so not recently. Of course, footprints could
be easily magicked away. I gripped the handle tighter.

"A fortnight. Just the one time," came Naleiri's answer. "No one has come
back. Aila, let's go." Her voice was pinched with fear.

The clearing suddenly felt eerie, compounded by the stillness and barrenness
of winter. As I turned to follow Naleiri, who was already moving back toward
the path, it caught my eye; across from me, one of the largest oak trees marking
the border between the cottage clearing and the beginning of the forest. Its
trunk left bare of snow, was black, as if someone had torched it. My eyes traveled
up the trunk. It was covered with what looked like black scorch marks, and in
the center of each, was a brown pulsing pustule, oozing a bright red goo that
looked like congealed blood.

"Naleiri, look," I called over my shoulder, pointing at the diseased tree.
Her light footsteps followed. "Ugh..." I covered my nose, trying to block out
the pungent, fermented smell. "What happened to it?" I inspected the oozing
discharge without touching it.

Pain coursed across Naleiri's face. "It's sick." She reached a hand up tentatively.

"Naleiri..." I warned, not sure if whatever this was could jump species and
spread to us.

Ignoring me, she gently placed her palm on an unmarred section of bark and
closed her eyes. Warmth radiated from her touch and the oak seemed to sigh in
response. Tears welled in her eyes when she turned back to me. "It's dying. Its
energy is so weak... like it's bound behind some invisible chain."

Without a second thought, she got to work circling the tree, scanning the trunk for wounds. She dropped to her knees, investigating the black mark and the ground around the trunk. "The roots are fine," she said, looking up after her inspection. "Whatever this is, it started from the outside, something topical, and it's working its way in, squeezing the life force out of the tree as it goes." She indicated the ooze as she finished her diagnosis.

"Okay... so what does that mean? What do you want to do?" I was at a loss, but her face was set with determination.

"We're going to save it."

Bewildered, I just stared at her, waiting for her to explain.

"We can cut it out. We just need to remove whatever is causing this, and the tree will be able to heal itself." She held out her hand expectantly, her eyes on my dagger.

A little wary of being unarmed while Naleiri worked on the tree, I begrudgingly turned the knife over to her. Naleiri got to work swiftly, angling the knife at the top of the first bulge. She sliced into the tree, hesitating after the first cut. I'm sure the tree had screamed in pain.

"Do you want me to do it?" I offered.

"No...I got it." She took a deep breath and continued. She was methodical. It only took a few minutes to completely remove the pustule, which dropped to the ground and throbbed rapidly for a moment and then deflated and went still.

"It needs a living host," I commented, observing the lifeless ooze on the forest floor. The exposed wood beneath the pustule had turned a sickly gray. Naleiri scraped at it with the knife, peeling the wood like an orange rind until it became a healthy tan color. Then, without pausing, she set in on the next wound.

The sun had moved to its highest point by the time she'd completely cleansed the tree of the parasitic growths. Despite the new gouges exposing bare wood up and down the tree trunk, the tree somehow looked healthier. Naleiri handed the knife back to me, surveying her work. "It's still very weak. But its energy is not trapped anymore. We did it." She beamed, smiling broadly.

"You did it. I just stood here," I said, smiling back. "I wonder what—"

But Naleiri's face had gone pale, her eyes staring blankly at the forest beyond the oak.

"Naleiri, what...?" I followed her gaze. Every tree past the clearing's border had the same oozing pustules and blackened trunks. Every single tree. The bushes around them peeking out from beneath the snow were also blackened and shriveled. The forest was dying.

"Naleiri... Naleiri!" I called louder, trying to shake her from her trance. I placed a firm hand on her shoulder and pulled gently. "Naleiri." Finally, she faced me. "We need to leave." It was all I could do to keep the edge of panic from my voice. Whatever could do this to an entire forest was extremely powerful, and I had no desire to confront it, especially with only a tiny dagger.

The branches shuddered above us. "It's some kind of darkness, a phantom. Not the creature that entered our cottage with the woman. Something else. Something...worse." Naleiri looked up at the oak. "It had a name once, but the forest has forgotten it." Her eyes filled with tears again. The joy she'd displayed moments before, gone. "They say not to come back here. It's not safe anymore."

As if to echo the trees' sentiment, a gust of wind whipped up, ushering us back into the clearing and toward the path to Aodhen.

19

Darkness swirled around me, biting at my heels like angry hounds. I tried to brush it away, but its tendrils wrapped tightly around my ankles, holding me in place. I tripped, falling to all fours where the darkness struck out quickly, sensing an opportunity, grabbing at my wrists and pinning me to the ground.

Frantically, I scanned the smothering blackness that enveloped me, looking for anyone to call out to. My eyes strained. I peered deeper into the dark, hoping. Forms started to take shape around me. Trees. I was surrounded by great, looming trees all tilting their bare branches toward me, each one dripping with red ooze. They bent lower and lower; the ooze almost touched my back. And then, a blinding flash of white light lashed the darkness, pulling it away with another, softer darkness.

I ripped off the covers. Sweat drenched my pillow. I sat for a moment, recalling yesterday's events. Naleiri and I had stopped at the library after we trekked back from the forest. We scoured book after book, looking for an explanation for the diseased forest, the red ooze, or the cryptic message about the nameless creature that could inflict this kind of blight. Nothing.

I could tell by the gray sky that it was morning and almost time for me to get ready to meet Kyran. It would be our first time seeing each other since our steamy meeting in the portrait room. I made up my mind before going to sleep that I would ask Kyran about the forest. Maybe this was the "situation" he was planning for.

<hr>

He stood just inside the ring, wearing his usual training attire. His shoulder-length hair was pulled back in a loose knot. A wide smile spread across a rather haggard face. His eyes were more tired than I had ever seen them.

Not waiting for words to be exchanged, Kyran was to me in two big steps, gripping me in a tight hug and planting a soft kiss on my lips. "I missed you," he whispered, cradling my face between his hands as he stepped back from his kiss.

My resolve slipped slightly as I allowed the words to come out. "I missed you too."

It wasn't a lie. I had thought about him often, fruitlessly trying to figure out the "situation." Just days ago, I could hardly think of anything but his urgent kisses and his firm hands exploring my backside. Today, I was consumed by another obsession: a choking darkness and a crimson ooze that was killing my forest. "Is everything okay? Did you and Cyrus plan for whatever the situation is?"

His eyes darkened slightly as he answered, "Not quite."

Unable to stop myself, I plowed forward. "Does the situation have anything to do with the trees dying in the forest west of Aodhen?"

"What?" He looked genuinely perplexed.

I briefly explained Naleiri's and my outing the day before, describing the eerie stillness, the blackened trunks, and the oozing pustules. I left out the part about the cottage intruders, as that might lead to more questions. Naleiri and I had considered the possibility of that part being connected to me being an Elemental. Kyran's face gradually became graver as my story continued.

"I asked you to stay safe, Aila." Disapproval flared in his voice. "Didn't you learn your lesson about the forest the last time you went in there alone? Why do you think I set you up in Aodhen? To keep you safe," he finished, answering his own question.

My defenses reared. "First of all, you can't 'keep' me anywhere. Secondly, I wasn't alone; I was with Naleiri. Thirdly, nothing happened, we're fine. And lastly, you are completely missing the point. Something is killing the trees in the forest. A creature of some kind. In your land, right next to your city! What are we going to do to stop it?" My tone became more intense with each point I made.

"We...are not going to do anything. I will bring this information to Cyrus and my father to decide how to proceed," he said flatly.

Seething, but not giving up so easily, I pressed, "That's right. I forgot you can't think for yourself."

He flinched. Maybe I'd gone a little too far. But I didn't care. I continued, "So what is the situation then, that has all of you so preoccupied that you missed this happening right in your own backyard?" I waited expectantly.

"I can't tell you about that," he said, pleadingly.

I hadn't wanted our reunion to be this way. He didn't know why this was so important to me. He couldn't know that I believed this could all be part of what happened to me three years ago. It was personal. He didn't know, because I didn't tell him. I couldn't.

I took a deep breath, letting it out slowly, feeling myself calm. I brushed past him. My voice returned to its normal volume as I said, "We can hash this out later. Let's get to training."

He seemed reluctant to leave things unsettled but eventually turned to the twin sai on the ground. "Alright. Show me what you've learned."

I demonstrated the various combinations he had taught me in our first twin sai lesson. I had perfected these simple maneuvers with ease. My demonstration became more intricate as I weaved in the strikes and parries I'd learned from the book into graceful combinations.

Once I finished, I eyed his sword leaning against the wall mischievously. "You know... you won't be able to tell what I've really learned through demonstration alone. I need an opponent..." I eyed the sword and raised my eyebrows at him, feeling adrenaline start to course through my warmed body. A challenge.

He followed my gaze to the sword and hesitantly marched over to it. "Are you sure?" he asked.

"Are you scared?" I countered, my smile growing.

He twirled the sword once, deciding, and then waved his other hand. A white sparring ring appeared on the ground beside us.

Upon entering the ring, I slid naturally into my fighting stance. Kyran did the same across from me. A whistle sounded in my head; then, the circling started. I knew he would have me make the first move, both as a fighting technique but also because I still saw the hesitancy to spar me in his eyes. I would use it against him.

I charged, knowing he would expect me to throw a jab like he taught me. Instead, I dropped quickly to the ground and spun my left leg out in a fan-kick, knocking his front leg forward and throwing him off balance. Spinning the twin sai in my hand to grip it so it created a lethal dagger with the point jutting out to the side, I swung a backwards hook toward Kyran's face. He raised a strong forearm, blocking the strike. We were both on our feet again in moments. His hesitancy was replaced by concentration now. I smirked.

He didn't wait more than a moment to initiate his own attack. I saw the telltale sign of his back foot pivoting ever-so-slightly as he launched himself faster. Much faster than the behemoth of an Eleiyon I'd fought last time. He raised his sword over his head and drove it down in an arc. The motion gave me enough time to lift my twin sai, making the middle prongs cross in an X. I used the strength of both arms to block the strong sword blow with the right side-prong. My arms reverberated with the impact as the weapons clanged together.

This was what I had been waiting for, what I had left out of my demonstration. I slid the right sai down his blade, twisting it to lock the blade in place as I pivoted to the outside and hooked the left sai's side-prong on the other end of the sword blade. With a final movement, I pushed up with the right sai and twisted down hard with the left, lifting the sword from Kyran's grasp and disarming him. His sword flew over my left arm and fell to the ground. Not done, I quickly changed my hand grip again and continued my outside swing, ending with my left sai inches from his throat and my right aimed at his gut. Only then did I lift my focus to his face.

He looked thrilled. "I'm impressed!" He smiled widely. "Cyrus can't even disarm me when I have a blade. You're a natural with the twin sai. Can you show me that disarming move slowly?" Genuine excitement coated his question.

I walked him through the technique, showing him the appropriate footsteps and correcting his grip on the sai.

We sparred the rest of the morning. Our physical combat acted as a much-needed release for the tense emotional exchange that had marked the beginning of our session. Kyran only won one round and never managed to disarm me. Dripping with sweat, we stepped back from the ring.

"I don't think there's any more I can teach you, Aila. I could show you the other weapons, but what's the point? You should clearly stick with those." He indicated the twin sai in my hands.

Was he ending our sessions?

"Magic!" I blurted without thinking. "You could teach me to spar against an opponent with a gift."

His eyes jerked up to mine. Something between surprise and anger crossed his face. "Why? It's too dangerous. Besides..." He stepped closer to me, exchanging whatever emotion he had felt for desire. "I'll protect you. You don't need to learn how to fight someone with a gift."

Bristling, I argued, "It's not about protection. I want to do something. I want to fight. Protect the ones I love. The place I love." *Figure out what happened to me and my family,* I added to the list in my head. This was the closest I had come to revealing the truth behind my desire to learn to fight to anyone but Naleiri. As the words tumbled out and images of the blackened forest and Naleiri's tear-filled eyes slipped across my mind, I knew they couldn't be truer.

He tilted his head slightly to the side with a look nearing pity that sharpened my anger even more. "Aila, I don't want you to fight. I don't want you looking for trouble. It seems to find you pretty well all on its own."

He had no idea how true his words were.

"You are just one girl. With no gift." He spoke more softly now, as if the volume with which he delivered his next words would lessen the blow. "You are talented with the twin sai, I admit, but you're not a soldier." He spoke soothingly, placing his hands on both of my arms where he massaged firm circles.

My heart fluttered; my body warmed at his touch; my anger and indignation wavered. It was so easy to succumb to my own desires when I was in his arms. I stood on my tiptoes and grazed his salty neck with my nose, planting soft kisses along his exposed throat. I wouldn't give up that easily. "So, are you saying there is no way then...for someone like me to defend against someone like you. Someone with a gift?" I whispered seductively in his ear.

"You are impossible," he growled back, sliding his hands from where they were on my arms to my waist.

"If there is, wouldn't it be best that I know it?" I asked sweetly in his ear.

"I still don't want you looking for trouble, Aila. How can I protect you then?" His tone was serious.

"Is it so impossible to think that I might ever be in a position to protect you?" I asked playfully, but wasn't sure I completely hid the note of sincerity I felt at the suggestion.

"Compromise?" he asked. He took my silence as agreement and continued with his proposal. "Tomorrow, we meet and do something unrelated to training, and you can ask me questions about sparring someone with a gift. Deal?"

I considered momentarily. "Deal." I smiled.

"I have to go to the main field now."

"And I'm not invited." It wasn't a question.

"I don't think it's a good idea."

We parted ways. The cloud of disappointment about not training with the Archai threatened my good mood, but I had to admit, I was proud of my newly acquired skills in the art of seduction.

———

Kyran kept his word, sharing more about his responsibilities and the training methods of the Archai. I learned about his duties to his father and his strained relationship with his mother, who wanted nothing more than a proper marriage and a grandchild. He discussed his distrust of the Eleiyon to the north, the Shades, and his skepticism at his father's desire to rebuild relations.

"Have you ever met Eleiyon from the other territories before?" I asked, genuinely curious about the other inhabitants of Kiakora. I'd never so much as stepped foot outside of Fira, and as Aodhen wasn't exactly known for its inclusivity of Eleiyon with gifts other than fire, I'd never seen anyone with other gifts.

"I have. Since the Treaty of Gifts, there hasn't been much cooperation between the territories, and not a lot of movement across borders. In fact, it's written in the Treaty that councils must notify the leaders of bordering territories if they wish to enter, even just to pass through," he explained. "I've had to confer with my counterparts in the south before; they completely lack a functioning government." He rolled his eyes. This was the second time he'd criticized Hawa's leadership. "And I've also had to meet with the Shades...more recently. About the forest. We share a much longer border," he added, by way of explanation.

This was as close as Kyran had ever come to sharing details with me about the Archai's movements and what he did with the information I'd given him about the blackened trees.

"And?"

"And a lot has changed in Kiromar since I last met with the Shades. More than I would have guessed...And that's all I'm going to say on the subject," he said firmly, ending the conversation.

I still hadn't convinced him to spar with me using his gift, and he glowered at me each time I suggested it.

"Let's just imagine for a moment that you're not there to save the day. What chance do I have in a real fight against an Eleiyon with a gift? An Archai, for example," I pressed, unwilling to give up so easily.

"First of all, the Archai answer to me, so that will never happen."

"But if it did," I insisted.

"If it did... there's very little you could do, especially against an experienced fighter. Your best bet would be to try to get your opponent to expend his or her energy. Magic, like everything else, is connected to our life force. It is very possible, particularly for a novice fighter, to expend so much of their energy through magic that they literally cannot produce more of it without recuperation." He paused a moment as if another thought just occurred to him. "The only other options are binding curses or enchantments, both of which take a lot of practice to weave correctly and an enormous amount of power, depending on the strength of the magic one is trying to bind," he added. "Unlike the Mangi, who are known for their spell-weaving abilities, Eleiyon tend to rely heavily on their gifts, and as a result, many have not learned this magic," Kyran explained as we strolled through the House of Fira's manicured grounds.

Our conversation ended as we rounded a bush the height of Kyran. It was trimmed in the shape of dancing flames. My next question caught in my throat as a I laid eyes on a massive stone statue of Liro. Ironically, instead of fire spouting from its mouth, a stream of water poured out, falling into the fountain's base below to be recycled. The statue was meticulously carved. Each scale etched into the stone, covering its impressive length. The statue looked fluid; the bends and curves of the giant dragon's body seemed intrinsic, resisting the stiff nature of the material from which it was sculpted.

"Have you ever visited the Mound Ruins?" he asked, drawing my attention away from the stone sculpture.

"Where the Eleyi of Aodhen used to live? No, I've not been there myself. Naleiri has told me about it, of course." *In one of her rants about the Archai,* I finished in my head, deciding not to voice the fact aloud. The tension between the two of them was thick enough.

"Let's go. There's actually a shortcut through the grounds." He nodded behind him toward a line of trees peeking out from behind the palace. He grabbed my fingertips, stiff from the cold, and pulled me onto the garden path. "When my family built this palace, they used parts of what the Eleyi had created: the burbling streams that brought fresh water to the Eleyi's homes were rerouted to water our gardens," he explained.

Sure enough, the sloping hills on the far side of the grounds melted into unnatural mounds along the tree line.

"Wow..." I whispered into the eerie quiet. Massive trees loomed above the mounds. Instead of having been cleared away, the mounds were made amongst the trees. Some of them using the roots to create gnarled doors. "Why don't we continue to build like this?" I asked, thinking of the fabricated wood houses and the sprawling city of Aodhen, completely cleared of the surrounding forests, except this single grove of trees.

"Simple, really. Nature fights back...The Eleyi used their powers to manipulate the trees. You'll find Kiakora is not so amenable to us," he responded defensively.

"Maybe…" I couldn't deny that what Naleiri was capable of was anything short of amazing. "I…" Kyran tugged at my elbow, pulling me away from the rest of my thought.

He clutched my arm tightly, eyes aflame with longing. The same eyes from the training field, and the portrait room. "It's nice being here, away from…from everyone." His warm breath on my face sent chills down my spine.

Pulling me again, gently this time, he led me into a strong embrace. His lips found my neck. The hard, sweet pinch of his teeth nibbled my throat. Our bodies entangled again like the twisted roots of the trees around us. His cold hands pressed against my bare back before sliding down the front of my pants.

Every part of my body was on edge, waiting in anticipation. The familiar warmth seeped into my groin, clouding my thoughts and cloaking them with desire. His fingers felt deeper, searching for the wetness I knew he would find.

"Wait…wait. I'm not…" What? I'm not ready? I want this. Do I? "I…"

"Shh." Kyran's body stiffened, saving me from deciding how I felt. He pulled his hand out quickly, igniting two crackling flames in each hand.

His eyes peered past me into the thickest part of the grove. I spun around, searching for whatever had interrupted us.

Only a menacing quiet met my gaze.

"Kyran…what is it?" I hissed, my heartbeat elevating. My hot breath released a puff of gray smoke into the winter air.

Kyran pressed his finger to his lips. He was scared. He stepped forward, placing himself between the grove and me.

Then I saw it. A wisp of black smoke curled around the trunk of a towering pine. Sinister ebony tendrils latched onto the trunk, like long, jagged spider legs harvesting an unlucky victim.

The brown wood dulled in response as if its life were being sucked from it. Gaping holes appeared and then swelled into brown pustules that immediately began leaked bright red ooze. This was it. The darkness. The thing that was destroying the forests.

Kyran stood rigidly in front of me. The fire was a flaming ball in his palm now.

"What are you waiting for?" I breathed fervently.

The blackness froze. A single thick strand separated from the mass and rose, turning toward us. It swayed, cobra-like. There was no question. It could see us.

Slowly it glided forward. It didn't have eyes, but I felt its heavy gaze. I knew, beyond a doubt, that it had no interest in Kyran. I was frozen. Waiting. Trapped in some kind of trance.

A wall of flame burst from Kyran's hand, ripping me from my stupor. The wall shot up, higher than either of us.

The sentient smoke paused its advance as if to decide whether it was worth continuing through the flaming impediment or not. It held my gaze a moment longer, and then, with a sudden forceful gust of air, it retreated. It disappeared completely, leaving both Kyran and me planted behind the firewall, our hearts still hammering.

Kyran didn't waste time. "Aila, let's go. Quickly."

"You don't need to tell me twice," I said, turning back toward the palace. "What was that?" I asked once we returned to the gardens, feeling a sense of security from the pristine hedges. I couldn't shake the disembodied stare. Whatever it was, it was pure evil.

"I don't know," Kyran replied. But his voice betrayed him. He looked distant, like he was piecing information together. This was the second time that I knew for sure he wasn't sharing everything.

"Aila, I'm sorry to do this again, but I..." he started.

"You have to go...yeah, I figured."

"Do me a favor, though, Aila. Please don't leave the city limits until I figure out what's happening. We may not all be as safe as we think we are." He planted a soft kiss on my right cheek, then my numb nose, followed by my left cheek. "It's cold. Go home and get inside," he said simply before hurrying toward the House of Fira.

I started in the opposite direction, but I had no intention of returning home. I was going to find answers for myself.

———

"I'm telling you, it could see me. I don't know how, because it just looked like black smoke, but it was alive. And it was looking at me," I explained to Naleiri in a hushed whisper.

We'd nestled ourselves in the aisle across from the scrolls, books discarded around us in lopsided piles. We'd been through all of them looking for some description that could be what I'd just witnessed.

"There has to be something," I said desperately, turning the pages of yet another giant volume fruitlessly.

"I can't believe it was in Mound Ruin, whatever it was. It's much closer than we thought. The birds were right...and Kyran didn't say anything?" Naleiri asked for the third time.

"No," I repeated. "He said he didn't know what it was, but..." Should I tell her I thought he was holding back? She already distrusted him. I interrupted my own thought. "We should go back to Mound Ruin. Maybe we can find something, a clue. Maybe to track it, or—"

"What? Aila, come on. Do you have a death wish?" Naleiri asked incredulously. "This is out of our scope. Let Kyran handle it."

I saw my opportunity. "Do you actually trust him and the Archai to handle it, Naleiri?"

She opened her mouth and closed it again, swallowing whatever thought she'd been about to share. Her eyes mirrored the serene skies as they held my own, assessing my resolve.

"Fine. A compromise then. The ball is tomorrow. We'll confront him about it there. Ask him what he knows and the Archai's plans to deal with it."

She looked pleadingly at me, begging me to just accept reason. I calculated my options.

"Deal," I finally decided.

Naleiri signed in relief. "Good." She smiled brightly.

I spent the rest of the day combing through texts, ancient and new, for anything related to the strange disease afflicting the trees. I was flicking through a useless chapter on various species of parasitic moss when I felt someone behind me.

"First twin sai and now Uscata Moss. You have quite the eclectic set of interests," Caeru trilled over my shoulder.

I closed the volume with a thud and spun to face her. Maybe she would know. After all, she was older than some of the forests themselves. Deciding to lay everything out, I asked boldly, "Do you know what's happening to the trees?" I posed the question innocently. *Let's see what she was willing to share on her own first.*

A gloom passed over her crystal eyes, and her jaw tightened behind her faded blue skin in what could only be interpreted as anger. She knew something, all right. "What do you know about it?" she countered.

Deciding that what I really wanted was answers, I broke the silence first. "I know that the forest is sick. Dying. I know that the trees are scared to talk about the black smoke that is causing it, and that the forest is no longer safe." And although a stab of pain struck my chest as I thought it, I added, "And I know the House of Fira is not doing anything to stop it. I must help," I finished with a crack in my voice.

In her typical fashion, Caeru assessed me silently before speaking. "Kiakora used to be a place governed by nature. Powerful spirits of the trees, the mountains, and deserts ruled, helped by magnificent, brilliant creatures of the lakes and skies. We all lived in harmony here. It sounds like a storyteller's tale, but it's true. There was a balance. The Mangi call it 'Han'ara,'" she translated. "Then the Eleiyon came. And when they came, they left open portals to other worlds; incarnations of death and decay were allowed to enter Kiakora. For that, the Eleiyon directly responsible were banished by the Protectors, locked for eternity in exile where they couldn't continue to wreak havoc," she finished.

I'd never heard this version of Kiakora's history.

As if reading my mind, Caeru continued, "Your stories have forgotten this. They've forgotten what was unleashed on Kiakora, and I'm not just talking about evil creatures. Han'ara meant that suffering had reason; beings had purpose. The Eleiyon brought with them selfish desires, a lust for power, and an appetite for betrayal and destruction the likes of which had never before existed here."

She held her long-fingered palm out and breathed something into it. Blue smoke swirled into a hovering sphere. As she continued speaking, forms took shape in the swirling mist performing Caeru's story. Small white seeds rose out of the blue smoke and nestled themselves in the hearts of the ethereal Eleiyon figures. "The Protectors recognized the threat the Eleiyon posed to Han'ara and gave future generations a gift from their own magic, their life force. They tried to forge an innate connection to Kiakora for the Eleiyon. But instead of honoring that gift, the Eleiyon used it to pillage the land further. They continued, in their own way, to conquer nature. To ignore the power held within every rock and branch." The misty forms reenacted her story, chopping down the wispy trees and damming the rippling streams. Soon a towering blue city stood in their place. "Eventually the native species of Kiakora, creatures that had walked this land since its birth, all but disappeared. I always thought the Protectors, like the Mangi, retreated into themselves, leaving Kiakora to fight evils alone."

I felt an unexplainable sense of shame. "I didn't know all of that," I whispered. "I suspected we weren't native to Kiakora... but I didn't know we were responsible for... for..."

Her eyes softened. "You are but a child, Aila. The powerful Eleiyon have hoarded knowledge away from the masses since they arrived here. To control knowledge is to control thought. And they know that." She closed her hands, and the floating sapphire city disappeared in a puff of smoke. "Truth has been erased from the collective thought of the Eleiyon long before you were around. For so long in fact, that the Eleiyon had to create stories to fill in the gaps, stories that became beliefs, and beliefs that became history. And the truth was lost, swept into these dusty shelves... You are not to blame," she finished softly, sadly. "I digress..." She paused again.

I was quiet, silenced by the truth of Cearu's lesson. I turned over each new piece of information, reassembling Kiakora's history in my mind, like a bridge to the past. "You said you always *thought* the Protectors retreated after banishing the evil from Kiakora...were you wrong? And what does that have to do with what is happening in the forest now?" But even as I asked the question, dread crept into my soul as a sinking feeling pressed on my heart, because I already knew the answer.

She continued as if I hadn't spoken. "The Land of the Banished, Nagrimar... It's a place even we've only heard of in stories. It exists at once as part of Kiakora and separate from it, shrouded in magic. Those there can never escape..." she claimed. But the doubt in her heart surfaced. "It's impossible to escape. What it would do to your soul, to break that kind of bind... But there have been...rumors. Of an evil sweeping through the forests in the north. A bodiless rot. That could be him. A torn fragment anyway. These are things that haven't been spoken of in the memories of any living Mangi. I thought maybe..." She drifted into her own thoughts for a moment, leaving me trying to piece the blanks together. She looked at me fiercely, returning from wherever she went. "The forest is lost. You cannot reverse what has been done. And with the forests dying, more evil will descend on Fira."

I thought of telling her about the intruders in the cottage. *Maybe more evil was already here.* Caeru gazed past me for another moment. Then she whispered, more to herself than to me, "This is a sign of things to come. This is proof that he has escaped. And he's brought others with him."

"Who is he?" I didn't understand the reference.

"There are more powerful forces at play than you can possibly imagine."

Fear gripped my heart at her sudden change in demeanor. "Caeru, who is he?" I repeated.

"Thalen. We all believed that he was still in Nagrimar. He must have escaped. I don't believe...but what else could explain it? It has to be."

Did Kyran, Cyrus, and the Lord of Flame already know about this? Was it only coincidence that the sudden disappearance of my memories aligns with the reappearance of evils that haven't traversed Kiakora in living memory?

Caeru's voice pulled me from my endless cycle of questions. "You can't reverse the decay, but that doesn't mean that there's nothing you can do. I don't know how Thalen did it, Aila, but the ancient world is stirring. Soon, we will all have to choose a side. Thalen is not the only one preparing." *What did she mean? Who else was there? The Archai?* "Everything you see has been thought of, created, fought for, by someone. There are those of us who are content to live passively in the world. And there are those of us who insist on shaping it. Who are you?" Her piercing gaze struck my core. Then she turned away.

"Caeru," I called to her back. "Who are the Protectors?"

A faint smile played on her lips for the first time in the conversation. "Let's just say not all of the Eleiyon's stories about Liro are complete nonsense."

20

Gillie arrived the morning of the dance with instructions from Kyran. We were to meet him on the stone steps of the House of Fira. I had been so distracted by Cearu's story and how I would confront Kyran, that I had completely forgotten about festivities of Solnas.

I padded down the stairs toward the kitchen, stopped at the window, and was flooded with festival reminders. The city was already alive with movement. Residents adorned their houses with last-minute decorations. They mounted strings of lights and wreaths made of pine needles and coral berries.

Solnascor was different than the Festival of Flame. It was celebrated across all Kiakora, not just in Fira. It was when Kiakora was farthest from the sun. The celebration marked the passing of time, but also the official start of Kiakora's journey closer to the sun, the bringer of life. Many Eleiyon exchanged gifts at midnight to celebrate the precise moment when a new cycle of life would begin. Naleiri and I never did. Instead, we celebrated the way the Eleyi and the Forest Nymphs did.

I preferred the quiet ceremony to the grandiose festivities of Solnascor. It was as a reminder of the cycle that all living beings experience. The ceremony was simple; Naleiri and I would wander down to the stream outside of the cottage.

We'd create a fire and gather the other elements: a cup of water from the stream, dried leaves from the ground. The fire represented our lives, a time-bound display of energy. We would pile on a few dried leaves, which curled and twisted under the heat of the flame, until they disintegrated into ash. Finally, at the exact moment Kiakora would start her new cycle, we would pour the water over the fire, extinguishing it, sending smoke into the sky. We covered the remains of the fire with dirt, and then Naleiri would recite the Solnas prayer: *all energy that comes from the land, returns to the land.*

The scrape of a whisk against a metal bowl sounded from the kitchen. The welcoming smell of cooking breakfast wafted toward me, luring me away from my window perch and back to the present. Naleiri was already awake, whipping up what looked to be an epic breakfast feast. Waffles and scrambled eggs were already set aside. Steam rose from their respective serving dishes. She was slicing fresh strawberries and piling them neatly onto a platter.

"Good morning. Happy Solnas!" She smiled widely.

"Happy Solnas. Wow! You outdid yourself. I would have helped," I added, snatching a strawberry from the dish.

"Hey, wait until I'm done." She jabbed the knife at my fingers. "I invited Gillie to join us for breakfast this morning, and I'm pretty certain I managed to convince her to say yes last night," she said proudly.

As if in response to hearing her name, Gillie timidly entered the kitchen, her eyes concentrated on the floor.

"Good morning, Gillie. Happy Solnas!" Naleiri beamed from where she stood behind the counter.

"Happy Solnas," Gillie said quietly, red tingeing her slender cheeks as she looked up to meet our gazes.

"Come in. Take a seat," I said, gesturing to the stools that lined the counter opposite Naleiri.

Gillie nodded as she walked to a stool, and Naleiri placed a cup of steaming tea in front of her.

"We're happy you decided to come," Naleiri ventured again, trying to stoke a conversation.

"Of course. You are both too kind for inviting me to join you for your celebratory breakfast," she responded formally, hugging the mug tightly in both of her tiny hands as she brought it to her lips. As I surveyed her, I was overcome with curiosity. *Where was she from? How did Kyran find her?*

Deciding a blunt approach probably would not be the best, I asked, "So, how long have you worked here?"

"Oh, it's been years now...yup, four years. Master Kyran, His Highness...he brought me here...after everything," she finished cryptically, taking another sip of tea.

"After what?" I asked, waving off Naleiri's disapproving glance.

Gillie's eyes flicked to mine. Her soft face was touched by sadness, evidenced by the slight droop of her lips and the crease of her brow. "My village was in Fira's northern forests, near the Kiromar border. We were attacked in the middle of the night. The entire village was ransacked. Our houses were set on fire. There was so much smoke." She paused her recollection, taking a shuddering breath before continuing in a whisper, as if speaking of it would summon whoever, or whatever, was guilty of the horrors that haunted her. "I was in the stable, a couple of our mares were in labor..." she explained. "But I heard it. Everything." Her wide eyes filled with tears. Her squeaky voice trembled as she struggled to continue. "My family, we are not warriors. We don't have any gifts to fight...And she came with a small army and two massive...things..." Terror permeated every aspect of her features as the memory came back to her.

"What things?" I pressed gently, reaching out to hold her hand, hoping the gesture would give her enough courage to finish her tale.

"I...I don't know. I've never seen anything like them. Even in stories...I never imagined... They are creatures of pure evil...I can't..." She shook her head as if to rid herself of the memory.

"It's okay," Naleiri said softly, reaching across the counter while rebuking me with another of her looks.

Gillie sat for a moment, gathering her thoughts before continuing. "Anyway, they destroyed everything. The woman, she was looking for something. She killed my family. And the creatures, what they do, is worse than death...I...I was such a coward...I just stayed...watching. I didn't help any of them." She lowered her eyes.

"No one would blame you." I patted her back in an awkward attempt at consolation. I was never good at sharing emotions, a fact that frustrated Naleiri to no end. "I'm happy you're here now. Safe."

She looked up at me through a veil of tears that transformed her wide eyes into glassy orbs. "Yes. The Archai found me in the stable. They must have been tracking the raiders. His Highness, Lord Kyran, was with them. And he brought me here." She lifted her trembling hands to take another sip of tea.

"It's Solnascor," Naleiri interjected happily, putting a swift end to whatever other details remained in Gillie's story. "Enough depressing talk. Let's eat some waffles and chat about the cute store owner across the street. The one who sells milk," she said lightly, plopping two huge waffles onto each of our plates. Gillie giggled, graciously accepting the waffles and the change of subject.

I would have been happy to keep asking questions and gathering more information about that night, about the woman and her strange creatures.

Instead, I listened to their banter about the dairy shop owner and one of the stable hands who Gillie was enamored by. I couldn't get Gillie's story out of my head. The fire. The piercing screams. It was all too familiar to the visions that plagued me nightly. *Could the same thing have happened to my town, and my family? If so, why could she remember everything so clearly while I couldn't recall a single moment from before three years ago?*

Gillie's account was also proof that Kyran and the House of Fira knew much more than Kyran was sharing. Caeru was right. *What if it was all connected?*

Gillie said the woman had been searching for something. *Was it the same woman that entered our cottage?*

———

The Solnas Ball was set to begin much earlier than I'd expected. Gillie stayed to help get us ready. She had a hidden talent for hair and makeup that she was all too excited to exercise.

Naleiri was first. Gillie chose a shimmering gray eyeshadow that made Naleiri's eyes look like the boundless sea under a haze of smoke and clouds. Her red hair was pulled up in a sweeping bun spiraled on top of her head. Gillie left loose curled tendrils that framed Naleiri's face, echoing the slips of twisted fabric that fell from her waist. She was radiant.

Naleiri finished admiring Gillie's work in the bedroom mirror before heading downstairs to wait for me. Gillie surveyed the gown now spread out on the bed. I slipped into the chair and she set to work immediately. Her slim fingers grappled with my shoulder-length hair, attempting to pull the comb through the curled strands.

"Nothing too intense, Gillie. I want to still look like me underneath," I warned.

"Done!" Gillie squeaked with excitement after what felt like ages. She lifted a small brush from my lips. "Wait...I want you to get the full picture." She reached for the dress and handed it to me. Once the dress was on and Gillie was satisfied, I turned to the mirror.

I almost didn't recognize the Eleiyon who gazed back at me. She was at once regal and refined, but also wild. Something untamed rumbled beneath her polished surface.

My face glowed; a touch of bronze shimmer at my cheekbones brought out the auburn freckles that dotted my cheeks. Gillie echoed the bronze on my eyelids with dramatic black lashes and a deep burgundy lipstick. I loved my hair.

The top was pulled back into a knot. Gillie had braided four small braids tight to my scalp that crisscrossed through my hair to meet at the knot. The rest of my hair came down in two tight braids, where Gillie weaved in thin gold ribbons that complimented my dress perfectly.

A braided gold strap fell across the nape of my neck and my bare shoulders, holding the forest-green fabric that billowed across my chest, shielding my mark from view. The dress ran uninterrupted but for a single slit in the center, between my breasts, which fell freely behind the loose fabric. The airy material cinched around my waist and hips. As I moved, the long slit that traveled from the floor to my upper right thigh revealed my muscular leg. Gillie added a braided gold band to my ankle that only showed when I walked. I turned to examine the back. The dress plunged from the gold braid at the top down to my waist, exposing my entire back and pooling in a small fold that sat on top of my bottom before hugging my hips and flowing outward.

I looked like I belonged at the Solnas Ball. I looked elegant, but natural, like I was a stencil cut straight out of the most beautiful forests in Kiakora.

"Wow, Gillie... I look..." I stared speechlessly at my reflection.

"Beautiful," Gillie finished. "Now go... I don't want you to be late. Kyran...I mean, His Highness' jaw will be on the floor when he sees you."

I blushed slightly at the obviousness of my relationship with Kyran. Showering Gillie with more thank-yous, I left the room to join Naleiri downstairs.

21

The House of Fira was decked out beyond imagination. The already pristine gardens seemed to have been manicured even more; not a stray branch or fallen leaf could be found. Glowing orange orbs of swirling fire hung from the trees, and rows of lights lined the entrance to the grand stone staircase, warming it even on the brisk winter evening. A black carpet with maroon and orange designs was laid out to welcome guests.

Kyran was nowhere in sight.

Despite our heeled feet, Naleiri and I arrived on foot. A narrow path I hadn't noticed before, skirted out beyond the front of the house. Ornate carriages of all colors lined the drive, dropping off elegantly dressed Eleiyon: the wealthy and powerful families of Fira, I presumed. Some popped out of thin air instead, appearing on the landing of the stone staircase next to the black carpet. The Archai must have created a portal for guests arriving from far across the territory.

I suddenly felt inadequate. A fraud dressed in a costume attending a ball I had no right to take part in. Naleiri clasped my hand and pulled me toward the entrance, shedding the inkling of doubt I felt.

A couple just arriving from a carriage marched up the stairs. The woman wore an iridescent white gown with matching earrings and ostentatious jewels around her neck. Her partner was dressed in all black. A pompous voice floated across the steps. "They hardly attempted anything at all this year," she said, casting a haughty, disapproving glance at the beautifully decorated grounds. "Remember, dear, they had a server with drinks greet the guests upon arrival last time?" Her partner simply nodded in agreement.

Naleiri caught my gaze and rolled her eyes.

The oak door opened to reveal an entirely unrecognizable foyer. Streams of never-landing flames shot around the crystal chandelier, sending shards of light sparkling through the entryway. The black carpet continued straight through the foyer into a huge open ballroom that had not been there the last time I'd visited.

Music beckoned us to the room. A full orchestra dressed in solid maroon played a joyful tune. Servers in black and orange moved amidst the guests who milled about the cavernous hall, almost all of them already carrying drinks. No one had ventured onto the dance floor yet. It seemed they were content to mingle with Fira's other socialites. I spotted a three-tiered fountain splashing on the opposite side of the room. A server dipped each of the tall tube-shaped glasses from his tray beneath the flowing rose-colored liquid,. Next to the fountain was a massive table. A few guests were ladling heaps of decadent food onto their plates while other servers were refilling their own trays. At the very end of the room was a raised table with throne-like chairs ornately decorated with black velvet and gold trim. A smaller, slightly lower table was set up just before it, piled with gifts. Solnas presents for the Lord of Flame.

All eyes in the room followed us as we moved toward the center. I couldn't blame them; Naleiri was breathtaking beside me in her glowing yellow dress. She grabbed two sparkling glasses from a passing server and handed me one.

"Cheers," she said before taking a long sip.

I scanned the crowd for Kyran. I spotted him engrossed in conversation. His normally tousled hair, slicked back into a neat pony. He was entertaining a small circle of Archai, commanders, each boasting pins and medals attached to their suits over the breast opposite the Archai triangle.

Kyran smiled effortlessly, chatting with the group, all of whom laughed at whatever joke he had just made. Glancing up, he caught my eye and excused himself.

Kyran was undeniably handsome. I admired his strong, muscular body as he made his way across the room to Naleiri and me. His eyes traveled up and down my green dress, his pupils darkening. He didn't even glance at Naleiri until he was right in front of me, clutching my fingertips.

"Ladies." He acknowledged Naleiri now with a nod. "Welcome. You..." he said, turning back to me. "You look beautiful." I allowed his eyes to take in my bare shoulders and the provocative slit between my breasts.

I had the sudden urge to dance. Grabbing Kyran's hand more securely and offering my half-finished glass to Naleiri, I said, "Shall we?" Not waiting for an answer, I dragged him to the dance floor. Naleiri downed my glass with a shrug.

I felt Kyran's eyes devour my bare skin and travel down to the small dimples exposed just below my waist as he followed me to the dance floor. Whispers and speculation reached my ears, all some version of the same question: *Who is that with the prince?* Kyran didn't seem to mind the attention as he spun me into his arms and the orchestra kicked into an energetic number. His hand clasped my exposed back sending a thrill up my spine as he pulled me closer to his body. He twirled me in circles, my feet falling into a familiar rhythm I hadn't been aware that I knew. The sway of my hips came naturally as I stepped into each spin, following Kyran's lead. Over his shoulder, Naleiri chatted with a finely dressed man who had dared approach her.

"Everyone is looking at you right now," Kyran's voice grumbled in my ear. "The men all want you. The women want to be you...and here I thought I'd be the most popular attendee." Red bloomed in my cheeks. I glanced discreetly to either side. Sure enough, the stares confirmed Kyran's observation.

Turning back to him, his eyes twinkled with laughter. "It's only because I'm dancing with *His Highness.*" I coated the last two words in a thick layer of mockery.

"See..." Kyran twirled me out and caught me midway with a firm hand on my hip so that my backside was pressed against his front. Our hands still tangled in our paused spin. His hot breath tickled my neck as he spoke. "That's one thing I love about you. You don't treat me like a prince. You don't look at me the way everyone else does. It's one of the reasons..." His hand slid from my hip to graze my bare upper thigh as it peeked through the open slit in the dress. "Definitely not the only reason, but one of the reasons that I find you so...intoxicating." He breathed the last word into my ear so that my hairs stood straight on the back of my neck and a tickling warmth flowered between my legs.

Suddenly the room disappeared. I didn't care that we weren't alone or who was watching, or what they would think. I pushed my planned interrogation aside and spun to face him. Untethered lust shone in his eyes, and I know they reflected what was in my own. We had all but stopped moving to the music as we swayed, locked in an endless gaze.

"Ahem," someone coughed at my shoulder. We jumped apart as if zapped by lightning.

Cyrus.

"Sorry to interrupt." He didn't look it. "Aila..." He nodded slightly as he acknowledged my presence before turning back to Kyran. "The Lord needs to see you... now." He glanced across the now-crowded dance floor to the far corner of the room, indicating where they'd be waiting for him. Cyrus nodded curtly again before turning on his heel.

"Does that guy ever loosen up?" I joked, trying to lighten the mood.

"No. Not really," Kyran said softly, his eyes still following Cyrus' back as the crowd parted to let him through. He turned to face me, the playful twinkle and lustful look gone, replaced by hard eyes and a set jaw. "I have to go. It shouldn't be long... I hate to leave you here with all of these...vultures." He flashed a smile that didn't quite reach his eyes.

Behind his pretty smile were answers to the questions that bubbled inside of me. Everything Caeru had shared came rushing to the surface in a wave that I couldn't stop. "Is it about Thalen? Are you preparing to move against him? Or is it the creature that is destroying the forest? I know you know more than you're telling me. I know what you saved Gillie from," I whispered. A half-truth, but maybe enough to get him to give me something. Anything.

His face hardened more as he clenched his jaw. "You don't know anything. And it's not your place to ask those questions, Aila. You know I can't share our missions with you, and definitely not here. It would put us all at risk." He looked around uneasily. "Can't you just be happy with me? Why do you need to meddle in things that don't concern you? How many times do I have to tell you that it's dangerous?" He peppered me with the questions, anger rising in his voice.

"Things that don't concern me?" My own anger rebelled against my carefully crafted calm. "I was attacked by creatures that should be living in the Northern Mountains of Kiromar. Me!" My voice was verging on a scream. I took a breath to calm myself before continuing. "My forest...my home is dying from some unspeakable evil. You...you have disappeared for days at a time, and you're off again on some secret, dangerous mission and you won't tell me anything..." I hissed. I didn't mention the other nagging suspicion that my family and I were victims of the same horrors Gillie had experienced, and the reason for my obliterated past.

Kyran's eyes softened, but he still glanced around for eavesdroppers. "I'm sorry," he said quietly. "I wish I could tell you more. I do. But I can't. Not right now, anyway. Once we...handle it. Then maybe I can share more. Until then, please just do me a favor and stay safe. I can't worry about you on top of everything else." He leaned in to brush a gentle kiss on my cheek before turning to follow Cyrus' path across the ballroom.

The room grew silent around me. I watched Kyran walk away, as if through a dark tunnel. The crowd parted wordlessly, making way for His Highness. He navigated the room, heading straight to the hallway without so much as a backward glance.

Something clicked into place. My heart started to pound in my ears, or maybe it was my soul sensing I'd finally set it free.

Quickly scanning the room, I found Naleiri in her spectacular sunflower gown entertaining a flock of suitors. She would be fine for another few minutes. I hiked up my dress and followed Kyran who had just disappeared into the hallway. The guests did not step out of the way for me. Jostling against shoulders, I excused and pardoned my way to the far corner and slipped down the dark corridor and out of the ballroom.

As soon as I entered the hallway, the music from the celebration muffled completely. Another enchantment. The hallway was bare, its maroon walls dimly lit. I padded on the balls of my feet to the end of the hall to prevent the clackity-clack my heels would surely make on the tile floor.

The hallway opened to a large room. Toward the center of the opposite wall was a double door crafted in the same style as the portrait room upstairs. One was slightly ajar. I crept closer, crossing my fingers that whatever silencing enchantment had been placed on the ballroom hadn't been cast here.

I recognized Cyrus' growl first as it floated out of the partially open doors. I pressed my ear to the open space.

"It needs to be a covert mission. A small band of us. No more than six. That should do it. If the Arbori are aware of our presence there, they will alert whatever might be guarding it."

"And do we know where it is exactly?" Kyran's voice cut in.

"In the lake." Cyrus' voice was flat, but was that fear that blanketed his statement?

"It's a big lake."

"The legends all refer to a cavern at the center of the lake. We think around here," another voice I didn't recognize chimed in. I heard a soft tap of a finger on a table, indicating a spot on a map of some kind.

"What are your thoughts, my lord?" Cyrus asked. *So Kyran's father was there.*

After a moment's pause, a slithering voice I did not expect broke the silence. "I need what lies in that lake. Having it secures our safety and a position of power for Fira. Try not to be found out, but do what you must to get it," the voice rasped. "You leave at first light," the lord finished.

"Get Egan and Ash..." Kyran said.

"We should bring Luga for enchantments and Fintan for cover with the longbow," Cyrus suggested, cutting in.

"Agreed. We meet at the training field at dawn."

Chairs shuffled, and the crinkle of folding parchment sounded behind the door. Slipping away, the creak of the door opening sounded as I rounded the corner into the dark hallway. My mind raced faster than my legs could carry me. *A covert mission.* Wherever they were going, someone or something was guarding what they wanted.

I searched the crowd for Naleiri, wanting to be next to her before Kyran found me so as not to raise suspicion. I spotted her dress almost immediately. *What were they searching for?*

I ran the conversation over again in my mind. *Had I missed any clues as to what it could be?* Something so important that Kyran would leave tomorrow. Something to protect the territory and gain a position of power, Kyran's father had said. This had to be about Thalen and whatever Kyran and I had seen yesterday.

I pulled Naleiri away from a new group of hungry men who were all clearly hoping she would choose them for the next dance.

"Hey...what's going on?" Her tone changed as soon as she saw my expression.

I quickly recapped the conversation I'd overheard.

"What lake do you think they're talking about?" Naleiri asked, looking just as confused as I felt.

I racked my brain. I knew Fira had several lakes within its borders. The image of a shimmering streak of sunlight glinting off a surface so flat that it looked like a polished onyx gemstone flashed in my head. "Lake Luan. Kyran said it was a big lake and that's the biggest one I can think of. That must be where they're headed."

Storyteller tales jumped to mind; the forests around that lake were haunted. The lake itself was protected by a gigantic sea serpent. Every parent in Fira told their children those stories to keep them from wandering too close. *Were they real? Did the Lord of Flame want to steal from it?* Naleiri's alarmed expression told me she was remembering the same stories.

Kyran's vanilla scent reached me before I spun around. His face was grave. "Aila, I'm sorry to have to abandon you tonight, but I need to prepare for some... official business with the Archai." His hand caressed the side of my cheek. "I really enjoyed dancing with you." The sincerity in his voice almost wiped away my resolve.

"Let me come to Lake Luan with you. I can help," I pleaded. Naleiri choked on a sip of her drink, her expression turning from surprise to horror.

His blazing hazel eyes hardened to ice. "How do you know about that? Are you spying on me...?" His question confirmed my guess was correct. He was angry.

"I wouldn't have to if you'd share with me. I don't want to be left on the sidelines of this, Kyran." We'd had this argument before. *Hadn't I proven that I could handle myself?* I'd disarmed him, the leader of the Archai, in a match. Maybe he would understand my desire to join him if knew my true motivations. He knew that I wanted to save the forests, but that wasn't all of it. I had to discover what had happened to me. It couldn't all be a coincidence: Gillie's story; the Myriapods; the strange woman and her nameless beasts; the dying forests; and now, a secret mission to protect Fira. Perhaps the truth about what had happened to me might also be hiding in the depths of Lake Luan. I had to find out.

"Aila, we've had this discussion before," Kyran repeated the words I had just thought myself. "And I'm not having it again. You can't help us. You are not a soldier, and I don't want you in danger. I care about you. And you'll just distract me. Please...stay safe." With that, he turned and left me standing beside Naleiri, my cheeks burning and my heart on fire.

"Are you crazy? You want to go with him? Aila, I agree with Kyran. Stay here where it's safe. Aila? Aila? Are you listening to me?...Aila?"

Naleiri's voice was muffled, an inconsequential beating against a padded wall. I heard her but couldn't drag myself toward her voice. My entire self was transfixed by Kyran walking away. He would never see me as an equal. And even as the icy chains of truth tightened painfully around my numbing heart, I felt the deep roots of a small seed that I had buried in darkness. I had left it, malnourished and lonely, but it had grown steadily nonetheless, reminding me now of who I was, and that this brief respite from restlessness would always have been only temporary.

"Let's go. We're leaving." I grabbed Naleiri's arm and pulled her toward the foyer.

"Aila...Did you hear anything I said? Aila...stop for a second," she said firmly, planting her heels and refusing to walk further.

I sighed in exasperation, knowing what was coming.

"What are you going to do?" Concern marked her beautiful face.

"What I should have done from the beginning. I'm not going to sit by. I'm going to do something," I said, echoing Caeru.

It was already dark when we reached the stone staircase. Guests were still arriving. They passed in a blur as I hurried down the stone steps, Naleiri trailing behind me. It would almost be time for the guests to exchange gifts. In another reality, Naleiri and I would be preparing for Solnas. Instead, we raced through the deserted gardens of the House of Fira, the cold biting at our heels to spur us on.

"That's what I'm worried about. What are you going to do?" She sped up to walk alongside me now.

"First, I'm getting out of this dress and changing into something more functional. Then, I'm going to Lake Luan."

No hint of surprise showed in her face.

"Kyran and his squad leave at dawn. I need to be back here to follow them. Can you run to the library while I go home and get ready? I'll meet you there. I want to see if we can dig up anything on what might be waiting for us in that lake."

Naleiri nodded. I swallowed the argument I had prepared in case she protested, but she must have sensed it would be fruitless to argue. We parted ways; she continued to the library while I rushed home. Fear-induced adrenaline and excitement propelled me down the empty streets.

22

The House of Fira was still ablaze with Solnascor festivities when I returned. It was past midnight; perhaps gifts had already been exchanged and the evening was devolving into a merry soiree of drunken cheer.

Instead of entering the palace again, I hurried down to the training field where Cyrus said they'd meet at dawn. I'd have time to find my twin sai before looking for a hiding spot to wait out the sun. They agreed to bring along someone for enchantment. *Why? Did they expect wards to protect the Lake and whatever it was they searched for?*

Naleiri hadn't found anything about what powerful object might be hidden in the depths of the lake. She did find references to a giant sea serpent living in Lake Luan, but nothing to give credence to the bedtime stories parents told their children.

Cyrus seemed to think there was something to the legends, because he was worried about something being alerted by the forest species. *What had he called them? Arbori?* I'd been so preoccupied by what might be living in the lake, I'd forgotten to ask Naleiri to check into what could be in store for us in the forests around it.

I nodded off against the weapons shed, clutching my twin sai, my thoughts lulling me to sleep.

The crunch of footsteps on gravel woke me. I peered out from my hiding spot. Five figures approached in the pale morning light.

"Where's Luga?" Kyran's voice echoed across the empty field.

As if in answer, another shadowy outline appeared in the entrance.

"I wanted to double-check coordinates with Dagan. He thinks if we arrive here"—he jabbed a finger at the center of the parchment he was holding— "we can avoid the Arbori, but also get close enough to the lake that we won't have a long journey through the marshlands."

"The Mavtir hunt those marshlands. They can be just as bad as the Arbori," Cyrus added.

"Well, we gotta pick our poison, I guess," added one of the others who I couldn't see.

"The plan is to be covert. In and out. Nothing and no one need to know we are there. Once we're at the lake, Cyrus, Ash and I will go in. Egan, you'll stand guard on the shore, and Fintan, you'll find a spot to set up with the longbow. Stick to hand signals as much as possible to communicate. Fire is a last resort. Everyone should be armed," Kyran commanded. "With any luck from Liro, we'll be back here by nightfall."

Another moment passed. "Are we ready?" His face was stern as he surveyed his squad. No one objected. "Luga."

My heart shifted into gear, hammering against my chest. *This was it.* I moved into a crouch. My dagger was strapped to my leg, and Kyran's twin sai was secured in an X-shaped holster on my back.

Luga began a whispered chant. A breeze picked up, carrying the dust from the training field with it. I poised myself to spring out of hiding. Luga finished as a bright, swirling blue portal opened. I could tell it was different from the one set up for Solnas Ball or even the one Gillie used at the house. This would be temporary. Nothing from Lake Luan would be able to get through, and no one from here would be able to follow once it closed.

Kyran stepped through first, followed closely by Luga and the other three. Cyrus was last. Just as he turned to step through, I launched myself at his back. Flying over the small space between the weapons shed and the portal quicker than should have been possible, I tumbled into him as the portal snapped shut behind me.

———

Thud.

I spilled out onto the cold, hard ground after Cyrus.

He was on his feet in moments, sword drawn. Confusion replaced his normal sneer. Six shocked faces looked down at me. Cyrus' confusion turned to disgust. Kyran's wide eyes wavered between anger, fear, and surprise.

"Aila, what do you think you're doing here?" he whispered harshly, breaking the silence as he stepped toward me. His expression had settled on livid.

"What I must," I whispered back.

He searched my face. Fear returned to his mix of emotions, creating a secondary anger, that special anger one feels when someone they love has put themselves in danger or done something incredibly stupid. Perhaps in this case, I'd done a bit of both.

"I can create another portal, General. Take her back right now?" Luga offered from where he stood behind Kyran.

Before I could protest, Kyran spoke, conflicted emotions evident on his face. "No. We can't open a portal without alerting everything in the nearby radius. The element of surprise would disappear."

Kyran's face fell as he considered his own words. I was here now, and there was nothing he could do to change it. "Fine," Kyran said, resigning himself to the fact. "You have a new priority on this mission, Luga. Protect her." He nodded toward me. "Should we be discovered and things go south, create a portal and get her to safety immediately. Then come back to help the rest of us. Is that understood?"

Luga nodded. "Yes, General."

The other Archai's faces were alert but impassive. Orders were orders. If they felt any way about Kyran prioritizing my safety over their own, they didn't let it show. Cyrus, however, glared at me with a look that bypassed hostile and veered close to loathing.

"I don't need—" I began.

"Shh." Cyrus cut me off with a hiss. He put his forefinger to his lips and gestured around before pointing again to his ears.

His meaning was clear. *Talk about this later. The marsh is listening.*

It was only then that I took in my surroundings. I didn't see a lake. The distinct smell of mud and dampness clung to the air, making it at once thick and moist. The sun was rising through a haze of clouds to our right, over a faded tree line that I could just make out stretching along the eastern and northern edges of the marsh. Behind us was what looked like an endless expanse of marshlands. We were standing in a thicket of long, yellowed grass. The ground was hardened from the previous days of intense cold, but around us, in every direction, the land disappeared, giving way to murky pools of water. Judging by the small tips of grass piercing the surface, it looked like most of the pools would be knee-deep.

The view from Orchard's Clearing crossed my mind, helping me orient myself. The lake should be due west of here. I turned back to my reluctant squad. Did they know of a path through the marsh, or would we be wading through the cold water? It occurred to me that the black boots and thick socks I'd selected would not hold up. *Too late for that now, Aila.*

Luga knelt at Kyran's feet and whispered faintly. He did the same to each of his comrades before turning to me. Glancing at Kyran for approval first, he whispered again. A warming sensation wrapped around my feet, traveling up my ankles to my knees. They felt insulated, as if I'd just donned knee-high waders. An enchantment to keep us dry.

Kyran motioned me forward before signaling to the rest of the team to assemble behind us. Luga followed me, I assumed because of his new set of orders. Fintan, Egan, and Ash were next. Cyrus brought up the rear. We left the haven of dry land for ankle-deep water. The squelching of our boots in the muck was the only sound. It was an eerie quiet. I strained my ears for a single bird's song, the chirp of a cricket, or even an occasional croak from a bullfrog. They were all absent from the hazy marsh. It had the stillness of a winter's forest with none of the peace. This silence was foreboding, like a sleeping volcano biding its time before erupting in all its destructive glory.

A shriek above us broke the dense silence.

I'd heard that screech before. An image of a beautifully freckled face marched through my mind. She was panicked. She threw her cloak over a little girl as she rushed to take cover in a ditch. She whispered something as she peered up at the sky. I couldn't hear. I strained, trying to recall the memory, but it slipped away.

"There." Fintan pointed. Our eyes shot upward in unison, searching the skies for the origin of the noise.

Fintan pointed first. Three huge black birds flew in a small circle behind us. After a moment, their circle widened slightly. They were searching the ground.

Kyran made another series of rapid hand-signals. *Damn, I wished I'd asked him to teach me those in our training sessions.* I picked up that we would be changing course.

We headed straight to the tree line on the northern edge of the lake. The trees would provide aerial cover. Whatever these birds were, Kyran was willing to abandon his carefully planned route to avoid them finding us. Our pace doubled. Kyran was no longer selecting the driest routes, but plunging through pools of water, making a beeline for the trees, the birds' circle ever-widening behind us. Our straight-line formation broke as we jumped into yet another deep pool.

Icy water seeped into my black pants. The insulating enchantment must only have affected up to my knees because the frigid water burned my thighs as I followed Kyran soundlessly through a deep stretch, trying to keep up. Even though there was no current, the water felt thick, pressing against my legs, and making it difficult to move. Egan, Fintan and Ash were all ahead of me now.

Kyran had almost reached the other side. I tried to move faster. Working my legs, forcing them through the water. Then...

My left foot sunk deeper into the muddy floor of the marsh. I pulled. It was stuck. I pulled again with all my strength, trying to free it from the mud.

Something pulled back.

Terror flooded my body, elevating my heartbeat until it was the only sound I heard thudding in my ears. My imagination? It could have been just a root, or a long piece of grass twisted around my ankle.

I tugged my foot again. It didn't budge. Nothing. I breathed a sigh of relief. *Get it together.* I scanned the pool for the others. Cursing the Ancient One, I would need to ask for help. Luga was closest.

"Lu—" A vice-like grip clamped around my ankle, tightening. Then a heave that I felt in my hip socket pulled me beneath the murky surface.

Cold water filled my ear canals, muting any sounds coming from the surface. Had they noticed me go under? Something was clawing at my leg, searching for a better grip. It was going to pull me deeper.

I lashed out with my free leg. My foot connected with something hard. The vice loosened. I tried to wriggle my leg away from whatever had me, but it clenched down again around my foot. My lungs burned for air. I aimed another powerful kick. And another.

It let go. I spun to my stomach, making futile attempts to stand. *Hadn't this pool only come up to my thigh? Where was the ground?* Muddy water filled my vision as I opened my eyes. *The surface...Where was the surface?* My lungs screamed.

I beat my arms against the water. Flailing. I tried to kick, but my right leg felt like a leaden weight. Then my hands touched muddy ground. I was halfway down some kind of hole. I scrambled frantically but just slid further down. I was digging myself deeper. A muted glow rose above me. *The sun. The surface.* I reached out for it just as my lungs were about to give up. A jet of water propelled me toward the light. I kicked as fast as I could, and finally, my face broke the surface.

Air. I gulped mouthfuls. Relief set in. Kyran charged back into the water. I relished the air a few moments more. He was yelling something. His muffled voice didn't quite reach my frozen ears. Luga was close now, wading quickly toward me. They were all yelling. Telling me to move, I realized. Panic grabbed at my heart again as adrenaline pumped my body into motion. My leaden foot burned in the frigid water.

Something latched around my waist with the same strong grip as before. I couldn't move. Oily black arms with long crooked fingers wrapped around my body. I couldn't see behind me but based on the horror crossing Kyran's face as he watched, I knew it was something I didn't want to see.

My dagger! I fumbled for the weapon strapped to my thigh.

A growl, and the grip loosened. Luga was there. He dove, pulling the creature away from me. The surface was all splashes and slimy black limbs tangled with the cloth of the Archai uniform.

Then calm. The surface went as still as a tomb.

The others stopped behind me, waiting for Luga to emerge. Another moment passed. Cyrus and Kyran exchanged a wordless glance.

Then the surface broke, and Luga shot up with a gasping breath.

Oh, thank the Ancient One. Luga was my favorite of the squad. He was the only one who didn't look completely disgusted at the sight of me. Plus, I would never be able to meet Kyran's eyes again if Luga had died saving my life.

"Come on." Luga grabbed my elbow, pulling me out of my daze and toward the bank. The others had already turned to wade out of the water.

"What was that thing?" My voice was a croak even in a whisper.

"A Mavtir. Nasty creatures. They burrow pits in the bottom of the deeper pools and wait for their prey to step into one. Then they drag them deeper to feed."

I shuddered. *How close to a muddy grave had I come?*

"Thank you." I mumbled.

Luga's eyes softened as he cast a sideways glance at me. His lips tugged up in an encouraging smile. "Not bad for your first encounter. You did manage to free yourself...initially."

We reached the bank, dragging ourselves onto the ground. The cold air blew harshly against my soaked body. My pants were shredded below the knee. Streaks of blood were visible beneath the shards of clothing where the creature's claws had broken my skin.

Superficial wounds, I concluded as I inspected my leg further. My body was so numb, I couldn't even feel the stinging pain that would have clued me in to the scrapes earlier. I suppose I could be thankful for that.

Luga muttered something under his breath next to me. When I looked again, he was completely dry. Turning to me, he continued muttering. A delightful warmth spread over me as my clothes and hair dried.

"Thank you," I said again.

Strong arms embraced me roughly from behind where I was sprawled on the bank. The familiar scent of warm vanilla felt so out of place in the damp marsh. "Aila...damn. I'm glad you're okay." Then, "Thank you." I knew he was talking to Luga. If he was still furious with me for crashing his mission, I couldn't find a trace of it in his face as I turned to him.

"We need to move, now," Cyrus' deep voice rumbled behind us. "We made too much noise. Something will have heard us."

Kyran was on his feet in seconds, reaching down to help me up. "Single file to the tree line. As fast as you can...avoid the deep pools." He cast a final glance at me, triple-checking that I was in fact alive and relatively unharmed. "Let's move," he ordered, satisfied with whatever he saw.

Towering pines, as of yet untouched by the menacing creature in the Hafra Forest, marked the end of the marsh. Small bushes and lush green ferns spotted the ground, flourishing in the moist soil surrounding the lake and marshlands.

Cyrus, who had kept his eyes on the circling birds the entire stretch to the tree line, now turned to scan the forest's edge.

"Ozars," Luga revealed quietly. I guess we had bonded in our near-death experience. "The spies and messengers of the north. We've noticed them growing more confident lately, entering deeper and deeper into our territory. Mavtir would look like house pets compared to whatever evil they would bring from Kiromar to rain down on us if they knew we were here."

The slippery clutches of the Mavtir dragging me to a murky tomb came to mind, and I wondered what could be worse.

"From the north? You mean the Shades sent them? Why would they spy on us? I mean, I didn't realize relations between Kiromar and Fira had deteriorated that much," I asked Luga, surprised by this new piece of information.

His eyes betrayed him. They widened slightly, indicating he'd said more than he'd planned. "Things have never been great with the Shades, but it's not them we need to worry about anymore."

"Is it Thalen? Is Kiromar siding with him? Is that what this is all about?"

Luga looked like he'd just dived into the icy marsh waters again. Clearly, he hadn't expected me to know as much as I did. "I..." Luga sputtered.

"We'll follow the tree line to the lake and set up there," Kyran whispered, cutting Luga off before he could deliver a coherent response. "So far so good. It looks like our presence is still unnoticed."

The rest of us nodded, but I couldn't have been the only one who saw the doubt in Kyran's eyes.

<hr>

We stopped on the edge of the most magnificent lake. Despite the cold breeze that whipped around my legs and lashed my face, the lake's surface remained placid, streaked with the golden glare of the afternoon sun. The Ozars had evidently lost interest in the marshlands. The skies above us were lifeless. A small wave of relief passed over me for the first time since going through the portal.

Egan and Fintan left the bank for the dense brush at the base of the tree line, most likely staking out Fintan's hide site for the longbow. Luga unfolded a parchment from an inner pocket in his lapel. Cyrus, Ash, and Kyran hovered over his shoulder to look at the map.

"We originally planned on entering from here." He pointed, scanning his surroundings as he gazed at the map. "Seems to me we're hereabouts now. Puts us slightly closer to the center of the lake, actually."

"But at what cost?" Cyrus cast a wary glance at the looming forest behind us. "Let's move. We don't want to be out here past nightfall," he growled.

"Cyrus, you'll stay with Egan and Aila on the shore. Fintan will watch your backs for an ambush with the longbow. Luga and Ash, you're with me."

Cyrus opened his mouth to protest, thought better of it, and closed it again. He was not happy about staying on shore. I suspected my interaction with the Mavtir changed Kyran's mind about who was entering the water. Cyrus was on babysitter duty. I bristled against the thought. The last Eleiyon in all Kiakora I'd want watching over me was Cyrus.

"Luga," Kyran commanded, turning toward the enchanter. The familiar muttering sounded from Luga as he walked first to Kyran and then to Ash. Beads of sweat formed on his freckled forehead despite the winter chill as he finished.

"I'm sorry, General. We only have one hour. I'm almost completely wiped from earlier. Couldn't muster the energy to give us more time."

"An hour should be all we need. We'll make it work," Kyran said confidently.

They exchanged grave looks before the three of them waded into the shallow waters of Lake Luan.

23

Kyran and the others swam out until their heads were distant black dots on the horizon. And then they went under.

Only an hour. What if the legends were wrong? What would they do if it wasn't enough time? Somehow, I didn't think returning empty-handed was an option. The Lord of Flame's slithering voice hissed in my ear, *I need that object...*

Minutes that felt like hours passed.

Egan paced the shoreline in front of us. Cyrus stood next to him with his back to the lake, peering warily into the trees behind me. He'd been uneasy about the Arbori from the beginning.

"I don't like this," Egan whispered to Cyrus as he stopped pacing. I followed his gaze to the once again serene lake surface.

TWANG

It took me a moment too long to connect the sound to the arrow that flew through the air. Cryus' keen senses and experience had him diving to the ground, but Egan, who was still slightly turned to speak to Cyrus, grasped his neck where a long blue arrow now protruded from it. Spouts of blood gushed between his fingers as he fell to the ground.

Egan's eyes locked on my own. I was frozen, watching his mouth open and close in futile attempts to speak. Only gurgling and crimson bubbles came out. He fell to his knees first, then collapsed to the ground. His eyes as lifeless as the marshland skies.

As if in slow motion, I ducked for cover as well, diving to my right behind a moss-covered stone. The forest was quiet above me. *Where was Fintan? Cyrus?*

Scanning the ground, I followed the bushes past Egan's body to a large fern that grew on the slope leading up to the forest. Next to it was a fallen tree, mealy and moss-ridden.

There.

Cyrus' fingertip was just visible on top of the log. He'd been able to crawl to safety. At least I wasn't alone, cursing myself for the feeling of relief at Cyrus' presence. I turned my focus back to the forest. Adrenaline pumped my heart faster and faster. *Where were they hiding?* I couldn't see any sign of the wielder of the bow, or its companions.

Then I saw it.

The trunk of one of the pines moved. Or at least, a section of it did. A slender figure appeared to dislodge itself from the pine. The slim body looked like a piece of the tree come to life. Its skin was a muted brown. Its long arms were sinewy strands that seemed more like tangled roots than bones, having no skin to shield them from view. They twisted to form forearms and hands. A long, serious face held deep brown orbs sunk into eye sockets that surveyed both Cyrus and me through our respective hiding places, as if they weren't even there. Its head was crowned with a tall headdress of pine needles, twigs, and leaves, arranged in a way that was both beautiful and menacing. It held a bow in its right hand, and a quiver of electric blue arrows was slung across its back. An Arborian.

A rustle sounded from the right, and another Arborian emerged. This one was clearly a female, not quite as tall but equally slim. Ivy vines tangled her long hair in clumps, and she held a longbow in her left hand. A bow with a small orange triangle etched on its surface where the wood met string.

Fintan's longbow.

I gulped audibly. Two sets of dark eyes bore into us. I got the sense that there were more we could not see. Deciding that there was nothing else we could do, I stood. When the arrow didn't come immediately, I raised my hands in surrender. The two figures' heads cocked unnaturally, slightly off-center as they took me in.

"We're here looking for a way to save our forest," I said tentatively, my voice sounding much more assured than I felt. I figured these were surely a forest people. Perhaps our mutual love of the trees could get us out of this. "Something is killing the trees in the forests east of here. Something wicked. A foul, bodiless being," I continued. Their unyielding eyes, the color of the rich soil beneath my feet, shifted uneasily. "Have you heard of this?"

They turned toward each other slowly. The female gave a slight tilt of her head. Then the male figure gestured toward me with his long, knobby fingers.

Follow him. *Liro's balls.*

My legs trembled beneath me, but I managed to lift one, place it in front of me, then the other. A noise from behind the log told me Cyrus had stood, though I didn't dare remove my gaze from the Arborian in front of me. Faster than a dartfish escaping the net, the Arborian launched his blue arrow at Cyrus, where it stuck quivering in the rotting log. The message was clear: Cyrus was not welcome.

Okay, so I'd be alone. No big deal. The forest. They loved their forest, and by the look they'd exchanged when I'd mentioned the darkness, they had heard of what was happening near Aodhen. Whatever was hidden beneath the lake surface had to be something we could use to save the trees. The Lord of Flame had said it would protect Fira. What else would it be for?

I expected the winter crunch of the dried leaves on the forest floor as I followed the figures deeper but was met with a soft silence. The forest here was still lush and the ground was a soft bed of fallen pine needles and mud. Despite clearly being in peril, I didn't feel scared. My gut told me these two only wanted to protect their home, and as long as I wasn't a threat, I'd be fine.

The sun didn't reach this far into the forest. Unlike the Hafra, where the sun's golden rays cast leafy shadows that tickled the forest floor, everything here was dark and moist, as if the murkiness of the marshlands had penetrated the oldest and deepest roots. The trees were slippery. A layer of dew clung to the branches that were not already dripping with hanging mosses and various-sized fungi.

The Arbori didn't look back once as I followed them deeper. The darkness broke slightly, and a small clearing appeared in front of us. The cloudy sky just barely showed through the woven tree branches above us, but even this sparse light altered the forest clearing. Here the trees were not quite as wet-looking. The ground was cleared of pine needles, and instead, tufts of grass spotted the caked mud.

The tall Arborian stopped walking and turned to me. The female stopped alongside him; her wary eyes scanned my face. The tall one waved his arm toward the great pines on the opposite side of the clearing. Following his gesture, my eyes narrowed on the blackened trunks of the first trees. Bulging pustules dotted them, oozing their sickening goo. I looked behind me to where we had entered the clearing. The trunks there were strong and brown. Healthy. Untouched by the darkness. *Why would that thing have come this far only to turn away?*

"Have you seen it? The creature doing this to the trees?" I asked. "Did you fight it off?"

The blank stares of the Arbori continued, unfazed by my questioning. They were not going to answer. I shuddered at the thought of the floating cloud of decay coming anywhere near me.

The Arbori watched me intently, waiting.

"What do you want from me?" I tried again, hoping they'd give me some hint as to why they'd brought me here. Caeru said we couldn't reverse the rot. *Should*

I tell them that? I doubted this would be the news that would save Cyrus and me.

Maybe the rot couldn't be stopped, but Naleiri had saved one tree. It could be enough to show them how. I took a cautious step forward. The Arborian in front of me stood unmoving, but the female's finger slipped to her bow, where it stayed, ready.

Not sure if they could even understand me, I said, "I'm going to reach for my knife. My sister, she saved a tree back in our forest. I'll show you how." Taking their lack of reaction as a sign to continue, I slowly grabbed my dagger from the thigh holster. The female had an arrow notched and ready in such a fluid motion that I would have missed it completely if it had not been for the sharpened arrow that now pointed at me.

I locked eyes with her. Hers were cold and calculating. I sent as much sincerity through my stare as I could. I was unsure whether she felt it but could have sworn that her shoulders relaxed ever so slightly, even though her bright arrow was still poised for the kill shot.

The tree was blackened almost to my hips. Resting my hand on its trunk, I worked to clear my head of thoughts, trying to pretend that I wasn't with two creatures of the forest prepared to pierce me with a hundred arrows at the slightest wrong move.

Nothing. Straining, I listened harder. All I felt was the hard bark beneath my fingertips and the light breeze on my cheeks.

What did Naleiri feel when she touched the trees? What did she hear in the swishing of their branches? Mimicking what I'd seen Naleiri do, I closed my eyes. I imagined that she'd told the tree she was only helping, but that it would hurt. I sent the message down my arm, through my splayed palm. Perhaps the tree could understand me, gift, or no. I knelt at its base, eyeing the largest pustule, and dug my knife in, carving it out of the trunk.

I worked quietly, forgetting my lethal audience. My knife moved from pustule to pustule. This tree had as many, if not more, than the one Naleiri had saved near the cottage. When I finished, I stepped back from the trunk, noting my work. The tree was scarred. Missing chunks marred the usually uninterrupted bark. It could have been my imagination, but I thought the tree bent its branches faintly in thanks.

It was only then that I remembered the circumstances that had brought me here. Spinning around to face my observers, I jumped back, startled.

It wasn't just the two Arbori that accompanied me now. At least twenty other Arbori had emerged from the trees while I worked. It was only the gratitude I saw in their faces that kept my knees from giving out. My original two companions motioned to the two other trees behind this one, signaling for me to perform the same task. Realizing I had little choice, I started in on the next tree.

———

Sweat dripped from my brow despite the winter cold as I finally stood up straight. The muscles in my back ached from the hunched position I'd assumed while carving out the disease. I turned back to my onlookers, as the stoic crowd parted.

A tall, slender figure stepped soundlessly through the middle. The trees swayed as she walked, whipping her long white hair into a swaying mane that made her look even more goddess-like. She wore a simple crown of woven branches, but I could tell by the way the other Arbori dipper their heads as she passed that she was their leader. Her gray lips parted as she spoke to me. Her voice was at once breathy, like loose leaves carried on a light wind, and deep, like roots stretching into the soil.

"Zanvis. Aciasgi. Oni odiamospi alvarlesi lonea'a. Ortarci nui bolari eriasi ipra lai mala'a edi uroa erposcui. Osna estruia'i. Ewa aciasgi. Oni emoshi counteredena nui alomi neu uroa osquebi orpi iglossi. Hereta oni ingunoni treeni sua equi ecuerderi yi uroa toriessa osni allanfi. Ewa orrectoci lai aysa equi taesi fermedadeni oni esi anca evertirri onci agiami? Lynoa...eshechodi orpi quellosai howa yudari?"

Her language flowed over the wind as if it came from within it. Another voice chimed in, this one deeper. It came from the Arborian who'd led me here. "Queen Ramuwren thanks you. We could not save them ourselves. To cut a tree would be to rip the soul from our bodies. It would destroy us. We thank you. We have not encountered an evil like this in our forest for many eons. There are none among us who remember, and our stories fail us. Am I correct in saying this disease cannot be reversed by magic? Only...undone by those willing to help?"

"Yes, so far as I know." My voice rang out in the small clearing. Uneasy muttering followed from the crowd of Arbori. "But there is something. A powerful object that can protect our forests. It is hidden in Lake Luan. It's why my companions and I are here, in your forest. I believe what we seek can help stop this."

More muttering erupted from the crowd. Their airy voices carried a sharper edge now as they seemed to be arguing amongst themselves. The leader stood silent. Listening to her people, but not once taking her bottomless eyes from where they held mine.

"Astabi." Her breathless voice was clear and firm, silencing the growing rumble of voices. "Esi ermitirepi ia iti yi ia ourya ompanerosca neu asopi afesa astahi asli rillasi fo'a Lake Luan. Oli equi esi indfa ebajodi edi lai urfacesi esi arapi equi oli andleha uta. Esi ima onsejoca equ'i olosi uta terena. Lei onoceraci uta eartha."

A glow formed in the depths of her eyes. I couldn't look away despite the deep voice that spoke her translation. "I will allow you and your companions safe passage to the shores of Lake Luan. What lies beneath the surface is for you to handle. It is my advice that only you enter. He will know your heart."

Continuing as if her soldier had not spoken, the leader stepped, landing mere inches from me in two graceful bounds. Instead of looking at my face, her eyes dropped to my collarbone, where the mark blazed under my tunic. She stared at it intently as if she could see where it hid underneath the black fabric. Her knowing brown eyes flicked back to my face. I was close enough to see the purple veins in the whites of her dark eyes. They crisscrossed in thousands of tiny pathways, like the roots of a plant.

"There are those who seek to hide their true path, like the winter's snowfall does to the forest trail. Be careful you do not follow too closely when you cannot see where it leads." Her voice was a gentle whisper that curled around the foreign words as she released them in my tongue.

With that she stepped away, nodding to the two who'd led me here. The others silently melted into the forest, except for the female with Fintan's longbow. She whistled sharply, and a small male Arborian emerged, carrying an unconscious Fintan. "We will escort you to the shoreline, where it is easiest for you to enter the water. Your other companion will join us there."

I'd forgotten about Cyrus. A little nag on my conscious reminded me that I should feel the same wave of relief I'd felt earlier at the idea of Cyrus rejoining me unharmed. But the wave didn't come.

We marched down a narrow, winding trail that led us away from the clearing and back into the dense, moss-covered forest. The female Arborian brought up the rear, carrying Fintan over her sturdy shoulder, and her partner led the way, just in front of me.

His strong branch-like legs nimbly passed over the exposed roots and rocks. Despite the rigidity of his legs, he moved with a grace and finesse that reminded me of water. The path opened suddenly into a yellowed meadow. Dried grass poked at me through my leggings.

Across the meadow was a tiny shoreline, bare but for the dirt and pebbles littered atop it. A tall Arborian was already there, standing behind Cyrus, who knelt facing the water. I peered over the meadow grass, examining the figures.

Cyrus was kneeling, but not in front of the water; he was kneeling over a figure sprawled on the ground.

Kyran!

I pushed past the Arborian in front of me. *Liro's balls. What happened in that lake?*

I arrived at the shore, quickly taking in the scene. The Arborian faced Cyrus' back with an apprehensive look. He casually brought his gaze first to me and then behind me to his approaching kinsmen. Luga sat holding his face in his hands and resting his elbows on his bent knees. Ash wasn't there.

Kyran.

Kyran lay on the ground, his eyes closed. His matted, wet hair hid most of a bloody gash near his temple. *Please be alive.*

"Cyrus?" The single word held all my questions. It sounded distant even to my own ears, but Cyrus answered.

"He's alive. Wounded. Maybe internal bleeding judging by the bruising across his chest and stomach. We need to get him to healers." I disliked Cyrus, but his genuine concern for Kyran was clear. Whatever happened down there was bad enough that Kyran couldn't heal rapidly enough on his own. And Ash hadn't made it back.

"Luga, can you open another portal?" I asked, hushed and hopeless. I doubted if they could; they wouldn't have been here waiting for me. Based on Luga's appearance, he wouldn't have the power left to do it.

Luga just shook his head slowly.

"He's got nothing left," Cyrus added, confirming my thoughts.

Luga cast his eyes to the ground, ashamed.

My dislike of Cyrus returned as I defended Luga. "It's not your fault. You've done so much already. Who could have known..." My attempt at encouragement puttered out.

"We head east. If we leave now, I think we'll be able to make it far enough into the forest for me to create a portal by tomorrow," Cyrus cut in.

So he could create portals. But either his skill or power must not be as strong as Luga's if we needed to get that much closer before it would work. *Why hadn't Kyran introduced me to enchantments during any of our sessions?* I might be giftless, but I was still an Eleiyon.

Luga got to his feet. I looked back at the Arbori. They were no longer with us. They'd left Fintan on the ground and had fallen back to the meadow's edge. I hadn't noticed the third Arborian join them. With a small nod, they turned toward the forest. We were alone again.

"Let's move." Cyrus' deep voice pulled my attention away from the bare tree line.

"No." Kyran's voice was raspy from lack of use and the effort it cost him to speak aloud. "No," Kyran said again, clearer this time.

"You're in no condition to—"

"No." Kyran's stern command cut Cyrus off mid-sentence. "I know I can't, but I also can't return to my father empty-handed. I need to prove this to him." Every word seemed to cost him enormous effort. "I need to prove to him that I can take care of Fira. Prove it to myself."

I had to look away from him as he lay on the ground, helpless, pleading with Cyrus. He looked...desperate.

"You don't need to ask." Cyrus must have understood something I'd missed. After a moment's pause, "Of course I'll go."

I knew Kyran. The last thing he would allow, if he felt he had any other choice, would be for one of his Archai to face a danger that he himself wasn't facing. His inner turmoil was evident in each crease of his tormented face.

"No." I heard my own voice speak up now as if it came from another's mouth. Kyran's distress turned to outright agony as understanding dawned on his face.

"No," Kyran protested weakly, just barely shaking his head.

"I'll go." I continued, ignoring Kyran and looking directly at Cyrus. Kyran was the prince, but Cyrus would be the one making the decisions now. "The Arbori advised I go alone anyhow. Besides..." I took a deep breath, as I knew this would be the silver bullet that sealed my fate. "If anything happens to you, it'll be days before we can get help, trying to carry both of them and waiting for Luga's energy to return." Judging by Luga's condition, maybe even longer, though I didn't add that. "If I don't make it back, you'll be able to make it far enough to conjure a portal home by tomorrow. Give me a couple of hours. If I'm not back, start home without me." I could tell by Cyrus' expression he wouldn't argue. Whether he thought I could complete the mission, I very much doubted, but there was no denying the logic in my plan.

Only Kyran looked murderous. "No. Cyrus, no," he said again, making a vain attempt to get to his feet but falling back to the ground, clutching his stomach. "Aila...please. You can't."

I knew he only worried for me, that he didn't want me in danger. I looked at his agonized face. Kyran did care for me, perhaps more than I had realized. But even as this understanding dawned on me, another truth cracked the shell of what I thought I wanted, letting in another stream of light that nourished the seed that had taken root in my soul. Trying to keep me safe by holding me back, by keeping me in the dark, would never be enough for me. I'd been in the dark for far too long.

"I can, and I will." With that, I turned away from his lovely, mortified face and plunged into the icy waters of Lake Luan.

24

The frozen water pressed in on my legs as I walked out into the lake. Stinging currents shot up to my heart as if to check that it was still beating and giving it a jolting jump-start anyway.

What had I gotten myself into? I could barely swim. I waded farther into the lake, but the water didn't become any deeper. I could hardly make out the figures I'd left behind on the small shore. The Arbori were right. This was the ideal place to enter the lake. Maybe this sand bar would lead straight to the underwater cavern, and the Arbori knew it.

I was almost at the center of the lake and still only thigh-deep. Something slithered by me.

I paused. The lake was as placid as it had ever been and yet...

I peered down trying to see underneath. I was at the edge of the sand bar. Another two steps, and a drop-off would bring me to the fathomless depths of the middle of the lake.

A silent ripple shattered the surface, sending rings toward me. A giant blue tail shot straight into the air with such force and speed, it turned into a blur of color. I stumbled as I tried to turn back, but the tail changed direction as if it knew exactly where I was. As if it had indeed waited for me to get to this very spot. Maybe it had been a trap all along.

As fast as the tail moved, it was surprisingly gentle as it spiraled around me. The tail was covered in a plated armor of hard blue scales, adorned with a pointed golden crest that ran the length of it.

And then it tightened. Squeezing the breath out of my lungs. Strangling any hope of escape as it tried to force the life from my body before jerking and dragging me beneath the surface.

———

Water crushed my senses as I plummeted deeper and deeper, dragged by an endless tail. My eyes could barely stay open with the speed at which we were descending. I didn't have enough air left. I wouldn't make it. This was it. My lungs burned. It was like fire boring a hole through my chest, pushing aside the shadow as the burn surged forth.

The tail loosened almost imperceptibly, but I felt it. And then more. I saw the tail struggling against some invisible force through my half-closed eyes. Squirming, I wriggled myself free from the binds, leveraging the little space that had been created. It was dark. The marshland sun wasn't powerful enough to penetrate to this depth. I would never make it to the surface.

My lungs clawed at my chest, begging me to open my mouth and take a sweet breath of air. I resisted. A dark hole caught my attention just as panic started to set in. An entrance to some long-forgotten underwater cavern. There could be air. If only I could make it.

My lungs protested, but I propelled myself forward, willing my body to move. Another surge of fire from my aching chest, and I flew to the mouth of the cavern as if carried on wings of water. The dark entrance loomed in front of me. My only hope was that it might have air pockets. I swam deeper, catapulted forward by some strong, unseen current.

Light. A shimmering glow was a beacon above me. My arms clawed at the water. Up, up, until, with a gasping breath, I broke the surface. My lungs rejoiced with each subsequent, delicious inhale.

Now that breathing wasn't my top concern, I looked around for any sign of the blue tail or the gigantic creature it belonged to. *Nothing.*

The shimmering light came from glittering marcasite deposits embedded in the solid rock ceiling of the cavern. The otherwise blueish-gray rock encased the pool where I now tread water. The ceiling dripped with stalactites the size of small trees, and the only sound was the water lapping against the cavern walls. Across from me were outcrops that created a solid shore of rock. What was this place? How could it be here, like this? A precious air bubble in the middle of the deepest stretch of lake. It could only exist by magic. *Which means I'm in the right spot.*

I made it to the rocks and hoisted myself out of the water. My leaden arms complained at the effort, exhausted after my frantic swimming. I lay on my back for a moment, breathing deep, calming breaths. The glittering rock above me reminded me of a grassy meadow basking under a summer's star-strewn sky. This had to be the cavern we were looking for. *Had Kyran and the others made it this far?*

On the other side of where I now sat was a narrow passage. The ceiling dropped lower there, just over the opening. There were water-filled nooks and crags, but the surface appeared solid enough to pass through. I'd have to crawl. I got on all fours and inched my way down the tunnel. The frigid splashes of water bit at my palms. *For Liro's sake, it's cold. Having the gift of fire would be nice right about now, or Luga.* I mused as my teeth chattered together loudly.

. I scanned the wall for air pockets where the breeze I felt might be originating. I didn't see anything but solid rock. I squeezed through the final part of the tunnel. My breath caught as I got to my feet.

This cavern was enormous. If the stalactites in the other cavern were as big as small trees, the ones that decorated the ceiling here were the size of fully grown sequoias. The roof here dazzled as well, high above me, dancing over the turquoise water that pooled below, spanning the entire stretch of the immense cavern. Dark spots were visible under the water's surface, leading to even more unexplored caverns, I suspected. On the opposite bank, a deep pocket was carved out of the wall, and in its center, a stone pedestal rose out of the ground.

That's it. It must be.

I examined the small embankment where I stood, hoping my reconnaissance would prove fruitful. However, neither side offered even the smallest of paths around the water. The only way to the other side was through.

"Come on, Aila. This is why you jumped through the portal, isn't it. This is what you've been yearning for." My whispered words of encouragement echoed in the hollow cavern.

But doubt tugged at my mind. It was too easy. Sitting there, literally offered up on a pedestal. Unguarded. Then again, I had almost been drowned by a massive tail and only found an entrance to this tavern by chance, and the guidance of the Arbori who had also almost killed me. Maybe this was it. I'd already gotten past the hardest part. Just cross the water, grab whatever was inside the pedestal, and get out. *I can do this.*

Tentatively, I placed my foot in the water. Expecting a surge of cold to arrest my heart, I was pleasantly surprised to find the water quite warm. Another secret of this strange place. I waded in, up to my shoulders, before the ground disappeared beneath my feet. I'd have to swim the rest of the way.

I hugged the wall, deciding to go around the exterior ring of the pool, rather than crossing through the middle, even though it would take longer. Something about being close to a solid surface provided a shred of comfort. I made my way carefully around the edge of the pool, moving much more quickly in the bath water of this cavern than the ice water in the other.

I arrived at the far embankment where the raised altar stood and climbed out of the water. Not sure what to expect, I crept toward the pedestal. It looked smaller from the opposite side of the pool, but standing next to it now, it easily rose to my chest. I peered inside.

Laid across the bottom, resting on a small stand made of stone, was a broken metal shard. *Was this it?* A broken piece of metal smaller than my hand? It couldn't be.

I examined it closer. It was shiny. The polished metal caught the light of the sparkling ceiling. The stone stand looked like it had been carved precisely to hold this artifact. On a second examination of the shard, it appeared to be a piece of a sword or a weapon of some kind.

I didn't need to figure this out. How it could be used to save the forest. Why it was so powerful. I'd ask Kyran later. My task right now was simply to retrieve it and get back to the shoreline. Quickly and alive.

Taking a deep breath, I reached in and grabbed it. I froze with the object in my hand. Half expecting the ground to quake or the water levels to rise, I sighed with relief that nothing happened. Turning back to the water's edge, I came face to face with the owner of the giant gold-spiked, blue tail.

A sea dragon towered above me. Its monstrous head nearly scraped the tips of the stalactites. I was only seeing a small portion of its body. The rest was still coiled, concealed in the bottomless pool. It was magnificent in all its terror. Its body a continuation of the tail, but ten times as thick, mostly blue, but gold scales here and there made a streaking design that led up to its head. Its mouth was open, revealing gleaming rows of jagged teeth. Swirls of gold scales decorated the rest of its fierce blue face. And its eyes. Bright golden orbs aflame with anger watched me. Its ears pressed flat against its skull, reminding me of a soundless hiss from a very large cat.

When it spoke, its mouth remained still; instead, the booming voice rang in my head, in every part of the cavern, bouncing off the glistening walls. "Why are you here, little Eleiyon? Didn't you learn from the fates of your companions? They now lie abandoned and broken, fed to the water."

I trembled beneath the weight of its stare as he confirmed Ash's fate. The creature blocked the entire pool. I wouldn't escape it twice, that I knew.

"Our purpose is bigger than any one of us," I called in response.

"Many have tried to claim what you now hold in your hands. All declaring allegiance to some grand purpose. But I can see who they truly are. Their intentions as dark as the deepest depths of this lake. They come for power, glory, revenge. They cannot hide what is in their hearts."

"And what do you see in my heart?" Queen Ramuwren's words came back to me, emboldening me to ask.

In a single, swift movement, the creature's head dove straight down until it stopped in front of me. I gazed directly into its golden eyes, each one bigger than my entire body. My reflection stared back. Mesmerized by its terrible beauty, I just stood still as it surveyed me.

We looked at each other. I noticed now, just under its jaws, red lashes streaked the otherwise flawless, blue neck. Burn marks. As if ropes of fire had lassoed the dragon's neck. I remembered those burning ropes from the training field back home.

Kyran.

For some unexplainable reason, despite the certain death I now faced at the jaws of this creature, shame flooded my soul for what Kyran had done, trying to chain such a majestic creature. Without thinking, I said, "I have a salve. Not enough to cover all your wounds, but enough for the rawest parts. It will protect them from infection and aid in the healing."

The golden eyes blinked curiously. "You would tend to my wounds, even as I promise to kill you?"

"What do you see in my heart?" I asked again, wondering at my own boldness.

Slowly, I untucked the small bottle I had stored in my tunic. Naleiri's recipe. I'd made it countless times using the ingredients the forest provided. The dragon cautiously moved its body forward to the shore's edge where I could reach it.

I examined its injuries. On either end of a particularly angry lash were two severe burns. The fire had completely scorched off the protective scale, leaving raw skin that oozed and bubbled with the beginnings of blisters. I had just enough salve for those two areas. Reaching out ever so slowly, I looked at those bright eyes for assurance. The dragon closed them in approval.

A loud hiss echoed through the cavern as I dabbed the salve on the first spot. I spread it, completely covering the first wound. I moved on to the second before stepping back from the giant. It watched me curiously, no doubt contemplating how it would kill me now that I couldn't be of any more use to it.

"And what do the Eleiyon want with a sacred treasure of Kiakora? One that I am sworn to guard and protect?" Its question echoed endlessly in my head.

"There's a darkness spreading in the forests near Aodhen, and even here, right on the shores of Lake Luan. We believe this object can help stop it." He was quiet for a moment, considering every word I'd spoken.

"Hmmm. Says who?" His ethereal voice curled into a menacing whisper.

My mouth opened to respond and tell him about Kyran and the Lord of Flame. About Ramuwren, the queen of the Arbori. Then I closed it again. None of them, not one, had actually said what the purpose of the object was. No one had told me it could be wielded to combat the darkness that plagued the forest.

I struggled to recall the conversation I'd overheard on the night of the ball, standing outside the room with my ear pressed to the opening. The Lord of Flame said, *It secures our safety and a position of power for Fira.* He hadn't said anything about the bodiless creature or about the decaying trees. I'd jumped to that conclusion myself. *What had Queen Ramuwren said? About following a trail too closely?*

I looked back at the dragon swaying in front of me. What else could Kyran's father have meant by *securing our safety?*

"The Lord of Flame and the prince say it will be used to protect Fira." This at least I knew for sure. "I will use it to protect Fira." I paused a moment, considering what to say next; "I give you my word."

"This object does not belong to Fira, nor to any one territory. It belongs to all of Kiakora."

"Then it will be used to protect all of Kiakora," I claimed with more certainty than I could hope to demand.

"And what is your name, protector of forests?"

"Aila."

"Hmm. I've not heard of you before. Not on the whispers of the waves nor carried on the breath of the leaves that fall into my lake." His soothing voice was a whisper reaching back in time, into his millennia of stored memories, checking to see that his statement was in fact accurate. "Who are you to claim this?" He asked the question I feared he'd ask. I didn't have any authority to promise this.

"I...I am no one," I admitted. "I am not someone you would have..." Of course, he wouldn't know of me. I wasn't a ruler. Not a leading general, or even a lord's heir. I was certainly not someone who could guarantee what I'd just promised. And he knew it.

His golden eyes followed the same path as Queen Ramuwren's had, settling on the hidden mark under my shirt. "You are, no more and no less, than what you believe, Aila."

My name sounded strange on his tongue. He imbued it, somehow, with power that I knew I could never possess.

"What's your name?" I couldn't help the foolish thought. He reminded me of the stories... "Are you Liro?"

"HA." A booming laugh resounded in my ears. "I have not been asked that for ages, when I used to roam all the waterways of Kiakora... I've been called many names in the eons I've hidden here, guarding these waters. Liro is one of them. But before that, I was called Baku."

"Are the stories of Liro...of you, true? Do the elemental gifts come from you?" I asked.

"Yes and no."

"I don't understand." This was my chance to piece it all together. To find out what was happening now and what happened to me three years ago. It had to be connected. All of it. "I don't understand," I said louder.

"I am the gift of water. The gifts all of you Eleiyon share come from each of us, each of the Protectors," he explained.

"If our gifts come from the Protectors' powers, does that mean if something were to happen to you, we would lose the gift of water?" I tried working it out aloud.

"On Kiakora, life, power, energy, whatever you want to call it...it doesn't disappear. It simply changes form. There are some who know how to harness that process, pause it at the exact moment that the spirit becomes energy. But yes...if that were to happen, that gift would cease to exist as we know it. Luckily, we are nearly impossible to kill," he added, his long jaw curving upward, doing nothing to soften his fierce appearance.

"Why did you do it? Why give the Eleiyon gifts?" Perhaps this could have all been prevented.

Sadness tugged at his features now. He was quiet, a faraway look on his face. "We believed that being bound in the same way to Kiakora that we are, the Eleiyon would abandon their destructive tendencies. We were fools..." he said softly. "It was a decision made without fully understanding the ramifications. Without knowing how those gifts would evolve once unleashed. The gift of shadow, for example, comes from the gift of fire. Yourself, the Elementals, another evolution." His golden eyes once again fixed upon my mark.

I shifted uncomfortably. I couldn't forget why I was here. "Caeru said there are rumors of an escape from Nagrimar."

Baku stilled; the weight of his full focus trained on me held me immobile as well. "What do you know of Nagrimar?" he asked.

"Not much," I answered honestly, trying to rack my brain for information.

"Nagrimar is a place but also a condition. Along the eastern edge of Kiakora, the banished walk amongst us as if behind a veil, watching life unfold in the outside world but unable to participate. A creative application of a magical bind, if I do say so myself," he explained. "The four Protectors combined our powers to create Nagrimar. We wove our powers together so tightly, so intricately, nothing would be able to escape."

"Then how—"

"A loophole. Nothing that we have ever seen, nothing that existed would have been able to escape, unless...unless they were willing to become something else," he said slowly.

"Like what?" I asked, confused.

"To escape would not only require an individual to wield enormous power, but it would also mean he or she would willingly rip apart their being and not know, or care, what form the different pieces would take on the other side," Baku said gravely.

"Is that what's plaguing the forest? A piece of...of...someone that escaped Nagrimar."

"Yes," he confirmed. "And to stop it, you must stop the source."

"The source? I don't..."

"Ahh...the journey is yours, Aila. I have no more answers for you."

"But I..." I had so many more questions. The forest, the darkness, Kyran's mission, Baku's quest. It was too much. I wasn't strong enough.

But I had to be. I shuddered at the image of the bodiless smoke that had stalked Kyran and me at Mound Ruin. I pushed aside the screams that forced their way into my dreams nightly and I held on to my mother's voice, onto Naleiri's shimmering eyes as she looked helplessly at the blackened tree trunks in our forest.

I looked up at Baku, mastering my doubts. I pulled from an unknown well of strength and uttered, "Baku... I have no right to promise this. No claim to power. But from the deepest reaches of my soul, I swear to you, if this object can help save the forests and Kiakora, I will do everything in my power to see that it is done."

"You may have no claim to power, Aila, but do not confuse that with having power you've not yet claimed."

Baku's glare lingered on my face. His golden eyes stared with an intensity that penetrated my body, my mind, and my soul all at once, leaving me bare and breathless, as if I'd just revealed the most intimate of secrets to a stranger. I knew then that he possessed the magic to break my mind as easily as his body had the power to break my bones.

But instead, he sank slowly beneath the water's surface and disappeared as soundlessly as he'd come.

25

D arkness had fallen by the time I reached the shoreline again. It was abandoned. No sign of Kyran or the others.

I must have been gone longer than I'd thought. I unsheathed my dagger and carefully cut my sleeve at the elbow. Tucking the metal shard into the detached sleeve, I slid it into the leg holster. I returned my dagger to the holster, where it now fit more snugly and tugged to snap the strap closed, securing both items against my soaked thigh.

I wasn't surprised that they weren't still here waiting for me; they probably had little expectation of my return, especially since their last glimpse of me would have been Baku's gigantic tail pulling me underwater. They might have left as soon as I went under, recalling Cyrus' doubt-filled expression. He, at least, never thought I'd make it out alive.

The dense silence of the marshland night pressed down on me. I needed to move. The plan had been to travel east, just far enough by foot to allow Cyrus to conjure a portal back to the House of Fira. An odd track marked the mud in front of me. It was an uneven dotted line. The same track led eastward off the shoreline and into the marsh. This had to be Kyran. Someone was supporting him, and he was dragging his right leg, clearly unable to put his full weight on it.

Well, at least this would be easy enough to follow. They'd headed directly east. They would have to cross a small part of the marsh, and then they would be in the forest. Cyrus must have decided speed was of the utmost importance; otherwise why risk any part of the marsh?

The marshlands at night were just as eerily absent of sound as they were during the day. No owls hooted greetings to the starry sky; no rustle of raccoons or foxes scavenging for food. I felt conspicuously alone as I maneuvered quickly, using the moon's light to avoid the murky pools of water.

The metal shard felt heavy on my thigh with the weight of responsibility I now carried. I'd made a promise. How could I hope to see it through when I knew the object would be turned over to Kyran's father as soon as we arrived back at the House of Fira? Why had Baku trusted me? Why had Queen Ramuwren trusted me?

I felt like I was back, submerged in the frigid water of Lake Luan. I was in over my head, not knowing which way was up, which would lead to the surface, and which would lead to certain doom. I didn't want to admit it, but both Queen Ramuwren and Baku had sensed my mark. I had felt it in their stares. They knew I was an Elemental. Could that have been what saved me? This stupid mark? An involuntary chuckle escaped my mouth, breaking the night's silence. How ironic. The mark I've been hiding for years for fear it would bring certain death to my doorstep is the thing that saved my life.

Maybe they expected a powerful Elemental, one who could wield all the gifts of Kiakora. Surely if anyone can save Kiakora, it would be an Elemental. But that wasn't me. I had no gifts, no magic. I couldn't even perform simple enchantments. Despite my desire to make a difference, I was weak. I cringed, hating the wave of truth that washed over me. I was not the awaited savior of Kiakora.

The forest's edge loomed ahead. A single bright spark lit the darkness, a traitorous beacon dotting the dark horizon. That was them. They must have stopped to camp for the night to regain their strength. Kyran's condition might have worsened. Cyrus wouldn't have risked prolonging their journey if he had any other choice. I doubled my pace.

The crackling of the campfire was the only sound I heard as I approached the site. Cyrus' hand rested on the hilt of his sword, his eyes alert but tired. He scanned the forest and marshlands for any sign of attack.

Fintan was still passed out on the ground. Luga looked slightly more animated than earlier. He rested his back against a log facing the embers. And there was Kyran. He slept on a headrest made of rolled clothing, his arms crossed over his wounded chest. He was in the midst of a restless sleep. Even in the few moments I watched, he tossed and turned, signs of suffering marked his face with each strained movement.

I needed to warn them of my approach. The last thing I wanted was to make it this far only to be a victim of friendly fire. Though I used that term very loosely with Cyrus. Once in range, I pursed my lips and let out a low whistle. Cyrus was on his feet at once, sword drawn. Luga stayed seated, but his hand sat ready on his weapon as well.

I whistled again as I walked closer, making my approach particularly noisy, hopefully making it obvious that I wasn't someone, or something, that intended harm. I stepped into the illuminating glow cast by the fire, finally revealing myself.

Cyrus' eyes widened with surprise. I couldn't help the smug expression that I plastered on my face as I sauntered over to join them. Luga smiled up at me. "Glad to see you made it, Aila." And he did seem genuinely glad.

"How is he?" I nodded toward Kyran, whose eyes remained closed.

"He'll make it. But we need to get him to a healer soon. Tomorrow morning ideally. That's why we chose to make camp. Weren't making good enough time carrying these two, especially with Luga's energy spent. And the longer we take, the more his condition will worsen. Luga thinks if we rest tonight, his power will return enough for him to conjure a portal home," Cyrus explained from where he still stood behind me. A moment's pause, and then, "Did you get it?"

The question hung in the air between us as I decided if I would answer him honestly.

"I did."

Luga's eyes widened as I'm sure Cyrus' did the same behind me. I'd guessed correctly. They hadn't expected me to return at all, let alone with the object in my possession.

"Let me see it," Cyrus demanded as he circled back to the fireside.

"Everyone will see it when we arrive back at the House of Fira safely," I added coolly. I had no intention of flaunting the object around here. Too many silent eyes could be watching us now. The metal shard felt hot against my thigh, as if aware we were discussing it.

Cyrus may have considered arguing the point, but instead he simply shrugged and sat back down on his log.

"How? How'd you do it?" Luga asked above the crackling. Cyrus couldn't feign disinterest as he looked at my face, waiting to hear the details.

I knew Luga's real question, though he was polite enough not to say it. How did you do it with no gift, returning relatively unscathed, when Kyran ended up severely injured and Ash was dead at the bottom of the lake? How had you not only escaped but succeeded where they had failed?

A tug at the corners of my lips would be the only emotion they got from me. "Luck, I guess," I said dryly, deciding that was the most believable explanation I could offer. I'd figured out on the solitary trek to the campsite that I could not trust them. Queen Ramuwren said Baku would see my heart, my true intentions. What had he seen in Kyran's heart then? That had to be the reason

I was released when they weren't. If Kyran really wanted the object to protect Fira, Baku would have given it. Wouldn't he? An uneasiness settled in the pit of my stomach as I thought about it again, remembering the queen's warning.

Seeing that I wouldn't be adding any other details, Cyrus finally spoke. "Get some rest. Both of you. Let's pray to Liro that we'll get out of here at first light."

Acrid smoke burned my lungs.

A blur of movement passed in front of me. I blinked, trying to clear my eyes. The fire still crackled. Louder now. Closer. As if it were right on top of me.

Then the screams.

I tried to get up, but a shooting pain in my stomach had me doubling over.

More smoke. More shadows. I had to get up. To run. I wasn't safe here. There was pressure all around me as shadows squeezed me tighter. Tighter. Get up. "Get up!" I shouted to myself.

I was running now. Running away from the smoke and shadow. It was still dark. Then, bright golden eyes appeared out of the gloom. I knew those eyes. Then the massive blue head emerged from the smoke. I ran faster still, but Baku's head kept my pace. Then Queen Ramuwren appeared, running alongside me in graceful, gliding strides. I couldn't get in front of them. The smoke and shadow were becoming thicker. Heavier. I couldn't see. I couldn't breathe.

Baku took a deep breath through his gigantic jaws, and a gust of wind washed over me, clearing the smoke. Freeing me from the shadow that grasped my mind. The shadows parted on the breeze.

I sat upright. The sting of cold air told me I was awake before my heart registered it. I was still leaning against the log beside the campfire where I'd nodded off the night before.

The soft gray light of dawn now blanketed the marshlands. Cyrus watched me intently from his perch. I could tell by the purpling bags under his eyes that he hadn't allowed himself even a moment of sleep.

Kyran still lay unconscious on the ground. Spasms of pain washed across his handsome features. Fintan was sitting up, his head in his hands as if he were recovering from a long night of ale-drinking. Whatever the Arbori had done to him seemed to be finally wearing off. Luga wasn't near the fire, which I took as a good sign of him having regained enough energy to at least wander away from camp.

As if in answer, he stepped back into view. "Glad to see you're up, sleeping beauty," he teased; his voice had returned to its full vibrant tenor.

"Likewise," I responded dryly.

Luga smirked as he crossed the small camp, extending a hand. Grasping it firmly, I let him help me to my feet. Shooting pains ran the length of my legs as my muscles woke from the much-needed rest I'd given them.

"Damn..." I stretched, bending at the waist and touching my flexed foot.

"Yeah. Tell me about it. I'm sore in places I didn't even know I had," Luga grumbled.

"So, what do you think, Luga? Can you conjure a portal and get us out of here?" Cyrus' gruff voice broke in.

"I think so. Not sure how long I'll be able to hold it, so let's be ready to move as soon as it opens."

"Right. Aila, you and Luga will help Fintan through. He's still a little shaky on his feet. I'll take Kyran. We ready to move?"

"Ready," Fintan responded. Luga and I merely nodded.

Luga set to work, muttering under his breath. Fintan got shakily to his feet. I scooted over, letting him place his arm across my shoulders for balance. In a single swift motion, Cyrus lunged to hoist Kyran over his back.

A bright blue portal appeared in front of us. Without hesitation, Cyrus walked through with Kyran. Luga grabbed Fintan's other arm, supporting his weight as we followed Cyrus. Energy coursed around me, rising in my eardrums. Then the portal closed with a pop.

We were at the entrance to the House of Fira's infirmary as dawn erupted over the western sky.

26

Relief flooded through me, and it was only then that I realized how scared I was that we wouldn't make it back here. Wasting no time, Cyrus kicked open the infirmary doors and brought Kyran inside. The rest of us followed.

Two nurses bustled into the room. One was old and squat with graying hair tucked behind a white bonnet that contrasted with her dark skin. She motioned to the other nurse, directing her to gently guide Kyran's head onto the infirmary cot as Cyrus set him down. The other was tall and slender, much younger looking. Her brunette hair was knotted tightly at the nape of her neck, and her pointed features gave her a haughty air. *Good thing bedside manner wasn't based solely on appearances.*

Fintan and Luga took a seat on the other cots. Cyrus and I remained standing where we were, leaving just enough room for the healers to work.

The squat one stepped away from where she had begun to undress Kyran. "This will be a few moments. I'm assuming the rest of you are healthy enough to wait?" Despite her phrasing, it was not a question. "Good. Please step back," she said to Cyrus and me. "We need privacy." With that, she muttered something under her breath and waved her hand. White curtains sprang from nowhere around Kyran's bed. With a final look, she drew them sharply, cutting off any view of Kyran.

"I'm going to give the report," Cyrus said matter-of-factly to the rest of us before quietly slipping from the room.

I plopped down next to Luga. I knew Naleiri would be worried at this point, but I had to make sure Kyran was alright. Besides, I needed to talk to him about his father's plans for the object that now rested on my thigh. Surely, I couldn't just hand it over without knowing what they would do with it, especially after everything I'd promised Baku.

The conversation I'd had with Caeru in the library came back to me. *Ancient stirrings.* She'd said things were in motion to combat Thalen. Baku had confirmed an escape from Nagrimar. It couldn't be a coincidence that the House of Fira was moving to secure some ancient magical object. It only made sense; they were also preparing to fight for Kiakora. To save it. *Right?*

"What is the object for, Luga?" I whispered to my wilting partner. "Are we going to use it to save the forests?" I couldn't keep the desperation out of my voice.

Luga's eyes saddened for just a moment, but long enough for me to recognize the truth. Whatever the object was being used for; it wasn't what I thought. "I honestly don't know, Aila. And that's the truth."

"What if what you're doing is wrong? You just blindly follow orders? No question?"

"Yes, Aila. I do... that's what it means to be an Archai," he said softly. His explanation was firm but tinged with what might have been regret.

Cyrus was giving a report to the Lord of Flame right at this moment, telling him that the object was in my possession. All I could do was hope Kyran got better faster than Cyrus could give his report.

Fatigue clouded my thoughts. Baku's golden eyes bobbed ahead of me, guiding me through the frigid waters where I was being chased by another set of eyes. Bright green ones.

198

"His Highness wants to see you." A gravelly voice dragged me from my peaceful slumber. Cyrus loomed above me. Sun streaked through the windows in the bright infirmary. The white curtains were gone, and so was Kyran. *Liro's balls. I'd missed my shot.*

"Where's...?"

"He's fine. They healed him. He's resting in his chambers now. He'll be sore for the next few days, but no lasting damage."

"What about Fintan and Luga?"

"They'll also be fine. The Arbori used poison from Dendro Needles. The healers gave Fintan Macaria to detox his body. Luga just needs to rest, like you. But first, I need you to answer some questions for the Lord of Flame."

I could have sworn he smirked as he spun on his heel, not bothering to ensure that I was indeed following him. I scowled as I got to my feet and walked after him.

———

Cyrus led me through the hollow, echoing halls of the House of Fira. The dark maroon walls felt imposing, almost suffocating, as I walked through them now, as opposed to the warmth I'd felt when I was with Kyran. That seemed a lifetime ago now.

I considered what Cyrus' versions of events to the Lord of Flame might have been and cringed. I'd spied on them, jumped through the portal to join secret Archai business. It hadn't occurred to me until now that I might actually be in some kind of trouble.

The hallways were never-ending. They all looked the same, minus a portrait here or candelabra there. I couldn't orient myself. We finally turned a corner at the end of another hallway and came abruptly to a large oak door. Cyrus reached up and rapped on it loudly. The knocks echoed in the cavernous halls.

Once, twice, thrice.

The door creaked open as if of its own accord. Cyrus waved an arm, motioning for me to enter.

Gulp. My fluttering heart would surely be heard in the relative silence of the halls.

I stepped cautiously through the doorway, passing Cyrus. The door clicked shut behind me. I spun quickly at the sound. No Cyrus. He wouldn't be joining me, and I wasn't sure if I felt better or worse at the fact. I turned back to face the Lord of Flame.

For some reason, I expected the quiet slithering voice I'd overheard to belong to a small man. Instead, an imposing figure stood before me, as tall if not taller than Kyran. Where Kyran's face was kissed by the sun and his hair streaked with blond highlights, his father's face was pale. Dark brown hair crowned his head, just as I'd seen in his portrait. His features were pointed and intense, verging on evil. There was not an ounce of kindness in his face. Unbridled power emanated from his eyes as he gazed down on me.

"So, you're the Aila I've heard so much about." The slithering voice I remembered hissed through the quiet room.

I was alone. My fate belonged to the man across from me, and no one could help me if things went sour. The room looked to be a study of sorts, with bookshelves lining the walls and a large desk behind where Kyran's father now stood. A book as big as the ones Naleiri and I organized in the library lay open on its surface. And of course, a blazing fire raged along the wall. Flames, to be harnessed by the lord in a moment of need.

My eyes flicked back to the Lord of Flame. "I guess. What have you heard?" I tried to sound sweet, casual. Why was my damn heart pounding so traitorously? *Breathe.*

"It seems my son has taken a liking to you. Spending countless hours training you, putting you up in one of our homes in the city... I admit, I thought the training a colossal waste of my son's time and never thought anything...fruitful would come of it. Guess I was wrong." He smirked, pacing toward me as he spoke. "I wasn't sure then, but now it's quite clear who was outside this room the night of the ball." He took an audible waft of air near my shoulder. "Yes...the sweet combination of black violet and champaca, tinged slightly now with marsh muck, of course. But I can't blame my son, I suppose."

I shuddered. I hadn't realized with all the twists and turns and long hallways following Cyrus that I'd ended up back in the room outside of the Banquet Hall.

He waited a moment. I decided that silence was the safest path forward, so I keep my mouth shut, doing my best to maintain eye contact. I had nothing to hide. *Nothing to hide.*

"Cyrus tells me you retrieved my object." *My object.* The entitlement that coated his tone was enough to spark my own temper. *Hold it, Aila. You can't win here.*

I swallowed the words that swelled in my mouth... "Did he now?"

"He had an interesting tale, actually. You were ambushed by the Arbori, it seems. One captured. One killed. The Arbori aren't very fond of me or my Archai. But you? You were taken, and somehow managed to be released. Escorted, in fact, to the shoreline.... My son..." He spit the words out. "My son failed to retrieve the object himself. But you succeeded. Two unlikely escapes. No gifts. How is that?"

"Luck isn't the answer you're looking for, I take it?"

His cold eyes snapped to mine. Sensing I needed to offer something more substantial before this went from bad to worse, I said, "The Arbori are worried about their forest. Just as we are. When I told them the object we sought could help, they let me go." I shrugged. It was essentially the truth.

"And in the lake?"

"The same. I don't think Ba...the dragon is our enemy." I don't know why, but it felt wrong to share Baku's name. I continued with my story, "His job was to protect a powerful object and make sure if it is ever used, it is used to help Kiakora. We were trying to take it. Simple as that. Once I explained to him that we were searching for the object to protect Kiakora, he let me go. That is what we are trying to do, right?" I couldn't hold back the question that nagged at my soul since retrieving the object. Since I saw the look in Luga's eyes.

"Of course," he spat. "It will be used to protect our land. We are part of Kiakora, so... You've done Fira, and me, a great service."

Before I could stop myself, I added, "But what about the rest of Kiakora? The object doesn't just belong to Fira. What about what's happening in the north?"

His icy laugh filled the study. "My, you are determined... And what, may I ask, did my dear son tell you the object was for?" His words were still casual, but they coiled around me, waiting for the right moment to squeeze.

I answered honestly. "He didn't." The Lord of Flame smirked in response, his coils loosening slightly.

And I realized how foolish I had been. I didn't know what the object was going to be used for. I jumped through the portal out of selfishness, not purpose. I was restless and wanted to be included in something that mattered. I wanted to find answers about my past. And now I'd contributed, but I had no idea to what.

"All of Kiakora is not my problem." His hiss turned, hardening into a sharp, sour point as he returned to the earlier question.

"You would sacrifice the rest of Kiakora for yourself?"

"Not for myself. For the future of Fira. For you, for Kyran. And yes, I guess there's a certain selfish benefit to me."

Baku knew this would happen. He warned me that the House of Fira would claim the object just for Fira. What was it? What did it do? How could I keep my promise now? I shook my head as if that might alter what I was hearing.

"You can't...I can't just..."

"You are overcomplicating matters, Aila, my dear. Is it really so different than what you would do in my position?"

"No. I wouldn't…I wouldn't let the world fall to protect myself." I said it defiantly. I knew I would use the object to help Kiakora if I could. If I knew what in the firestorm it did and how to use it. There wasn't a doubt in my mind.

"Your friend… Naleiri, is it? She works in the library. Beautiful girl…" he drawled. My heart beat faster. I didn't like the menacing tone in his voice or the way it wrapped around Naleiri's name. He knew who she was. Knew where we stayed. Where we worked. Of course he did. We were living off his fortune. "You love her very much. And would do anything to protect her. To keep her safe." It wasn't a question. "You're making the same choice right now. By giving me that object." His eyes dropped to my thigh, as if he could see the shard hidden beneath my dagger. My face burned. This wasn't a choice. It was a threat.

"There's nothing to be ashamed of, dear. Any time we have power, whether it comes from within, or from…possessions, we have choices to make. Those choices aren't always easy. But they are necessary."

I was numb. The tightness in my chest constricted my airway, moving silently to my throat, where it burned. The truth in his words seared the back of my eyes until tears threatened to betray me.

I submitted. Just like that. I so easily gave in to my selfishness, letting it corrupt my choices. I'd failed Baku quickly and completely, and what's more, it didn't feel like such an awful thing to do. To save Naleiri. Maybe there was some truth in what he said. Maybe all we have is an illusion of choice.

I walked, trance-like, behind Cyrus. He led me away from the study. Hallway after hallway. One melted into the next as I mindlessly followed him, drowning in my own thoughts. The holster hung heavy against my leg despite being lighter now. Even if I wanted to try to make this right, I'd lost all my bargaining power when I gave up the object. I was back where I started: a powerless Elemental watching events unfold around me.

Cyrus cracked a door open in front of us and ushered me inside. I barely registered the warmth emanating from a fire blazing in a black hearth to my right. The room was empty. That was all that concerned me. I needed to be alone. I couldn't face anyone. Part of me just wanted to go home, but I didn't have the energy to protest.

A huge white bed sprawled across the center of the room, forcing the small round table into the corner next to the window. Solid black curtains were drawn, making it impossible to tell whether it was day or night. I wanted nothing more than to lie down and rest. Instead, I sat at the foot of the bed, facing the flames of the fireplace.

I watched the fire burn, and yet, the wood appeared untouched, as if coated with some flammable but protective jacket. Blue flames licked the logs, but there they sat, quite literally in the middle of a raging inferno, failing to be consumed by it. I tried fruitlessly to remember who told me that it was blue flames that burned hottest. The amber twists of flame danced across the logs. It seemed like something so wild, fire. Unruly, unyielding, and yet, here it was, completely contained. Mastered.

I wandered over to the table in the corner where a couple of books were piled, unopened. I brushed my fingertips across the smooth leather of the top one. *Ancient Kiakora*, the faded blue title stretched across the top.

"There are some pages missing from that one." His deep voice startled me. I snatched my hand back, as if I had been caught stealing. I turned.

Kyran stood near a second door that I'd missed in my first take of the room. His hair was wet from bathing. He dabbed at the dripping tendrils with a small white towel. He walked toward me slowly. He was bare-chested, wearing only thin black pants that revealed the deep grooves of muscles around his pelvis. He was completely healed but for the angry red marks around his chest, reminders of his encounter with Baku.

I turned away from him slowly, drifting back to sit on the foot of the bed. The fire recaptured my attention. Through my daze, I felt a mixture of anger and pity for Kyran. My head spun with memories of everything that had happened between us. Maybe he really did care. Maybe he was doing what he said, just trying to protect me. Maybe he knew exactly who his father was. But he accepted it. Or maybe behind his easy smile and air of bravado, he was just as scared of his father as I was.

His smooth hand found my cheek, caressing it softly, coaxing the silent tears from my eyes. He didn't ask me what happened or why I was crying. For that I was grateful. Perhaps this wasn't such a surprising reaction to a meet-and-greet with the Lord of Flame after all.

Exhaustion took over. My limbs hung heavily at my sides. I vaguely registered that I was still wearing my damp, smelly clothes from Lake Luan. I wanted a bath. I wanted to rest. Reading my mind, Kyran scooped me into his arms and carried me to the other room, where a large white tub filled with steaming hot water beckoned my aching, tired body to enter blissfully.

I didn't know how long I stayed in the hot water. Long enough for both my hands and feet to prune. Kyran had given me privacy, sensing my desire to be alone. We hadn't exchanged a single word.

An oatmeal-colored tunic and pant set was folded on the counter. At this point, I'd stopped questioning the little bits of magic that appeared throughout the mansion, enabling a life of convenience. The fabric was soft and hung loosely from my body.

Finally ready to face Kyran, I gently turned the knob to leave the steamy sanctuary. Kyran was sitting at the round table with *Ancient Kiakora* open in front of him, which he closed as he took in my arrival.

"How are you reading right now? Every inch of me is exhausted."

"Me too. Believe it or not, it calms my mind when I have a lot of thoughts racing around."

I just nodded, taking my previous seat on the edge of what I now knew was his bed. "You have a nice room," I said lamely.

He surveyed the room for a moment. "I guess I do," he agreed. He got up stiffly, clutching the chair for support before he made his way over to me.

"Are you still in pain?"

"A little sore. But, overall, no. The healers are the best in Fira and did a fantastic job, as usual."

"What happened?" I'd promised myself that I wouldn't be the one to open the conversation about what each of us had experienced in the lake, but curiosity took over. I had to know what had happened between Baku and Kyran. Silence sat between us for a long moment.

"We couldn't find the entrance to the cavern," he began. "We were swimming for a while, at least half of the time Luga had given us. The maps led us to underwater caverns, but each one led to another and another." I remembered the dark shadows beneath the surface of the final pool where I'd found the object. "We were almost out of time when I saw another entrance. This one seemed bigger, darker somehow. Ash and Luga were behind me. Or so I thought. I turned to show them what I'd found, but they weren't there. Luga was already moving a little slower, having spent a lot of his energy just getting us all there. So, I just assumed they'd fallen behind a bit. I swam back the way I'd come, looking for them." His throat bobbed as he swallowed, taking another moment to collect the details from his memory. This was it. This was where he encountered Baku.

He stared at his open palms in his lap as he spoke. "When I found them, they were both fighting a giant creature. Aila, it was huge. A sea dragon with blue scales and golden spikes. Each one bigger than me. I mean, I'd heard the legends, but no one, not even with the Eleiyon's long memories, no one could confirm them firsthand. I knew the possibility, but to be honest, I assumed most of the creatures from the legends had left Kiakora, if they had ever even existed in the first place. But this...this dragon was more gigantic, more marvelous, and more terrible than any of the images I had conjured up as a little boy listening to those stories..."

He sat with his thoughts another moment. When he started speaking again, his eyes were wider. "It had Ash coiled in its tail and was thrashing her about, like a stray dog ripping a limb free from its prey. Honestly, I'm not sure if Ash died then and there. Her neck could have snapped from the whiplash or her spine could have been crushed. Maybe that's better than drowning..." he contemplated quietly. "Luga had his sword out and was trying to pierce the tail to free Ash, but it was moving so wildly, and Luga... I don't think he had any energy left at that point to call on his magic. I know he blames himself. But it was me. If I'm admitting the truth, it was me. I was in such a rush to find the entrance, to secure the object and get out of there, I just...left them. I..."

His voice caught with a crackle as he hung his head, staring determinedly at his smooth palms. He traced the swirls of his fingerprint with his opposite thumb. I slipped my own hand into one of his, squeezing it gently. He took on so much responsibility, so much blame. A surge of anger toward his father erupted in my chest. I didn't care who Kyran blamed, I knew whose fault all of this was.

Responding to my touch, he continued his account. "I just attacked. I couldn't see its head. I just blindly sent out a blaze to the part of the tail holding Ash. At first its plates offered some protection against the flame. Of course, we are always going to be at a disadvantage underwater, but most of us are trained to add magic to our flames to overcome that weakness somewhat. But it wasn't lessening its grip no matter how much power I put behind my flames. So, instead I sent swordfire, thinking I might be able to slice through whatever those scales were made of. That worked. It squirmed, and Ash fell free, but I couldn't get to her. She was sinking, but I couldn't reach her, because the creature's head appeared. Aila...Its eyes were...medallions, alight with an intense fury I haven't felt before, and I knew...I knew it would kill all three of us if it hadn't already succeeded in killing Ash."

I remembered those golden eyes. I tried to recall what I had seen when I looked at them. I was terrified, yes, but I didn't see rage or fury. I saw wisdom.

Ages of knowledge captured behind those eyes and an intense curiosity...about me, I realized. About whether I was the one to be trusted with whatever he guarded.

Kyran disrupted my realization as he continued, "I sent out a fire lasso to try to harness it, just like any beast, I thought if I could control its neck..." He stopped again, shaking his head. "Stupid. Stupid to think that I could...by myself...I thought it worked for a minute, because it did let out an ear-wrenching shriek, but somehow...it somehow used my own lasso. My power." Kyran's confusion was palpable as he worked through what had happened himself. "I've never seen anything like it. It encased the flaming rope, my flaming rope, in a tornado of water. The water-tornado sped up the length of the rope to my hand, where it spun me so violently, so quickly, I barely knew what was happening until I was wrapped in chains of fire and water. They tightened around me until I couldn't move. I don't know if it was that or the spell wearing off, but my lungs screeched for air at that point, and I was sure I was going to die. I felt my ribs crack. And those eyes... He just stared at me, watching the light fade from my face." He paused, letting his story sink in. "Luga saved me. With his last bit of energy, he managed to wrench me from its grip and propel both of us out of the water and onto the shore."

Kyran's version of events were heavy. I understood his fear. I had faced Baku. When had it become so difficult to figure out who was good and who was bad? Everything was upside down. Kyran had watched his friend die in front of him. Would I have reacted any differently if it had been Naleiri? But then again... What had Baku seen that made him react the way he did?

Gently, I reached up to Kyran's devastated face. Stubble was starting to poke through his typically smooth jawline. He blinked. His face a question. I knew the expression because I wore it myself when I looked in the mirror. What did I think of him? And I didn't know the answer. I couldn't decide if I loved him or hated him or feared him or pitied him. I couldn't name the swell of emotion that rose in my chest and clenched around my hammering heart.

And so, I kissed him. Deeply and completely.

I wanted to forget about this day. About what had happened under the lake and in the forest. What I had promised. What I had done. What I had lost. I kissed him to forget what it was to think.

His arms were around me in seconds, urgently stroking my back and feeling the warm skin beneath my clothes. His hands found my hips. He lifted me and squeezed handfuls of my flesh, bringing me to straddle his body. Our kisses were more frantic. I ran my hands in his damp hair, taking in gulps of his sweet vanilla scent. I breathed him in deeper. The warmth spread from my chest, down my body to just between my thighs, where a sudden urge gripped me.

I was on my back, sinking into the fluffy comforter. Kyran pressed his lips against my neck, planting firm kisses down my jaw. "Are you sure?" he whispered, nuzzling my neck.

"Yes," I breathed.

"You have no idea how long I've wanted you. Dreamt of this exact moment, of having you." His demeanor changed, transforming from the calm, reflective Kyran to something more animalistic. He ripped off my shirt hungrily, freeing my breasts. My hair tumbled down my shoulders and chest, filling the space between us with another wave of vanilla from the soap I'd used. His eyes devoured my exposed body lying under his, consuming every part of me.

Then his darting eyes locked, rigidly focused on something. His whole body froze, and his expression transformed to shock, verging on terror. He stared fixedly at my collarbone. My hair had fallen away to reveal my bare chest and shoulders.

And my mark.

Gasping, I found the discarded shirt lying next to me on the bed. I clutched it over my chest, once again hiding the mark.

"Kyran...I..."

"You're an Elemental?" His voice was a low whisper of disbelief. "All this time and you didn't...what are your powers? Have you been pretending this whole time to not have any gifts? Is that how you escaped?"

"No, Kyran. No. I can explain. I don't have any gifts. No powers. I'm not trained in any magic. I never lied about that. The most training I've ever received has been combat training...from you. I just..."

"How do you know you don't have gifts then? Have you been tested? Maybe you're just untrained and they're dormant right now..."

"No, Kyran...I don't want...I just don't have any powers, okay?" Besides, even if I did, I wouldn't remember having them or how to use them anyway, and I didn't feel like getting into that little detail about my past with him as well. "It's just dangerous, you understand. For Eleiyon like me to...to share this. But it doesn't affect anything. It doesn't change anything. I..."

"It changes everything. What do you mean?" He sounded incredulous now. His voice rising.

"Shh. Keep your voice down. Please." I couldn't keep the desperation out of my voice. "I---"

He turned, exasperated now, as if losing his patience. "You're an Elemental. From Fira. You very well could be the last Elemental in Kiakora. My father would know, he's been searching."

"Your father has been searching for Elementals? Why?" A trickle of fear seeped into my heart as that slithering voice once again invaded the chambers of my mind. Caeru could say what she wanted about Thalen, but something inside told me the Lord of Flame was just as bad, if not worse. And he was already here.

Kyran continued as if I hadn't spoken. "You could have powers that just need to be unlocked and honed. I mean you could be a weapon for—"

"No, Kyran. You're not listening." I said firmly, cutting him off mid-rant. "I don't have powers. No one can know what I am. No one. It would put a target on my back. Not even your father can know." *Especially not your father.*

"But we could use you. The west. Fira. You could help us protect the territory, and with an Elemental joining the Archai, we could try to save the forests too..."

"Kyran! Stop. Just stop! Do you hear yourself? You can't tell anyone about this. They will come looking for me. Anyone who wants a shot at power, or a bargaining chip." The sinking feeling in the pit of my stomach returned as I recalled what the trees had told Naleiri about the woman in the woods searching our cottage. Why had I buried that information for so long? What else could she have been looking for if not for me?

Silently cursing my stupidity, I glared back at Kyran. "Do not tell a soul. I trust you, Kyran." *But did I?* Even as the words left my lips, I knew they were a lie. The pit turned into an endless black hole trying to suck me inside. I kept my voice from wavering, "I need to leave...now."

Kyran blinked above me, realizing the awkward position we were still in and what had transpired between us. That moment of passion was ages ago. If Kyran had something he still wanted to say, he thought better of it and moved aside. I shoved past him and out of the room.

Sugsack! What in the firestorm had I been thinking? Sugsack. How could I have taken off my shirt?

I cursed myself for the moment of poor judgement as I practically ran through the House of Fira's courtyard. I folded my arms across my body, tucking my bare hands under my arms. It was freezing, and, of course, I had no coat. Nothing but the flimsy outfit from Kyran. *Liro's balls.* Naleiri was going to kill me. This put her in danger too, I realized, my stomach dropping impossibly lower.

I swung open the front door and barged into the kitchen. Naleiri spun around, wide-eyed, clearly startled. Her jaw moved to finish chewing a bite from the half-eaten sandwich she was holding.

Swallowing, she finally found her voice. "What in the name of Liro, Aila? You scared me half to death. I was getting worried." She studied my face, which must have gone as white as the Eastern Mountains. "Aila, what's wrong? What happened?" She hurried to my side, ready to comfort me, not knowing I didn't deserve it. I slid into the stool, not daring to look at her.

Tears blurred my vision. I tried to stare through them at the marble countertops, tracing the grey lines etched across the cream-colored surface.

"Aila...Aila. What happened?" Her voice come to me muted, as if I were underwater and she were yelling from the surface.

Slowly, I brought my eyes to meet hers. Her surprise was replaced by fear and concern. She just waited. I loved that about her. She always gave me time and space. Never prying. Never pressuring. But always there. "He knows," was all I could bring myself to say.

"He knows? Who knows what?"

"Kyran...He knows what I am." I let the words thicken between us. And then, "And I think he might tell his father." I hadn't let myself think it until this moment, but I knew it was true.

Kyran's loyalty was to his father before Fira, before Kiakora, and certainly before me.

Naleiri was still sitting quietly next to me. Absolute terror was written all over her face, but as was typical of Naleiri, she remained calm. "We need to leave. First thing tomorrow. We need to get far away from Aodhen...maybe even out of Fira," she finally said.

I merely nodded. I had concluded as much on the trip over. Aodhen was off limits, and perhaps none of Fira would be safe for me now, especially considering Kyran's father had been searching for Elementals.

"You look awful. Let's pack what we need and get an early night tonight. We're going to need it. We should leave before dawn," Naleiri advised.

My body remembered how tired it was. I forced myself from the stool and trudged up the stairs. I stared blankly into the closet. What would I need?

My possessions were minimal: a few pieces of worn clothing, some books I'd borrowed from the library, and a cloth pack. That should do it. I made a mental note to shove everything into the pack when I woke up. All I wanted now was my bed.

———

The night was crisp and dark. Only the light of the full moon shining above lit the path.

Soft moss stuck between my toes as I padded barefoot through the woods. The sounds of the night greeted me. Owls hooted from a branch nearby, leaves rustled in a soft breeze, and the cicadas played their twangy song.

The world spun, disorienting me. Suddenly, I was on the ground, peering through pricker bushes at the back of a kneeling woman who faced three figures shrouded in smoke and shadow. I rubbed my eyes, trying to clear the blurry vision.

A sudden flash, and a high, unending scream rent the air...

27

I shot upright in bed, drenched in sweat and panting as if I'd just run from our cottage to Aodhen twice over. Something felt wrong. My room was quiet. Thanks to the sound buffer enchantment, I couldn't hear anything from the city streets. Judging by the darkness of the room, it was the middle of the night. I'd passed out midafternoon and hadn't stirred since. Naleiri must have let me sleep and had probably gotten all our food and supplies ready on her own. The pit in my stomach was wider, making it impossible to think of anything else.

I was a plague. Everywhere I went, I eventually brought destruction. Whatever happened to my family, I was sure now, more than ever, that it had to do with this stupid mark. Naleiri would always be a target. As long as she stayed with me, she would never truly be safe. Naleiri had another option though. But she would choose to stay with me, that I knew.

She always told me that it would be me who would eventually grow tired of the quiet life. I'd have to make the choice for her. And not to pursue adventure or freedom or whatever it was I felt missing from my soul, but to keep her safe. To keep her away from me. I needed to leave. Now. Before she woke up. It was the only way to ensure her safety.

Resolved to my decision, I slid out of bed. I snatched the items I'd collected earlier and threw them in my pack. I left my bedroom, shutting the door softly. A small pack sat outside Naleiri's closed door, prepared for dawn, confirming my suspicions. I slowly snuck down the stairs, careful to avoid the creaky third step that would surely wake Naleiri.

I went into the kitchen. There had to something I could scrounge up for my journey. But the cabinets were largely empty. Naleiri had probably packed most of what we had already. "Naleiri, you couldn't have left some apples? A loaf of bread maybe?" I whispered under my breath, trying to reason out my annoyance. Naleiri didn't know that I'd try to sneak off in the middle of the night. I closed the cabinet with a quiet clack of wood on wood. Something shuffled behind me.

I spun around. Gillie stood in the entryway to the kitchen. I breathed a sigh of relief that it wasn't Naleiri waking to thwart my plan. "Gillie? What are you—" Then I saw the basket in her hand. Peeking over the rim were a couple of apples and two loaves of bread.

"I keep forgetting. I'm sorry, I didn't mean to call you." I crossed the kitchen to take the basket from her. "Thank you." She nodded in response.

"Where are you off to so late, madam?" I didn't want to tell her too much in case she felt the need to report to Naleiri. There was one other stop I wanted to make before getting as far from Aodhen as I possibly could before dawn.

"The library. Caeru has another great reorganization idea. I wanted to get an early start. Thanks for this," I said again, holding up the basket.

The library was dark but for the ever-lit candles in the main entry above the desk. I had come prepared to pick the lock the old-fashioned way but was pleasantly surprised to find the door open. Who would come to steal a bunch of books anyway? *Me.*

Something Baku had said made me think. He said he was sworn to guard the object, but he hadn't always stayed in Lake Luan. Caeru had said the same thing. He was one of four Protectors. Our children's stories had just gotten it wrong; His name wasn't Liro, it was Baku. And he wasn't a dragon of fire, but of water. And Kyran's book. The title was *Ancient Kiakora*. He was looking for the other Protectors.

Baku was called on eons ago to protect that shard. What if the other Protectors had been called to do the same? The metal shard I'd found beneath Lake Luan was just that, a shard. What if there were other pieces? What if that shard was just one piece of a larger, more powerful object? That would explain why the Lord of Flame was after it, and Thalen might be after the same thing. These were the stirrings Caeru had mentioned. If the pieces were put back together, what would it be capable of?

I hadn't quite figured out how I fit into all of this, but it couldn't be a coincidence that there was a renewed search for Elementals the past few years. That the woman who searched my cottage raided villages in Fira in the years since Caeru said Thalen escaped. All I knew was that I couldn't let the Lord of Flame get his hands on all the pieces of that object. Maybe I'd lost Baku's shard for now, but I could thwart the Lord of Flame's plans by finding the other pieces first. And that might be the only way to restore the faith Baku and Queen Ramuwren had placed in me.

I had no clue where to begin looking or if this hunch was valid or not. My best guess was to find out where other ancient creatures of legend might be hiding. There had to be something about the protectors of Kiakora in this library, even if they were just legends. Kyran had said he'd heard stories of Baku when he was a child. It had to be enough to go on. All I needed was a destination.

I knew where I wanted to start my search, having organized most of these volumes myself. I pulled out three massive texts and sat down cross-legged on the floor, bringing the first to my lap. I flipped through the yellowed pages. I had no idea what exactly I was looking for. A legend? An image? Something about creatures, ancient guardians of Kiakora.

Shoving the book aside, I reached for the second. The cover was brown, embossed with swirls of blue, gold, white, and red. I skimmed through the first couple of pages. Old maps of ancient Kiakora were sketched across them. The territories were there, but the borders we knew today hadn't been included yet, dating the book from before the war. I gently turned the thin pages, skimming one after the other. Then, I saw Baku. It was a black and white rendering, but unmistakably him. He was magnificent, even without his shimmering blue scales and striking spikes of gold.

The blurb beneath his image read:

The sea dragon Baku is said to have eyes of gold that can see through skin and bone, lies and enchantments, to the true nature of a being. It is colossal in size and, while it does possess extreme physical strength, its true power lies in its ability to discern truth. It can enter minds and manipulate the powers of lesser creatures. It is strongest in water, and most believe if it still lives in Kiakora, then it dwells in Lake Luan.

I remembered Kyran describing what Baku had done. A being's nature? What had he seen? Curiosity threatened my motives. I could seek him out again. Ask him what he saw in Kyran, and in me.

Focus, Aila.

It would be a waste. I'd lose time returning to Lake Luan. Plus, I'd have to admit to Baku that I'd given up the shard and had no idea how I was going to fulfill my promise. Baku would take one look at me and know the truth of what had happened. What would he do then?

I turned the page. A map of the Hawa Sandsea. I scanned the caption. Nothing about creatures. It didn't make sense. Why would a description of the Sandsea follow Baku? I turned back, my fingertips on the bottom corner of the page. I moved my thumb, *Page 1114.* I turned back to the desert page. *1119.*

Kyran said that there were pages missing from his book too. My mind spun, and a rustle behind me had my heart in my throat and my hand on my dagger.

"Admirable reflexes, Aila. Although I've been behind you for a couple of minutes now." The high lilting voice surprisingly soothing to my jumpy nerves.

"Caeru, Liro's balls. You scared me." I snapped the book shut, though I was pretty sure she saw the page I was on.

"Baku. Hmm...Interesting midnight reading," she said, confirming my suspicions.

"Yeah...I came across it before and couldn't sleep tonight, so I thought I'd check it out," I replied lamely.

"Sure. Baku can have that effect," she whispered.

I jerked up, startled, searching her knowing face. My hand tightened slightly on my dagger, which I realized I was still clutching.

"Relax, girl. I'm not after you. Did you get it?"

I studied her face a minute longer. It was the same crinkled, yet strikingly beautiful, face I'd come to know. "I did...but I don't have it." Shame flooded my face again as I thought of the promises I'd made. "The Lord of Flame has it now."

A flicker of anger flashed across her face before she was able to compose her features. "I see." She couldn't mask the disappointment in her voice. "The fact that he gave it to you means something," she pondered, more to herself than to me.

"How do you know all of this? I mean, how do you know I didn't just take it from him?"

Caeru laughed. "It would require a lot more than a couple of Archai to take something Baku didn't want you to have." Kyran's story of his fight with Baku confirmed that. She continued, "Still, now the House of Fira has it."

I dropped my gaze to my feet, shame burning my face.

"Did you find what you were looking for? Or was the information...lacking?"

I looked up again. It was the second time Caeru surprised me with how much she knew. "It was you? You took the pages?" Caeru only nodded. "And from Kyran's?" She nodded again, this time a small smile played on her lips. "But why?"

"It would be disastrous if certain information fell into the wrong hands. Your legends already talk about Baku, you just have some of the facts wrong. I'm sure you've already realized that." She paused, confirming that I had, in fact, realized that Baku and Liro were one in the same. "So, there was no sense in hiding that part, besides it would have raised suspicion if all of it went missing. Once I found out what the House of Fira was up to, I took any information I could find about the other Protectors."

I was right. Kyran and his father were after more of these ancient objects, and they were being protected. I could redeem myself. I could find these objects before they did and...and do what?

"What is it anyway? The object?"

"It is only one piece of an object both terrible and wonderful. A dagger that, if rebuilt, can slice worlds."

"How many pieces are there?"

Caeru pulled several yellowed pages from behind her back in answer. They crinkled as she unfolded them and offered them to me. "Like I said, sides are already making their moves, but Thalen and the Lord of Flame are not the only ones playing the game."

I took the pages, turning the top one over. A creature more frightening than Baku stared back at me. It was another black-and-white image. Jagged limbs extended from a colossal body that looked as though it had been carved from the side of a glacier. Its fingers were jagged peaks of solid ice, and although there was no color in the eyes set in its stony face, something told me they might glow red with fury.

The caption read:

I had so many questions. Who was Caeru really? Why was she here in Aodhen? All of them threatened to tumble out, but if I asked, assuming she decided to answer, I would be here much longer than I wanted. The most important task at hand was to get out of Aodhen. Tonight.

A sense of urgency rushed over me, pushing the questions aside. For whatever reason, maybe because of these pages, or the fact that she knew about Baku, but deep in my heart, I trusted Caeru.

"I need to leave, Caeru. Tonight. I'm taking this book if that's okay." It was not really a question, as I was already shoving it into my overloaded pack. "I need you to do me a favor. I need you to keep an eye on Naleiri for me. Please. Don't tell her I came by, just keep her safe. Please."

Understanding dawned on Caeru. "They know you're an Elemental?" Her tone changed. It became serious, hushed, and business-like. "Yes. You need to leave Aodhen. Now!"

"I know...I am."

Her eyes traveled to my pack. "I have something I'd like to give you before you go." She turned abruptly and disappeared down one of the aisles. Faster than I'd thought possible, she returned in front of me, holding out her hands. Lying across them were twin sai, unlike any I'd ever seen. They each had a bound leather handle, worn to the point of small indentations made for slender fingers across the grip. The blades themselves were a cloudy crystal, opaque white in some areas and utterly translucent in others. Where traditional twin sai blades were straight and smooth, these came to three crooked points. They were deathly beautiful. "Take these. It is tradition for the grower to name the blade in Mangi culture. These were mine. Its name is *Frostbringer*. They are imbibed, though I'll let them share their own secrets."

I stared at the glorious gift Caeru presented, her arms still outstretched. Raising a shaky hand, I gently stroked the closest blade. A bright blue spark erupted from the tip of the center prong, making me jump back in alarm.

"Ahh...a sign. They will serve you well, I think," Caeru whispered.

Reaching out again, steadier this time, I grasped the two blades and tucked them into my pack.

"Thank you."

Caeru simply nodded. "I'll do what I can to protect Naleiri. Go, now." She ushered me toward the stairs. I slung the heavy pack across my shoulder and hurried down the dimly lit staircase. *Caeru must believe that the Protectors have the other pieces. I'll go East and find Tuwha.*

I reached the floor, where I skidded to a halt. In front of me were two giant beasts, the likes of which I'd never seen before. They were...glowing against the dimly lit library. Their bodies resembled gigantic lions, but where the shaggy mane might have been, two blue horns curled up, curving inward and ending in sharp points. The one on the right flicked its haunches, revealing a blue, snake-like tail that ended in what could only be described as a suction cup. The cup twisted toward me, like a scorpion's stinger. It was filled with hundreds of smaller suction cups, all writhing independently, giving the appearance of little mouths snapping hungrily at their prey.

Between them stood a tall, slender woman carrying a double-edged battle axe. Beautiful, if it weren't for the scornful expression marring her otherwise flawless features. Kneeling at her side in a crumpled ball was Naleiri. Tears streaked her terrified face. Her mouth opened in waves of silent sobs muted by some enchantment. And out from behind the tall woman stepped a timid Gillie. Our eyes locked. I expected to see guilt or shame in her expression, but her eyes were filled only with terror.

"Please..." she said weakly.

"Yes. Fine. You may go," the woman answered briskly. Gillie gave no more than a second glance at Naleiri and me before she ran out of the library, the final sting of her betrayal landing with the thud of the door.

My heart dropped to my knees. Naleiri. I knew without asking that these were the beasts the forest wouldn't dare speak of. They were an indescribable evil. This was the woman who'd entered our cottage, who had been searching for me all this time.

"You're not the easiest to find." Her voice was unnaturally sweet, like the nectar of a Pitcher Plant, seducing its listeners into an early death.

"I didn't know anyone was looking," I responded more bravely than I felt.

"Hmm." Her cold eyes assessed my cloak and the pack I was still shouldering. "Doubtful."

The sucking tails of the two beasts swayed like cobras, opening and closing their hungry mouths. Naleiri's silent whimpers crashed against my soul even though I failed to actually hear them.

What can I do? I thought briefly about the twin sai in my pack. Why hadn't I taken out the back-strap and worn them? Everything I'd learned in training with Kyran flashed through my head. Combat. Blocking punches. Dealing knock-out blows. Weapons training. Being pinned by an attacker. Not one hostage scenario.

A loud crack sounded on the balcony above us. All five pairs of eyes traveled upward. Caeru was standing on the railing. Her white hair flowed out in a windless breeze. Her old face, normally soft, hardened into a look of pure hatred as she gazed upon the scene below her. She jumped, landing cat-like in an effortless fighting stance.

The woman and her beasts shifted their attention to her. Without another moment's hesitation, Cearu shouted, "Kahu Igni!" She blew something from her hand. Azure flames exploded from her open palm, speeding toward the woman. The flames coiled around her body, locking her arms at her side like a constricting serpent. Her eyes widened in surprise and fury. The two beasts prepared to attack, but Caeru whispered another enchantment, holding up her left arm. The creature's paws stopped mid-step. Even their suction tails stilled. They were completely immobilized.

Caeru turned to me. "Go, now. Quickly. Get her out of here. I can't hold them for long...but long enough. GO!" She turned her attention back to the three foes who were clearly trying to break whatever hold Caeru had on them.

Naleiri was already on her feet, running toward me. The back exit. Without a word, I grabbed her hand as she reached me. Both of us were thinking the same thing. The back exited to a side alley, two streets over from the forest path. We could make it to the forest. There could be enough places to hide there. How much time could Caeru give us?

———

Naleiri and I ran silently through the frozen streets. No one was out. The streets were deserted as if we were the only ones who hadn't received notice to stay indoors. We made it to the forest path before slowing our pace slightly.

"Are you okay?" I whispered, finally deciding I could risk asking.

Naleiri just nodded. Was she still under the enchantment? Then, "What were you thinking, trying to leave without me?" Anger pulsed in her wet eyes.

"I'm sorry, Naleiri. I was trying to keep you safe. To keep you out of all of this."

"Well, that worked out beautifully, didn't it?" she said crossly.

I winced. I'd left her unprotected and unaware. Alone. Maybe worse off than if she's just come with me.

"I'm sorry," I said again.

Her gaze softened as she walked over and hugged me tightly. "Don't do it again. We're in this together. You and me. Always." She gave me another tight squeeze before letting me go.

"So, Caeru is badass," she whispered softly as we returned to a light jog, heading deeper into the dark woods.

"Yeah... who knew?" I said, although, I was beginning to think we'd only seen the tip of what Caeru was capable of.

We were heading due west. The exact opposite of the direction I'd wanted to go. The Eastern Mountains of Rimean might have answers about the second Protector and perhaps another piece of the dagger. We could hide in the forest through the night; then at dawn, we could circle back along the outskirts of Aodhen and head east. I mapped the new plan out as we walked.

The thinning trees jerked my thoughts away from plan-making. We were almost at our old cottage. "We should break from the main path and get away from here. Just in case she escapes Caeru. Let's not make it too easy for her." Naleiri nodded in agreement.

We veered left, leaving our accustomed path behind. My hand found the small dagger on my thigh as I recalled, from first-hand experience, the other dangers that lurked in the forest after dark. My ears pricked at every rustle and crinkle, hoot or screech.

"It's fre...fre...freezing." Naleiri chattered behind me. I turned. She was wearing a simple long-sleeved shirt and pants. The same thing she'd had on when she'd been dragged forcefully from her bed.

"Liro's balls, Naleiri." Her frame shivered next to me. "Okay, let's find somewhere to make camp. I have some blankets in my pack." We walked a little farther before Naleiri's voice broke the silence again.

"There's a cave a few yards out this way. Empty, I think." She cocked her head sideways, listening for something only she could hear. "Yup, a few bats, but most are out for the night."

"Lead the way." I gestured for her to move in front of me, thankful for her gift.

Naleiri, led by the trees, brought me to the opening of a small cave. It would do for the night. I didn't want to go too far in this direction anyway before starting to veer back east. I pulled the two blankets out of my sack and handed the thicker one to Naleiri, who took it gratefully.

I dozed off within minutes. Images of blue flames, green eyes, and soulless creatures danced through my dreams. I awoke startled. Naleiri nudged my shoulder.

"Wha—"

She held her index finger to her lips and nose, telling me to be quiet. A small bat sat perched on her other finger. I squirmed slightly at the hook-like claws grasping Naleiri's skin. She pointed to the mouth of the cave and used her middle and index fingers to indicate someone walking. "It's here," she mouthed soundlessly.

She let the bat loose. It flew up to its ceiling perch to settle in for the coming day. I grabbed my dagger and got slowly to my feet, crouching low. We were cornered if she found us here, no chance of escape.

I motioned to Naleiri, pointing to both of us and then to the forest south of the cave. She nodded in understanding. We crept to the opening and peered into the endless night. I couldn't see anything. There were no signs of movement. No sounds of approaching feet. But that didn't mean they weren't out there. I trusted Naleiri's bat more than my night vision.

Signaling to my left, I let Naleiri know to follow me. We crawled as quickly and quietly as possible. I winced at the sound of each cracked branch or crunch of a dry leaf underfoot. Not more than a few moments after we left the cave, there was a loud rustle behind us. I froze. Naleiri did the same next to me. Footsteps. Heavy ones.

We turned and ran full speed, not waiting to hear any more. I no longer worried about careful footfalls or snapping branches. The footsteps behind us were loud, more like a galloping. It was unmistakably the pounding of heavy paws hitting the ground. Terror gripped my chest as I pushed my legs harder, urging them to move faster.

There was a clearing ahead. I could see in front of me now. The curtain of pines had broken, allowing moonlight to shine through. Naleiri and I tumbled out of the brush and into the clearing.

The cottage. Our cottage. We'd somehow circled around and ended up back here. And in front of us, across the clearing, was the woman. She smirked, still holding her axe menacingly. Its blade gleamed in the moonlight.

Herded. We hadn't made a mistake; we'd been herded back here. Behind us, another shake of bushes and snap of branches, and one of the beasts emerged from the cover of the forest. I looked around involuntarily. There was no sign of the second creature. I guessed Caeru had taken care of it. I wondered briefly what happened to her. If she was alive.

I reached for my dagger. The thigh satchel was empty. *My dagger!* It must have fallen out in my run through the woods. Naleiri and I pressed our backs together. The woman and the beast closed in, backing us up against the cottage where we'd have no escape route.

I looked around frantically. The cottage. The trees bending toward us, their leaves flipping in outrage at our circumstances. This was too familiar. The woods. The darkness. I half expected to see looming green eyes emerge from the forest line. A loud, blood-curdling screech from a large oak tree drew our attention. A vulture-like bird with bat-wings easily spanning the length of my entire body clung to a branch with its massive talons. An Ozar, I realized, remembering what Luga had called them.

"Ozars. Handy birds. They'll report everything that happens here to Thalen. There's no point in trying to run anymore. We all see you now. There will be no escape."

I bumped against the cottage. That's it. As far as we could go.

"I don't want your friend, Elemental." The woman's voice rang out clearly in the night. "I promise I'll leave her unharmed if you come with me now."

What option did I have? I scanned my surroundings again. What could I use for a weapon? *Nothing.*

The axe! It was still there, lodged in the wood pile from when I'd last used it to cut firewood. I'd never make it there before they attacked Naleiri. I had nothing. I disconnected myself from Naleiri despite her protests and stepped forward. My hands balled into fists at my sides. "What do you want with me?" My voice sounded steadier than I'd anticipated. I took another step forward, feeling four pairs of eyes watch my every move.

"I want to take you to Thalen. That's all. A short trip to Kiromar," she crooned sweetly, a devilish smile twisting her pale features.

"If I come, you'll leave her alone?" I nodded toward Naleiri, who was shaking her head violently, tears pouring from her eyes.

"No! Aila, No!" she shouted from behind me. I ignored her, refusing to break the woman's gaze.

"You have my word." The feigned innocence in her voice as she pressed her hand to her heart in a manufactured display of sincerity was all I needed to know. Naleiri would not make it out of this whether I surrendered or not.

Okay, new plan. I will fight. What had Kyran said? *Everything can be a weapon.* His deep voice floated in my head, and as much as I despised it now, I remembered the hand-to-hand combat training session. *You need to be ready for anything.*

A sharp rock protruded from the ground near my left foot. Without considering it further, I lunged for the rock. I slid toward the creature on my knees while chucking it with all my strength straight into the gaping, sucking mouth at the end of its tail. It squealed and fell to the ground writhing in pain.

Its tail was its weakness.

I used the moment of distraction to race to the wood pile and grab the axe. It was steady in my hands. I walked back toward the woman, closing the space between us. A green shimmer lit the darkness. It came from the blade of her axe as she lifted it in a battle-ready stance. The mocking sneer slipped from her face as her cruel black eyes assessed the new situation.

Naleiri touched the back of my shoulder. Her fingertips warmed. I'd seen her do this a million times before. She was calling her power, asking the forest to help us.

Another screech split the night air. This one very different than the death squeal released by the injured creature. This was a natural part of the night. Two huge snowy owls dove down from a hidden perch. They attacked the writhing lion's face, pecking at its eyes. Just as they swooped away to avoid the lethal tail, an army of at least seven raccoons attacked the lion's legs and paws. One launched itself onto the creature's back, biting and clawing mercilessly.

The woman let out an impatient growl, and stalked toward us, gripping her axe.

"Naleiri, when I say so, you need to run." Without waiting to hear the protest I knew would come, I said, "I mean it, Naleiri. When I say so... run.

"Now!" I lurched forward, raising the axe above my head.

Naleiri took off in the opposite direction, sending me the tiniest surge of relief as I brought my axe down. The woman countered with her own axe. Green sparks flew at the collision. I'd never practiced with an axe before, sending another silent curse to my training sessions with Kyran. The woman shoved off my blade, bringing her axe back up to a striking stance. I mirrored her movements, circling her, waiting for an opportune moment. She was nimble, lighter on her feet than Kyran or anyone else I had faced before. She might be able to match my speed. We circled each other for what seemed like an endless moment. Why wasn't she attacking?

She didn't want to hurt me. She wanted to take me. Alive. She was buying her time. For what... Naleiri! Had she escaped? The lion creature was gone. It had managed to fend off the last of the raccoons.

I let out a yell of frustration and rage, sprinting forward in a head-on attack. At the last moment I crouched, sweeping my leg out to trip her in the same movement I'd done effectively with one of the Archai. My leg didn't quite reach her, but I felt a surge of warmth in my chest and a gust of wind that emanated from my foot and swept the woman off her feet. My momentum perhaps? Or had she tripped in her own anticipation of the attack? No matter. She was on the ground. I lunged forward again, my axe raised in a killing blow. She rolled out before I could strike, hopping to her feet effortlessly. A smile played on her lips.

"You've got some fight in you, Elemental. I didn't think this would be so much fun."

Then she stood, dropping her axe to her side. Confused, I followed her gaze behind me. The creature had Naleiri, its tail poised to strike. I didn't want to imagine what those suction cups did to someone. *A fate worse than death*, Gillie had said. My heart froze. The creature marched her closer to the waiting woman. Naleiri's eyes went from me to the woman and back again, clearly calculating our options.

"Okay. I'll go with you. No fight. Please. Please, just let her go." I dropped my axe.

"No!" Naleiri shouted. Before I could object, she stomped on the creature's unsuspecting paw and twisted away from its striking range. The creature raised its other clawed paw to slash across Naleiri's chest. As she moved to her left to avoid the impending strike, the woman swung her axe, lodging it deeply into Naleiri's stomach.

Time stopped.

As if in slow motion, I watched the woman retrieve her axe. She turned to face me. My only thought was to get to Naleiri. My friend. My sister. Naleiri's eyes found mine as she crumpled to her knees, cradling the gaping wound in her abdomen. Blood drenched her shirt and pooled on the ground. She kept her eyes on me.

Something surged inside me. Something I had never felt but, perhaps, always knew was there. I leapt toward the creature. A breeze carried me, catapulting me over it, toward Naleiri. Out of instinct or maybe just blind hope, I raised my left arm toward the creature and the woman, making a sweeping motion as if they were clutter on a kitchen table. The gust of wind that followed my arm blew them both off their feet and across the clearing. I landed next to Naleiri, who was still staring at me, choking on the blood that was filling her mouth and slowly trickling from the corner of her lips.

"Take it," she gargled. She pressed something hard and cold into my trembling hand. "Take it," she said again. I looked at her soft face, normally a bright white powder, like a blanket of snow shining in the gleaming rays of the sun, now pale and muted. Her eyelids fluttered, trying to stay open.

"Naleiri, please," was all I could say as I gripped her hand with one of mine and used the other to cradle her head. And then her body shuddered with a last breath and the light left her eyes.

The world stopped spinning. There was nothing. Only her lying in my arms and the hole that was ripping through my chest.

And then anger. I was the angry storm that whipped through the forests, felling trees and houses. I was the raging sea that tormented fishing boats and surged on unsuspecting shores. I was the fire that sped through my veins, burning my heart. The tightness in my chest spun the wind and water and fire into a swirling orb that encased Naleiri and I. The woman and the creature looked at us, wide-eyed. The ball continued its furious spin, shielding us for the moment, threatening anyone who got too close. And then it dropped.

The woman's mouth curved into a sneer as she raised the axe again. Just as she was about to lunge, a ball of fire struck her from the right, sending her toppling through the clearing. My head snapped up to see soldiers charging forward, wielding balls of fire. Soldiers from the House of Fira. *Archai,* somewhere inside me registered blankly.

The woman took one more look at me, as if etching my face to memory, and then disappeared. The creature turned and retreated into the depths of the forest. My gaze returned to Naleiri, lying almost peacefully on the ground. The trees seemed to bow with the loss, their heads lowering to show their respect. I looked at my blood-soaked hand and what was cupped inside. She'd given me a necklace. A sharp tooth embalmed in hardened amber and encased in the finest of vines that webbed around the gemstone leading to a braided black cord. The amber glowed slightly and then darkened. I closed my fist, turning back to Naleiri.

I didn't know how long I knelt there, looking at her lying lifeless on the ground.

<hr />

Strong hands gripped my shoulders. I hardly registered them as they pulled me away from Naleiri's body. As if through a haze, I watched Archai spill into the clearing. The choice to rebel against the grip finally came as if from the depths of a murky swamp. I lunged against it as I watched several Archai surround Naleiri and lift her up, carrying her with them to wherever they were going. Away from here. Away from me.

The embrace tightened, preventing me from escaping. Not entirely aware of my own movements, I surged forward again. All I could think was *get to Naleiri.* I had to get to Naleiri. The hands held me back in an unrelenting grip. Sound dulled around me. Someone was shouting my name, and then a blow to the back of my head. I welcomed the darkness.

28

My eyes fluttered open. A pounding ache at the base of my skull reminded me of how I'd gotten here. And of everything else.

Naleiri.

I was in some kind of dungeon. Stone walls, twice my height, pressed down on the small room. There were only two sources of light: a small rectangular window, placed high enough on the wall that I couldn't see out, and a candle. Sunlight streamed through the window, telling me it was day. The flickering candle was set in a glass sconce fixed to the wall beside the door. Fire. No one would leave fire in a prisoner's cell expect the House of Fira who, in their arrogance, would believe themselves the only ones who would be able to use it.

I was on a small, thin cot shoved against the wall. I looked down at my hands, still coated in dry, crusted blood. Naleiri's blood. Flashes of the power that surged out of me sped through my mind: air, water, fire. I had powers. Why couldn't I remember anything about them? How to harness them? Maybe if I had remembered...maybe I could have saved Naleiri.

Naleiri. My chest turned to a block of ice. What had they done with her? The swarm of Archai had taken her away without so much as a word. I walked over to the door and jangled the knob. Locked, of course. It was solid iron, probably as thick as the stone walls in which it was set. I turned back to the bed. My pack sat on the floor. It looked unopened. Whoever had brought me here had decided it wasn't worth searching. Caeru's crystal twin sai would still be in there. The pages Caeru had given me as well. That seemed like ages ago now. Caeru was also probably dead. Protecting us. Me. All of this was because of me.

Naleiri's bloody, gurgling mouth. Life faded from her body as I held her. I had watched it leave. *The necklace!* She'd handed me a necklace with her last breath. Frantically, I reached for my throat. An instinctual reflex, as I didn't remember putting the piece on. My neck was bare. I patted down my chest, feeling the pockets of the tunic. My heart lightened at the small lump in the fabric. I pulled out the tiny amulet on the braided cord. The sharp tooth was seemingly frozen forever in the orange stone.

An iron bar slid across the other side of the heavy door, jarring me out of my daze. It swung open and Kyran walked through.

I hadn't expected the wave of hatred that writhed in my chest at the sight of him. I wasn't sure what I expected.

"I'm sorry about Naleiri," he said softly. The first thing out of his mouth was her name. I wanted to spit in his face.

Instead, "Don't. Just don't." I couldn't stop the tears that welled in my eyes as I gazed at his perfectly manicured face. His clean-shaven jaw and his hair pulled back in a neat bun. He looked well-rested and recovered compared to the last time I'd seen him. What had that been, only last night? Two nights ago? Time had slipped away from me.

"You have powers." It wasn't a question.

I just stared up at him silently.

"I'm on your side, Aila. I can help you," he pleaded, stepping closer to the cot.

"What does the House of Fira want with me?" I let the question linger, relishing in the hurt that crossed his face. Not "you." The "House of Fira."

There was no he and I anymore. He was one of them and that was it. "These are very different accommodations than I've had in the past."

Ignoring my jab, he said, "My father plans to turn you over to Thalen, just as Drata would have done." I straightened slightly at hearing her name. *Drata.* "You're an Elemental," Kyran continued, unaware of my reaction, "and being the ones to actually turn you over would be....better for us. We'll gain Fira favor in Thalen's eyes. A move like this will protect us when he invades." He said all of this objectively, robotically. It was as straightforward to him as laying out the most obvious points in a military strategy. Collateral damage. That's all Naleiri and I were to him and his father. It was the first time I felt like I had gotten the entire truth from him.

"He's already invading. What do you think is happening to the forests? The raids?" I said angrily. How could he be so naïve? "Why does he want me anyway?"

"It's not about you. He wants Elementals, and you happen to be one. Maybe the only one left in Kiakora. The last of a kind... We hand you over, the attacks stop, the darkness goes away. You wanted to save the forests; this is how you do it."

I simply nodded, too infuriated to speak.

He fell silent for a moment as he contemplated my expression. Unreadable, despite the roiling hatred that fought beneath my skin's surface. I looked down at my hands to prevent giving him anything he could use.

"Aila...Aila, look at me. Please." And against my best efforts, I looked up at his beautiful, traitorous face. His expression was pained, "I think I love you, Aila. And I can save you." If the past day had not cast doubt on my ability to judge character, I would have believed he was being genuine. "Future protection from Thalen and demonstrating our allegiance to him by turning you over is an option, but pure power is a better one. Having an Elemental on our side? Having you stand with us? Even Thalen would think twice about sending any more of his minions down here. I know I can make Father see it that way. And then you wouldn't have to leave. You could be here...with me. We could be together." He reached for my folded hands. I ripped them back before I had to endure his touch.

"I would rather spend eternity as Thalen's prisoner than waste another moment *standing* with the House of Fira." My voice broke. Not from fear or sadness, but from an intense, quiet rage that smoldered in the depths of my soul. "You don't know what 'love' is. And how could you? With the father you have." The pang of pity I'd felt for Kyran before didn't come. He'd lost that privilege. "You and your father will get what's coming to you. I'll make sure of it." My voice was no more than a hushed whisper, but the ring of my promise echoed in the empty stone chamber.

I saw Kyran clearly, as if for the first time. Where I once saw confidence, I now saw privilege; where I saw deference for tradition, I now saw intolerance. I always knew it was there, hidden beneath the excitement, the newness of my relationship with him, and the sense of purpose our sessions gave me. But I had been wrong. And Naleiri had known it. She'd tried to tell me. Where would we be now if I had only listened? Kyran's kind hazel eyes hardened. He scanned my face once more before turning on his heels and reaching for the handle.

"Suit yourself." He paused another moment, holding the door ajar.. "He won't keep you as a prisoner, you know. It's the House of Fira or death." The door closed behind him with a loud, metallic clang.

Alone again. I sat back down on the cot, staring at nothing. "Then I choose death," I whispered to the cracks in the stone wall.

Thoughts about my apparent powers chased images of Naleiri's lifeless body through my head. I couldn't know exactly how long I sat there, but it must have been hours as moonlight rippled through the small rectangular window, creating a spotlight on the floor of my prison. I mindlessly followed the grout lines, tracing them with my eyes, envisioning an escape from some imaginary maze. I waited for panic to set it, but it didn't come.

The door swung open behind me with a crash, but I didn't turn around. I didn't care what was coming for me now. A set of rough hands grabbed my shoulder as another forced a rag over my mouth and nose. A sweet smell filled my nostrils, clouding my senses and dimming the gleaming spotlight on the floor. And before I could register anything else, I was once again enveloped in darkness.

Voices sounded all around me, mingling with the crackle of a fire and the sounds of the night forest. I was outside again. Perhaps it was the proximity to the campfires or some enchantment, but I felt warm despite the frost-covered ground. I was in a cage. Metal bars surrounded me on all four sides, connecting to solid metals slabs both above and below me. I searched for a hinge, a latch, a door of some kind. It was seamless. No spot of weakness. No opportunity for escape. Nothing.

The blurriness cleared from my vision as three figures took shape. I recognized two of them: Cyrus and Kyran. The other was just as tall, his features soft despite being set in a firm jaw. He was listening intently with eager eyes, revealing his desire to prove himself.

"We leave you here. It's three days' march to the northern border, where Thalen will meet you. He doesn't trust us; sent his Shades down here to make sure we deliver." His face twisted with disgust. "You outnumber them; if they try anything, do what you must to secure the...prisoner." He had to pause to think of the word. To describe what I was to him now...*prisoner.* "She doesn't leave the cage. She's our only bargaining chip; I want you to personally hand her over to Thalen." The third soldier placed his fist over his chest, indicating his acceptance of Kyran's orders. Cyrus and Kyran nodded in farewell and left the camp without a second look at me.

I rose slowly to my feet. The cage was high enough for me to get into a standing crouch. I was in an Archai camp. Fires crackled all around me with groups of soldiers congregated around each one. I scanned the figures I could see for a familiar face, maybe Luga or Fintan. Neither of them was there.

I looked more closely at the groups gathered around the scattered fires. Now I saw the group Kyran had referred to. They huddled around the fire closest to me, dressed in dark charcoal uniforms. Unlike the form-fitting leather worn by the Archai, these were made of linen. The pants were loose-fitting except around the calves. They were designed for swift and silent movements, made for stealth, not for combat. A light breeze parted the branches above the group of gray-uniformed Eleiyon. The light of the moon snagged on an embroidered insignia marking the chest of one of the solders. It was a crescent moon cradled in an open, upside-down triangle. I'd seen that symbol before. It was the same one Drata had on her chest. I shuddered. I wouldn't be able to escape before arriving in Kiromar. Kiromar was here. They already had me.

Panic started to replace the numbness I'd felt since Naleiri died. This was really happening, and I'd be face-to-face with Thalen soon. Perhaps once he realized I'd be of no use to him, he'd feed me to Drata's beasts.

"She's awake," a gravelly voice said from behind me. I spun around quickly to face two stout Archai. The owner of the gravelly voice had an ironically smooth face, giving him a young, innocent impression. The other Archai was round at the midsection and red in the face.

I eyed the flask of booze in his hand as he responded to his friend. "Shall we have a bit of fun with her then?" His words slurred together in a drunken song.

The other smiled back with a wicked glint in his beady eyes. "What'cha say, girlie? Wanna come out of that cage and play with us?"

I thought about sliding back down to the floor of the cage and ignoring the taunts altogether. But then they'd leave me alone, with no opportunity of escape. My best bet...my only bet was to get them to let me out.

"Where are you taking me?" I asked innocently. I wanted to know how much of Kyran's plan had been communicated to his Archai.

"You must know, or at least have guessed it. Haven't you looked at our friends over there?" he answered, nodding toward the men dressed in gray.

I gulped. The two men smiled with satisfaction at the fear clearly plastered on my face. "How long until we arrive?"

"Three days, girlie. Then, you're all theirs." He looked again at the gray group huddled around the fire, and if I hadn't already been examining his face, I might have missed the momentary look of fear that slid across it.

I had three days to figure out something. Caeru said everyone would be choosing sides soon. Kiromar had chosen Thalen, and despite the look of disgust on Kyran's face, clearly the House of Fira had also made some kind of bargain. They wouldn't turn me over until they were recognized as the captors, and the Shades would escort us all the way to ensure our arrival. Whatever tenuous truce this was, neither party trusted the other completely.

"Hey, Shadoworms! Let her out. Let's have a little duel with the all-powerful Elemental." His tone was mocking. The Archai knew that I was untrained.

The Shades all turned at the man's request, contemplating the idea. Another Archai spoke up. He was the one who had been talking to Cyrus and Kyran. The one in charge. "That's not part of our job, Lorcan. She's supposed to stay locked up until we get her to the border. General's orders."

"Well, goody two-shoes, aren't you. The general isn't here, is he now?"

One of the Shades smirked, clearly entertained by the Archai's banter. I looked back to the Archai in charge. His furrowed brow smoothed as his lip turned into a mischievous smirk. "Fine...let's see what the Elemental's got. One duel. But back in the cage immediately afterward." He gave a small nod granting permission. *So much for orders.* "Who's gonna take it?" he asked.

The young, smooth-faced Archai named Lorcan grinned widely. "She's mine."

The rest of the camp had become aware of the conversation and were looking on with anticipation. A Shade stood by the cage and grabbed one of the bars. I gasped as what I believed to have been solid metal, disintegrated, transforming into moving shadows, each of which scattered back into the night. I straightened ignoring the ache in my lower back. No sooner had I done so than another black shadow slithered around my wrists; tendrils reached out and yanked my hands together, clasping them in cuffs.

Bewildered by the shadows that now synched my wrists in a vise as strong as metal, I looked up at the Eleiyon before me. I'd heard of Shades before. Of course, I had. And in theory, I knew what their gifts were. But to see it...to witness the shadows take form...I hated myself for thinking it, but it was an impressive power.

"C'mon then," the Shade said.

The soldiers created a makeshift ring with their bodies. They had all stopped whatever they were doing to gather around the circle. Lorcan, my opponent, stood waiting.

I walked shakily into the center of the jeering circle.

"Let's see what she's got."

"She's the all-powerful Elemental?"

"I heard she can't use her gifts."

"Give it to her, Lorcan."

I shut them all out, trying to focus on my opponent but trying harder to inconspicuously spot an escape route. All the attention was on me. I'd never be able to get out of here. Maybe if there were some kind of distraction while I was outside of the cage...but how could I do that without help?

Lorcan squared up across from me. My initial impression was correct. His stance revealed his inexperience. I assumed my own stance. His left hand curled up, and a ball of flame sped from one of the campfires to his hand. I swallowed hard. So, this wouldn't be like Kyran's combat training. This Archai planned on using his gift against me.

I tried to summon whatever power had surfaced after Naleiri's death. How had I done it? I'd felt the power surge forth as if it were breaking free of something. Warmth had filled my chest, and I'd been vaguely aware of the swirling elements around me. I'd turned it over in my head again and again since, but I was still at a loss for how I'd done it.

Lorcan arched his arm and launched a ball of fire right at my face. I ducked just in time to avoid it, but it boomeranged back to his waiting hand. A cruel smirk played on his lips. "I'm gonna enjoy this. All the fuss about the Elemental and she can't even counter a little fireball." He laughed cruelly, and the crowd joined in.

I circled him warily. This was a fight I couldn't win. I had no weapon. No gifts, that I was able to summon anyway, and even though I might have a chance with this guy in hand-to-hand combat, he had no interest in fighting me that way. He was going to rely on his gift.

That's it! Kyran's warning sounded in my ears. This Archai relied on his gift. He obviously was less experienced than the soldiers I'd sparred with before in hand-to-hand combat. All I had to do was get him to beat himself. Get him to expend enough energy that he wouldn't be able to use his gift.

I shrugged at my opponent. "That puny thing was a fireball? It didn't seem worth my effort." I said it loudly enough that the crowd could hear. A wave of *ooohs* erupted from around us.

In exactly the reaction I'd hoped for, the Archai shot out two balls this time, much larger than the last. I lunged forward, somersaulting between them, landing on my knees, and turning just in time to see one of the balls zooming back toward me. I flattened myself backward against the ground in a hero pose as the ball passed harmlessly over my chest.

Jumping to my feet, I launched myself in a direct onslaught, swinging my leg in a powerful roundhouse kick. He dodged it, though I hadn't really expected to land it, just distract him long enough that he'd lose his fireball and be forced to conjure another. *Success!* He lost control of the fireball, and it flew into the crowd, where an Archai diffused it. My opponent conjured another ball of flame; this one, he fed with energy, hoping to deal the final strike.

I could have attacked as he took his time adding energy to the strike, but I waited, letting him add more and more of his power to the ball. *That's it.* Again, he launched the ball, and again, I maneuvered around it. He was a novice, that was entirely clear now. His attacks were repetitive and predictable. Another ball. Another miss. One after the other. He was able to reign in some of them to relaunch while others flew wildly past me into the crowd.

The last ball blew past my shoulder and into the bare branches of a tree before exploding in a shower of sparks on the onlookers below. Lorcan tried to produce yet another, reaching out to call the flames from the surrounding campfires. Sweat poured down his brow as he struggled. Nothing. This was the moment I'd been waiting for. Not hesitating another second, I lunged forward again with a sharp jab to his exposed chin. I didn't let up. I threw combination after combination of punches and kicks. He blocked some, but most found their mark.

I felt the crowd's energy shift from mere amusement to actual excitement as our battle intensified. I landed a particularly skillful combination with a powerful right hook to the gut. He collapsed to his knees, clutching his stomach and gasping for air. I stood over him. Victorious.

"What's that say about you then? Being beaten by an Elemental who can't even use her powers?"

Just then, a cold pressure crept around my wrists before pulling them together sharply behind my back. I was back in cuffs before I could get any ideas. A Shade appeared at my shoulder. "Let's go, girl. Back to your cage. Fun's over."

The crowd had already begun to dissipate, having lost interest in the fight once they realized there wouldn't be any more bloodshed.

"I'm coming for you tomorrow, sweetie. Don't get too comfortable," another Archai called from the remaining observers. He had greasy, slick-backed hair and a thin frame, but something told me that he'd put up a more difficult fight. No matter. This was what I needed. Another chance outside of the cage. "And I won't make such a rookie mistake."

"Looking forward to it," I called over my shoulder as my wrists needled into the small of my own back, urging me to follow my captor. I climbed onto the base without protest, and the bars of shadow emerged from the surrounding darkness. I had until tomorrow night to figure out how to create a diversion that would give me a chance to escape. Maybe there was a chance that I could play them against each other. It might not be too difficult to conjure up some conflict and slip out in the ensuing chaos. With that comforting thought, I dozed off, leaning against the hard bars of my cage.

29

Tonight's campsite was much the same as the previous one, a small clearing in the middle of the forest. I ate the slop they shoved through the bars, simply because I hadn't eaten the past two days. Hunger stabbed at my insides. If I didn't look at what I was shoveling into my mouth, it was bearable. Then, I waited. After dinner, the soldiers broke out the wine and alcohol. Once they finished gorging themselves, they'd come for their entertainment.

Sure enough, the plump Archai from last night sauntered over with a Shade, the same flask clutched in his meaty hand. The smooth-faced Archai I'd defeated was nowhere in sight. "Hope you got some rest, girlie. You're gonna be needing it for this one."

With a wave of the Shade's hand, the bars melted away again, leaving me standing on the metal base. I could make a run for it now. Most of the rest of the camp hadn't made their way over yet and were still distracted with food and drink. It was only these two Eleiyon who were paying attention to me. I considered it for all of three seconds before X-ing it out. I wouldn't make it to the edge of the camp without some kind of distraction to give me a head start. I'd thought on it all day, and the only thing I'd come up with would be risky. I wasn't even sure I could pull it off. *You don't have a choice, Aila.* I took a deep breath, stepped off the base and headed toward the ring.

The greasy Archai was waiting for me, a wicked grin already plastered on his ugly face. My heart fluttered. It was less from the idea of facing this opponent and more because of what I needed to accomplish to have the slightest chance at escape. The Archai flexed his fingers, his knuckles cracking noisily as I took a deep breath and stepped into the circle.

I could tell immediately that this fight would be very different. My opponent found a fighting stance like my own. He wasn't squared up, leaving his body vulnerable to attacks. Instead, his stance was slightly sideways, creating an even narrower frame for me to target. He had experience in hand-to-hand combat. The strategy I'd used last night would not work here.

We started to circle each other. His eyes tracked my every movement. He assessed my foot placement, the angle of my chest, the height of my shoulders. He would notice and capitalize on any vulnerabilities he saw. I did the same. Three times around the circle, and then he took a quick stutter-step toward me. Instinctively, I took a minuscule step back, breaking my evenly spread gate slightly. My foot caught on a raised root, and I tripped. He seized the opportunity, forming a disc of fire and flinging it at me. I managed to back up just enough that the disc grazed my raised forearm instead of my cheek. The smell of singed flesh filled my nostrils as I yanked my arm back in pain. I didn't have time to nurse the wound; he charged me, leaping in the air, knee raised in what would be a stomp to my neck. Without thinking, I rolled under him, coming to my feet on his other side. He landed, already facing me, having turned in midair. His arms rose again as he resumed his fighting stance.

Liro's balls. That was too close. For my plan to work, I have to live through this stupid fight.

I needed to be on the offensive. He'd known about the root and forced my misstep at the precise moment when I'd trip over it. He'd been surveying everything, not just my stance: the ground around us, any imperfections he could exploit. He found one and used it. *What else had I missed by concentrating only on him?*

We fell back into our circling rhythm. He was an opportunist, that much was clear. So, I would give him an opportunity.

As our circling continued, I made a mental note of where the exposed root was. My biggest advantage in this fight would be his underestimation of me. When I came back around to the root, I feigned the same mistake, stumbling slightly and purposely taking my eyes off my opponent. I was ready for the fire this time. I flattened myself completely to the ground as the fireball passed over me. I knew he would follow with a physical attack. As he came, I spun my legs out, twisting my hips and using the momentum to propel my other leg over. I bent and kicked back with all my might, connecting with his knee. It buckled. He dropped to the ground with a grunt but was already backing away before I could finish my attack. Both of us were on our feet again within moments, harboring only minor wounds.

"Let's go, Konel. Finish her!" a voice shouted from the crowd.

Had he just been playing with me? As soon as the thought entered my head, Konel smirked and shot out a rope of fire from his hands. He must have kept an ember alive for this. I'd seen it before. This was one of Kyran's favorite moves. The rope sped toward me; a hissing snake ready to wrap itself around my body. Reacting purely on instinct, I reached out and grabbed hold of it.

Instead of the searing pain I expected, I only felt warmth. I clutched the end of the rope, raveling it in my palm until I had a strong grip. I wasn't sure how I was doing it, but I held onto the warmth in my hands, letting it flow through me. And then I pulled.

Konel flew forward in surprise, still connected to his end of the rope. The fire felt natural in my hands. I urged more of my own warmth from my chest, sending it down my arms to my palms. The fire glowed blue and surged, shooting back up the rope like an ocean wave. It reached my opponent, who yelped in pain, dropping his end of the rope. It hit the ground and fizzled out. I stood frozen, shocked at what I'd done.

Now...I had to do it now! And I could. It had only been an idea before, a far-fetched one at that. But now, I knew I could do it. I turned toward the closest fire, searching inside me for that familiar warmth. I found it in my chest and clutched it with my mind, willing it to grow as I focused on what I wanted, a single flame from that fire.

And then, I was blinded.

Darkness glided over my vision like a descending veil. My last sight was of my opponent on the ground, still recovering from the shock of my counterattack. Then pain.

A strong blow landed on my cheek, and then another. My nose broke with a sickening crack, forcing me to drop to my knees. The rusty taste of blood poured into my mouth from my gushing nose. Noise erupted around me. Or maybe it had been there the whole time.

My head spun as star sparks burst in my blackened vision. The sounds became muddled as my ears rang from the blows to my face. I felt around the ground, trying to orient myself through touch and memory. And then I was choking on air, gasping for breath as another blow struck my ribcage and knocked me the rest of the way to the ground. Voices competed with the high-pitched hum in my ears. Then someone dragged me to my feet.

"That's enough. She goes back in the cage. You won. It's over." A deep, raspy voice said calmly from behind me.

My body screamed in pain as the hands clutching my armpits pulled me backward. I was stumbling blindly, supported by the disembodied voice of my captor and rescuer. A slippery sensation tickled the bridge of my nose, and then the veil was lifted. It was still dark, but I could see. The light from the campfire illuminated the bustle of the onlookers returning to their sleep sacks for the night. My nose throbbed, and my ribs ached. The slimy thickness of blood coated my chin and mouth.

"Here." The Shade supporting me reached over, offering me a small black cloth.

I took it, placing it over my nose. The blood flow had turned from a gush to a steady trickle by now. As I wiped myself up and staunched the bleeding, I surveyed the Shade who led me back to my cage. He was dressed in all black instead of the dark gray the others wore. A hood covered his head. Fabric from the hood wrapped around his neck, obscuring the lower part of his face completely. I could only see the brown skin of his nose and his dark eyes, which, despite being as black as a crow's feathers, glimmered against the darkness as if they too were alive.

He brought me to the metal base before loosening his grip and gently guiding me to the floor. I held up the cloth he'd given me, offering it back even though the throbbing returned as soon as I lifted it from my face. I didn't want anything from them.

"Keep it. It has Macaria. Press it to your nose and it will speed the healing of your bones. I didn't hear your ribs crack, so you'll probably just be sore and bruised tomorrow." He was matter-of-fact, but not cruel.

"Thank you," I said begrudgingly, replacing the cloth. "Hopefully I'll heal enough to stand a chance against whoever wants their entertainment tomorrow," I added, my voice dripping with sarcasm.

His dark eyes just stared down at me. I couldn't read them. He lingered another moment before turning back to the camp. The bars formed behind him as he walked away. "Get some rest."

I knew what he was thinking, because I was thinking it myself. I'd have to be very careful tomorrow night indeed. If the Archai did want another duel and suspected I'd be able to harness fire again, they wouldn't play around with me anymore. I'd probably just lost my only, best shot at escape.

Silently cursing the Shade who'd slipped a veil over my vision, I lay down on the hard ground, holding my stomach with one hand and pressing the cloth to my face with the other. It would take a miracle from the Ancient One for me to get out of this alive.

———

The next day passed uneventfully. As predicted, my ribs were sore, but I could still move. My nose felt like it was back to normal. True to his word, the cloth the Shade lent me did the trick.

The closer we got to the northern border, the stranger the Archai began to act. They were shiftier, walking in groups of three or four, their eyes scanning the surrounding area. The forest had changed as well. The crisp, frigid air was replaced by a warm fog. I'd always thought of winter as a place of silent stillness. Frozen in time, like a fossil, waiting for the thaw of spring to reveal what had been waiting under the surface. Not here. Here, despite many trees being bare, the amount of green was overwhelming and proof of the life that still surrounded us. Evergreens and pines stood guard. Fluffy moss clung to their trunks and branches, giving them a soft, otherworldly appearance. Dewdrops sat happily on the moss, making this cool, wintery jungle feel more alive than the bare forest we'd come from.

"We'll make camp here tonight. Should reach the border soon. Not two hours' walk. We turn the girl over and put enough space between us and this place to finally get some sleep." The broad-shouldered Archai had his back to me, speaking to a small group of soldiers, likely commanders, each of whom went off to inform their respective squads of the plan.

One more night. I was mere hours from Thalen and whatever other evils he'd managed to unleash. I had no time to solve this impossible problem. The panic I expected to come as I stared at the thick bars of my cage didn't. Instead, a heavy resignation settled over my chest. If they let me out to duel again, they wouldn't be as careless. I wouldn't get the chance I needed. My opportunity had been last night, and I'd failed.

The journey north had the opposite effect on the Shades. Although they kept to themselves, they were more lively and more confident in their surroundings. I searched the group for the black-clad soldier who'd intervened last night but couldn't find him. Like it or not, I owed him, at the very least, my healed nose. *If not more.* I recalled the raspy voice that stopped the beating before it really started. Who knows how far the others would have gone. But...why bother? He put the bars back on my cage. He was turning me over to his boss, whose plan was surely to execute me. The trickle of gratitude I'd felt for the faceless Shade vanished just as completely as the bars of shadow around me.

I munched on a mealy apple, a hardened block of cheese, and stale bread that had been shoved through the bars of my cage.

"It's our last chance to have some fun with you, girlie. Daigh here will go easy on you, so don't you worry too much," he said between hiccups and burps that smelled of wine. He swayed back and forth, barely able to stay on his feet. *Why can't I have a go against you?* I'd probably just have to sit back, offer him another bottle of wine, and wait for him to pass out.

The bars melted away, and I hopped down from my small prison. My feet touched the ground with a jolt to my still-sore ribcage. The crowd seemed more agitated, and more drunk, than the past two nights.

"Hey!" A deep, raspy voice silenced the onlookers. "Why do you Archai get to have all the fun? Should be a Shade's turn to have a go with the girl, don't you think?" A murmur of agreement rustled through the gray-clad group.

No, no, no. The cold feeling of the shadow shackles sliding across my wrists and the sudden darkness of the veil over my eyes sent my resolve scampering.

I feared the Shades' gift much more than fire. I did not want to face one. The crowd parted.

It was the all-black Shade who'd helped me last night. Had he just been trying to save me for himself? Another wave of hate spilled over me as I looked at him with all the contempt I could muster.

"Seems fair," the broad-shouldered Archai finally said.

"Hey! C'mon, Captain. I was—"

"That's enough. I said, it's fair. Get out of the ring," he commanded. "Which of you will duel?" he asked the Shade.

Before there was any discussion, the captor-rescuer said, "I will."

My heart sank to my feet.

The crowd grew quiet around us as the Shade entered the ring. The Archai seemed to be in awe of the Shades' gift as well. Or maybe, deep down, they feared it as much as I did. The merriment dimmed to undivided attention on the ring. The Shade across from me moved differently than any Archai I'd sparred with before. The closest would have to be Kyran, but even he didn't move with the ease of my new opponent. His stride was effortless, his foot placement, perfect. Not a single sound came from his feet. He moved with cat-like precision. This was a man trained for stealth: to strike and then melt away into shadow.

It was dark. Not the time of day when Shades were at their strongest, but the dancing flames cast enough shadow for him to have something to work with. I racked my brain for anything I'd learned about fighting Shades. But we'd never discussed the weaknesses associated with the different gifts. Kyran was so adamant that I wouldn't have to learn to fight Eleiyon with magic. Something told me that this guy would not fall for either of the tricks I'd used with the other two.

My opponent started circling, cuing me to do the same. He was still covered head-to-toe in black fabric. Only his eyes were visible, and even they seemed masked by shadow. I couldn't determine where exactly he was looking, which would have been helpful in anticipating his attacks; I switched to his feet. He moved methodically, as if he knew every inch of the ring.

I bumped into something solid. My momentum made me fall sideways, and whatever the object was caught my following foot as well, taking me completely off-balance. My palms touched the ground first, breaking the fall before my legs caught up. What had I fallen over? Nothing was there.

Quickly regrouping, I turned to face my opponent. Sure enough, his hand was raised slightly. With a tiny twitch, shackles of shadow sped toward me. I was on all fours as the cold I dreaded slipped around my wrists and ankles, pinning me to the ground.

The audience's laughter rose around me. They were enjoying this humiliation. I tried to pull, to resist the cuffs, but it was as if I'd been stapled to the forest floor. I'd been here before. This position. In my dreams. The trees had bent toward me and the ooze. I couldn't move. I'd been trapped then as well.

This time, a swirl of darkness spun around my head, whipping my grungy hair around my cheeks before turning opaque and blocking the rest of the onlookers from view. And then a chilling whisper. An ethereal voice in my ear, the voice of shadows: "When I say, run east. Do not stop. I have friends waiting to help you. When I say..." The swirling stopped and the voice left. I'd heard that voice before. Where had I heard that voice before?

My vision cleared, and there was my opponent standing over me, a cat deciding whether to end its game with a mouse or continue toying a bit longer. I couldn't read his expression. His eyes were blank, his face still hidden beneath the black cloth. I braced myself for the blow...

And then a loud screech tore through the ink-blot sky. Not a scream of pain, nor was it the screech of an Ozar. It was a battle cry, like an eagle's signal of triumph, claiming its prey for all to hear.

I looked skyward. Beautiful white wings, wider than any of the Archai were tall, swooped into the fire light. The gigantic wings carried a slender figure. Her jet-black hair was shoulder-length on one side and shaved completely on the other, giving her a warrior's ferocity that contrasted her angelic wings. She wore a quiver on her back and launched arrow after arrow at the unsuspecting camp in an unrelenting assault.

Just as she drew the soldiers' attention, the campfires around us flared bigger than ever, casting long shadows from the sudden chaotic movement of the soldiers. Instead of following their owners, the shadows turned on them, grabbing weapons, restraining the soldiers from retaliating against the beautiful, winged archer. Another figure entered from behind her on foot. He wore a hood that covered his face, and he wielded a long sword. As he twirled it in the air above him, it set fire, becoming a flaming torch, which he thrashed against the wave of Archai. Fire raged as a coldness crept up the back of my neck, sprouting goosebumps down my spine.

"Run. Head east. Now!" The familiar whisper tickled my ear.

My opponent stared at me intently, unperturbed by the evolving situation around us. His eyes were intense, urging me into action. But he stood completely still.

I sprang to my feet. This was it. By my doing or someone else's, this was what I had been waiting for. My distraction. My escape. *Go east*, the voice had said. *Friends were waiting.* Friends? What friends? The only friend I had in the whole world was dead now. I had no friends. Without another thought, I ran. My body ached; my legs were tired; my brain was foggy from lack of food; but I ran...west.

I thought I heard a groan of frustration from behind me as I hurtled over fallen bodies, dodging blows from soldiers amidst the chaos of the ambush. I ran straight toward the tree line. The forest would offer some cover at least. *Almost there. Just a bit farther.*

Something snagged my boot, and I flew face-first into the hard ground. The air left my body with a thud. I tried to scramble to my feet, but my boot was still stuck. I looked back. An Archai was also on the ground, grasping my ankle, and another charged toward us, unsheathing his sword from its holster.

"Where do you think you're going, girlie?" he shouted as he approached. I tried to wriggle free, but the other one had me. I kicked harder, expecting to hauled to my feet at any moment. Instead, their snide, triumphant faces simultaneously turned to fear as the color drained from their skin.

Deliberate footsteps sounded behind me as the soldier released my ankle and scurried to his feet. Stepping next to me was the black-clad Shade. The cloth over his face had come off, revealing a sharp, mahogany jawline covered in scruffy, black stubble. His eyes still swirled like bottomless pits. With the scarf gone, his muscled arms were visible as well as the jagged points of a black chest tattoo inching up his neck and poking out from under his collar. His fists clenched in tight balls at his side.

As he opened his palms, something bubbled behind his eyes, and the tattoos slid down his arms like snakes. They glided past his open palms and, in a whirl of movement faster than the blink of an eye, took shape into two, solid black weapons. In one hand, a short sword and in the other, a swooping double-edged weapon: a sickle on one side, an axe on the other. His black eyes smoldered with hatred.

"Aila. Run," he said quietly, without looking at me.

My name felt easy on his tongue, like he'd said it before. I got to my feet hurriedly and, without a second thought, sprinted toward the trees just as the Shade raised the sickle over his head. The commotion of the campsite drowned in the darkness of the forest as I ran full-speed through the trees. I'd gone west, exactly the opposite of what the voice had told me. Now I was happy I'd chosen to defy it since I was certain the disembodied voice belonged to the Shade that even the Archai seemed to fear. Yet, he'd saved me not once, but twice, I reminded myself. *Still*. I couldn't shake the cold, pressing darkness I'd felt as he pinned me to the ground in that ring.

I wasn't sure if anyone had seen me leave besides the two Archai soldiers. I paused my outright sprint to listen for potential pursuers' footfalls behind me. Silence. Only my heavy breathing sounded over the dense quiet of the forest.

Turning forward to continue my escape, my heart jumped as a stunning Eleiyon stepped out from behind a tree.

She was tall and slender. Her midnight skin contrasted strikingly against the white outfit she wore tight to her muscled body. Knitted socks folded over her knee-high boots, and a long, thick cape with a loose hood draped over her head. Her eyes twinkled just as brightly as the stars in the night sky.

"Aila...stop. It's okay." Her smooth, melodic voice instantly put me at ease. It was a voice I could listen to forever, or just until I drifted off into a blissful sleep. My guard went back up immediately. I'd heard of sirens leading Eleiyon to their doom using only the sound of their enchanting voices. Instinctively, I reached to my thigh. *Liro's balls.* The dagger was gone, of course. I slid into my fighting stance. The woman across from me didn't mirror my actions. Her face was kind, her voice soothing as she said, "I'm going to reach behind me..." Ever so slowly, her arm stretched behind her. *My pack!*

She tossed it to me. I caught it without taking my eyes from her. She raised her hands cautiously. "I'm a friend. I'm here to help."

I gripped my pack, trying to assess what was happening. Was this the friend the shadows had referred to? I eyed her suspiciously before relaxing my stance and slipping the pack over my shoulders.

"Good... I'm Bana. We need to move. Quickly." With that, she turned and started speeding through the forest. She was fast, but I could keep up. She moved nimbly between trees, looping us around the campsite to bring us back east while staying far enough away that we wouldn't be spotted. Had the Shade been behind my escape? Had he coordinated this rescue?

I shivered, recalling his tattoos crawling down his arms to form solid weapons. Even with that kind of power, it was only him and two others taking on an entire camp of trained Archai and Shades.

Bana and I ran for an unknowable amount of time, as the moon didn't reach here. We ran until not a single sound met my ears. "We will rendezvous here," Bana said quietly, slowing to a complete stop near a moss-covered boulder.

I eyed her white outfit, searching it for the crescent moon insignia. "Are you one of them? A Shade, I mean?"

"Definitely not. Do I look like one?" She mockingly checked her clothes for signs of Shade contamination. She reminded me of Naleiri.

"No...I guess not." A small smile cracked my lips. The first I'd felt in days. And it felt like a betrayal.

"The Shade in all black..."

"Manu."

"Manu. Is he the one who planned all of this?"

"We all had a hand in this one. Our circle, I mean."

"The winged archer?" I said.

"Ha! Winged archer? That's cute. She'll like that. That's Asfa. She's a Saga. Decedents of the Sagari, the flying warriors."

I'd only ever heard of the Sagari in storyteller legends.

"And Kage. The one with the fire sword...he helped with the distraction so you could get out of there. They'll be here. Once they can get away safely without bringing any undesirables along."

I turned from Bana, scanning the night forest for signs of movement. Instead, two floating yellow eyes gleamed in the darkness. Behind them, a huge mass formed. I could make out the rosettes dotting the creature's black, silk fur. A jaguar. It stalked toward us.

My heart thundered behind my ribs as my adrenaline soared. I backed away slowly. The jaguar circled us, not taking its eyes off me.

"Kika," Bana's calm voice said from behind me.

"Huh?" I asked. The hammering of my heart faltered at Bana's nonchalant reaction to the giant feline joining us.

"This is Kika. She's with us. Well, with Manu, but she puts up with the rest of us," Bana explained.

As if understanding, Kika turned away from me and, in a single bound, leapt from the ground to a thick branch that hung over the clearing above us. She lay down, one massive paw dangling, seemingly relaxed. Only her twitching ears and bright yellow eyes signaled her alertness as she peered into the pitch-black forest.

Once I got my heart under control, I tried to piece it all together. Bana sprawled against the boulder, surveying the forest with an extra set of eyes unnecessarily, as I was certain Kika would detect any newcomers from much farther away than she could. The House of Fira was working with Thalen. Thalen was in Kiromar. Kyran betrayed me to his father. The Lord of Flame saw an opportunity to gain favor with Thalen by turning over an Elemental, knowing he'd been looking for them all these years.

I cursed myself again for being so careless with Kyran. A small part of me knew that Kyran could not have known his father would turn me over. But it was a very small and insignificant part of me. Because the rest of me wanted to rip Kyran's heart out for betraying me and putting Naleiri in the middle of it.

There were still so many unanswered questions. Why did Thalen care so much about Elementals? What did the House of Fira want with the dagger? And, now perhaps most immediately concerning, who in the firestorm was this group, and what did they want with me?

"They're here." Bana's clear voice interrupted my hypothesizing. She lowered her foot, which had been resting against the boulder as we waited. I peered into the darkness, looking for whatever sign had alerted Bana to her friends' arrival. I looked up; the branch that held the jaguar moments ago was empty. A twig snapped, and a swoosh of giant wings folding sounded in front of us, finally notifying me of the new arrivals.

A tall, lean Eleiyon stepped out from behind a tree. He was dressed like a Shade, but something about him told me that he wasn't one. He had flaming red hair, cropped low to his head. His young face had a boyish grin that lit up his pale skin. Next to him stood a magnificent creature. *A Saga*, Bana said. She had the body of an Eleiyon, but folded behind her back were large, white, feathered wings. She was wearing sky blue-cloth and brown fighting gear, with a matching headband tied across her forehead. Her heavy-lidded eyes were wary as they surveyed me from across the clearing.

"This is Kage and Asfa." Bana said, pointing at the recent arrivals in turn.

"Nice to meet you, Aila," Kage said in a friendly voice. Asfa nodded in acknowledgement but didn't speak.

"Likewise," was all I managed.

Kika reappeared behind them, making Kage jump. "Sugsack, Kika."

"Scared?" Asfa asked, hiding a smirk.

Kage let out a shaky laugh. "Of the overgrown housecat? Nah…I just can't get used to her creeping around… She's so…" Kage grasped for the words to describe exactly what Kika was.

"Cat-like?" Asfa offered, her smirk turning into a full smile. Kage rolled his eyes.

"Where's Manu?" Bana asked, interrupting their exchange.

"He's finishing up. Said to go on ahead. He'll meet us at home," Kage answered.

Bana nodded and walked toward us. She made a sweeping motion with her hand, as if drawing a circle in midair. A bright blue portal opened just like the one Luga had made to transport us to and from Lake Luan. Asfa stepped through first, followed by Kage. Bana gestured for me to go next. I turned to see if we'd be joined by the apex predator, but she'd already disappeared into the night. Bana fell in line behind me, and the portal closed with a pop. I was once again submerged in darkness.

30

"What's he doing anyway?" Bana's clear voice sliced the darkness first.

"He has a couple of questions for the Archai. Can't blame him for not wanting to waste this opportunity to get some answers, can you?" Asfa responded.

"Do they know it was us?"

"Senko and his crew definitely knew. Though I don't think any of them will be making it back to share the news," Kage smirked. "Not sure what the Archai know, honestly. Part of what Manu is trying to figure out, I'm sure. From my time there, I'd say if the Archai know, it's only the royal house —the Lord of Flame, his advisor Cyrus, and his son, of course, General Kyran."

My hair stood on end as Kage casually mentioned Kyran's name. I agreed with Kage's assessment, though. Kyran and Cyrus know much more about a lot of things than they cared to share with me or with the rest of the Archai. A spark lit the darkness and Kage, holding a burning flame, led us through an underground tunnel. *So he had the gift of fire.*

We walked in a line down the narrow tunnel until flickering lights ahead told me we were reaching its end. Sure enough, the tunnel opened into a cavernous space with dancing candlelight. Smaller tunnels, like the one we just left, led in different directions. Despite being little more than an underground hole, the cavern felt cozy and warm and somehow welcoming. Exhaustion and grief were setting in, and all I wanted was solitude and rest.

Thankfully Bana grabbed my hand. Her gentle touch was reassuring, putting me at ease in this strange place. "I'm sure you have a ton of questions, and we'll give you honest answers. Right now, if you'd like. Or, I can take you to your room and you can rest first." Her voice was soft and kind. The other two just stood there watching me, waiting patiently for my decision.

"Rest sounds good," I said flatly, not caring to participate in pleasantries. Bana gave my hand a gentle squeeze and nodded as she led me down a corridor to our left, leaving Kage and Asfa behind.

I sat on the bed for a long time. The quilted blanket spread smoothly across the mattress. Not a single crease. I absentmindedly grabbed the corner that draped over the edge, fiddling with the single loose thread that gave away its patchwork beginnings. I'd sat on another strange bed three years ago when my life was torn apart the first time. Had it only been three years that I'd lived with Naleiri? We'd become closer than friends in that time—sisters.

I remembered awakening to sit across from her on my thin cot, watching her sleep peacefully as I tried to piece together what had happened. Naleiri stirred, her eyelids fluttered open to reveal blue orbs.

"Hi, you're new here." The first words she'd said to me.

"Yeah…I arrived last night, I guess," I'd answered, unsure of where "here" was.

"I'm Naleiri. It'll be great to have another girl around. What's your name?"

"Aila," I answered, happy that at least my name jumped right to mind.

I'd followed Naleiri through Aodhen that day as she delivered washed clothes to the wealthier residents. I walked in a silent trance, looking for something that might trigger my memory.

"I'm not from here either, you know," Naleiri confided that night. We both sat on her cot, chatting into the night.

"I made my way here after my tribe was attacked. It was the Archai, burning the forests for the Ancient One only knows why. My mother and grandmother both...they didn't make it." She paused sadly before asking, "What about you?"

I searched my mind, checking every nook and cranny for hidden memories that could answer her question. It was an answer I knew but couldn't recall. "I don't remember...I know certain basics about who I am, but my family, my past, where I'm from and why I'm here—it's all gone." My eyes had filled with tears then, just as they did now. The soft trickle down my cheek brought me back to the small, empty room.

It flickered with candlelight. It was the walls that gave away the fact that I was actually underground. All the furnishings felt very normal, and above-ground-like. A comfortable twin bed, a small wooden dresser with three drawers for clothing. A desk and chairs stood across from the bed, and an oval mirror in a black frame hung above it. Candle sconces adorned the walls on either side of the door, and other candles were scattered about the room, sitting on the desk, the dresser, and the small bedside table.

My heart was the barren cave this place once was. Hollow. A pervasive emptiness settled in my soul where everything I'd loved used to be. I couldn't feel the aching that let me know I was still alive. That I was still here. The wretched pain I'd felt right after Naleiri died was gone, replaced by a void. The tears that had been my constant companions over the last couple of days had dried up, leaving me with only a sensational loneliness that I knew was wrong, if only because of its contrast with the soul-splitting pain I'd felt before.

Sleep eluded me. I stared blankly ahead, wanting answers but not finding the energy to look for them.

I felt him before I saw him. Manu stood at the doorway, dressed in black pants and a loose black shirt that revealed the whirling tattoos on his biceps and peeking out from his neckline. They looked like shadows moving across his dark skin, swirling into different shapes and then stopping, as if deciding this was the intended design all along.

"How are you?" His raspy voice echoed in the small room. Or maybe it just ricocheted in the emptiness of my soul, the sound waves bouncing off the deserted chambers of my heart.

I dragged my eyes to look at him. His face was in darkness again, this time from the shadows cast by the candles. Even still, I could make out the stubble of his beard growing in and his dark eyes. They looked at me with what could have been concern, before whatever emotion it really was melted back into shadow.

He stepped forward cautiously. Involuntarily, I shifted further back onto the bed, shrugging my shoulders up as if to block an oncoming attack. He stopped at once. "I'm not going to hurt you." His voice was soft, maybe even pained. The feelings that I thought had been emptied rose to the surface, and an even, deathly calm voice rolled from my mouth.

"You don't wear the same crescent moon insignia the other Shades wore." It was not a question.

"That is Thalen's symbol. It has nothing to do with being a Shade," he explained calmly, but an edge of anger laced his words.

I nodded blankly, deciding I didn't care enough to try to untangle the relationship between the Shades and Thalen's followers. "I know it was not you who betrayed me or imprisoned me. I know it was not your power that bound my wrists and kept me in a cage of darkness for days. But I can still feel it; the restraints of shadow; the pressing darkness in my ears and over my eyes. When I look at you, that is what I see. My captors. My prison. You are shadow...you are darkness."

I looked at him then and held his gaze, pouring every emotion I felt into that stare. My rage; pain; fear; helplessness; I poured it all into my eyes as I looked at him. I saw the flinch that showed my words had hit their mark before he turned and left the room.

And maybe he didn't deserve it. And maybe he was my scapegoat for every-thing else that had happened these past few days. But what I felt was real. And it was easier to hate. And it was easy to hate him. And so, I did.

<hr>

I woke up starving. The candles still shone dimly on the walls of my room. It was impossible to tell the time of day down here.

My pack was on the floor next to an open archway that I hadn't bothered to explore earlier. As I entered, candles ignited with enchanted fire, illuminating a simple yet elegant washroom. A large black basin tub sat in the middle, con-trasted with a small, white marble washbasin on the other side. I quieted my growling stomach, deciding that my stinking armpits and greasy hair were the higher priority. Grabbing my pack and selecting a comfortable pair of dark green leggings and a beige form-fitting tunic, I returned to the washroom, happy to see that the tub had magically filled with glorious hot water.

Feeling somewhat myself after the bath, I strapped on the back holster and loaded it with the crystal twin sai from Caeru. I wouldn't be caught off guard again. A lesson learned too late. Carefully, I took out the amulet Naleiri had given me and held it in my palm before placing it back in my pack, not ready to put it on. Somehow wearing it felt like admitting she was really gone. I headed back down the narrow tunnel to the large cavern, where I paused in a pool of light. A bright blue sky shined above me; the tips of huge green trees tickled the nimbus clouds that stretched across its expanse.

"Feeling better?" Bana's lilting voice startled me. I spun around to find her standing in the right-most tunnel.

"Better. I'm starving though." I decided once again to ignore normal man-ners. I turned back to admire the ceiling.

"We call it the Skylight. It's enchanted to create a window to the surface. It's an exact mirror of whatever is happening up there," she explained.

We headed down the corridor. An opening to my left showed a cavernous hall full of chairs and desks. Toys were stacked up to the side and a small group of children played with a ball. Screeches of delight and bouts of laughter floated toward us. To my right, another big room where adult Eleiyon were scattered about, performing a variety of activities; a small group of women were sewing, another couple were playing some kind of card game; a group of men chatted in the corner while still others cleaned gleaming weapons.

"Community Room," Bana offered by way of explanation. "We're not very big, but our numbers are significant enough. After Kiromar fell to Thalen, we led the survivors here. Over the years, others have joined our little rebellion. Outcasts from the other territories mostly. Here we can live an almost normal life. The kids can play, get exercise in the Main Hall. We work in the Community Room, sew our own clothes and such. It's best for the community to be as self-sufficient as possible to avoid unnecessary travel to surface towns."

I swallowed my surprise. When had the north fallen to Thalen? "I hadn't realized there had been a battle for Kiromar. I didn't even know about Thalen until a few days ago."

"Yes...the House of Fira is good at controlling what its citizens know," she said as she continued down the corridor. "It wasn't a battle really. Kiromar was already being pulled apart from within. There were many who resented the open borders, who thought outsiders coming in from the rest of Kiakora were weakening the north. Many viewed tolerance as a burden." She paused her account to face me. "His arrival was insidious. He stoked the hateful thoughts that were already being spoken behind closed doors and whispered under breath. When the time came, he had an angry following that was ready to tear Kiromar apart. They attacked...turned on their own. They follow him now. They were the ones in gray at the camp, wearing his symbol. Those that survived, fled. We brought them here."

"You created this place?"

Her face was pained as she spoke. "We did. Kage, Manu and I. Asfa came to us later. Manu noticed the changes in Kiromar before the rest of us. His father was our leader. But no one, not us, not even his father...we didn't believe him. When it happened, he was the only one who knew what to do. Who had a plan. He'd probably been hatching it for years, just in case."

"What happened?" I ask quietly, entranced by this story that I'd never heard.

"Manu's father had information Thalen wanted. He was tortured for it. Manu tried several times to save him. He failed. Ultimately, Drata used her despicable beasts on him. Turned him into something worse than a corpse." Bana's voice dripped with contempt as she spoke about Drata. "Anyway, we built the Refuge, that's what we call this place, to save who we could. And to bide our time. Figure out what's happening and make our move." She turned and continued walking. I guessed that was all I was getting out of her. For now, at least.

We reached a brightly lit kitchen. Stacked off to the side were shelves upon shelves of green plants. There were herbs and spices, and trays of lettuce and cabbage. Vegetables and tubers lined the bottom shelves. "Aeroponic farming. You'd be surprised what can grow underground with the right concoction of nutrients and a little bit of spell-weaving," she explained, as I examined the shelves of greenery.

I stifled my amazement again at what they'd been able to build here. I was about to ask about the spells when a loud laugh drifted from an open archway on the other side of the kitchen. It was a banquet hall filled with rows of long tables and benches, some of which were occupied with Eleiyon eating and talking animatedly. Off to my right was another short corridor ending in a small room. Debating voices drifted into the open space. Curiosity trumped the grumbles, and I slipped quietly down the corridor, semi-aware of Bana following quietly behind me.

"I'm just not sure why it makes sense to do this now. We just finished a high-profile job. It's going to draw a lot of attention," Asfa was saying.

"We need to. I didn't get a hold of any Shades last night. We have no idea what they know or what they're planning. We need to interrogate them," Manu's gravelly voice replied, sending shivers up my neck.

"And the Archai?" Asfa asked.

"Nothing. If the Lord of Flame has a plan, we'll have to go into the House of Fira itself to hear about it. They're keeping their soldiers in the dark," Kage answered. "But they're making moves. Now we know where the west stands. Best case, they can't be trusted to give their allegiance to anyone but themselves. Worst case, they've already sided with Thalen," Kage said. "They're up to something else though. Neither the general nor Cyrus were in the camp. If Aila had been their top priority, they would have been there," he finished persuasively. And then as an after-thought, "All the more reason to go north and learn what we can."

"Bana, can you please talk some sense into them," Asfa said without looking up at our entrance. I thought they would stop discussing their plans at the sight of me, but they didn't.

Slowly, Bana answered from where she stood next to me. "I think we need answers..." Asfa jerked her head up and stared at Bana with surprised eyes. "But," Bana continued quickly, "Asfa is right. Eyes will be on us right now. We just made a big move. It might behoove us to wait..." Her voice trailed off at Kage's angry expression and Asfa's smug one. Manu sat in the back corner, fingering a small knife with Kika lying at his feet. His face was unreadable.

"A compromise then?" They all turned to me in surprise as my voice broke the tense silence. "The Shades and Archai, at least, are already making moves. We don't have the luxury of being cautious..." Asfa turned on me ready to interject, but I continued before she had the chance. "But we don't need to be reckless either. Why not go north? Two or three of us. Not on a raid to capture, just to eavesdrop. Learn if there's any movement from the Shades, any orders to march. Just observe. I overheard Kyran and Cyrus in the camp one night. They didn't seem too happy about working with the Shades, but that doesn't mean the Lord of Flame hasn't struck up some kind of truce. We can see if there's any evidence of the Archai working more closely with the Shades than we might realize. We can't afford to be caught off-guard, especially not if the Shades and Archai are indeed working together." I ended my point, but before anyone could comment, I added, "And we're at a disadvantage, until we know exactly what they're after and why they're after it... Unless we already know that?" I ended with the question I really had for the group and cast a glance at each of them in turn. What did they know and what would they be willing to share with me? I refused to be kept on the sidelines this time.

They exchanged looks before Bana spoke. "We know that Thalen is after you and that he will try to find you. He's obsessed with killing Elementals. He's been searching for the past several years, since his escape from Nagrimar, but the truth is, the Eleiyon largely wiped-out Elementals millennia ago. You very well might be the last one in Kiakora. And he will not stop until he has you. I am certain Drata and her soulsuckers are trying to track your trail as we speak." I swallowed the flutter of fear and rage that swelled in my throat at the mention of Naleiri's killer.

Bana continued before I could ask any of the thousands of questions I now had. "As for the House of Fira and what deal they possibly have with Thalen, we have no idea. You might have more insight on that than we do," she ended, not bothering to hide the assessment in her eyes.

"Other than the broad strokes... you know, total world domination," inter-rupted Kage.

They all looked at me, waiting.

"Why?" It was the question I kept returning to. It was the one, of all the others, that kept rising to the top. "Why is it so important to him to find Elementals?"

Asfa and Kage looked at each other. Manu's hood was up, but I could tell he was staring at his booted feet. Bana looked at me with a mixture of pity and concern.

"What is it?" *What were they not saying?*

Silence.

Bana, Asfa and Kage all seemed to be waiting to see how Manu would respond. He'd been quiet up to this point but somehow still commanded their respect. What had he done to earn it?

Manu set down the knife he'd been fingering and looked at me from beneath his hood before he answered. "We don't know. The most I've been able to piece together is this. It started with my father. Ten years ago, he noticed changes in Kiromar. Subtle things. Creatures descending farther and farther down the mountains. A change in the forests: dying trees, fleeing animals. He didn't know about Thalen then. He went searching for answers in the Ancient Forest." It was the first time I'd seen any trace of real emotion on Manu's face. I knew what happened to his father and felt like it was a secret I shouldn't know yet, not until he was ready to share it. "I don't know what they told him. But I know that he wasn't the only one who heard it." *The Ozars. What had Luga said?* Thalen's *spies. That's why Kyran had been so afraid of them.* "When my father returned home, the coup had already started. Thalen was there, ready to take his place with a mob of traitors at his back. They'd already killed so many innocents. My father didn't fight. He thought if he gave in, the rest of his people would be able to escape." Manu's voice was a quiet rage as he recalled memories only he could see. Kika raised her head at the shift in his tone, as if Manu's rising anger stoked her own. Manu paused his account before turning to face me. "Needless to say, that didn't happen. My father was tortured. Whatever the Ancient One told him, Thalen thought there was more to it. Ever since then, we've been watching his moves, trying to figure it out. We know he's after Elementals, but we don't know why, and he's too powerful to stop. He's not of Kiakora. He's one of the original Eleiyon. We need help, an army, something to stand a chance against him."

"How do you know about him? How did you discover he escaped from exile?" It didn't seem like information Thalen would share as part of his takeover.

Bana answered this time. "Caeru told us."

My head spun. Cearu. Caeru from the library? She was working with them. They were all in on this and I was kept in the dark? But I was the one Thalen was after. Anger started to bubble to my cheeks.

Bana continued as I tried to control my rising temper. "Caeru is older than all of us. Older even than the Lord of Flame or Manu's father. When Thalen escaped, the Mangi sent her here to learn what was happening. The last time he was free, he almost tore Kiakora apart."

Caeru had said that the House of Fira and Thalen weren't the only ones preparing. I hadn't thought...she was gathering information on their movements, their motives. On me. It all made more sense now.

"If Thalen is one of the original Eleiyon in Kiakora, how is he still alive? I mean, that was before the war, how is that possible?" I asked. We lived a long time, but we were not immortal beings. I couldn't imagine any Eleiyon that old was still among us.

"It's another part of the puzzle. But, let me ask you, does it matter," Asfa spoke up brusquely. "I mean, does it really matter, Aila? How we know what we know? How old he is? What happened to lead us to this point? The facts are, you are an Elemental, Thalen is here, and he's after you. The House of Fira is up to something, in collusion with him or on their own is to be determined. Are you with us, or not?"

She was right of course. It didn't matter how we all arrived at this juncture. Here we were. Caeru had told me *soon we'd all have to choose a side.*

"I am." They were my best option right now. I thought of the yellowed pages Caeru slipped me in the library; what I knew about Baku's shard and what I suspected about the dagger. It looked like Caeru hadn't given them this piece of information either. If there was one thing I learned so far, it was not to trust anyone with everything, not until you are absolutely sure of their loyalty. I'd hold onto this information a little longer.

"Fine. It's settled then." Asfa nodded, clearly annoyed and picking up the original thread of the conversation. "Manu and I will go north tomorrow. See what we see." I was about to object and insist on joining them when Asfa added, "The smaller the better. I can get us there quickly with no magic." She nodded at her great white wings folded across her back. "And Manu can listen discreetly, better than any of us. We can be back in two days. If anything is worth exploring further, we can make plans from there."

Kage didn't look happy at the idea of being left behind either, but he didn't object.

"So, it's decided then," Manu concluded finally.

Only silence answered him. He stood from his chair. The others also rose.

"I'm starving," Kage said loudly, putting his big hand on his stomach.

My stomach growled impatiently. "I was just going to take Aila to the kitchen," Bana responded with a smile, and I was certain she heard my stomach's rumbles.

31

The next two days passed surprisingly quickly. The Refuge was much bigger than I'd initially realized.

Bana showed me the Combat Room. It was a huge cavern covered with padded mats, devoted to practicing and honing combat skills. Twelve pairs could easily spar in the room at once, though it was deserted when we first entered. Lining the walls were weapons cabinets with every type of blade, ball, or bow imaginable. On the far side, three pedestals stood, each with a small indentation that held a single element: fire, water, and sand. The elements, without Eleiyon to manipulate them, stood placidly corralled in their carved containers.

Just as we were about to leave, Kage entered, leading a small group of Eleiyon children, no older than five. They ran excitedly onto the mats, seemingly unaware of our presence. The atmosphere was suddenly energetic and youthful. Excited shouts and giggles echoed from the children in the cavernous space. Kage led them to the center of the room, where they all sat down. He stood in front of them and raised his hand. A ball of fire flew from its pedestal straight into his waiting hand. I couldn't stop the involuntary flinch my body made at the sight of the fire wielder.

The kids all clapped with delight, like it was a magic show. He called a small girl up. She had short blond pigtails and rosy cheeks. Kage held out his open palm, where the orange flame danced happily. Tentatively, the girl stretched out her small hand and touched the flame. I expected her to snatch it back in pain, but she held it there. Her brow furrowed in concentration. She stared at the fire. Finally, she withdrew her hand, and a tiny flame hopped from Kage's palm to hers, where she willed it to the center. The other children watched, engrossed, almost holding their breaths with anticipation at their classmate's efforts.

"Now, grow it," Kage commanded. "Slow and controlled, like we talked about."

The small girl gave a determined nod before returning her focus to her hand. Nothing happened. A minute passed. And then another. Then, quite suddenly, the flame brightened. It doubled in size, then tripled. The girl was sweating now. Her forehead creased as her eyes drew together in concentration. The flame was larger than a small pumpkin.

"Try to shape it," Kage instructed.

The girl raised her other hand as if to mold the flame into a circle, the way a potter would shape clay on a wheel. I realized she was trying to create a fireball. The wildness of the flame fought back, refusing to be tamed. It grew. Its rogue tips stretched taller and taller. The girl pushed more of her energy into her effort, which only fueled the flame more, making it grow bigger than she could handle. Her nerves won out as her forehead loosened, and she looked up at Kage for reassurance. In that moment, she lost control; she tried to refocus, but the flame had other plans as it continued to swell. Just as she realized she no longer had control, Kage squeezed his palm closed, extinguishing both his and the girl's flame.

"Training," Bana's voice interrupted my thoughts. "Manu usually does it, but since he's not around... Lily is the only one with fire besides Kage." She indicated the pigtailed girl who returned to the ranks of her classmates. "We found her and her father in a village not far from here. It had been raided.

Everyone killed except for them." I thought of Gillie's family and of my own. Even though I couldn't remember, I was starting to feel like I was getting answers about my past. "The others are mostly Shades. Their families escaped with us, helped us build this place."

"What about you?" I asked, turning to face her.

She was dressed in a silver tunic today. Her eyes trailed to the left momentarily, not quite meeting my gaze. She pushed away the quiet sadness that had settled there.

"You said you weren't a Shade," I pushed.

"I'm from Rimean," she said, returning her gaze to meet my own. "This is my home now. We've all been walking a fine line between protecting it and trying to stop what's going on out there." She nodded toward the surface. "That's why Asfa was so against going, you know. She thinks it's more important to protect our home than to try to save Kiakora." A dark shadow passed over her eyes. "She gave up believing it could be saved a long time ago. If I'd been through what she has, maybe I would too...Sometimes I think she does what she does more for our sake than believing it will make any difference."

It felt strange to be talked to so candidly by a stranger. I knew more about their plans, their reasoning, from the past three days than I'd ever learned with Kyran.

"What's your gift?" I asked, suddenly curious about the stunning Eleiyon before me.

Without a word, she raised her hand. The air between us suddenly went frigid. My breath turned to smoke, and my nose tingled with cold. She twisted her hand, and tiny ice balls appeared suspended in the air between us. "Cold, snow, ice...pretty much anything winter."

I'd never seen anyone with that gift before.

"All Eleiyon's gifts are derived in some way from the four basic elements. I've heard that a connection develops over time, between Eleiyon and the natural world that surrounds them. It's why my gift isn't that rare in the east," she added, as if reading my thoughts. This was an example of the evolution Baku mentioned. "It's much rarer there to see a female Eleiyon trained in her gift...They don't let us," she clarified. "Seeing young Eleiyon train together like this, the girls and the boys...even the dream of it would be prohibited back in Rimean." She smiled sadly.

"Well, I don't think I've ever been trained in my gifts either. Up until a few days ago, I didn't even know I had power. I mean, of course I knew I was an Elemental from the mark, but I just thought I was a Nulk...that they were dormant or something. I can't remember anything about my life before three years ago. It's... It's like a dense fog in my head. I feel my memories sitting there. Sometimes, I can even catch glimpses, but I can't fit the pieces together. It's just..." I grasped for the words but couldn't find them either. "Just out of my reach," I finished frustrated.

Bana turned to face me. There was something else in her eyes. Was it pity? She looked like she wanted to say something more but decided against it. I cleared my throat awkwardly, hating the emotional exchange we'd just had. She seemed to feel similarly because she added, "Let me show you the library." She walked past me. I turned to follow, ensuring I didn't trail too closely, leaving some private space for our thoughts.

"Do you ever leave here?" I asked Kage over dinner that night. "I mean, besides for raids?" I was starting to feel trapped despite the labyrinth of spacious rooms and the enchanted skylight in the main atrium.

"You get used to it," Kage answered sympathetically. "Honestly, it doesn't even occur to me that we're underground anymore. It just feels like home." Kage shoveled in another mouthful of mashed sweet potatoes. "We do go above ground though. There are strict rules on how to leave and return, to prevent any unwanted guests, but..." He shrugged, adding, "Honestly, we don't hardly need to worry much about being followed considering where we are."

"And where is that exactly?"

Kage took a big swallow before answering, "We're under the Thoir Woods. Some of our tunnels go right up to the eastern border. Not a heavily trafficked area of Kiakora, that's for sure."

I conjured a mental map of the world. I'd never been this far east before. Despite still being in Fira, apparently, I felt like a stranger in a foreign land, wanting to explore the new sights around me.

"Asfa and Manu return tomorrow. Once they get back, we can escape to the surface for a bit. If you're dying to get out of here, we can probably make sure it won't kill you." Kage grinned at his own joke. "I wouldn't mind running into some of those Ember-eaters again, showing them what can really be done with the gift of fire."

Bana gave him a threatening look.

"What? I'm just saying I wouldn't mind it. Not that I'm gonna go looking for trouble," he said, raising his hands in mock surrender.

"You better not," Bana said. Her look softened slightly, but an air of disapproval still hung on her words.

"Well, I'd love to get out tomorrow. Archai or no Archai," I announced.

Kage grinned widely, spooning in his last mouthful of food before letting the silverware clatter to his dish. "Sounds like a plan."

Asfa and Manu returned mid-afternoon the following day. Manu's feline companion was notably missing, though no one seemed concerned, so I gathered it wasn't unusual for her to come and go as she pleased. We all went straight to the small room off the kitchen corridor.

"Well?" Bana asked as soon as we were all inside the room.

"Nothing exciting," Asfa announced, flopping into a chair by the fireplace hearth.

"Well, that's good," Bana replied.

"We confirmed what we suspected about Drata," Manu continued. "She and one of her monsters are already back in Fira, scouring the forests for Aila. They think she'll return to Aodhen," he said matter-of-factly without looking at me.

For some reason, he still made me uneasy. He looked tired. His black hair twisted in two tight braids on his scalp, the ends of which hung past the tops of his shoulders and lay against his chest, an observation I'd missed when I first met him because of his hood.

"One beast? Where is the other?" Bana caught the detail I'd missed. She had two of those foul creatures when I'd seen her last as well.

"Dead. Didn't make it out of Aodhen the night Aila was captured apparently," Asfa stated.

"Caeru. She must have managed to kill it." They turned to me in unison. "She fought them at the library, giving me and...and Naleiri a chance to escape." My voice caught on her name. It was the first time I'd said it aloud since she died.

"We need to find out what happened to her," Bana said, concerned. "I haven't heard from her since then."

"On it. What else?" Kage asked, turning to Manu and Asfa. "The Archai?"

"No word on the Archai or the House of Fira's intentions. Either no one knows, or no one is talking. My best guess is whatever uneasy deal they'd struck rested squarely on turning over an Elemental, and since that didn't happen..." Manu shrugged.

"Only problem is that might mean both Kiromar and Fira, the Shades and the Archai, will be after her. Plus, that soulsucker Drata," Asfa said solemnly.

"I get the sense there's more going on than just rounding up an Elemental," Manu said, more to himself than any of us. "Why would the House of Fira risk this alliance now? And what is Thalen waiting for? Is he not going to invade until he is sure he has all the Elementals?"

"The sickness." The words were almost a whisper coming out of my mouth.

"What?"

"Fira's forests. They're dying. You must know..."

"Yes, we've seen it. My father noticed something similar in our forests. It's one of the things that prompted him to go looking for answers. How do you think that relates to Thalen's plans to invade?"

"Well..." I began cautiously. It was only a theory, and it only made sense in my head so far. "Caeru told me the thing causing it, it's really him. Well, part of him. Part of Thalen. Maybe he's realized he can use what he's become to his advantage." I looked up at their blank faces. "We know Kiakora draws power from the land itself. Even some of us, some Eleiyon, can draw power from different parts of nature," I said, thinking of Kage's fire, Bana's gift, and Naleiri's ability to commune with the natural world. "If he can weaken the natural world..."

"He weakens us. And any natural defenses," Kage finished my sentence.

"How can we stop it?" Bana asked, horrified.

Asfa shook her head. She didn't know. I thought about sharing my journey to Lake Luan and the recovery of the metal shard. Baku told me the only way to stop it.

"Sounds to me like the next best bet is to get into the House of Fira, see what we learn from them," Kage suggested nonchalantly.

"And I suppose you're volunteering for this" Bana said, a twang of disapproval returning. Kage just shrugged.

"The Archai are going to be on high alert now. I'm not sure—" Asfa started.

"You and Manu just went north. How is this any different?" Kage argued before Asfa could finish.

Asfa's temper rose as she responded. "The difference, Kage, is that we could keep our distance and observe. You're talking about full-blown infiltration. An undercover operation, in the heart of Fira no less. For all we know, Drata is snooping around there as well, and we're not entirely sure what other forces are at play."

"I can do it. They'll never know..." Kage snapped his fingers, lighting all five of his fingertips like a match. "I blend in."

Asfa rolled her eyes, and Bana just shook her head, worried.

"Let's think through our options. We can come back to this tonight. After dinner. Okay?" Bana suggested, trying to calm the rising emotions.

"Fine." Kage said, and the flames disappeared. He got up, pushing his chair out with a groan. "You coming surface-side, Aila, or what? I suddenly need some air too." With that, he left the room.

We walked silently down the narrow corridors that were quickly becoming familiar. The atrium with the enchanted skylight told me it was a clear, crisp day on the surface.

"You might want to get something long-sleeved. It's a bit chilly outside," Kage recommended, eyeing my bare arms. "I'll wait here." He indicated the opening of the tunnel that led to the surface.

I hurried down the other corridor to my room. My pack sat on the bed, the contents spilling out from the last time I'd rustled through it. I found my thickest tunic, pulling it on over the shirt I wore. Something fell to the ground with a clatter.

I bent down and picked up Naleiri's amulet. My heart tightened with a swell of sadness. I closed my eyes and clutched the amber stone, letting memories of Naleiri bounce happily through my mind. This time, instead of returning the amulet to my pack, I reached up and clasped it securely around my neck, tucking it gently beneath my clothes, where it rested against my bare skin, just above my heart.

"We only enter and leave through this tunnel. It's the only part of the entire place where the enchantments allow for portals," Kage explained as we made our way down the exit tunnel. "Of course, the great thing about portals is you have to know where you want to land in order to open one...makes concealing a secret community that much easier."

"What if you don't know how to make a portal? Is that the only way in and out of this place?" I asked, suddenly feeling claustrophobic.

Kage spun around to face me. I could just make out his boyish grin in the darkness.

"We don't advertise it because, well, you know, kids...they'd be going and coming for a game of Dare Dash. But yeah, we're going to leave by foot now. Come on..." He gestured for me to follow.

We rounded several bends to get to this point, which shielded the area from any ambient lighting or noise traveling down the tunnels from the main community.

"We created this spot just for this," Kage said from ahead of me. "As an additional safety measure. If someone does manage to create a portal, they'd have to know where to go to find us. There are some fake tunnels shooting off in random directions leading to nowhere. Asfa wanted to add booby traps and Krech Dragons, but Bana convinced her that it wouldn't be the best idea with the kids and everything."

I suppressed a giggle. From what I'd learned about Asfa so far, I was hardly surprised. She was objective, tactical, and blunt; a devoured Eleiyon child here or there at the jaws of protective dragons would be chalked up to collateral damage by her calculations.

We arrived at the end of the tunnel. Solid rock face surrounded us. I turned curiously to Kage, who had a sly grin. "If you know what you're looking for, it's easy to find," he said as he reached toward the right wall of the tunnel. His fist closed around something, and just as it did, a ladder appeared, as if out of thin air. "Simple concealment enchantment. Only those who already know its location can see it."

"From what I've gathered, enchantments, especially complex ones like that, require a lot of power and skill to maintain. Which of you...?" I let the question linger, not sure how to phrase it correctly.

"You're not wrong. This isn't a complex enchantment, really. A little drain on the energy to have it constantly working, but more than manageable for a skilled spellweaver. Bana is by far our strongest." Admiration shone in his eyes. "Eleiyon from Rimean are known for their enchantment prowess...well, the men anyway."

That was the second time I'd heard Rimean described in such a way. "Is it really that bad out there? How did Bana learn?"

"Thankfully she had a brother who didn't see eye-to-eye with their village elder. He trained her at night, showing her how to harness her gift, manipulate the weather around her, and eventually how to channel her powers into spells and enchantments." He looked sad as he shared these details about Bana's past. "The rest of her story is hers to share," he said firmly after a moment. "But she's definitely the strongest spellweaver amongst us. Then Manu, then me. I know enough but wouldn't trust my spells to keep our home safe." He started climbing up the ladder. He called back over his shoulder, "You have to remember, it's not just about the complexity of casting a particular spell, or even the energy it takes to maintain it. It also must be strong enough to withstand other Eleiyon trying to break it. Bana always says when you cast a spell, you must cast it imagining that someone out there is trying to undo it. She's something special all right." And as I followed him up the ladder, I got the sense he was much more interested in Bana than he let on.

The climb was short. Again, we arrived at a solid rock ceiling. Kage muttered something, and a wooden door appeared above us, lying flat with an iron bolt and handle. "Same idea," Kage explained. "It's a password. Right now, it is *Moonbloom*, Bana's favorite flower." My suspicions about Kage's feelings were confirmed. "The door will only reveal itself when you say it aloud. And only a few of us know it. Bana changes it regularly as a precaution. You never know who is listening. Thalen has agents everywhere, especially in the forests," Kage added darkly.

Kage lifted the hatch. Sunlight streamed in and greeted my face with a sweet kiss. It wasn't even that sunny, but compared to the underground world, it felt delicious, like walking into the just-baked golden crust of an apple pie.

I basked in the winter rays. "I don't know how you all do it. To live for so long underground, I'd go crazy," I added.

"Constantly being on the run gets old," Kage answered simply. "There are tradeoffs for safety. For what we have down there." He shrugged as if the choice wasn't really a choice at all.

The forest around us was quiet. We'd come back south after we'd walked through Bana's portal outside of the camp that night. The air was cooler and crisper than it had been farther north, and the drapes of moss no longer coated the tree trunks.

"So this is the Thior Woods?"

"Yup. About as far east as you can go and still be Fira. Actually, the kitchen and dining hall are technically under the border of Rimean," Kage added as an afterthought.

We walked side-by-side through the forest. It was sparse compared to the forests at home, or even the ones we'd traveled through on the way to Kiromar. Pines and firs here were more massive than any trees I'd ever seen. Straight, sky-scraping trunks shot up from the ground. The pine branches formed a triangle, as if to write on the sky.

The silence was nice. Kage seemed lost in his own thoughts as well. Probably still fuming over the denial of his request to infiltrate the Archai. I couldn't blame either of them. Undercover with the Archai would be difficult. Kyran and Cyrus trained with their soldiers almost daily. The Archai knew each other. Of course, if it was done quickly and carefully, before anyone realized a stranger was amongst them...but then again, Kage knew everything. If he were captured and tortured for information, that would put the whole Refuge at risk. But to know what Kyran, Cyrus and his father were planning now... To know exactly why they betrayed me, why they wanted the metal shards and what they planned to do next. If Kage could get us that information, wasn't it worth the risk? I debated the pros and cons of each option as we wandered through the woods.

Something rustled above me, and I felt a tug on my mind, as if my thoughts were snagged by some invisible fishing rod. I looked up in the direction of the tug. Nothing. Only bare branches swayed in the light winter breeze. I turned to continue walking and felt the tug again. I spun around, looking frantically into the sky. The tug became a gentle coax, a nudge on my thoughts. I followed it, sending my own thoughts down the line connecting to whatever was on the other side. Then, a gentle whisper. It was the sound of leaves swaying in a fall breeze. "Stop walking. There is a camp up ahead. Archai. They're looking for you." The voice stopped, and the tug disappeared just as suddenly as it had come.

"Aila...what the —-?" Kage said behind me.

"Shh." I placed my finger to my nose, cutting him off, not removing my eyes from the branches above us. I waited, listening for more, searching for that line. I'd just heard a tree. I was sure of it. I'd seen Naleiri talk to trees countless times. I'd witnessed her respond to the same invisible hook. *I could hear trees. How is that possible?*

"There's an Archai camp ahead of us. They're searching for me. That way." I pointed, indicating the direction the tree had shared with me.

"What?" Kage asked, looking baffled. "An Archai camp? How do you know?" he asked suspiciously, but his hand now rested on the hilt of his sword.

"The trees..." I whispered, still trying to work through it myself. "A warning from the trees," I said again, recalling the warning they'd given Naleiri so long ago about the strange woman in our cottage. A warning we all but ignored.

"We need to go. Now," I said firmly.

Kage looked around, perplexed but on edge. He grabbed my hand as we marched back toward the hidden entrance. "I didn't know you were Eleyi."

"I'm not. I mean, I haven't been. Before. I—" I stammered, because the truth was, I didn't know what to think. "It's all just happening so fast now. I don't know...I don't understand." Three years of nothing and now, suddenly, I was an Elemental with powers being hunted by Thalen and all of Fira. And I could talk to trees?

We didn't speak the rest of the way back to the Refuge and even as we maneuvered through the narrow tunnels. Kage brought us to the Banquet Hall, where Manu was sitting. He wanted to report the proximity of the Archai camp.

Manu sat alone at the end of a table against the wall. A cup of tea and an untouched chocolate pastry sat in front of him. I felt a sudden pang in my chest at seeing the pastry. Naleiri's favorite. Manu held a book open, with the cover facing the table, preventing me from seeing what it was. Kage slid onto the bench opposite him while I remained standing awkwardly next to the table.

"Reports of an Archai camp, not far from here," Kage announced.

Manu looked up from his book. Concern colored his eyes, but otherwise, his expression was neutral. "You saw them?"

Kage cast a quick glance at me before answering, "Not exactly."

Manu looked between Kage and me. Then, apparently deciding not to question it, or more likely, deciding he would ask Kage later when I wasn't around, he closed the book. "Let's check it out."

They left without another word. Kage gave a curt nod as he passed me and left the hall. The book still sat where Manu had closed it, the cover now visible. It was a map of Kiakora. Inside the western territory was a dark mass outlined with a yellow border. Curiosity trumped manners, and I opened the book. The Archai's triangle marked the inside cover.

Caeru had given Manu this book. I was sure of it. I didn't understand everything that was at play here, but Caeru told me about the dagger for a reason. Baku gave me his shard for the same reason. The key to end all of this, to stop Thalen was that dagger. And Caeru gave me everything I needed to find the other pieces.

The truth was, that I couldn't do anything alone. I needed help. And even though I didn't like the idea of working with a Shade, Manu and his crew did seem like my best bet. And they hadn't done anything to deserve my distrust. Not yet anyway.

32

The tunnels were darker than normal. I didn't pass a single person as I strolled down the winding corridors toward the Banquet Hall, where I'd figured they'd all be eating dinner. I worked through what I was going to say. I would share what I knew about the metal shard and Baku. I'd admit that I'd turned over an indescribably powerful object to the Archai and that it was now in the hands of the Lord of Flame. I'd tell them my suspicions for where Kyran and his father would go next.

The Banquet Hall was full, buzzing with merry chatter and the joyful tinkle of cutlery on dishes. I hadn't realized there were so many of us down here. There had to be at least forty Eleiyon at the tables, of all ages. Children, who'd finished eating earlier than their parents, sprinted up and down the aisles between the long benches, playing an imaginary game of cat and mouse.

I scanned the tables, looking for the familiar faces of the group that made this whole community possible. Not there. I retraced my steps toward the training room. Voices coming from down the small corridor stopped me in my tracks.

"I'm telling you...she said the trees told her about the Archai camp. And Manu and I went back out afterward and checked. Sure enough, there was a camp."

"Elementals don't have that power—" Bana started.

"Well, she does," Kage said firmly.

"Are we sure she's an Elemental? I mean, are we just taking the Archai's word for it that they got the right girl in the first place?" Asfa asked.

"No." Manu's raspy voice entered the debate. "She grabbed a fire lasso in a duel with one of the Archai in the camp. She was able to match its energy."

"Then what?" Asfa asked.

"I don't know," whispered Manu into the room after a moment of silence, as if saying it too loudly would make the chance of it disappear.

"What could it mean? I could look in the library," Bana spoke up softly. "There are probably enchantments, ancient magic maybe. Do the Saga have any stories like this?"

"No," came Asfa's brisk voice. "But like you said, there are other kinds of magic. Older and more powerful than the gifts the Eleiyon wield."

"It's just too much of a coincidence," Bana stated, her voice becoming stronger. "She's been tangled up with the House of Fira. Who knows what all she knows that she's not revealing. There happens to be something different about THIS Elemental, the one we rescued from being turned over to Thalen. And she's the same one you—"

"Enough. Speculating is a waste of our time. We've hit a dead end. We need answers. I only know of one place now that we can get them," Manu said quietly to the room.

"No. No way. It's too dangerous to go there right now. I mean, Manu, you and Kage just found an Archai camp at our doorstep, and they are only one of three groups looking for us. And you want to traipse across the entirety of Fira?" This was the first time I heard Bana lose her temper.

"Are you suggesting what I think you're suggesting?" Kage asked, ignoring Bana.

"The Ancient One," Asfa declared quietly.

"It's time. We've been holding off on doing this—"

"That's because it's dangerous," Asfa cut him off.

"Manu. Please think about this. Asfa is right. Even if we make it unde-tected across Fira with Archai, bounty hunters, and Shades looking for us, the forest itself is waiting. Everything in there is designed to kill. We could very well go on a quest for answers and not come back at all!" Bana finished.

"Sounds like an adventure." I could almost hear Kage's grin as he spoke.

"We go. We've sat here for too long hoping things will change. No one will save us. We need to save ourselves. Start planning it out." Manu stated finally, ending the debate.

My head was reeling as I stepped back from the dimly lit hallway. I quickly padded down the corridor and made the left that would lead me back to my room. My thoughts were jumping like popped sweet corn on every kernel of information I'd overheard.

I played back the conversation in my mind. What had Bana been about to say? I needed answers, and I didn't want to wait until they tested me enough to reveal them. Besides, if everything Bana and Asfa said was true, I needed to leave tonight. I couldn't risk any of them going and not returning. The community here, all the Eleiyon they'd saved, they relied on them. I wouldn't have more death on my conscience.

***

Night fell over the Refuge. The stars twinkled on the enchanted ceiling of the atrium, watching me as I tiptoed quietly toward the exit Kage had shown me earlier. I found the end of the tunnel and sure enough, the ladder had already materialized for me. I climbed, heading toward the hidden hatch at the top.

"*Moonbloom*," I whispered, hoping Bana hadn't changed the password yet. The door appeared. *Yes!* I slid the bolt, pushed the door open with a loud creak, and climbed out.

As far as I could tell, from how Kage described our location, I was still far enough north that if I headed directly west, I'd pass north of Aodhen and avoid the city altogether. The Ancient Forest was on the other side of Lake Luan. The complete opposite side of the territory. Thankfully, the Archai camp I'd found was just north of here, so if I moved quickly, I could avoid them too. *Unless they were heading in the same direction as me.*

I'd have to put some distance between us tonight so that I wouldn't have to keep looking over my shoulder. The forest was quiet. Not the peaceful calm of winter that I'd grown to love, but an expectant calm. It was heavy with anticipation of what was to come.

I wasn't the best at navigation. Most of what I'd learned about the forest around Aodhen had, admittedly, been the result of fortunate accidents or trial and error. I'd spent a lot of time exploring, running through the forest, walking to Aodhen or to Orchard's Clearing, to the small meadow where I gathered herbs, or to the stream that wound around the cottage's perimeter. This was different. I had a destination, and I didn't have the luxury of time. A mistake could lead me too close to Aodhen, or on a perpendicular path with the Archai, or something much worse.

Naleiri had told me stories about the teachings of the Eleyi, and how everything they did, all their traditions and beliefs, were tied to the natural world. One night, in Orchard's Clearing, she'd pointed out Karu, the Guiding Star. "Most Eleiyon," she'd said, "have forgotten about this star. They don't think they need it. A simple enchantment can get them where they want to go. But we always look to Karu. It's constant, immutable. It will always guide you if you remember to look for it."

I peered up at the sky now, trying to locate the Guiding Star the way Naleiri had taught me so long ago.

"Find the star that glows orange. Two to the left and one up...there," I whispered. Now that I'd picked it out, it clearly shined brighter than the other stars in the sky, and I was surprised that I hadn't seen it right away. According to Naleiri, this star would always lead to the land of the first Forest Nymphs. The north. Which meant, if I wanted to head due west, I'd need to turn ninety degrees to my left. I mumbled to myself in the darkness. Confident in my first planned attempt at navigation, I set out into the night forest.

<hr>

A twinge of guilt settled in my chest as I walked farther from the secret site of the Refuge. They'd been good to me, not to mention rescuing me from torture and certain death. They told me the truth when I asked for it, or at least some of it anyway. They clearly hadn't told me everything, but could I blame them? Neither had I.

Perhaps our paths would cross again. I was certain I wouldn't be able to find the entrance to the Refuge again. Even now, I'd gone far enough that I didn't trust myself to recognize the exact place in the forest that hid the underground sanctuary. I cast an involuntary look over my shoulder, tucking away the nagging feeling. I turned and continued walking.

"Is your plan to go all the way to the Ancient Forest on foot?"

I jumped, startled by the sudden intrusion.

Manu leaned casually against the trunk of tree in front of me. His long braids emerged from his hood where they fell over his shoulders. He took a bite of an apple as he sauntered over to me.

My spine stiffened as he neared. For some reason, I couldn't dissociate him from the other Shades, the ones who'd kept me in three miserable days of darkness. Why had it been so easy for me to see Kage differently when he had the same gift as the Archai? As Kyran?

Deep down I knew the answer. Fire was familiar. It was something I understood. Something, apparently, I could wield myself. Shadow was foreign. It was a gift I'd never witnessed until it was being used against me. It felt dark and unnatural, like anyone possessing that gift must be as cold and lifeless as the shadows they controlled.

"I'm not going back," I announced firmly, though I was certain if Manu wanted me back at the Refuge, there would be very little I could do about it.

"I know." My eyes flicked up to meet his, surprised by his response. His face was also beautiful. Though not in the same way as Kyran's. It was more rugged. It was the difference between the shimmering surface of the ocean and the jagged peaks of snow-capped mountains.

"I need answers." I said flatly.

"We all do." After a moment, he added, "The journey is too long and too dangerous without a portal. There are eyes everywhere between here and there. You'll never make it unnoticed." He pointed a long index finger to the trees before continuing. "The Ancient Forest itself is treacherous. Many who venture there never return. And that was before Thalen. The forest protects itself. Now, with everything that is happening, who knows what it will be like." As if to emphasize his point, Kika emerged from the darkness behind him, a personification of night itself. Her yellow eyes shone brightly, like two stars plucked from the sky.

He was right, of course. I recalled the deathly screech of the Ozars. "So, what are you saying...? We need answers. And that's where we can find them." *I have to go.* I left it unsaid.

"I'm saying...I'm asking. Can I join you?"

I stared at him for a moment. It was one of the last things I wanted. It would be nice to have company, and sure, a portal would make things a whole lot easier, but I'd much prefer Kage or Bana to him. I shrugged indifferently. Besides, I doubted it was a genuine question. He would probably just follow behind me anyway.

"Great." And one of the first smiles I'd seen, creased his normally stoic face, making it much more breathtaking than either the oceans or the mountains.

We landed in a meadow, near an outcropping of rocks. The small clearing separated two forests. The one behind us was what I was used to, like the one near Aodhen. A deciduous forest with a mix of maples and oaks that stretched their bare branches straight up to the sky. The air was frigid and crisp, a clear indication we'd returned to the heart of Fira. But the forest in front of us was like nothing I'd ever seen before. A cloudy haze hung over lush green plants of all sizes that bent and folded this way and that, creating an impenetrable barrier. Leaves the size of Eleiyon children adorned the tallest trees. There was no other word for it: it was a rainforest.

A misty haze clung to the trees in front of us but dissipated entirely at the clearing's border. It was magic, an ancient magic rooted in Kiakora and kept alive for eternity. The Ancient Forest.

A sense of foreboding crept over me as we neared the edge.

"Are you ready?" Manu asked softly, casting a sideways look at me and Kika. He wouldn't push me. If I changed my mind now and decided to turn back, he'd take me. And for some reason, despite it being the exact opposite of what I wanted to do, it put my mind at ease knowing that it was an option.

"Let's go." I took a deep breath and stepped into the forest.

The trees teamed with life. Birds squawked loudly overhead, cicadas sang into the dense canopy and monkeys swung playfully from the high branches. It seemed...untouched by everything outside its borders. It was like it existed in some protected glass sphere, unreachable by Thalen, by the darkness, or by Eleiyon.

Naleiri would have loved to have come here. I imagined the warmth emanating from her body as she chatted merrily with monkeys or felt the memories of one of these ancient trees. I smiled sadly to myself. Kika bounded playfully through the dense brush ahead of us before disappearing entirely.

"She'll be back," Manu assured, seeing the worry that creased my brow. "She's happy to be here. This was her home originally, you know...My father found her here in the rainforest, abandoned. He took her home with him. Gave her to me..." he explained, the same sadness creeping into his voice that had been there the last time he spoke of his father. I wanted to ask him more about what had happened, but I held my tongue.

"What do you want to ask the Ancient One?" Manu's voice broke through the forest ambiance, trying to normalize this strange place.

I turned to him sheepishly. "Besides how to stop Thalen?" I asked, applying a matter-of-fact tone to disguise the truth that I did indeed have other things I wanted to know. Things about my past.

He shrugged. "The question I have for the Ancient One is how; how he could have escaped Nagrimar. It's supposed to be impossible." He looked genuinely frustrated. "I've scoured libraries across the territories looking for something... I can't find a loophole anywhere. And if what you said Caeru told you is true, how do we kill him?"

We marched on in silence for a moment. "What do you think it means, that I was able to hear the trees the other night?" He stopped wading through the dense brush and turned to look at me.

"Have you ever been able to...communicate with the natural world before?"

"No. With Kage was the first time."

"What about now? What do you hear?"

I blinked and looked around. I'd been so caught up in gaining information from Manu, I'd completely forgotten to see if I could connect with the forest. It was the perfect place to try. "I'm not sure I can. Control it, I mean."

"Clear your mind. Take a deep breath and feel the power inside of you. It's like a small kernel, an ember maybe, tucked inside of your soul."

I remembered the warm sensation I'd felt in my chest each time I'd tried to use a power, and even times I hadn't been consciously calling to my gifts. Memories of escaping Baku's tightening tail with a sudden surge, or my fight with Drata where I vaulted through the air. Had I been calling on my gifts all this time and not known it?

I closed eyes and breathed deeply. The air was humid. Its thickness caught in my nostrils. I reached to touch the closest tree trunk. An ember sparked inside my chest, just as Manu described it, traveling down my outstretched arm toward the tree.

"You shouldn't be here," an old voice bellowed from the ground. I felt the vibrations of its bass in my bones. "This forest is not friendly to your kind. Leave now, before you can't leave at all." The voice quieted into a slow, low hum before disappearing altogether.

My eyes cracked open as I dropped my hand. My heart fluttered with the adrenaline of the connection.

"Well?"

"A warning. It says...it's not safe for us here. We're not welcome and...we should turn back."

"Nothing we didn't already know," he said as he continued a moderate pace through the foliage. "But I'm glad you're making progress at commanding it."

It hadn't been a fluke. I could really connect with nature. Why were my powers only revealing themselves now? I mused as we traveled deeper into the forest. A bright red something in the periphery caught my attention, pulling me from my thoughts.

It was a plant unlike anything I'd seen before. Green at the base with a crimson stalk shooting straight into the air, topped with a yellow bubble of liquid. It stood at least as high as my chest. There wasn't just one of these peculiar plants, but an entire grove of them blossoming in the undergrowth. Bees buzzed from bubble to bubble, gathering nectar while small, curious mammals scurried on the ground at the base of the unusual plants. They had long hoses where mouths might have been, most likely to slurp up the yellow bubbles. I stepped cautiously toward the grove. Another step. Another.

A firm, calloused hand clasped my wrist gently. "Careful," Manu whispered. "This looks like—"

But whatever it looked like, I didn't hear. A not-at-all-gentle, sticky vine clamped around my other wrist. From behind the red grove of sticky stamen, a massive, almond-shaped plant rose up. The vine started to reel me into its base. The clam-like plant opened its mouth, revealing a blood-red inside lined with sharp spines that dripped with yellow saliva. The bubbles weren't nectar; they were beads of saliva, luring animals to its lethal jaws. It yanked at my wrist, pulling me free from Manu's grasp. Another vine shot up and latched onto my other wrist.

"Manu!"

He took a step toward me, but he was stuck too. Vines had wound around his feet, immobilizing him. Panic took over. I was being reeled into the gaping mouth, like a helpless trout on the wrong end of a fishing rod. Manu could handle himself.

I turned my attention to the vines binding my wrists and searched desperately for the ember in my chest. I threw all my energy into my search, trying to find the bead of warmth and send it toward the grappling vines.

At last, I found it. "Stop!" I shouted down the connection. "Stop! Please. We're here to help."

"And you will help..." a bone-chilling voice answered. "Your bones will nourish my body; your fat will lure more of our forest friends to join us. It has been too long since we've had such a large meal..." The shrill voice transformed into a vicious cackle.

My legs were bound now as well. Despite my struggling, I was pulled closer and closer. A warm breeze touched my face, and I realized, with another bout of panic, it was the plant's breath. A morbid question popped into my head as I looked at the gnashing jaws. Would I be mashed to bits by the giant spine-like teeth, or would I sit, clamped inside the bubbling saliva-filled mouth as my body decayed?

I lashed out against either option but couldn't break free. I was in the air. The vines held me high above the ground. It was going to drop me into the open mouth, like a long-awaited delicacy. The vines squirmed up my chest and face. Tightening. Constricting my breathing and immobilizing me to the point where I couldn't struggle against my restraints anymore. And then darkness as they sealed off my eyes.

There was a squelching sound, and I hit the ground with a thud. The vines loosened and fell away from my body. I turned in time to see Manu, his black weaponry drawn at the end of each arm. He moved quicker than I'd seen any fighter move. Another spin and the last of the tentacle-like vines fell to the forest floor. The gaping mouth opened in a shrill scream. Manu jumped into the air, arcing his axe over his head and bringing it down on the plant with a sickening crunch. The plant quivered momentarily before sliding away, completely cut in half.

Manu turned to me. The concern disappeared from his face as soon as he saw I was okay and already getting to my feet. The black weapons faded to dark shadows that crawled back up his arms. As they traveled, they formed various geometric shapes and tribal lines until settling on a final design that extended the length of his arms and spread across his broad chest, peeking through his collar at the base of his neck.

He reached out his hand to help me to my feet. I grasped it, allowing him to pull me up. I was unharmed, but my knees trembled with adrenaline, which I tried to mask by looking anywhere but directly at Manu. Remnants of the carnivorous plant were strewn across the grove, and the beautiful red plants now looked angry as they began to wilt.

"Thanks," was all I could say.

"Let's go." He dropped his hand from mine as he brushed past me.

<hr>

We avoided hacking through the forest, knowing we were already unwelcome guests. I followed Manu silently, watching the muscles in his sculpted back through his sweat-soaked shirt as we made our way slowly through the dense underbrush.

"We should rest here for the night," Manu called back after hours of silent trudging.

I could barely see the sky through the canopy of leaves, but it was still clear that night was descending on the forest.

"Luckily it's too warm to need a fire," Manu continued. "I doubt the forest would take too kindly to that." He hopped down from a massive boulder he'd been using as a perch to scan the surroundings. "This is as safe a place as any." I surveyed the area. He was right. The outcropping of the boulder kept the undergrowth from the immediate area, creating a small clearing where we could sit and lean against the rock, protecting our backs.

I didn't object. I was exhausted, and besides, we were in the forest now. Night would come regardless of whether we stopped or not, and I'd prefer to be in a place that looked semi-safe rather than stumbling through a forest of flesh-eating flora. And if those were the plants, what of the other creatures that called this dreaded place home? I plopped down against the rock, my back and legs moaning in appreciation. A shadow cast by the tree branch above us danced on the ground in the dimming light. Suddenly, it went unnaturally rigid and then darted off.

I turned to Manu questioningly.

"Sentries," he said simply.

"How do you know where we're going?" I asked after he sat for a minute, leaning up against the boulder next to me.

"I don't for sure. My father mapped it out years ago, before he came here. I remember watching him comb through book after book in our library, looking for information on the Ancient Forest. It's a place everyone has heard of, but where no one goes, so a lot of the information is theoretical. The portal we went through brought us to the edge closest to where the Ancient One should be, and just a straight hike in from there."

"HA!" My barking laugh was loud against the darkening forest backdrop. "Easier said than done, huh."

"Well, definitely if you take unplanned detours," he said slyly.

"Tell me about it. Now I know how my carrots feel," I muttered under my breath, just loud enough for him to hear.

He chuckled. "Well, if we get too lost, we always have Kika." He nodded to the boulder above us. I almost jumped out of my skin at the sight of the massive cat lounging lazily above us, licking the bottom of her giant paw. Now I understood why Kage struggled to get used to her. I hadn't heard any sign of her approach.

Manu continued, clearly unsurprised by Kika's arrival. "We can make it to the Ancient One tomorrow if we move quickly. The magic here is too thick to create a portal, and even if you could manage to create one, you wouldn't be able to weave through the maze of spells and enchantments here," he said, anticipating my next question.

We sat in silence for another endless minute. "Your father was looking for a way to stop Thalen too?" I asked softly.

His face went distant. Grief tugged at his eyes, which were looking not at the forest in front of us but at some far-off memory. "Yes and no. He didn't know it was Thalen. He saw the darkness causing the diseased trees and believed it was a sign. He wanted to know how to save them and our home, Kiromar. He wanted to know what was coming," he said finally. "He came too late." Bitterness coated his tone as he tossed the clump of dirt he'd been mindlessly crumbling in his hand.

I wanted to press further. What exactly happened to his father? What were those last moments like when Thalen confronted him?

"What—"

"We should rest. We still have a way to go tomorrow...and we can't be sure how difficult the journey will be." He put a definitive end to our get-to-know-you session.

I was about to protest when I felt a gentle tug on the back of my neck, making my nerves tingle. I looked up to see Kika's starry eyes peering down at me. I tried to locate the kernel of warmth again. It was easier to find this time. A quiet strength emanated from Kika. It had a slight edge to it, a warning, and although she didn't say it, I knew she was telling me that if I pushed Manu too hard for answers about his past, I'd push him away completely.

Questions circled my mind, one chasing the other. But I was tired. My legs ached, and my eyes drooped. *Rest wasn't such an awful idea*, and I drifted off to sleep.

33

"Where is she?" The woman's shrill voice pierced the night, rising above the crackling fires and screams from the other houses. The smell of charred flesh punctured the comforting scent of burning wood, filling the night air with foreboding. Smoke and ash hovered over the blazing houses in the center of town. A slight breeze started to blow the cloud eastward.

"I don't know who you're talking about," a woman croaked from the ground. Figures crowded around the crumpled mass.

One of the figures, a woman, spoke. "You don't have as many friends as you think you do in this little pigsty of a town...People talk..." Her lip curled up with disdain as she eyed the burning village. Her pale, slender fingers toyed with the blade of her double-edged axe.

One of the others landed a strong kick to the woman on the ground, who whimpered at the impact. She groaned in pain as she rolled to the side, clutching her stomach. Then a swift movement and a flash of green lit the sky as the woman twirled the axe above her head.

"Aila...Aila!"

My eyes fluttered open to Manu's face looming inches from my own. His hands gripped either shoulder shaking me awake. "It's okay. It's okay. You were having a nightmare...a pretty intense one by the sound of it," he explained softly.

Drata. She'd been looking for someone. And the poor woman on the ground had refused to help her, even though it had cost her life.

I blinked back the tears that swelled in the corner of my eyes. Who had Drata been looking for? I swallowed the only answer that floated to the surface. The reason I was always having these nightmares. The reason I couldn't recall a single thing about my past. The reason that Drata was still searching for me.

Manu's hands felt like life support braces, roots grounding me to the real world, reminding me that I was living and breathing. I found my voice. "Ahem..." I cleared my throat and tested the steadiness of my voice inconspicuously, or so I hoped. "I'm sorry. I have..." Still shaky. "Ahem...I have vivid dreams sometimes," I finished quickly, offering a partial truth.

He let his hands slip from my arms, and I thought I detected disappointment in his eyes as he backed away from me. "No need to apologize. I didn't want to wake you, but I'm pretty sure you would have brought every creature in earshot to our feet if I let you continue much longer."

My cheeks warmed with embarrassment. *Liro's balls.* "Hopefully I didn't embarrass myself too much," I said shyly, allowing a sliver of honesty.

"We need to get going anyway. It's just about dawn." He nodded toward the barely visible stretch of sky above us. He tossed me a satchel of nuts and dried cranberries, which I snatched out of the air. "This is all I had time to grab. I was in a rush...someone left quite unexpectedly." He flashed a lopsided grin as I knocked back a handful of the snack mix. It was a first sign that maybe he wasn't so serious all the time.

We resumed our slow march through the dense forest. Kika had disappeared again. I followed Manu distractedly through the dusty sunrise, barely noticing as he picked his way carefully through the ever-thickening jungle. My thoughts kept turning to my dream. The gleam of the axe blade in the moonlight; the woman's terminal defiance; and the flash of green that silenced the rest of the memories. Manu could get whatever answers he wanted from the Ancient One, but I had my own agenda.

The foliage was starting to thin out the deeper we went into the forest, something I registered as being counterintuitive. It was as if the forest was the outer barrier, protecting whatever lived at its center. My boot squished as it sunk into ankle-deep mud.

"Ugh," I groaned, lifting my mud-laden boot in the air.

"We're close," Manu said, looking back at me. "There's a marsh at the center of the forest where the Ancient One is." Fear lodged in my throat. A marsh. The inky coils of the Mavtir curled around my hands again, dragging the terrifying memories from Lake Luan to the present.

"A marsh. My favorite..." I mumbled, trying to let the sarcasm calm my nerves. Manu looked back at me, a question almost formed on the tip of his tongue. But he turned his head, deciding against asking it. He seemed to have just as many questions for me as I did for him but was equally unwilling to voice them. We were on opposite sides of a canyon, completely ignoring the bridge that connected us.

Manu was right. We weren't in the marsh long before it transformed into a pond-like oasis. The ring of reedy marshland surrounded us, followed by the band of thick rainforest. We were at the center.

Dark green lily pads decorated the pond's clear surface. The croak of bullfrogs added to the chorus of cicadas and mingled with the tweets and whistles of the birds in the branches above. Mist hovered over the surface of the pond, and despite being just as warm as the rainforest around us, I felt a chill in my bones and a static in the air.

It was an indescribable pulsing energy radiating from the clearing that let us know we were in a deeply magical place. At the center of the pond was a grove of three massive river cypresses. Their thick trunks were partially submerged in the water, and the ends of their moss-covered branches dipped, tracing the water's surface.

"That's her," Manu whispered, not taking his eyes from the three trees. I followed his gaze back to the grove. They were ancient indeed. The light brown of their trunks looked like fossilized bones.

As I peered at the trunk, mesmerized by the color, the bark shifted. I blinked. Again, I stared at the trunk, where I could have sworn there had been movement moments before. Maybe the heat of the rainforest had made me delirious.

"Did you...?" My unfinished question hung in the air as the bark shifted again and the face of an old woman materialized in the trunk of the front-most tree.

The Ancient One's wrinkled face was formed by the folds in the bark, her mouth, a notch in the tree's otherwise smooth surface. "It's nice to see you, Prince of Shadow." Her voice was soft but grating, carrying countless eons of experience.

"Likewise," Manu called back clearly, bowing his head slightly, though careful not to break eye contact with the Ancient One. I mimicked the bow, forcing myself to hold my gaze steady as well.

"And your guest...ahh...the Elemental." Her pupil-less eyes assessed my body, my face, and, as I'd come to expect after both Baku and Queen Ramuwren, the mark hidden beneath my tunic.

Before I could respond, two other faces appeared on each of the trunks on either side of the first. To the left of the old woman's face was a child's. The bark on her tree had gone completely smooth to form the plump, youthful cheeks of a young girl. Despite her appearance, her eyes were old. The other was somewhere in the middle, not old, but not young. Her features were sharp and angular, fiercely carved out of the trunk. Her eyes were slits, making her smooth, bold features angry and threatening.

"Your father was not satisfied with our answers then, Shadow Prince?" the young one asked, a dangerous tone playing on her words.

"Quite satisfied," Manu said softly. "I'm sorry to say, he's gone. Though, you already know that."

"And now his son comes seeking more...so soon? You already have a gift from our forest." I turned to my left where Kika lurked at the edge of the clearing.

"It's been ten years. Much has changed; new answers are needed...and yes, an invaluable gift," Manu responded. I admired his confidence. The three faces had all but stripped my courage.

"Only ten years..."

"The same time passes differently, sister" the old one interjected.

"You with the riddles. The same is different. Different can be the same. Just speak candidly, Seyi!" the young one mocked.

"Not changed, Shadowmaster, rather, much has now been revealed," Seyi stated.

"What we are saying..." cut in the young one, "is that you should not have returned here. The forest is no longer safe; not for you, not for us," it explained with a note of exasperation.

"We know. That's why we're here. None of Kiakora is safe anymore. Not with the threat of the House of Fira. Not with evils escaping from Nagrimar. We are here to end this once and for all. We seek your guidance, your advice on how this can be stopped. Forever."

"Ha! Kiakora's history is strewn with the Eleiyon only acting in the interest of the Eleiyon. Betraying Kiakora, betraying each other. Your kind only sews death and destruction." The young face turned angry, her high voice slicing across the pool.

"Not all Eleiyon, Cali. There have always been those who would be fair amidst the foulness of this world," countered Seyi.

"Parasites. A plague," Cali muttered under her breath, no louder than the faintest whisper of leaves in a soft breeze. Then louder, "As I told your father, tell me why you are deserving of our help."

"But you did help him. You told him something that could save our home. He was... erased before he could share it with me. Help us, as you helped him."

I listened half-heartedly to their banter, but I couldn't shift my focus from the third face. Her eyes were lifeless, unlike the other two; she stared unblinkingly back into my own.

"We will hear your questions now." Her voice was both deep and feminine, sending ripples across the water's surface. Her mouth didn't move, but her words echoed in my head. I turned to see if Manu had heard it too. One look told me he had. He also faced the third tree.

Manu opened his mouth, but it was my voice that cut across the water. I had the feeling that the third face had been talking to me, even if we had both heard it.

"Why can't I remember anything about my past? What happened to me?" I finished the questions quickly. This wasn't why we came here, but I needed to know.

It was the old woman who answered as the other two looked at me discerningly. "I hope you did not journey all the way here to ask us questions you can answer amongst yourselves."

"I...I don't know what you mean. I—"

"Next question," Cali interrupted.

So much for closure. I didn't know what kind of answer I'd expected, but I needed something more than this.

It was Manu's turn. If he was annoyed by me usurping his opportunity to speak with a personal question, he didn't show it. "What did you tell my father?" His strong voice carried across the water.

"Prophecies are funny things. They are given in the past, speak of the present, and can determine the future. But they are so fickle. One word from us could change it. Undo it. Ensure it...I always discourage my sister from giving them to you, Eleiyon, because you take them so seriously," Seyi said coyly.

"A prophecy? You told him a prophecy?"

"A prophecy is true when we reveal it, but one word, one choice, can alter the course of events entirely. Retelling the prophecy to you now...could render it false."

"Tell us."

Seyi didn't break our gazes either as she contemplated it and then said, "Go ahead, sister."

I expected the echo in my head this time as the third spoke again. "I am Veyo. I see what is to come. It is very...unorthodox for me to retell a prophecy. Though I do admit, I am curious to see what you will do with it." She closed her eyes. A cold wind whipped through the oasis, sending shivers up my spine and blowing loose strands of hair across my face. The crackle of energy curled into the wind as Veyo spoke into our minds:

An enemy both new and old
Will stoke fears, and make them bold,
Shadows will fly and the North will fall
As evils escape and cross the wall.
She who tames the wind and rides the floods,
Who bends mountains and has fire in her blood.
She who hears the whispers of trees,
Is the same who holds the key.
There are five pieces of one that she must wield,
And only to her will the darkness yield.

The wind stopped abruptly as Veyo concluded the prophecy. The echo of her words pounded in my head. An Elemental. They were the only ones who could wield more than one elemental gift. Thalen was exiled millennia ago, when Nagrimar was first created. In fact, he was the reason it even existed. But he has returned. He was the enemy, both new and old. And he was after Elementals to prevent this prophecy from ever coming true. *He's after me.* I thought of the trees' warning outside the Refuge. Could I be...? No. I wasn't trained. I wasn't powerful. There was no way...

But Manu spoke the question I couldn't even voice in my head. "Is Aila the Elemental in this prophecy?" And even as he asked, I wasn't entirely sure I wanted the answer.

Seyi spoke this time. "The truth is prophecies are intimately woven together with free will. Parts of this prophecy have already come to pass, and others may never happen. As for your question..." Her eyes shifted to meet mine. "You are an Elemental; you're alive during the time of Thalen; can you defeat him? Will you defeat him? Those are questions only you can answer, choices only you can make."

"The five pieces of one. This thing that can be wielded by the Elemental, what is it?" Manu pressed.

"Ahh," Cali cooed, her previous impatience having subsided. "A powerful and ancient magic, older than this world, protected by just as powerful and ancient of a magic. If it is ever again constructed, its wielder would be... unstoppable."

The dagger. Now at least I knew how many other pieces to look for.

"It could be a tool or a weapon," added Seyi.

"To build or to destroy the future," Cali chimed in.

"But what is it? What are we looking for?"

"This is the second time you've asked a question you already have the answers for." Cali's anger flared up again. "Our patience is waning."

Manu didn't know about the dagger. But I did. They said we already had the answers about my past. Did Manu know what happened to me? Before I could speak, Manu cut in.

"What is the House of Fira doing?"

Cali answered, "The Lord of Flame has always been concerned only with power, his power. It's all-consuming..."

"If he is not careful, it will consume him," added Seyi.

"Before this is over, he will sacrifice his family, betray his territory, and risk Kiakora, to hold on to it," said the third.

"That was not my question," Manu said firmly. I was shocked at his candidness with the three trees.

"No, I suppose it was not," said Cali slyly. "Thalen and the Lord of Flame are each concerned with the prophecy..."

"Though a different piece concerns them," Seyi added vaguely.

My heart pounded. The piece of the dagger I'd taken from Baku and all-but-willingly turned over to Kyran's father was like an arrow in my chest. Shame burned my cheeks, and I felt the third face's unwavering stare.

"You already know of what she speaks." Veyo's voice sounded in my head. I could tell from Manu's lack of attention that she was speaking only to me. "If he finds all the pieces, we are doomed. The prophecy will be lost; hope will be lost; Kiakora will be lost."

Her words echoed endlessly in my mind. *What had I done?* I'd handed over the first piece of the puzzle. I was certain the Lord of Flame already suspected what I'd learned. That the pieces were guarded by the Protectors. *Find them, find the dagger.* The library in Aodhen, scouring the world for ancient texts, curating and organizing them—it all hadn't been for some societal enlightenment. It had been to stockpile eons of knowledge into a single place and cut it off from everyone else. They were the only ones searching for it. They weren't searching because of the prophecy; they'd dug up legends about this ancient powerful object and were out to find it. And Thalen was too concerned with finding the Elemental to worry about finding the dagger.

Kiakora hadn't simply forgotten the stories of this dagger or the Protectors; the House of Fira had stolen them. And no one knew what they were missing...until now. My heart jumped to my throat as it dawned on me. I was more than just a pawn in Kyran's father's game of allegiance with Thalen, though I served that purpose well; I was a loose end.

Another surge of wind lashed against my face, yanking me out of my thoughts. The three trees' faces had gone blank, and their branches swayed ominously.

Then they were back.

"You must go...now," said Seyi.

"Wait...I have more questions."

"There's no time," Cali added, a touch of sorrow in her otherwise smooth face.

The old tree was conflicted. Then, as if they each arrived at the same conclusion in unison, they took turns, picking up where the other finished.

"Removing the shadows of your past will illuminate the path forward," Cali said.

"Isn't it from the height of the mountain that we understand the depth of the sea? Share your secrets with each other if you hope to survive," Seyi added.

"Your thread, and that of the Shadowprince, have become intertwined with Kiakora's tapestry. If you pull a single thread, you risk unraveling the whole design." I knew Veyo's voice sounded only in my head. "You are misguided, young Eleiyon. Shadow does not come from darkness, but from light." And then her voice boomed forth across the pool for all to hear "Go. Now! We know our fate; the fate of Kiakora is still being woven."

With that, the pool went placid, and the faces disappeared back into the ancient cypress trees.

Manu's eyes darted past me. I heard it now. A loud whacking and a wave of voices tumbled out of the dark forest. We started backing away slowly, eyes trained in the direction of the approaching voices. The flash of swinging machetes appeared first, and then the army of Archai emerged from the forest on the far side of the pool. Kyran and Cyrus in the lead.

My eyes locked on Kyran's. Shock froze my feet in place.

"Aila..." Manu whispered at my side, urging me to back further away. "Let's go...now!" he demanded.

But I stood there. Frozen. And then, Cyrus let out a surge of fire, creating a ring around the oasis, encircling us. We were trapped. The fire caught on the tall grasses of the marshlands. It snapped both Kyran and me out of whatever trance had held us.

"Aila!" Kyran called. "Come with me. Join us. We can fix this, together. We can make things right." More Archai emerged, hacking at the underbrush and sending spouts of flame across the pool.

Screams reached my ears, echoing endlessly in my blood. High-pitched screeches of agony made my hair stand on end, and I realized what I was hearing. The screams were not Eleiyon; they were from the forest. The trees. The grasses. The charred brush withering in the heat of the flames. Tears welled in my eyes as I stared across the hazy pool, surrounded by the smoldering forest. I sent every ounce of hatred I could toward Kyran, and toward Cyrus and the rest of the Archai with whom I'd once so desperately wanted to belong.

Warmth exploded in my chest, and the calm waters of the pool rose up and rushed toward the burning marshlands in a roiling rage. Without thinking, I waved one arm to the right, sending the waves to extinguish the flames, and with my left, the rest of the waves gathered speed and rushed into Kyran and the others on the far side of the bank. As soon as the waves landed, an army of shadows advanced on the recovering Archai.

"Aila, let's go. Now!" Manu tugged my elbow. Despite the urgency in his tone, his touch was gentle, a suggestion, not a mandate, as he let me make the decision to turn away.

We broke into a full-speed sprint, racing back into the dense cover of the rainforest. Behind us, the fires raged once again, burning everything in the small oasis. I risked one glance at the three strong cypress trees, consumed in thick black smoke as flames lapped at their ancient roots. Tears stung my eyes as I ran. The three sisters, the Ancient One. They'd known what was coming and kept talking to us.

And I was filled again with boiling hatred for the Lord of Flame. He'd come to destroy the only other place, besides his library, where Kiakora could come for answers. Where someone who was looking could find information to stop him. And I was done making excuses for Kyran. I watched the flames dance in his eyes as the Archai burned the oasis around us. Its ash was on his hands as well.

"Aila. Stop...I need to get my bearings. This forest will trap us, suck us farther in if we don't move purposefully." Manu looked around, trying to find something familiar, something that would indicate where we were and where we needed to go.

A snap of a twig breaking underfoot and a swish of something brushing plant leaves sounded in front of us. *Kika.* It was the first time the massive cat brought me a sense of relief.

Come. I felt her tug me into the forest behind her.

"She knows how to get out of here...They didn't come here for me, but I'll be a nice bonus," I said, referring to the charging Archai. "We need to move, now."

Kika turned and bounded through the rainforest with us on her heels. The thick smoke from the burning flames followed us, pursued by the crashing and thwacking sounds of the Archai.

———

With Kika's help, we made it out of the forest much more quickly than it took us to travel to our destination. We broke through the final dense boundary of the Ancient Forest, escaping into the comparably sparse meadow. Kika had already spun around, looking past us with sadness.

Following her gaze, I turned and let out a gasp. The rainforest was ablaze. Thick gray smoke clouds rose above the trees. The only part seemingly untouched was next to where we now stood. Tears rolled freely down my cheeks. All the life lost in those flames; it wasn't fair.

"I'm sorry," I whispered to Kika, because I didn't know what else to say. "I'm so sorry." *Cali was right.* The Eleiyon only brought suffering.

Kika approached me slowly. Her beautiful, silky coat stretched tight over her muscled body. I reached out a tentative hand. She nuzzled her big head under it, bringing the rest of her body closer as I knelt to the ground, embracing her in a hug. "I'm sorry," I whispered again, allowing the warmth in my chest to find its way down to her.

Kiki's sadness wrestled with her resolve. A strong, clear voice purred back into my shoulder. "We must stop them."

I looked up at Manu, who was staring down at us with a curious expression.

"There's somewhere we need to go first, before we go home." Manu's voice broke the connection between me and Kika. He looked apprehensive but re-solved as he muttered something under his breath and a blue portal materialized in front of us. "Let's go, quickly. Before anyone can join us."

I stepped through first, savoring the temporary weightlessness as space folded around us, a nice break from the heavy world we had to live in. Kika followed me, and then Manu. With a final whiff of charred wood, we disappeared into the darkness with a pop.

34

Kika's ears perked up attentively in the dusty gray clearing. The sun was still toying with the idea of tucking itself behind the horizon. Tall trees surrounded the tiny village in which I now found myself. The wooden houses, typical of the western territory, appeared all but abandoned. Some were still intact, but many had been burned down to their foundations.

"Where is everyone?" I asked, dreading the answer.

"Dead. Gone," Manu replied, walking down the gravel road that cut through the center of the small, deserted town.

Kika prowled in front of us. Her long, lean figure, every inch of her toned body, prepared to pounce at a moment's notice. Her yellow eyes took turns scanning the tree line and then the rows of empty houses, searching for any sign of an ambush. Manu walked slowly in front of me, lost in his own thoughts. He didn't expand on his two-word answer.

"Where is this? Why are we here?" I called up to him, hoping he'd let me in on his solo reveries. Why had we taken the time to stop here after what we just witnessed in the Ancient Forest? "We need to get back to the Refuge and warn the others."

He didn't answer. We continued our silent walk through the ghost town. The road ended abruptly up ahead, just before the forest's edge, leaving a small area of green grass between it and the last house on the street.

I slowed to a stop in front of it. Two big bushes bordered the steps to the front porch, and another couple of smaller bushes led off to the left toward the forest. The house looked like all the others: wooden, minimalistic, vacant. It wasn't burned the way some of the others were, but it was humble and long deserted. But I gravitated toward it, like some kind of magnet.

Slowly, I grasped the rickety railing and placed a foot on the stairs. I don't know what I expected, but nothing happened, other than the dilapidated wood creaking under my feet. Without bothering to see what Manu and Kika were up to, I continued into the small house.

Everything was coated with a layer of dust. There were white plates stacked on a towel next to the washbasin, drying from a last meal. To the right was a door to a bedroom, and in front was a staircase leading to a tiny loft. Something drew me up the stairs. The room at the top had a bed pushed up against the far wall, under a single window. There was a desk piled with odds and ends as well as three clay bowls.

I lifted one up. It was empty. All three of them were empty, but they reminded me of the pedestals back in the training room at the Refuge from which Kage had drawn fire to teach the children. I turned the small bowl over in my hands. They were laden with imperfections, slightly lopsided, the glaze thicker in certain areas.

I set down the bowl in exchange for a cuff bracelet hiding behind a tiny satchel of stones. The bracelet was dyed with four colors: green, yellow, blue, and orange. Strands of colors led to the center, where they swirled together in a single circle so that it was impossible to separate each line from the other.

I felt connected to it. Something about this bracelet, this room, the entire house, it felt like...

"Home." Manu said, startling me. The word rang in the empty house, and as I listened to its echo, it settled in the hollow spot in my chest, and I knew it had always belonged there.

"This is your home," he said again. And as he said it, as I heard it, I knew it was true. It was like finding a missing puzzle piece and sliding it into the waiting empty space. I fastened the leather cuff on my wrist.

"How do you know? That this was my home, I mean?"

"I tracked you here...three years ago. I knew Thalen was looking for Elementals and Asfa heard rumors of a 'last Elemental' in a small village on the outskirts of the Hafra Forest." He was looking down as he spoke. His voice was soft but clear. "By the time I arrived, they were already here. Attacking the residents, questioning them about you..." He raised his eyes to meet mine. "They had your mother. I tried, but I couldn't..." He didn't say it, but the apology resonated in his voice, clinging to each heavy word that passed between us. The crumpled woman on the ground from my dreams. The flash of green light. It was her. My mother.

"Why don't I remember?" I had been there. I knew it now. The images that ran through my mind when I slept, those were memories of a horrible night. The night I'd lost everything, apparently, including my ability to remember it.

Manu looked at me full in the face now. His eyes were sad. He crossed the small room to stand in front of me. The top of my head just reached the bottom of his chin. He lifted his calloused hand to my temple. His touch was so gentle, like the soft brush of dried summer wheat. My eyes closed involuntarily against his touch. And then I felt it. Like a fog lifting from a morning landscape, allowing the sun's rays to illuminate the beading dew on each blade of grass. Dew that had always been there, but the light was just now touching. My memories returned, becoming clearer and sharper as the shadows receded. My past. My home. My gifts. My mother. That night. The tears pooled behind my lids, forcing them open. Bright, startling green eyes stared back at me.

My heart dropped to the floor as I backed away from him, knocking into the desk where the clay bowls clashed against each other. Everything came flooding back, as if a dam had pent up my memories and then suddenly exploded, letting them gush forth.

———

That night I had awoken in my dark room. This room. The recovered memory played like a song in my head.

I hadn't been sleeping well. The wind seemed to enter my room, swirl near my bed, and tug me gently to the edge of town. That night, I'd let the wind win. I slid from my bed and quietly padded down the creaky wooden stairs toward the front door. I passed my mother's room on the left. The door was ajar. Her body was a quilted hill, rising highest at her hips and sloping downward to her legs and feet.

Hindsight was a cruel gift. This was the last time I'd see my mother peaceful and unbothered. Had they come in and dragged her from her sleep? Had she woken at the noise and gone outside to investigate? I tucked the quiet memory of my mother's sleeping, sloping figure safely away.

I stepped onto the gravel road, the small stones jabbing at my bare feet. I did this often. My feet barely objected to the stones but rejoiced as the ground became soft dirt and grass. I wandered past the tall trees that marked the edge of town and the beginning of the forest. A small stream sprinkled past, climbing over the rocks and amid the small knolls. This was my favorite part of the forest. The meeting of all parts of the natural world— the forest, the wind, the water— all nestled here in peace.

Serenity was shattered as a scream tore the night. More terrified screams. They were coming from the town.

And even though I knew the way this story ended, I couldn't help the worry in my chest. My mother. I had to get back to her. And as I relived the memory, I knew my worry was pointless, but it persisted.

The wind whisked me back to the village, carrying me several bounds with a single leap. Each footfall was light, barely there as the wind scooped me aloft again. I was almost back at the forest's edge when something snatched me out of the air, grabbing me tightly by the crook of my arm. I fell backward onto the soft ground. Above me stood a beautifully dark Eleiyon man, draped in a black hood. His face dripped with sweat, and his piercing green eyes shone with fear.

They were the same stabbing green eyes that looked at me now in the present. I'd looked up at those eyes that night, searching them for answers.

His now-familiar, gravelly voice spoke. "Aila, listen to me."

"How do you know my name? Who are you?" I interrupted. The conversation replayed in my head; I now remembered every word.

"Aila, listen to me. You need to run from here. She's after you. They all are. Head to Aodhen. Now."

"What? What are you talking about? Who is after me? Why? My mother, she's in the village. What's happening?" The questions tumbled out of my mouth, leaving him no chance to respond. I tried to get to my feet, but Manu held me down with a forceful foot to the chest.

"Aila. I need you to listen. There's no time. I will go and help your mother, but I need to know you have left safely. Please. I will find you in Aodhen. Leave now." He lifted his foot and held out a hand to help me up.

"I'm not going anywhere. I need to find my mother." I pushed past his outstretched hand and headed to the village. His soft footsteps followed me closely, but he didn't object. The trees thinned at the edge. Dark smoke hovered over the burning houses. Some villagers were outside, fleeing the smoldering remains of their homes. Others were strewn lifeless across the ground. I gasped at the damage that had been done in a matter of minutes whilst I'd been in the forest.

Manu tugged my elbow again. "Aila. Please wait." He searched my face. I only saw sincerity in his expression. "Let me go. I'll find your mother and bring her to you. Wait here. Let me make sure it's safe. I beg you."

I watched his back as he turned on his heel and walked out of the forest. He walked with a limp and clutched his side for a moment before steeling himself with a deep breath and straightening his back. He was wounded. His tattoos whirled down his arms as he melted into shadow.

He reappeared from the darkness beside my house. Just as he was about to round the corner to climb the porch steps, a horse whinnied in the street, drawing my attention. Two soldiers dressed in maroon Archai attire– one on horseback, one sheathing a sword that glinted briefly in the fire light before disappearing– stood in the road alongside a pale-faced, slender woman with a double-edged axe . They hovered above a kneeling woman who was hunched over, clutching her stomach. "Mother," I heard myself whisper. She was already injured.

"I don't know who you're talking about," the woman croaked from the ground.

"You don't have as many friends as you think you do in this little pigsty of a town... People talk..." the woman said. The soldier that had just sheathed the sword kicked the kneeling woman, who let out a cry and crumpled to the ground.

Terror gripped my insides. Had I just watched this and done nothing to stop it? I balked at my past self.

Manu hesitated, clearly debating what he should do. He wasn't going to help her, I realized. He was just going to leave her there, defenseless. I moved a step for-ward, out of my crouched hiding place behind the tree line. He saw my minuscule movement and shook his head ever so slightly before stepping out from behind the house.

The woman looked up nonchalantly as Manu approached.

Drata.

"Ahh, Manu. I thought you might be here. Misandree is barely a dot on the map though. I dare say, I feared we might miss you." She toyed with the shaft of her axe as she spoke in her sickly-sweet voice. But you are here. Which means we're right in being here as well. Tell me...where is our mutual interest?"

Manu seemed unsurprised by Drata's greeting. He stood casually facing the group, his face a picture of pure hatred. If he was scared, he didn't look it.

"My wound slowed my pace, Drata. You all arrived here before me, so your guess is as good as mine. But you know I wouldn't dream of missing a chance to…reconnect." His eyes flicked to the horseback rider. His tattoos slithered down his forearms, almost imperceptibly.

As the dismounted Archai turned to address Manu, his face became visible.

It was Cyrus. I knew there was something about him, something I never liked. He was a filthy, backstabbing traitor. My heart hammered against my chest as I listened.

"Tell us where the Elemental is and we'll leave the rest of the village, and its people, unharmed," Cyrus demanded.

"Isn't this your village? Are we not in Fira? You should be protecting these people from the likes of her." Manu jerked his head toward Drata, who wore a face of mock insult.

"The way you protected the north?" the hooded Archai countered. If eyes could kill, the soldier would have been long dead with the icy stare Manu gave him. He continued, "I'll take it that's you refusing our offer?"

Another Archai on horseback rode up to the group. "Sir, your orders? Are we letting them flee?"

The hooded soldier turned back to Manu. "Last chance…"

"I just arrived, as you have witnessed, and have yet to find anyone. It seems I may have some trouble doing so anyway, considering your rampage." He motioned to the burning houses and scattering residents.

"Fine. Have it your way." As the hooded Archai turned back to the recent arrival, his hood slipped from his head.

Kyran.

My stomach jumped into my throat as Kyran's face shone in the darkness. I suppressed the nausea that threatened to spill my insides.

"Round them up," Kyran ordered.

"None escape," Cyrus said coldly.

The Archai gave a curt nod and galloped back to the village center to relay orders to the waiting group of soldiers. After a moment, they turned in unison on the defenseless villagers and began a series of relentless assaults. Manu swallowed, turning back to face Cyrus, Drata, and Kyran.

"So, we're really going to do this then, Manu?" Drata sung sweetly. "Why not join us? Why waste your time with this weak filth?" She kicked the crumpled mass on the ground, who let out another groan. "You don't need to make the same mistake your father did." She walked toward Manu calmly, no longer toying with her axe but getting ready to brandish it.

I almost missed it. Manu's black weapons swiftly took shape in his waiting palms. His short sword in one hand and the scythe-like weapon in the other. Drata's axe blade glowed green momentarily, and then it was just streaks of blinding light as she attacked Manu, swinging it overhead. The glowing axe blade struck the matte black sword.

Manu was smoke and shadow as he wielded his two weapons like they were extensions of his own limbs. His movements were effortless as he bobbed and weaved to avoid Drata's blows. Drata countered each blow, dancing nimbly on her feet. Cyrus joined the fray, but Manu's skill was beyond even the two of them together.

Kyran attempted to join, but just as he shifted in his saddle, a shadow leapt out of the night, startling his horse. It whinnied and arched on its hind legs before sprinting off in an uncontrollable gallop, Kyran still on its back.

The three of them were engaged in battle. They were distracted. I could get to my mother and bring her to safety. Rising from my crouch, I tried to leave the tree line, but something was there. An invisible wall blocked my way forward. I punched it, pushed it with all my strength, but I was trapped. A solid barrier kept me hidden from view in the trees. Tears of helplessness streaked down my face as I pounded against the wall, cursing Manu.

Manu continued his duel with Cyrus and Drata. They twirled around each other in a death dance. Why didn't Cyrus use his fire? Then I realized. Because of the shadows it would create.

Manu was injured on his right side. Both Cyrus and Drata knew it, and as experienced fighters themselves, they exploited it. All their blows were to the right, forcing Manu to block strikes on that side.

After a particularly powerful blow from Cyrus, Manu's knees almost buckled. The barrier flickered. I punched through it once. Then again. Then it disappeared entirely. Without a second thought, I raced toward my mother. I could make it. I could save her. Just as I was about to come into view, I was knocked back into one of the bushes next to my house. What in the firestorm? I tried to get to my feet again, but slippery, cold shadows held me back, wrapping themselves around my feet and arms.

Manu was doing it and fighting them at the same time. The energy and concentration must have been enough to tip the scale in his opponents' favor, because Cyrus landed a punch to the face and then Drata's axe thudded into the Manu's already wounded side.

He fell to his knees as a sharp whistle sounded from where the other Archai had gathered.

"They found someone," Cyrus' deep voice called to Drata, who stood over Manu. Her eyes blazed with adrenaline.

"Finish him." Cyrus left to join the mob of Archai.

Drata raised her axe above her head, and just as she tensed to bring it down, Kika sprang from the darkness. She landed on Drata's back, clamping her jaws around Drata's axe-wielding wrist. Drata screeched in pain and dropped the axe.

Kika leapt off, placing herself protectively in front of my mother and the kneeling Manu. Her ears flattened to her head as she let out a menacing hiss.

The sharp whistle sounded again from the other side of the village. Drata grabbed her axe from the ground as she tried to staunch the bleeding from her wrist with her clothing.

"This is not over, Manu," Drata said quietly before turning to follow Cyrus.

Rain fell, landing on the embers of the houses, making the smoke even worse. It fell harder, creating muddy puddles along the unpaved road where my mother lay. I struggled against the shadowy restraints.

Manu crawled to my mother. He turned her on her back, revealing the fair, freckled face that looked so much like my own. The face I remembered now as the one who had taught me to harvest; who taught me to control and train each one of my gifts; who had warned me that who I was made me a target; who had cooked the most delicious mushroom pies. My mother. Her blue lips moved, saying something to Manu. He shook his head. She said it again, clutching his firm hand with her trembling one. A last word formed on her lips: "Please."

Then her hand went limp. Manu turned to me. Only sadness was in his eyes. My own tears mixed with the rain, and I cried so much that even the deep puddles of rainwater would have tasted of salt.

"We need to leave, now," he said, and his green eyes were the last thing I saw as he lifted me in his arms.

The same ones that looked at me now as I opened my own tear-filled eyes in the tiny bedroom.

———

I tried to back away from Manu but bumped against the wall. I was confused. What had he done to me?

"It was you?" The question came out weaker than I would have liked. I was hurt. And it sounded like it. How had I let myself be tricked again? Stolen my memories, my past, my identity. Who looked at me in the face countless days, knowing who I was and what had happened to me, and chose to just let me flounder in darkness.

And Kyran. I remembered the feel of his soft lips on mine, his greedy hands all over my body, and I suppressed another wave of nausea.

"Your eyes?" It was trivial, but it's what came to my mind. I would have remembered the bright green eyes. His eyes had been dark until moments ago.

"Shadows can be useful as more than just sentries or restraints," he answered.

He'd known that those eyes would trigger my memory. A memory that he ...that he did what to?

He answered before I could ask the question. "An enchantment. Two actually. One to hide your past from yourself. And one to bind your powers. Though, admittedly, your powers are stronger than even I expected. They've broken through several times." He couldn't help the admiration that laced his words, even as he answered solemnly.

"But why? Why do it? Why leave me in the dark for all this time?"

"Your mother." The final image of her popped into my head, her shaking hand grasping his. The desperation in her eyes and her last word "please." She'd asked him to do it. He'd refused at first. But she pleaded with him. Her dying wish was to protect me.

But still. How long had he planned to lie to me? The Ancient One had said to trust each other and let go of our pasts. How could I ever trust him now?

"I'm sorry, Aila. I should have told you sooner. I still think about it. About whether it was the right thing to do in the first place... I tell myself it was. That a mother knows what's best for her daughter. That Drata, Kyran, and Cyrus had gotten too close and would have found you. That what I did kept you safe, at least this long..." He stepped back, giving me more space. "Your mother said that if you knew, if you remembered, that you would go after them. That you would die trying to get revenge. I brought you to Aodhen where I knew Caeru could watch over you."

And she was right, of course, as mothers so often are. Naleiri was the one looking for justice, wanting to do the right thing. I looked for opportunities. I tried to protect the people I loved, and I would break the rules to do it. I had before. And yet, everyone I cared about died to protect me.

Or maybe it was to protect an idea of who I might become...some kind of hero, a savior of Kiakora. But I wasn't. I wasn't the hero everyone needed.

"I'm not the one everyone wants me to be," I said softly, voicing the terrifying truth that haunted me. My mother, Caeru, Naleiri. They'd all sacrificed themselves for me.

"Remember what the Ancient One said. You don't have to be the Elemental from the prophecy. That's not important. Your choices are. What you do with your time in this world, the decisions you make, that's what will ultimately tip the scales in favor of what's good and just. Our choice to keep fighting," Manu finished softly. He stood across the room now, giving space for his betrayal to settle between us.

"There are things about your past that you need to explain. Answers you owe me. Like why you were wounded. About what happened in Kiromar when Thalen took over and how you escaped." I needed these answers. I needed to understand how I fit into the larger story. The tapestry of Kiakora, Veyo had called it. Manu and I were linked; she'd said as much. And I needed to understand his past just as much as he knew mine.

"I don't forgive what you did. And I certainly don't trust you. But I believe we both want to save Kiakora, and I think, like it or not, we're on the same path now." With that, I pushed past him and down the stairs of my abandoned home.

Kika was still standing guard as I walked out the front door, the sun and I bidding the day farewell together. Kika's ears twitched at my arrival. I sensed her disposition; she was uneasy.

"Manu," I called into the house. He hadn't followed me out of the door. "Let's go, I—"

"I thought you might turn up here," a low voice rumbled, emerging from the tree line. It filled me with dread. Kika let out a menacing growl as she turned to face him and the small army of Archai behind him.

Cyrus rode into the graveled street. He looked just as he had in my memory, sitting atop a strong chestnut horse. His maroon hood was situated on his head, reminding me of the last time I saw him here. The night he'd killed my mother.

Manu appeared at my shoulder.

"Manu. I admit, I didn't realize we'd had her under our noses for so long. You must have found that amusing. Not until word reached us that a Shade helped her escape did I put two and two together. Figured you might be stupid enough to bring her back here."

Kika let out another warning growl as she paced back and forth in front of us. Manu's tattoos were angry whirlpools on his forearms.

I loathed every inch of Cyrus. His pompous face with his stark features. His cropped hair that was just as dark as his heart.

"It's fitting, really," Cyrus taunted. "That it should end here where it all started. I'll gut you and leave you face-down in the dirt, just like I did your mother." The gleam of the sword blade in the firelight sliced through my memory, severing whatever ties I had on my emotions.

He killed my mother and had returned to do the same to me. But I wasn't the weak girl he remembered from training. I wasn't the powerless Elemental they'd caged back in Aodhen.

Kika and Manu were ready to fight. They were waiting for me, I realized. Waiting to see what I'd do. They would take my lead.

I reached over my head and grabbed the hilts of my crystal twin sai. Rage coursed through my body to the point that I barely registered the blue glow of the crystal weapons as I charged Cyrus. Manu and Kika were right behind me, teeth bared, and weapons drawn.

The moment of surprise in Cyrus' eyes disappeared as he blocked the glowing blue blow. I twisted backward and sent a tendril of warmth down my arm to his horse, beckoning it to buck and dislodge its rider. It obeyed. With a loud whinny, it rocked back and forth, launching Cyrus from the saddle. He landed cat-like on his feet.

I wasted no time in charging him again. This time, I jumped, letting the kernels of warmth in my chest burst forth. A gust of wind carried me in a twisting dive. I slashed my sai through the air. Cyrus dodged, but not quick enough. The blade split open his cheek. I watched in shock as the skin on either side of the gash turned blue, then purple, as if it was frostbitten. *Frostbringer.*

The moment was enough to distract me from the Archai who came up behind me. A slip kick knocked me over, and a fireball blasted the crystal sai out of my left hand. I sprung to my feet. Cyrus and the other Archai circled me like a pair of wolves. Behind Cyrus' shoulder were Manu and Kika, taking on the other horde of soldiers. He and Kika moved as one. The black jaguar wove in and out of Manu's shadows, using them as cover. She disappeared into a cloud of darkness only to reappear with a lethal swipe of her giant paw. Manu fought with his black blades, standing back-to-back with his own shadow, which morphed between something solid to land blows and something ethereal to dodge.

The elemental powers glowed in my chest. I wasn't afraid. I sent a gust of wind knocking the nameless Archai off his feet. Cyrus blocked it with a shield of flame. He was more skilled with the gift of fire than I was, even with my memory restored, but I could make things difficult for him. Summoning the orange warmth forth, I siphoned a flame from Cyrus' shield. It felt natural in my palm as I fed it more of my energy, until it was as large as my fist. Then, I shot it at Cyrus in a burst of continuous orange flame. Cyrus was quick. He met my fire with his own. The two jets clashed with a shower of sparks. It was like a tug-of-war in reverse, as we each battled toward the other, pushing our flames to reach our opponents.

Cyrus was stronger. His flame slowly devoured mine, surging closer and closer to my open palm. Just as I thought it might reach me, Kika lunged across my field of vision, knocking Cyrus to the ground. His flame vanished. I let my own die out. Cyrus blasted a fireball at Kika's chest. She howled and sprang off him in pain.

Kika's attack gave me enough time to locate the sai Cyrus had knocked from my hand. I grabbed it and threw it at him, sending a gust of wind, urging the blade to fly faster than a diving falcon, so fast that Cyrus couldn't block it as it thudded into his chest. He flew backward, the force of the impact lifting him off his feet. I clutched the other sai, prepared to have to deal another blow as I walked slowly to where he lay on the ground.

I stood over him. I wasn't shocked this time to see the grayish-purple circle on his skin around the blade. The sai was buried to its hilt in his chest. The purple circle of frostbite grew, radiating from where my sai penetrated his body, turning his skin the color of dried lavender flowers. His jaw quivered silently as his lips and nose changed color. And then he went still. As still as ice.

Whatever feeling I might have expected didn't come as I examined his frozen body. Not the familiar warmth of anger, or even the burn of intense fury. Instead, a cold hatred seeped into my bones, like the clinging chill of winter. He'd shattered my heart into thousands of unrecoverable pieces.

And I would do the same to him.

I knelt unceremoniously and grabbed the hilt of the sai. It was stuck firmly in his frozen body. I twisted the blade in a single swift motion. Cyrus' body cracked under the pressure. Like a frozen pond bearing too much weight, it broke into pieces.

"Let's go! Now!" an Archai shouted from my left. I looked up. Two Archai retreated into the forest. I surveyed the scene. Manu had left half the soldiers lifeless on the ground. He didn't pursue the escaping Archai but ran to us instead. His eyes glanced over the fragments of Cyrus, but he didn't say anything, moving quickly to Kika.

"Kika! Are you okay?" he asked, cradling the injured Kika in his hands.

I crawled over to examine the angry red wound on Kika's chest. Her hair was singed by the blast. I felt the calming warmth trickle down my arm, feeling for Kika's energy. It was there, dulled but still quite strong. "She'll be fine. We'll get her back to the Refuge and put a salve on it, to prevent infection."

Manu nodded. "Right. Let's not waste time. Who knows when they'll be back...or what else might be coming now." He lifted Kika and conjured an escape portal.

As I stepped into the portal behind Manu, a flash of movement above me caught my eye. Buzzards were circling.

35

Kika limped slightly, favoring her injured side as we followed Manu down the familiar tunnels. I got the sense that she was not happy about being back underground.

Manu led us to the small room that had become the place to strategize. He walked straight to the back corner and took his usual position, one leg bent, his foot on the seat, the other sprawled out in front of him. He toyed with his knife, waiting for the ensuing discussion. Kage was sitting at the table. He shifted uneasily as Kika prowled by him and headed to the ledge in the back of the room near where Asfa stood. Kika leapt up and situated herself so that she was not laying on her burn.

"Ouch! What in the firestorm happened to Ms. Kitty?" Kage said, noticing Kika's wound.

Manu's eyes flicked sharply to Kage, though he didn't answer. Kika let out a hiss, flattening her ears to her head, and he slid his chair away.

"She doesn't like that nickname," Asfa chuckled. "I give you permission to take a chunk out of his leg if he gets too annoying," she said lovingly to Kika.

Kage assessed Kika uneasily before turning to me, apparently deciding that Kika would not leap across the table and eat him. Bana stood by the door, looking nervously between me, Manu, and Kika.

"Okay, well, it seems we've missed out on a lot," Bana said calmly from the corner. "Spill...tell us what happened."

I recounted our journey through the rainforest and then shared what the Ancient One told us as well as the prophecy. Tears fell from Bana's eyes and Asfa cursed as we told them about the Archai's arrival and what they'd done to the Ancient Forest.

I paused there, deciding how much of the rest of the story I wanted to share. "We stopped in Misandree."

Bana took in a sharp breath that revealed she knew more than she had let on. I'd suspected as much. She was not only Manu's second in command, but his counsel.

"Got my memory back," I continued. "Misandree is my home. Oh, and Cyrus and a bunch of Archai showed up there. We fought them off before coming here. Cyrus is dead. Kika got hurt. We'll need to get her a salve for that burn." I would share just enough. They didn't need to know everything, and by the looks on Kage's and Asfa's faces, Manu had left them in the dark as well.

"So, what now?" Kage asked.

"Now we make our move," Manu finally spoke. "We can't hide forever. It's been long enough. We know the House of Fira's priority and we know Thalen's. We aren't quite sure why he hasn't invaded yet, but presumably, he's waiting for the other territories and Kiakora to weaken. The one thing we know for sure is that it will happen. And soon. Our best bet is to figure out where these ancient objects are and beat the Lord of Flame to them."

"And how do you suppose we do that?" Kage asked.

This was it. My turn to be honest. To trust. "I have an idea of where the pieces are. And I know for sure where one shard is..."

"How do you know that?" asked Asfa suspiciously.

"Because I was the one who retrieved it from its Protector, Baku, in Lake Luan."

Silence.

"And where is it now?" Bana asked, though the fear in her voice indicated she'd already guessed the answer.

"The Lord of Flame has it. I gave it to him." There. I said it. A weight lifted from my chest as I spoke the words aloud. But as it rose from my chest, it settled between the five of us in the small room. I'd tried to bury this truth, hoping it didn't matter in the grand scheme of things. But it did. And I had to set it right.

The room was heavy. Only Kika's soft purr filled the air. It hadn't been intentional, but it was a betrayal. I'd furthered the Archai's cause, making whatever plan they'd hatched that much easier to accomplish. The four of them were judging me, the same way I'd judged Manu.

Kage broke the silence first. "The Archai will be expecting us to go there. If they know you spoke to the Ancient One, and they know Aila's with us, then they'll assume she's told us about the shard. They'll be waiting for us to come."

I agreed with Kage. "So, we let them expend their resources protecting it from a threat that isn't coming right now. We go after the other pieces. They don't know what I know," I explained. How could they know that Cearu had been manipulating the strings this whole time? They couldn't know about the torn pages she'd given me or the book she'd snuck to Manu.

They all looked at me expectantly. "Baku had the first shard. He is one of four Ancient Protectors of Kiakora."

"Of course," Asfa whispered. The others looked at her with the same confusion.

"According to the stories," I continued, "all four Protectors disappeared around the same time, and no one knows why. Many even believe they died or left Kiakora altogether. We know that's not the case, because I met Baku, and he is very much alive. And he was protecting a shard. My guess is the other three have pieces as well. They all disappeared to protect the shards, keep them from Eleiyon like Thalen and the Lord of Flame."

"But what do these pieces make?" Kage asked. "What happens if someone gets them all?"

"The Ancient One told us it's a weapon of indescribable power. Thalen is more focused on the prophecy, and me, right now. But he'll be after the dagger as well. We can't let either of them get their hands on all the pieces to rebuild it."

"That's only four pieces," Manu spoke up from the corner. "The prophecy said five. The Lord of Flame's piece and the three other Protectors only makes four."

I'd thought of this. I had no idea where the fifth piece might be. Maybe one of the Protectors was guarding two.

"We need to start somewhere," Asfa responded. The silence in the room was a sign we all agreed. "The House of Fira will be trying to find the next piece to rebuild that dagger."

"The Protectors have been all but forgotten from our collective memory. That's why it was so important to the House of Fira to collect all of those books that now sit in the library in Aodhen. That's how they found out about the dagger. My guess is they also know about the Protectors. But Caeru saw to it that some of the specifics went missing. We might be able to beat them."

"So where do we go next?" Bana asked.

"One of the pages Caeru gave me said that the Protectors retreated to the part of Kiakora most connected to their innate power. For Baku, that was the largest, deepest lake... Lake Luan," I explained.

"And that means..." Bana ventured.

I looked at her squarely before answering, because I knew it would fall heaviest on her ears. It would be the last place in all of Kiakora she'd want to go. "We're going to the Eastern Mountains."

About the Author

Allyson Martinez is a former NYC high school English Language Arts teacher. She received her Masters in Literature from Hunter College and has written many, many stories in countless notebooks. She finally shares one of them with her debut novel, Kiakora: A Flame of Sorrow, the first book in a trilogy. Allyson enjoys traveling, exercising, and spending time with her husband and two sons. You can visit her online at www.kiakora.com or on Instagram (@kiakora_books).